I0788825

How to Be a Good Villain

Jamie Dalton

This edition of How to Be a Good Villain has a touch of spice. If you prefer it without, that is available on most online book retailers.

For all of us who live in chaos, we all have our critics. Their
disapproval doesn't make you a villain.
Unless they deserve it. Then villain on.

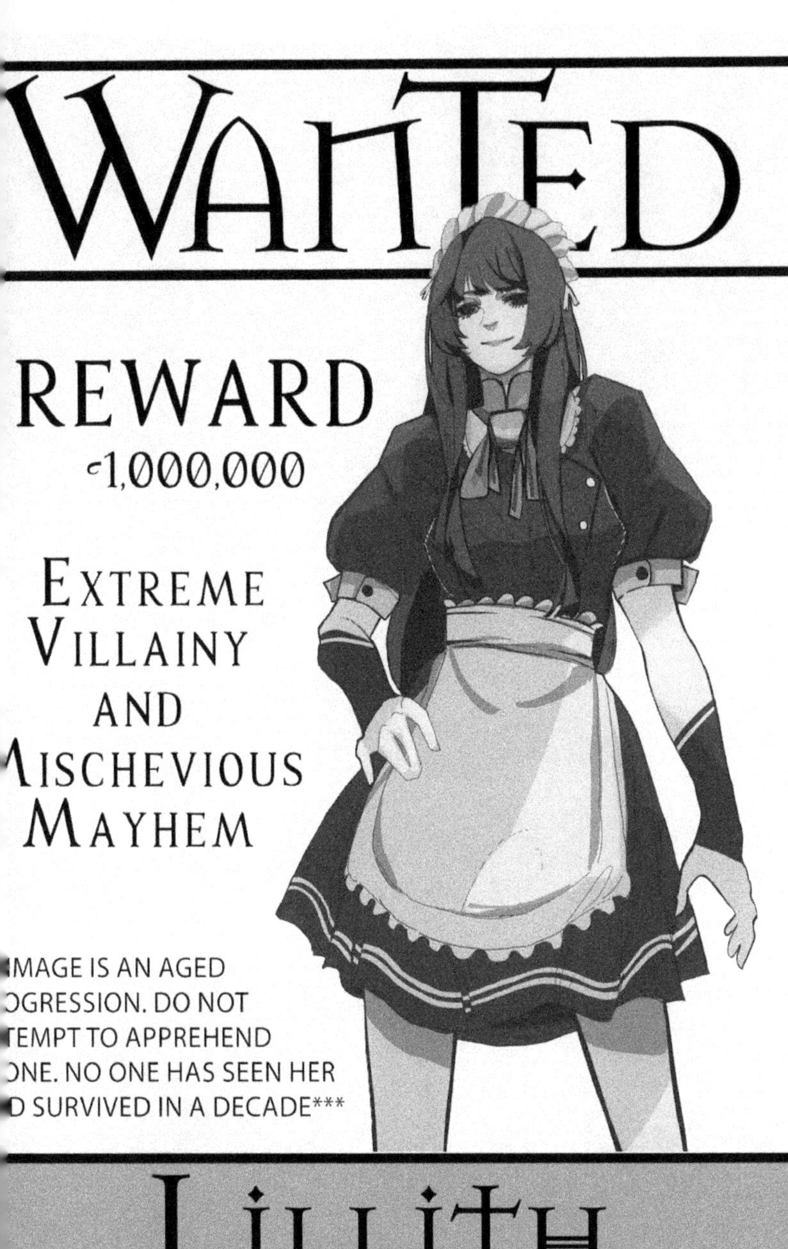

WANTED

REWARD
ᶜ1,000,000

EXTREME
VILLAINY
AND
MISCHEVIOUS
MAYHEM

IMAGE IS AN AGED
PROGRESSION. DO NOT
ATTEMPT TO APPREHEND
ALONE. NO ONE HAS SEEN HER
AND SURVIVED IN A DECADE***

LILLITH
SHADOWEND

Necia
Prince Asher's Home
Lillith's Lair

Rodel
Treterra

HELP WANTED

PRINCE ASHER SEEKS STAFF FOR HIS NEW ROYAL RESIDENCE. OPEN POSITIONS INCLUDE:

MAIDS—HARDWORKING INDIVIDUALS WILL MANAGE HOUSEHOLD CLEANING, LAUNDRY, MEALS, AND OTHER DOMESTIC DUTIES. DISCRETION IS REQUIRED. MUST PRESENT A MODEST, DUTIFUL APPEARANCE BEFITTING SERVICE IN A NOBLE HOME.

GROUNDSKEEPERS—MUST BE PHYSICALLY FIT AND ABLE TO PERFORM LANDSCAPING TASKS AS THOSE HIRED WILL BE RESPONSIBLE FOR THE UPKEEP OF ESTATE GARDENS AND EXTERIOR AREAS. KNOWLEDGE OF PLANTS/FLOWERS PREFERRED.

GUARDS—EX-MILITARY AND MERCENARIES ARE ENCOURAGED TO APPLY. MUST BE SKILLED FIGHTERS DE-

VOTED TO PROTECTING THE ROYAL GROUNDS FROM ALL THREATS. ABILITY TO WORK INDEPENDENTLY OR ALONGSIDE EXISTING SECURITY CRITICAL.

STABLE HANDS—HORSE EXPERIENCE IS REQUIRED AS DUTIES INCLUDE FEEDING, GROOMING, AND CARING FOR THE PRINCE'S PERSONAL STEEDS AND CARRIAGES. MUST BE COMFORTABLE WITH ANIMALS AND DAILY OUTDOOR WORK.

IN ADDITION TO GENEROUS WAGES, ALL LIVE-IN STAFF WILL RECEIVE ROOM AND BOARD WITHIN THE PALACE. THREE MEALS DAILY WILL BE PROVIDED. UNIFORMS AND ALL NECESSARY EQUIPMENT FOR DUTIES WILL BE SUPPLIED.

THIS IS A UNIQUE CHANCE TO DIRECTLY SERVE THE KINGDOM'S CHAMPION AND IN HIS OWN HOUSEHOLD. DAY-TO-DAY EXPOSURE TO PRINCE ASHER MAKES THESE ROLES HIGHLY COVETED. COMPETITION IS EXPECTED TO BE INTENSE.

ONLY THE MOST QUALIFIED CANDIDATES DEMONSTRATING LOYALTY, VIRTUE, AND AN IMPECCABLE WORK ETHIC WILL BE CONSIDERED. BE PREPARED FOR RIGOROUS BACKGROUND EXAMINATIONS.

SOME KNOWLEDGE OF THE PRINCE'S PREFERENCES/LIFESTYLE IS BENEFICIAL BUT NOT REQUIRED. THE ABILITY TO GRACEFULLY MANAGE MULTIPLE TASKS SIMULTANEOUSLY AND THRIVE UNDER PRESSURE IS KEY.

If interested in applying, please arrive at the east gate on the morning of the sixteenth for preliminary interviews. Bring all references and identification. Opportunities await!

1

Lillith

Being the most powerful being in the known world isn't all it's cracked up to be. I've spent my entire life trying to become the evilest, most powerful villain in the kingdoms of Rodel, Necia, and Treterra, and all for what? Fame? Fortune? It's not worth it. Frankly, I'm bored.

So what do you do when you have everything you've ever dreamed of, and you could rule the villains if you wanted to? Which I definitely don't. They're a bunch of needy, drama-filled, selfish, entitled, ridiculous fools. My family included.

You see what makes the other side tick.

I stride briskly through the bustling village square, weaving between merchants hawking their wares and children darting underfoot. To any passerby, I appear an ordinary peasant woman, indistinguishable from the scores around me in my modest gray cloak and blue linen skirt. Exactly what I want them to think.

I'm only passing through this nondescript village on my way to an important interview. Prince Asher, champion of the realm and icon of goodness, is seeking a new maid for his household. It's the perfect opportunity for me to infiltrate the prince's inner circle and ascertain what drives the insufferably virtuous.

What is the point of attaining such immense power if I have no worthy foes left to test it against? No, this prince's flawless reputation intrigues me. Perhaps I will find amusement in subtly corrupting his pure spirit from the inside.

As I turn down a dingy alleyway, eager to avoid the congested main thoroughfare, a meaty hand shoots out from the shadows and clamps around my arm in a vice-like grip. I let out a theatrical yelp as I'm yanked off my feet and shoved forcibly against the hard stone wall, packages dropping from my hands.

Three hulking men tower over me, their ragged faces obscured by stained scarves. Bandits. The one pinning me brandishes a wickedly curved dagger with casual menace. I spot various other weapons hanging from their belts—clubs, maces, knives. These back-alley thugs clearly mean business.

"Well, well, what do we have here?" the bandit holding me scoffs, his sour breath hot on my face. "Hand over your valuables, wench, and maybe we'll let you leave with your skin intact."

I force my body to tremble, widening my eyes in feigned terror. "P-Please sir, I have nothing of value!" I plead, injecting desperation into my tone.

Inside, I have to suppress a sneer at their arrogance. They have no idea who they are dealing with. I could obliterate them all in the blink of an eye, but I'm curious to see how this little drama will play out. Like I said, I've been a bit bored.

The thieves guffaw, clearly relishing my apparent weakness.

"She's a scared little lamb!" One chortles. "This'll be easier than swiping candy from a babe."

"Please, sirs, have mercy," I whimper, laying the desperation on thick. "I'm just a poor peasant girl!"

"Shut it!" The leader backhands me roughly across the cheek.

I grunt, more startled than pained.

How dare this filthy lout strike me! I have to fight the urge to loose my power and teach him a fatal lesson in manners. No, I will wait. All in good time.

From the alley entrance comes the clanking of armor. The silhouette of a warrior in the light, his sword gleaming, approaches. Ah, a so-called "hero" has come to save the damsel in distress. How trite.

"Unhand her, thieves!" the man proclaims loudly. "I shall save this poor damsel from your villainy!"

It takes everything in me not to burst out laughing. That has to be one of the cheesiest introductions I've heard a hero do, and I've heard plenty.

The bandits turn to this new threat while I continue to cower convincingly against the wall. With a roar, the brash warrior charges down the alley, sword swinging. He catches one bandit with the tip of his blade before the others set upon him. Clearly outmatched, the overconfident fool soon fails, and the gang of thieves quickly overwhelm him.

With a final anguished cry, the would-be hero falls lifeless to the grimy cobblestones. Crimson blood pools around his body, soaking into the cracked earth. What a waste.

The lead thief turns back to me, his dagger dripping with the deceased warrior's blood. "Now, where were we?" he purrs menacingly.

In that moment, I drop all pretense. My spine straightens, power thrumming through my veins. These pathetic fools have wasted enough of my time. I have an interview to get to.

With a small smirk, I crack my neck and flex my fingers. "Do you have any idea who I am?" I ask softly, my voice edged with danger.

The thieves pause, confusion breaking through their sneers. I almost laugh.

I throw back the hood of my cloak, magic swirling around me in a terrible vortex. "I am Lillith Shadowend."

At the utterance of my true name, all color drains from the mens' faces. They stumble back with cries of alarm, eyes bulging in naked fear. One even soils himself, the acrid stench filling the air.

"I beg your pardon?" one of the men asks, a slight tremble in his voice.

"Then beg."

Sneering, I drink in their terror with twisted delight. At last, fitting reactions to my power. These fools have threatened the wrong witch.

"What's wrong?" I purr, purple flames dancing along my fingertips. "Just moments ago, you were all bluster."

"Please, have mercy!" one thief sobs, falling to his knees before me. Pathetic.

"Mercy? Your friend asked the same before I burned his face off," I lie casually, relishing their renewed whimpering.

I have done no such thing... yet, but why not embellish a bit for the drama of it all?

"We won't tell anyone, I swear it!" another pleads desperately. "Just let us leave this place with our lives!"

I pretend to consider it for a moment, tapping one finger against my cheek. "Hmmm, how about... no."

With that, I unleash my pent-up power in a devastating wave. Purple-black flames erupt from my outstretched palms, slamming into the thieves like a rampaging inferno. Their forms disintegrate instantly, burnt to less than ash by the white-hot magic. The stone walls of the alley crack and blacken, warped by the intense heat. Smoldering embers float through the air like hellish snowflakes.

I lower my hands calmly and brush cinder from my sleeve. Such a shame about their garments. Those scarves really would have fetched a decent price at market, but the flesh beneath was riddled with lice and disease. No great loss there.

Stepping daintily over what remains of the foolish thieves, I emerge from the alley and stride toward the village square. Behind me, plumes of foul smoke rise into the sky like an accusatory finger. Shouts of alarm echo as villagers notice the carnage I nonchalantly unleashed.

Moments later, the heavy footsteps of approaching guards thunder down the lane. I turn smoothly, arranging my features into a look of innocence and distress—wide eyes brimming with crocodile tears and lower lip trembling. I'm the picture of a frightened peasant woman who has narrowly escaped assault in a dark alley.

A squad of guards rushes up to me, spears bristling.

Their captain, an imposing brute of a man, roughly seizes my shoulder. "You there, halt!" he barks. Flecks of spittle fly as he shakes me. "What happened here?"

My eyes fill with tears. "Oh, sir, it was awful!" I cry, my voice breaking believably. "These terrible robbers pulled me into that alley and threatened my life!" I bury my face in his tunic, shoulders heaving with manufactured sobs.

The captain awkwardly pats my back. "There now, lass, you're safe," he soothes.

I hide a smile against the grubby fabric of his uniform. Even the most hardened men are useless at comforting a crying girl. I have him eating out of my hand already.

After a few moments, I pull back, dabbing at my eyes with the captain's grimy handkerchief. "Thank you ever so much for rescuing me!" I gush. "Those men meant to defile me. I just know it!" More sobs wrack my body.

By now, the other guards have ventured into the alley to examine the aftermath of my handiwork. Chaotic shouts float back to us.

"Captain, you aren't going to believe this! They've been burnt to ashes!"

"The whole alley's been scorched black!"

"What kind of devilry is responsible for this?"

The captain's bushy eyebrows shoot up in surprise. He opens his mouth, no doubt to question me on how I have escaped such destruction unscathed.

But I cut him off, gripping his wrist tightly. I let real tears of exertion fill my eyes this time. "Oh, sir, please! I just want to forget this whole awful day!" My voice drops to a whisper. "Don't make me relive the horrors again."

The captain's face softens into a mix of concern and awkwardness. "Of course, of course," he murmurs gruffly, patting my hand. "No need for that. You just run along home now."

I nod and wipe the tears from my face as I leave the scene of the burned alley behind me.

***

"Miss Lilly Grimsbain?" a woman calls. Her silver-streaked hair is pulled back in such a tight bun that I'm sure she is doing it to keep her recently formed fine lines in check calls.

I raise my hand and look as innocent as I possibly can. "Here!"

Quickly, I stand and straighten the skirt of my dress before pulling my shoulders back, tucking the escaped black lock of hair back into my braid, and gracefully walking over to her.

My name may be Lillith Shadowend, but I can't get hired to work in Prince Asher Sunbash's home under my own identity. The golden prince, second son to the king of Necia, is the most noble hero of the kingdom. Where I'm the epitome of evil, he's the protector of the good and innocent. I'm pretty sure I'm his number one target. Too bad he has no idea what I look like. No one does. Rule number four of being a good villain—never leave any witnesses. Ever.

I follow the woman through a large wooden door and into a spacious office. The wooden floors are polished to a shine, and the walls are lined with bookshelves filled with aged volumes of literature. I take in my surroundings as I make my way to the chair opposite the desk where she sits, keeping my distance from the cup of tea and candles between us. The last thing I need is to accidentally get a reading of the woman or draw the flame's attention. Those would guarantee I wouldn't get the position.

She pulls out a fresh roll of parchment and dips a long quill into a small black bottle of ink. "Tell me a bit about your experience. Where was your last placement, and what did you do?"

"I've been working as a handmaid for many noble families around Necia," I lie.

Brow raised, she holds the quill over the crisp paper, clearly waiting for me to continue.

I quickly try to back up my story. "I have references if you would like."

"Let's hear them."

I rattle off names of people who don't exist, faces and stories woven from my imagination. Of course, I sprinkle in with one or two wealthy individuals from less prestigious areas of the kingdom. Rule number eleven—adding a touch of truth makes all lies more believable.

"My most recent placement was with the Ambrose family in the bustling city of Honeyvale. The Lady Ambrose was most discerning in her staff. For three years, I cared for her children and maintained her lavish home. One particular feat that stands out was the summer solstice ball Lady A hosted for dignitaries from across the realm. I helped coordinate every intricate detail for weeks. The event was hailed as one of the most extravagant balls in recent memory. Even the king sent praise for its splendor and entertainment."

Pausing for effect, I let a modest smile play at my lips.

"You've been working for quite a few households. What made you choose to come here?" she asked.

I swallow hard. "My previous employer told me of your need for a handmaid, and I felt it was the perfect opportunity to serve a noble family of higher standing. I gained much experience keeping such a high-profile household running seamlessly, but I felt it was time for a new challenge, to use my skills in service of an even nobler family if possible. When I heard of the opportunity here, well..." I trail off artfully, meeting the woman's eyes with an attentive gaze. "Serving someone as esteemed as Prince Asher would be an honor. I hope my qualifications are suitable."

Perfect. I spin the tale with just enough tantalizing details to pique interest without verification. Every gracious yet self-assured manner aims to charm—a perfect deception to cover my more sinister intentions.

That seems to satisfy her as she finally nods before writing something on the parchment. She looks back at me and says, "If you are hired, it will be on a trial basis. Is that acceptable?"

I keep my expression neutral. "Of course."

"Good." She gives a single nod. "We will provide you with a uniform and all other necessary materials upon acceptance into service."

The woman leans forward slightly, her eyes studying me carefully. She has an intensity in her gaze that makes me feel as though she is scrutinizing every inch of my soul.

I hold her gaze until she finally says, "If accepted into service in this household, you would need to commit to complete loyalty and discretion."

I nod quickly in agreement, but inside, I am churning with excitement. It seems they are the perfect target—powerful yet oblivious to who I really am.

***

My heart is pounding as I make my way through the forest toward the prince's home, my bag clutched tightly in my hands. The offer for the trial includes room and board, so I packed some of my belongings. I had to be careful not to leave anything behind that I wouldn't want anyone to find. Rule number six—never trust another villain. I also can't bring anything that might reveal my true identity in case someone gets curious and starts digging into my personal belongings.

In my quick ascent to the top, I avoided building relationships. Rarely does anyone I encounter survive long enough to tell anyone anything about me anyway. For most, I am merely a name that holds an ominous and dangerous end. That holds true for heroes and villains alike. The chances of anyone being able to identify me are slim, and if it does become a problem, I can always either make them disappear or disappear myself.

Over the course of clawing my way to the top, I developed a personal set of guidelines—my own "how to be a good villain" rulebook. By following these rules, I made myself powerful and eliminated any weaknesses that could be used against me. I spent most of my life identifying my vulnerabilities, finding ways to overcome them, or, even better, transforming them into strengths that only I can leverage to my advantage. My rules ensure that no one dares cross me, and if they do, they will find no footholds to exploit. Rule number ten of how to be a good villain—lean into your trauma. Use it to fuel the anger. Grudges feed your soul.

A cruel smile curves my red lips at the thought of corrupting the kingdom's precious golden boy right under their noses.

The building is not a mansion but a palace. Manicured formal gardens fill the area before me, and wrought iron gates mark the entrance. Stone walls circle the grounds like protective arms, and scattered throughout are odd statues with water spitting out of various parts of their bodies into pools of water. Whoever thought a naked young child statue peeing in a pool made appealing art has a more twisted mind than my own, and that's saying something.

Taking a deep breath, I trudge up to the door and put on the most sincere smile I can muster before knocking.

The door creaks open, and a tall butler peers out. He looks me up and down. "You'll need to use the servants' entrance around the side," he says in an authoritative voice. "One moment please."

The door closes, and I'm left standing awkwardly on the steps, unsure of what exactly I am supposed to do.

A few minutes later, the door again opens to reveal a bubbly blonde in a ruffled black dress covered by a cute apron. I don't know what makes me sicker—the fact that she seems to bounce without realizing it as she takes me in or that I'm pretty sure this is going to be my uniform too. It's so very... adorable.

The door creaks on its hinges as the radiant maid prances after me into the garden. "Hi, I'm Mairelle," she chirps breathlessly. "I heard you're new here! Who are you? Where do you come from?" Her words spill out like water from a fountain. She dances around me, her black dress swaying with each step. "I just got hired here, too, so we'll be seeing each other a lot! I mean, to be fair, everyone is new here. After all, the prince just bought the place!"

I open my mouth to respond to her questions, but she speaks too quickly for me to get anything out.

"We're very lucky here," Mairelle says as she continues to walk and talk in circles around me. "You see, the prince was given one one-hundredth of the hoard from the dragon Dizan, Eater of Sheep, and bought this place with it."

I can't help but feel a bit sad hearing that name. Dizan had been my next-door neighbor deep in the Zibath Mountains, where my lair is hidden. While we weren't exactly close, having someone nearby who respected my space was nice. Plus, dragons are an excellent deterrent for nosey villagers poking around. At least I still have the mountain trolls to draw their curiosity.

Mairelle's voice trails off as she looks at me curiously. "Is something wrong?"

I shake my head to clear my thoughts before forcing a smile. "No, I'm fine. Just a little overwhelmed with everything."

She nods understandingly before pointing out the servants' entrance. "Your room is on the third floor. You'll share it with two other maids, but don't worry. They're very nice."

She stops moving and stares at me expectantly. I eye her back, unsure of what she wants me to do. Then she offers a slight nod of her head in the direction of the door before bounding off in another direction.

The girl is quite odd, and I wonder if she is slightly mad. If that is the case, she just might grow on me.

I approach the door and once again put on my most pleasant smile before knocking. This time, an older willowy woman opens it, likely the head housekeeper from her attire. A longer dress, no frills or ruffles in sight. She looks me up and down before nodding curtly in approval and motioning for me to come inside.

"You must be our new maid," she says briskly as she begins to lead me through an impressive foyer toward a more secluded wing of the house.

Her movements are silent. Not even the click of her shoes echoes on the white glistening marble floors. From my experience, that usually means they have some experience as an assassin. I would know. My father was one of the best. I make sure to allow a small sound from my footsteps so as not to give away my own skills and take a mental note to keep an eye on the woman.

As we pass doors with gold handles and artfully arranged furniture, I marvel at how grand and luxurious everything looks, far more extravagent than any other home I have been in before. My eyes widen at the sheer number of grandiose imported items. Vases of flowers are everywhere. The ceramics, gilded mirrors, and lavish furnishings are of the highest quality. The smell of rich green grass and a hint of flowers drifts in through the slightly open window, and the faintest tinge of sweat tickles my nose.

I haven't been inside many homes of my victims, instead mostly spending time in my own home. Catching them off guard while traveling for mundane outings such as the grocer or the tailor means they have less protection, making them much easier marks.

We pass a grand staircase with a massive crystal chandelier and walk through a white-painted door into a much less ornate hallway. There are no paintings or any defining features like fancy handles in this section. The walls are a muted green, the color of a lime's peel. The floors go from white marble to a worn polished dark wood. I assume we entered the servant's corridors and follow her up several flights of stairs and down a confusing number of narrow hallways.

The woman stops outside of one particular door adorned with intricate carvings. "This is your room while you are employed here." She gives me a stern look. "You may call me Mrs. Umbernuckle. You will find your uniform in the closet. Please change quickly and meet me in the laundry downstairs. Always remember that you must conduct yourself accordingly while inside these walls."

I nod quickly in agreement.

Mrs. Umbernuckle turns on her heel and is gone before I have the chance to ask where exactly the laundry is.

I open the door to my new room and step inside. It isn't much larger than my bathroom back home, but its walls are painted a soft blue, and it seems well taken care of with a large wardrobe taking up one side of the space and three small beds tucked away in the corners. Curtains drape either side of the single window, a mirror hanging on one side, a small shelf with a collection of books on the other side. I will explore the books later.

After dropping my bag to the floor beside the wardrobe, I quickly undress and change into my uniform—a familiar black dress with ruffles along the bottom of the skirt, puffed sleeves, a crisp white apron, and sensible black shoes.

As I ready myself, my thoughts drift to my past training. I can still hear my instructor's stern voice echoing in my memory. "Magic is not innate. It is a discipline that takes mastery. While talent gives one an advantage, even the lowest peasant can attain power through dedication."

I know the truth of those words well. My own gifts have been born from natural prowess, but I have honed them to a razor's edge through relentless practice and study. I spent countless hours struggling through dense spell tomes, pushing my limits in secret. Now, my reserves are vast, yet I still keep up my studies.

My fingers dance as I reinforce protective warding spells upon my vessels of concealed magic. Despite my disguise, staying prepared in dangerous lands like these is important. I have worked too hard to rely on chance alone. Rule number nine of how to be a good villain—always have a plan D. B is never enough.

Taking one last look in the foggy mirror for reassurance, I gather my courage and begin my hunt for the laundry room.

I have always dreamed of infiltrating the prince's household, but I never imagined it would be so easy.

MYSTERIOUS ARSON SENDS VILLAGE INTO CHAOS

By Sir Justice Jab

A local village is reeling after a devastating fire of unknown origins tore through the main square yesterday, leaving three dead and untold damage in its wake.

The blaze erupted without warning in a crowded alley off the square, instantly reducing the narrow passage to a blazing inferno.

Three slain bodies were discovered in the aftermath, burned beyond recognition. From clothing remnants, they are believed to be members of a notorious band of thieves and

RUFFIANS WHO HAVE LONG TERRORIZED LOCAL MERCHANTS.

HOW THE OUTLAWS MET THEIR FIERY END REMAINS A MYSTERY. WITNESSES NEAR THE SQUARE REPORT HEARING SHOUTS AND SEEING PLUMES OF SMOKE, BUT THE EXACT SPARK IS UNCLEAR.

"IT JUST EXPLODED INTO FLAMES ALL AT ONCE," ELOISE, A FRUIT VENDOR WHOSE STALL BORDERS THE ALLEY, SAID. "WE ALL RAN FROM THE TERRIBLE HEAT. IT WAS WITCHCRAFT, I TELL YOU!"

THE FEROCITY OF THE SUDDEN BLAZE SUGGESTS MAGICAL ORIGINS, THOUGH NO SPELLCASTER HAS COME FORWARD. PRINCE ASHER HIMSELF AIDED THE INVESTIGATION BUT COULD FIND NO RESIDUAL MAGICAL TRACES OR ANOMALIES.

"A TRAGIC ACCIDENT, BUT NO EVIDENCE OF FOUL PLAY," HIS HIGHNESS STATED AFTER SURVEYING THE SCENE. HE POSITS STRAY EMBERS FROM A PIPE PERHAPS IGNITED LAMP OIL IMPROPERLY STORED IN THE ALLEY.

STILL, UNEASY TOWNSPEOPLE WHISPER OF DARK FORCES AND SINISTER HAPPENINGS. THREE THIEVES DO NOT JUST SPONTANEOUSLY COMBUST SIMULTANEOUSLY, THEY ARGUE, BELIEVING THAT A SURVIVING OUTLAW MUST HAVE STARTED THE FIRE TO CONCEAL ASSASSINATING HIS COMRADES.

OTHERS PROPOSE MORE MYSTICAL EXPLANATIONS, SUCH AS VENGEFUL SPIRITS, DEMONIC INTERVENTION, OR AN EVIL SPELL GONE AWRY. THEY SAY THE BLACKENED STONES AND UNNATURAL HEAT POINT TO MALEVOLENT MAGIC.

"MARK MY WORDS, A WITCH CAUSED THIS, AND SHE'LL STRIKE AGAIN," OLD FLORIA, THE TOWN FORTUNE TELLER, WARNED.

BUT PRINCE ASHER DISMISSES RAMPANT RUMORS OF SORCERY. "LET US NOT ASSUME MYSTIC MOTIVES WHEN SIMPLER CAUSES SUFFICE," HE CAUTIONED CITIZENS. "JUSTICE WILL RUN ITS COURSE IN TIME."

FOR NOW, THE OFFICIAL VERDICT REMAINS OPEN UNTIL THE FIRE'S TRIGGER IS DEFINITIVELY DETERMINED. THE DEAD THIEVES' KNOWN QUARRELS AND ENEMIES ARE UNDER SCRUTINY AS THE INVESTIGATION CONTINUES.

IN THE SQUARE ITSELF, A SHAKEN YOUNG WOMAN SPOTTED FLEEING THE ALLEY WAS QUESTIONED. THOUGH VISIBLY DISTRAUGHT, SHE WAS MIRACULOUSLY UNHARMED BY THE DEVASTATING FLAMES. THE WOMAN INSISTS SHE WAS ASSAULTED BY THE THIEVES BEFORE THE SUDDEN FIRE, BUT WHETHER HER ACCOUNT IS ACCURATE OR A GUILTY PLOY TO CONCEAL INVOLVEMENT REMAINS UNCERTAIN.

FOR NOW, LOCAL PATROLS HAVE DOUBLED TO REASSURE NERVOUS VILLAGERS AS SPECULATION RUNS

RAMPANT. PRINCE ASHER PLEDGES TO RESTORE ORDER AND IDENTIFY THE REAL CULPRITS.

"THERE ARE ALWAYS DEEPER FORCES AT WORK THAN MEET THE EYE, BE THEY MUNDANE OR MYSTICAL," HIS HIGHNESS ACKNOWLEDGED, "BUT JUSTICE ULTIMATELY PREVAILS THROUGH METHODICAL TRUTH-SEEKING, NOT RUMORS."

UNTIL FACTS COME TO LIGHT, FEAR HAS TAKEN ROOT AMONG NORMALLY PLACID VILLAGERS. THEY LOCK THEIR DOORS EARLIER, LEAP AT SHADOWS, AND AVOID THE BLACKENED ALLEY WHERE THE FATAL FIRE ERUPTED.

THE PRINCE'S CALMING PRESENCE HELPS KEEP WILD THEORIES IN CHECK, BUT AS LONG AS MYSTERY SHROUDS THE BLAZE'S ORIGINS, NERVES WILL REMAIN ON EDGE IN THE OTHERWISE PEACEFUL COMMUNITY.

FOR NOW, RESIDENTS SIMPLY HOPE NO MORE "ACCIDENTS" OCCUR TO STOKE UNEASE. ONCE OFFICIAL TRUTH EMERGES, THEY WILL REST EASIER KNOWING THE GUILTY PARTY HAS BEEN HELD ACCOUNTABLE FOR THE LIVES AND PROPERTY LOST.

2

Lillith

After some trial and error, I eventually find the laundry room located near the rear of the house, only to find Mrs. Umbernuckle there waiting for me with her arms crossed sternly over her chest.

"I see you made it," she says as I approach. "Now, let's get started. As a part of your job here, you will be washing all of the linens and the prince's clothing by hand. I expect you to use the special soaps and starch them properly without leaving any residue behind. If there is a stain, like blood or wine, then extra care must be taken when cleaning that particular item or room. Remember that most of these items value more than your annual salary, so be sure to take extra care."

She points around the room and demonstrates some of the techniques she suggests while speaking. Once our initial lesson is complete, she points to a large basket full of clothes.

"Your first task will be to clean those. His Highness just returned from a mission, so watch for stains carefully. When you are done, hang them on the lines over there and open the windows to allow the cross breeze to help them dry quickly. Then, come find me for your next job."

"Yes, ma'am. I will. Thank you," I mumble.

I wait to begin until she has left the room entirely. Hesitantly, I step forward and study the overflowing wicker basket. Exquisite fabrics of all hues and textures spill out from the top—deep red velvets, lush greens, silks, and ivory linens. I soon discover a less pleasant discovery, a crumpled pair of underwear with a streak of brown running down its back.

Quickly, I drop them back into the basket with a laugh. I refuse to touch those again with my own fingers. Unfortunately, I can't use magic to clean them because I have to be careful not to use too much magic, or else my magical signature could be picked up by someone. Apparently, Prince Perfect isn't so perfect.

Mrs. Umbernuckle said something about using lemon on some stains. I dig in the cupboards and find none. Disappointed, I go in search of the kitchen in hopes of finding one.

As I travel through the winding hallways and past the mysterious rooms, I'm filled with a sense of awe. Who knows what secrets these walls hold? A wicked laugh fills my mind at the anticipation of discovering every single one of them.

My heart races as I step into the kitchen, and something stirs. Instinctively, I stop in my tracks, my eyes desperately scanning the darkness until they lock onto the source of movement. Crouched on the cold stone floor is a small creature, its beady eyes fixed on me as it greedily devours every morsel it can find. The little thing is grotesquely adorable with its long ears and large eyes. What is it doing here?

I tiptoe closer. The creature stops in its tracks and turns to face me with a timid expression. I can feel its vulnerability and desperation.

"Come here, sweetheart," I say gently, motioning with my hand.

It hesitates for a moment before slowly walking over to me on two feet. Its skin is dry and tattered, a clear sign of starvation.

Taking pity on the poor animal, I scramble through the cupboards in search of something that might help it. I find a jar of peanut butter and a loaf of bread. It isn't much, but it will have to do.

After I tear off a piece of bread and spread some peanut butter on it, I hand it to the creature. It eagerly takes the offering and gobbles it up in seconds, leaving no crumb behind.

I smile, happy to have helped the little guy.

Suddenly, I feel something shift inside of me. It is like the air grows heavier and darker, and I find it hard to breathe.

The creature looks up at me with big, sad eyes, and I feel like it is trying to tell me something. I can't understand what.

"Hey, what's wrong?" I ask, reaching out to touch it.

As soon as my fingers brush against its skin, I'm hit with a jolt of energy so strong that it knocks me back a step.

The creature scurries away, disappearing into the shadows.

This is strange, but with the creature gone, there isn't much point in me pondering too much. There are no answers to be found at the moment, so I divert my attention to my original goal. After a few minutes of searching, I manage to find a lemon that seems perfect for cleaning stains, as Mrs. Umbernuckle had suggested earlier.

With the lemon in hand, I quickly return to the laundry room, where the basket of clothes, including the crusty underwear, await me. I place the lemon on a wooden table and, grabbing a small knife, slice it in two.

I eye the disgusting undergarment while contemplating how to go about this without actually having to touch it. A stick allows me to pick up the underwear, and I keep it far away from my body. With speed, I drop it onto the ground. Then, I grab half of the lemon and squeeze it onto the brown spots, trying to ignore the stench filling my nose. Hands on hips, I stare at the garment. Something isn't quite right. This will not be enough to remove the stubborn stains.

Suddenly, I remember something from my childhood. Adding salt to the lemon and leaving it in the sun removed many of my worst stains. I was quite the troublesome child in the best way. My clothes were rarely clean by the time breakfast was over, not to mention by afternoon tea.

I grab salt from a nearby cupboard and toss it onto the underwear. Unfortunately, the sun patch on the ground won't be enough. I'll have to find a more creative solution.

With the stick, I drag the underwear over to the door, trying not to breathe too deeply as I do so. Sure, it probably doesn't actually smell, but at this point, I'm convinced I can detect the slightest hint of poo wafting from it.

I open the door to the outside. Sunshine spills into the room, momentarily blinding me. Blinking away tears, I scan for somewhere to put the garment where it will get good sun exposure.

Nearby, there is an evergreen bush that is shaped like a heart. It seems as if it is in just the right spot to get good sunlight for most of the day.

Without hesitation, I drape it over the bush and step back to admire my handiwork. It now looks much more interesting with the white garment sitting atop like a patch over a broken heart.

With satisfaction in finally finding a solution, I clap my hands together and go back inside to work on the rest of the pile of laundry left in my care, content with a job well done.

Several hours later, I finally finish hanging the clothing. I'm exhausted. I require a snack and a break before I can start my next task.

I search the castle for Mrs. Umbernuckle but can't find her anywhere. With a sigh, I decide to head into the gardens in case she is outside enjoying the sunshine.

An ear-piercing screech echoes off the walls as I walk through the gardens.

Startled, I run toward the sound and stumble upon Mrs. Umbernuckle and a tall, muscular handsome man standing together. She looks angry and is muttering something at him while pointing behind his back.

The underwear!

The moment her eyes find me, she starts to scream. "How dare you leave his... his... clothing his... unmentionables out in the open like that? Do you know what could have happened if anyone else saw them?" She paces around in a circle, her hands on her hips as she continues to yell. "You are responsible for this mess! I can't believe you were so careless and irresponsible!"

The man meekly glances at the bush with the clothing before turning his gaze toward me. He seems amused by the predicament but tries his best to hide it behind a polite smile.

Mrs. Umbernuckle, however, waves her finger in my direction and continues to berate me for being careless and irresponsible. "This is not something that you can just ignore! You must take responsibility for your actions! As an experienced maid, you should know better than anyone how important it is to be careful with delicate items." She grabs my shoulder and gives me a hard look. "You need to understand that there are consequences for your mistakes, or else you won't last long here!"

I stand there, speechless. Already most of the stain is gone. I fail to see what the exact problem is.

Before I can respond, the man beside her steps forward, soothing Mrs. Umbernuckle. "Really, Mrs. Umbernuckle, it's fine. No one saw anything other than ourselves. There was no harm done."

Who is this man? I appreciate him helping me out, but in my personal experience, no one ever does something like that without their own personal agenda behind it.

"Prince Asher, please forgive her. She only started today," Mrs. Umbernuckle begs between sobs.

My jaw drops. It can't be. This is the hero prince of Necia? He is even more handsome up close than he is in paintings. His bright blue eyes twinkle as he smiles down at me, and my heart flutters as a lock of his long white hair blows across his face.

Mrs. Umbernuckle clasps her hands together, her eyes glistening with tears. "I'm so sorry," she says in a hushed tone. "I never meant for this to happen. I... I beg your forgiveness." She looks up pleadingly, her voice quivering.

Prince Asher waves away her apology. "You hung my clothing outside? How did that even occur to you?"

I shrug. "It's the most efficient way to get out particular types of stains. I've used it on my own clothing often. "

He nods thoughtfully and smiles. "That's pretty ingenious. I'm impressed. Although, perhaps in the future, we can put up a temporary barrier so those passing by don't get quite as good of a view of my underwear. I would even be willing to speak to the gardener about erecting a dedicated space where this could be done safely on a regular basis."

"Of course," I say, giving a slight curtsy.

He smiles again. "I very much appreciate your help taking care of my clothes. I won't forget." After pausing for a moment, he adds, "By the way, what's your name? In case I ever need it again."

"Lilly, your Highness."

"It was nice to meet you, Lilly. If you would excuse me," Prince Asher says.

I watch as he leaves, admiring the view before a cough pulls my attention back to the woman beside me.

"You're lucky, you know. Any other member of the royal family, and you would have just lost your head."

"Of course. You're right. It won't happen again. I promise."

I turn slightly so she doesn't see my smirk. Chop off my head? I would love to see them try.

Asher

As I leave Lilly and Mrs. Umbernuckle, an image of my underwear fluttering in the breeze on a nearby bush brings a chuckle to my lips. I shake my head in amusement, marveling at the servant's audacity. It is refreshing to encounter someone so unpredictable.

I make my way to the training yard, admiring the lush greenery of the sprawling field. A symphony of birdsong fills the air, creating a soothing atmosphere. Every step forward is light and effortless, like I am walking on a cloud. In the distance, the butler stands beneath a willow tree looking out over the idyllic landscape. The tranquil stillness has an uplifting quality, as if something good is waiting just around the corner.

"Ah, there you are, Your Highness," Mr. Rendfield greets me politely, offering a formal bow as he hands me my practice sword. His dark eyes hold a hint of mischief, but his demeanor remains serious, as it always does during our sparring sessions.

Hiring him as a butler was one of the first things I did to establish my own household. He is one of my most trusted people and the best sparring partner I could ask for.

"Thank you, Mr. Rendfield," I reply, taking the sword and settling into a ready stance.

Steel meets steel as we begin our dance, the sound of our blades ringing through the yard. I can't help but admire my butler's skill, his movements fluid and precise. There is something intriguing about his expertise that goes beyond his seemingly unassuming appearance.

"Your form has improved, Your Highness," Mr. Rendfield comments dryly as he parries one of my strikes.

"Thank you," I pant, grinning despite my exertion. "I have an excellent teacher."

Our mock battle continues, each of us trying to gain the upper hand over the other. Rendfield pulls off an unexpected feint and knock-away, causing me to stumble back in surprise. That move isn't one typically employed by a butler.

"Nice trick," I say, regaining my footing and launching another attack.

As we spar, I notice him using advanced techniques that go beyond our usual training sessions. My curiosity grows with each deft parry and riposte.

"Where did you learn that one?" I ask, genuinely impressed as Rendfield disarms me with a swift, fluid motion.

"Ah, well," he says, his voice betraying the slightest hint of amusement, "one picks things up here and there."

"I'm sure they do." I laugh.

As our sparring intensifies, there's a subtle shift in Rendfield's movements. He is no longer holding back. He is testing my limits. The air around us seems to crackle with energy as our blades clash and dance in the waning light.

"Your reflexes have certainly improved, Your Highness," Rendfield says, grinning, "but let's see how you handle this."

With a flick of his wrist, tendrils of shadow erupt from his sword, snaking toward me like living creatures. My eyes widen at the unexpected display of dark magic, but I refuse to let it mislead me, and I quickly sidestep the shadows, feeling a cold chill brush past my face as they narrowly miss their target.

"Interesting choice of distraction," I remark, keeping my voice steady even as my heart races.

"Sometimes, the most effective tactics are also the most unconventional," Rendfield replies, his eyes glinting with mischief.

We continue our dance of steel and magic, sweat beading on our foreheads as we push each other to new heights. I marvel at Rendfield's skill and finesse. Hiring him to take care of my property while I'm out is one of my better decisions. Most of my staff have unique skillsets that are best kept secret.

Finally, as the sun dips below the horizon and the first stars begin to appear, we lower our swords, breathing heavily from the exertion.

"Quite the workout today, wouldn't you say?" I pant, wiping the sweat from my brow.

"Indeed, Your Highness," Rendfield agrees, equally winded. "I trust you found it... enlightening?"

"Very much so." I chuckle. "But one word of advice, my friend. Careful with those dark arts. People might get the wrong idea about you."

Rendfield simply offers me a sly grin. "Of course, Your Highness," he says, bowing slightly. "Discretion is always key. Until next time, Your Highness." He bows once more before departing.

"Indeed," I murmur, watching him go and pondering the enigmatic man who serves me so faithfully.

Lillith

I groan in dismay, both at the sight of my two new roommates—they seem unnaturally pleasant—but also at the fact that I got in trouble. Who is Mrs. Umbernuckle to scold me? Her behavior is unacceptable for anyone working as a maid in my opinion, no matter the level they hold in the house.

And now, I am stuck in this room with these two, and I have no idea what to do with myself.

Mairelle, sensing my distress, springs to her feet and makes her way over to me in an instant. "Hello there!" she says brightly, her voice dripping with the same optimism that always seems to be radiating from her. "Remember me? I'm Mairelle. Who knew that we were going to be roommates?"

I force a smile, though it feels more like a grimace, and turn to the other woman. Where Mairelle is bright in every way from her hair to her behavior, this woman is almost the opposite. She has black hair and a much darker complexion. Her movements are far more stiff and reserved.

She stares at me with a carefully neutral expression. "Hello. The name's Cherry," she says curtly, her voice devoid of emotion.

I nod in acknowledgment but say nothing. I'm not in the mood to talk, and even if I had been, I don't think either Mairelle or Cherry would be interested in the dark thoughts that are swirling through my mind, namely of revenge and of getting back at Mrs. Umbernuckle. Of course, I can't do anything that would make me get noticed, but maybe a laxative slipped into her tea or coffee at the very least is in order.

Mairelle, however, either doesn't get the hint or doesn't care. She continues chattering away, her enthusiasm never fading. She speaks of all the wonderful things that have happened that day, of how she found the perfect charm to add to her bracelet and of how, just that morning, she has seen Prince Asher from afar.

While I am tempted to tell her that the prince has asked personally for my name and thanked me, I keep my mouth shut. Let's be honest, those small acts of wickedness feel oh so good, but this woman is already exhausting without me engaging in actual conversation with her.

Finally, after what feels like an eternity, she pauses, her eyes losing a bit of their shine. Maybe she realizes that her words have fallen on deaf ears. She glances over at Cherry as if seeking confirmation that I am not the talkative sort and then back at me.

"My apologies," she says softly, her voice gentle and understanding. "I didn't mean to ramble on so. It's just I'm so excited to have met you, and I'm eager to become friends."

I don't know what to say. Friends? I scoff inwardly, though I keep my face carefully neutral. I have never been the kind of person to have friends, and I highly doubt that either of these two would be willing to accept me as one, not when they know who I really am.

To my surprise, Cherry smiles and nods. "I'm sure we'll become friends in no time," she says confidently, her voice surprisingly warm. "It's nice to meet you."

I blink in confusion. What is she up to? Is she trying to make me feel better, or is there something else going on that I'm not aware of? I don't know, but I find myself strangely grateful for her kind words.

"It's nice to meet you both," I say, my voice surprisingly steady.

Mairelle beams, her eyes alight with pleasure, and Cherry gives me a small smile.

"Maybe we can do something together soon," Mairelle suggests, her tone hopeful.

I hesitate but then nod. Maybe spending time with them will help to distract me from my thoughts of revenge or possibly turn that focus onto them instead. Only time will tell. Of course, the prince will still be my main target. I need to figure out where to start with him. Everything is just too... perfect. Bleh.

"Sure," I say slowly. "That sounds like a good idea."

Mairelle claps her hands together in delight, and Cherry nods in approval.

"Wonderful!" Mairelle exclaims. "We'll plan something soon. I'm sure it will be loads of fun!"

I allow myself a small smile, though I can't help but feel a twinge of sadness. Fun doesn't seem like it is something I am capable of having. At least not in a way that would please them as well.

***

I'm on my hands and knees, my fingers raw and aching as they scrub at the stone floor of the hallway hard enough to make it gleam. The work is mindless, and it feels like an eternity since I've been able to think of anything more than the stubborn stains that refuse to budge. Several wings still haven't been cleaned up after the house was purchased, including this one. That is apparently my job.

It's lonely here, which I thought would be a blessing at first. Nobody here wanting to be friendly with me, nobody wanting to know more about me. I'm just here to clean, though obviously not very well.

I really miss my magic. My own home stays spotless thanks to my constant spells.

Something small scuttles across the floor, catching my eye. A woodroach, the size of a fingernail. It is strange, for this is an old castle and I have only ever seen them in the kitchens, usually in buildings surrounded by natural forests.

I watch it as it makes its way across the floor, and then an idea strikes me. If there is one, there will be many more. They will be my tools.

If I can call the woodroaches to the prince's bedroom, then they can stay there. If he steps on them or kills them, it will be a small act of evil. My entire purpose of being here is to try and get the golden hero prince to slip up and do something less than perfect. I can't start with anything too big. This is small and unassuming. It is, for lack of a better word, perfect.

I stand up, brushing the dust from my knees, and begin to make a plan.

First, I need something to lure them. I have some bread crumbs left over from dinner, and I scatter them around the hallway. Then, I kneel back down, close my eyes, and begin to focus my power. I have to be careful not to use too much, or I'll risk being discovered.

Slowly, the air around me begins to hum. I can feel the presence of the woodroaches as they gather around me, drawn in by the promise of a meal. I open my eyes. They're crawling around me, their small black bodies wriggling as they move. Now, I just have to get them to the prince's bedroom without being seen.

I move slowly through the castle, taking care to be as quiet as possible. My second day here, I made sure to learn where the prince spends most of his time. His study, where he sleeps, where he eats... all so when the moments present themselves I would be ready.

Finally, I reach the prince's room. I open the door and step inside then quickly scatter the woodroaches around the bed and around the room.

I stand back and watch as they begin to explore their new home, scuttling around and through the prince's bed. I've done it. I've taken a small act of evil and used it to my advantage.

Smiling to myself, I leave the room, satisfied with my work. I've done something that no one else in the castle would have had the cleverness or the power to do. Okay, yes, I'm probably the only one who would be interested in doing this, but that's not the point. I'm the only one who has the power to control the woodroaches, and I am determined to use it to my advantage.

Sometimes being a villain means doing something just for my own enjoyment, even if others think it immature. The trick to being a really good villain is not caring.

5

Lillith

A strange sense of unease annoys me as I make my way back to the hallway. The walls seem to close in on me, their secrets taunting me like whispers from the shadows. As Lillith Shadowend, villain extraordinaire, I have always been one step ahead of everyone else, but here, under the guise of Lilly Grimsbane, maid and general cleaner of floors and underwear, I am at risk of being exposed if I don't keep my wits about me.

"Surely, there's nothing to worry about," I mutter to myself. "Nobody suspects a thing."

Yet, that nagging feeling refuses to go away. Every time someone looks at me or speaks to me, I can't help but wonder if they know who I truly am. As a villain, even working as a maid wouldn't be possible. If I wasn't disguised as Lilly, the law literally states that I would have to be killed.

There's no other option. If you're born a villain, you live as a villain.

As I resume cleaning the floors, I can't shake the feeling that something is amiss. My instincts scream at me that danger lurks nearby, ready to pounce on any hint of my true identity. Not danger to myself but challenging my superiority. It is as if an invisible force guides me, urging me to follow it to the source of my unease.

"All right, intuition," I whisper, "let's see where you take me."

After placing the bucket full of dirty water and rags in the washroom, I follow my gut instinct to the back of the home. The air grows colder as I venture farther into the shadows. It's too quiet. I tiptoe through the darkened halls, trying to stay as quiet as possible so as not to alert anyone to my presence. My heart pounds in my chest with each step, and I strain my ears to listen for any signs of life.

"Who would guess," I muse softly to myself, "that Lillith Shadowend would be skulking around in the darkness like some common thief?" But if I want to protect my secret, I need to find the source of my unease before it finds me.

As I round a corner, I catch a glimpse of movement in the shadows. My breath hitches, and I press myself against the wall, heart pounding in my ears. Something is here.

"All right," I mutter under my breath, "let's get this over with."

Steeling myself, I prepare to confront whatever lay hidden in the darkness.

"Who's there?" I call out, my voice shaking slightly.

I strain my ears, listening for a response or any clue as to who might be lurking in the shadows, but all I can hear is the pounding of my own heart and the distant creaking of the old castle.

"Show yourself!" I demand, trying to sound brave and confident despite feeling anything but. "I won't hesitate to defend myself! I promise you will come out of this far worse than I will."

A soft chuckle echoes through the corridor, sending shivers down my spine. Whoever it is, they are clearly amused by my threat.

My mind races as I try to recall any villains who might recognize me from my past life as Lillith Shadowend, but their identities elude me. I prefer to keep to myself. Rule number six to be a good villain—never trust another villain. All the more reason to ensure my secret remains just that: a secret.

"Come now," says a raspy voice, finally emerging from the shadows. "Is that any way to greet an old acquaintance?"

As the figure steps into the dim light, I catch sight of their hand first. It is a ghastly sight. Rotting flesh clings to bone, some of it hanging in tatters like shredded cloth. The stench of decay wafts from it, making bile rise in the back of my throat. He must have touched the rot iron fence on his way in. A snort escapes me. What kind of idiot couldn't recognize rot iron or did and still chose to touch it?

"Acquaintance?" I spit, trying to keep my composure. "I'm afraid you've mistaken me for someone else."

"Ah, playing coy, are we?" The villain smirks, revealing a row of jagged, yellow teeth. "Very well, I'll play along, but know this. I am not the only one who knows your true identity, Lillith Shadowend."

My heart skips a beat, but I refuse to let my fear show. Instead, I force a smile. "Well, if you do know me, then surely you remember that I don't take kindly to threats."

"Threats?" He chuckles again, the sound as grating as nails on a chalkboard. "No, no, dear girl. This is simply... a friendly reminder."

"Your idea of 'friendly' could use some work," I quip, trying to buy time as I rack my brain for any way to escape this situation.

"Perhaps," the villain concedes, their rotting hand flexing menacingly. "But I think we both know that our past encounters were anything but friendly, and should your secret come to light, well, let's just say your life here will be far less... cozy."

"Is there something you want from me?" I ask cautiously, dreading the answer yet knowing I have no choice but to push forward.

"Ah, finally, we get to the heart of the matter." The villain's grin widens, revealing even more of those disgusting teeth. "For now, simply your silence. But soon, Lillith, very soon you'll be called upon, and when that day comes, you'd best not hesitate."

"Are you threatening me?" I growled out, clenching my fists at my sides. "Since you know who I am, you know very well how exactly that turns out for most people."

"My dear, your threats mean nothing to someone who knows your weaknesses."

What weaknesses?

"You and I both know that's a thinly veiled lie. You've got nothing."

"So you say." The villain smirks, stepping back into the shadows. "Until we meet again, Lillith Shadowend, the flame that dances in the darkness."

And with that, he vanishes, leaving me alone in the cold, dim corridor to contemplate the words he left with me.

Before I can turn, a flurry of movement erupts. One knocks over a suit of armor while another leaps out the window like a cat fleeing from a bath. The third villain, a lanky man with an eyepatch, tries to scurry away but trips over his own cape.

"Wait!" I call out, panic rising in my chest. "Don't—"

"Run? Why ever not?" Eyepatch answers, finally extricating himself from his cape. "Unless you're planning on turning us in?"

"Of course not!" I hiss, glancing around nervously. "You're making such a commotion!"

"Exactly," he replies, sneering at me. "We're causing a distraction so we can escape. It's called strategy, love."

"Quiet, both of you!" a new voice commands.

My stomach drops as Mrs. Umbernuckle emerges from the shadows, her willowy frame imposing despite her slight stature. She looks every inch the head maid, her eyes narrowed and her lips pursed in disapproval. If she notices the chaos that has unfolded moments before, she gives no indication.

"M-Mrs. Umbernuckle," I stammer, my heart pounding in my chest. "I was just—"

"Save your excuses," she snaps, silencing me with a wave of her hand. "I'm well aware of what you were doing, Lilly, and I must say, I'm disappointed."

"Disappointed?" I echo, searching her face for any sign of recognition or shared secrets, but all I find is stern disapproval.

"Indeed," she continues, her gaze flicking between me and Eyepatch. "You've both been entrusted with tasks of great importance here at the palace, and yet you insist on engaging in this... tomfoolery. I expect better from my staff."

I am confused. Eyepatch works at the castle? What does that mean for the other men?

"Of course, Mrs. Umbernuckle," I mumble, staring at the floor.

"Good. Now, Lilly, I suggest you return to your duties, and as for you," she adds, turning her attention to Eyepatch, "I trust you know your way out?"

"Like the back of my hand." He smirks and vanishes down the hallway.

"Very well," Mrs. Umbernuckle sighs, massaging her temples. "Lilly, see that this mess is cleaned up and then report to me in my office, and do try to stay out of trouble in the meantime."

"Yes, Mrs. Umbernuckle," I mutter.

"Good," she replies, her eyes never leaving mine for a long moment.

Then, she turns and strides away, leaving me alone with the wreckage of the villains' flight and more confused and suspicious of Mrs. Umbernuckle than I had been before.

But Mister Rotting Hand recognizes me doesn't mean Mrs. Umbernuckle knows who I am.

As I set to work cleaning up the chaos, a million questions race through my mind. How much does Mrs. Umbernuckle know? Is she one of them or merely an unwitting pawn in their game? And most importantly, how can I continue to keep my true identity a secret if everyone around me seems to be hiding something too?

Lost in thought, I miss the creature from the kitchen until suddenly it appears in front of me with a quiet pop.

I gasp and nearly jump as the creature gives me an almost apologetic look. Its long ears flop slightly as, wide-eyed, it casts a worried glance down the hall and offers a hurried motion in what I can only assume is the command to hide before disappearing again with a small pop.

The gentle rustle of her skirts is my only warning. Spurred by my desire to not be caught after wasting so much time, I find the perfect hiding spot behind a towering suit of armor. From there, I watch Mrs. Umbernuckle as she investigates the scene, her brow furrowed in concentration. She seems to glide gracefully across the floor, her willowy figure a sharp contrast to the chaos left behind by the fleeing villains.

"Curse my curiosity," I mutter under my breath, trying my hardest to remain silent and unnoticed. The air feels thick with anticipation, and my heart races within my chest.

Mrs. Umbernuckle kneels down to examine a discarded scrap of cloth. "This is peculiar," she murmurs, picking it up with delicate fingers.

As she scrutinizes it, I can't help but notice how familiar it looks, almost like it belongs to one of the villains' cloaks.

Could she be one of them? But if she were, wouldn't she have recognized me? Or is this all an elaborate ruse?

"Who goes there?" Mrs. Umbernuckle suddenly calls out, her voice slicing through the silence like a dagger.

My heart skips a beat, convinced that she has discovered me.

Instead, her eyes are focused on a small creature scurrying across the floor. "Ah, just a mouse. You gave me quite a fright, little one."

My pulse still pounds in my ears. That had been far too close for comfort.

Risking another glance, I see Mrs. Umbernuckle rise from her crouched position, her expression unreadable.

"Ah, well." Mrs. Umbernuckle sighs, pocketing the scrap of cloth and straightening her apron. "I suppose there's nothing more to be found here." She glances around the room one last time before turning on her heel and exiting the hallway, leaving me to breathe a sigh of relief.

"Close call, indeed," I whisper to myself, my heart rate finally beginning to slow.

As I emerge from my hiding place, I ponder the mysteries surrounding Mrs. Umbernuckle and the villains who have recognized me. One thing is clear. Keeping my true identity a secret is becoming increasingly difficult, and I have to tread carefully lest I be exposed.

"Time to focus on my duties and lay low for a while," I decide. I can't help but feel that my life is about to get far more complicated than I ever could have imagined.

***

I can't shake the feeling that something is off about Mrs. Umbernuckle, and the more I think about it, the more suspicious she seems. As I continue cleaning the floors, I notice her casting furtive glances my way, as if trying to gauge my reaction to her earlier investigation.

"Miss Lilly," she calls out to me, a thin smile crossing her face. "I trust you're finding your new duties... manageable?"

"Of course, Mrs. Umbernuckle," I reply with a tight smile of my own, my mind racing with unanswered questions. "I'm quite adept at adapting to new situations."

"Ah, good," she says, and I could swear I see a flicker of disappointment in her eyes. "Well, do carry on then."

She walks away, leaving me to wonder what her true intentions are.

Is she onto me? I scrub vigorously at a particularly stubborn stain. *Or is she merely testing my loyalty? Either way, I need to be cautious.*

Just as I am finishing up the task, a messenger appears in the doorway, looking rather flustered. "M-miss Lilly," he stammers, "you've been summoned by Prince Asher. He requests your presence in his chambers immediately."

"Thank you," I reply, curiosity piqued. "I'll head there right away."

As I make my way to the prince's room, I can't help but feel a mixture of excitement and trepidation. He has to have found the woodroaches in his room. I can't think of any other reason he would call me to it. How angry is he? Has he killed them and needs the corpses cleaned up?

I enter Prince Asher's sitting room, my eyes taking in the lavish surroundings. I had been so distracted by my mission the last time I was here I didn't really take in the room.Tapestries line the walls, depicting scenes of heroic battles and mythical creatures. A large fireplace crackles softly, casting a warm glow over the room. Plush velvet chairs sit invitingly by a small table laden with an assortment of delicacies fit for royalty and my roommates on two of them. A large wooden door connects to the room where I left my present.

"Please, have a seat." Prince Asher gestures to one of the chairs, his voice as smooth as silk. He appears to be the epitome of serenity, his white hair framing his strikingly handsome face. His vivid blue eyes seem to hold a secret wisdom that belies his youthful appearance.

"Thank you, Your Highness," I murmur, seating myself on the edge of the cushioned chair, unsure of what to expect.

As soon as I am settled, he turns his attention to my roommates, who sit on a long couch across from us. "Now then," he begins, rubbing his hands together briskly, "I've called you all here because we have a bit of a woodroach situation. Fear not. I will instruct you on the proper method of relocating them without harming the creatures."

"Woodroaches?" I ask, feigning innocence.

"First," Prince Asher says, reaching into a box on the small table and pulling out a large wood roach, unphased by its antennae waving in front of his face, "you must approach the creature gently, so as not to startle it."

He demonstrates his point, holding the roach tenderly between his thumb and forefinger.

"Next, offer it a small morsel of food, such as this," he continues, producing a tiny crumb from his pocket and extending it to the roach.

To my astonishment, the creature takes the offering with its spindly legs, nibbling contentedly. That little traitor. Was its stomach not filled already from my own offering?

"Finally," Prince Asher concludes, "once you've gained the wood roach's trust, simply place it in an appropriate location outside." He opens a nearby window, releasing the satisfied creature into the night air.

"Your Highness," Mairelle interjects, "why exactly are we learning about woodroaches?"

"Ah," he replies with a gentle smile. "I believe that all creatures have their place in the world, and it's important for us to learn how to coexist harmoniously."

"Of course, Your Highness," Cherry manages with a shaky smile.

"All right, let's practice what we've learned, shall we?" Prince Asher suggests, gesturing to the collection of woodroaches scuttling about in a terrarium on a nearby table.

"Absolutely!" Mairelle chimes in, her bubbly excitement serving as a welcome distraction from my internal turmoil.

"Good luck, ladies." The prince grins, stepping back to observe our progress.

I approach the terrarium cautiously, hyper-aware of every movement within the room. My senses are on high alert, ears straining to catch even the slightest whisper of suspicion while my fingers tremble as I reach for one of the roaches.

"Easy there, Lilly," Cherry murmurs, her regal poise a stark contrast to my own rattled nerves. "Remember what His Highness said—slow and gentle."

"Right," I agree softly, forcing my hand to steady as I offer the roach a tiny morsel of food. To my relief, it takes the offering without hesitation and without the need of magic this time.

"Excellent work, Lilly," Prince Asher praises.

My heart skips a beat. I glance at him, searching for any hint of mockery behind his kind eyes, but all I can see is genuine admiration.

"Thanks," I reply quietly, releasing the creature out the window before turning to watch my fellow maids attempt the same feat.

Mairelle coos at her chosen roach, her cheeks flushed as she successfully relocates it. Cherry, on the other hand, struggles to conceal her disgust, her lips pursed in a thin line as she reluctantly follows Prince Asher's instructions.

"Well done!" Prince Asher says as he walks to the door and opens it. "Now if you don't mind, please take care of the rest."

Mairelle squeals as she jumps on top of a nearby table at the sight of the hundreds of small brown bugs waiting for her. Cherry freezes. A blank mask slams down on her face. Fists clenched behind my back, I try to keep my face as neutral as possible. This is not how this was supposed to play out.

I can do nothing for the moment, though. I will do whatever it takes to keep my secret safe. I am here because I need a challenge, and the prince is turning out to be the perfect one. For now, at least, I will tread carefully, my every move calculated to maintain the delicate balance between my two identities.

6

Lillith

As I trudge down the palace hallway, Mairelle and Cherry flank me like two weary soldiers. Our faces are etched with weariness after a long day of relocating an army of cockroaches, a task so far beneath my magical potential that it feels like a cruel joke. What kind of person wouldn't just use their magic to get them out of their room or kill them all? From everything I had heard of Prince Asher before coming here, he obviously has enough power to do either. But no, instead he thought it best to have his maids come and relocate them instead. Can't he just be normal? I'm not even asking for full-on evil. We can get to that later.

"Ugh," I mutter, glaring at the polished marble floor as if it personally offends me. My brows furrow, and my lips purse in a tense scowl—my default expression when I am tired or irritated, which is basically all the time lately.

"Come on, Lilly," Mairelle chirps, her golden curls bobbing as she tries to put a positive spin on our situation. "At least we won't have to see those disgusting creatures again. Think of it as... character-building!"

"Character-building?" I snort, my sarcastic tone fully embracing my grumpiness. "Pretty sure I already have plenty of that."

Mairelle's eyes twinkle with mischief, and she laughs lightly. "Well, not all of us are so lucky to be overflowing with character."

No, some have far too much, including you. How could anyone possibly be so happy all the time about literally everything? No, not everyone here is like that. Mrs. Umbernuckle is quite the opposite. There appears to be no good side to get on.

I can't help but smirk at the thought of our enigmatic head maid. Ever since I saw her glide gracefully through the shadows, there was something about her that strikes me as suspicious. Is she hiding something? Or am I merely projecting my fear of discovery on the grumpy woman?

Cherry, our third companion in this cockroach-cleaning trio, shudders violently as we walk down the hall. She scratches her arm absently, as if she can still feel the phantom tickle of bug legs on her skin. Her dark hair hangs loose around her face, emphasizing her pale complexion, and her tall, willowy frame seems to sway with every step.

"Ugh, I think I'll never get over that feeling," Cherry groans, her normally regal demeanor momentarily forgotten. "I can't believe we actually had to do that."

"Believe it," I quip, still grumbling under my breath. "But, hey, at least we're done for now."

Our conversation lapses into silence, punctuated only by the occasional shiver or itch from Cherry. As we approach our room, my thoughts keep circling back to Mrs. Umbernuckle. Just what is it about her that sets off my inner alarm bells?

"Wait!" I exclaim suddenly, stopping short in front of our door.

Mairelle and Cherry both startle at my sudden outburst, and I can practically feel their eyes boring into me.

"I... I forgot something. I'll be back in a few minutes."

"Are you sure?" Mairelle asks, concern etched on her face. "You look awfully tired, Lilly."

"Positive," I insist, waving them off with an airy gesture. "Just give me a moment, all right?"

"Take your time," Cherry says, her voice soft and sympathetic despite her own discomfort. "Don't expect us to be awake when you get back. Try to keep it down when you come in, all right?"

Nodding in agreement, I turn on my heel and head away from my room. My curiosity about Mrs. Umbernuckle has reached its peak and nags at me relentlessly. I can't shake the feeling that there is more to her than meets the eye.

She seems so... otherworldly, and the way she moves, like shadows themselves are carrying her, is unsettling.

I tiptoe down the hallway toward Mrs. Umbernuckle's quarters, trying to remember everything I know about being stealthy without using magic. I have always been light on my feet, but this is different. I need to be as quiet as a ghost.

As I approach her door, I steady my nerves and focus on my goal. *Nothing ventured, nothing gained.*

I take another deep breath. Silently, I turn the handle and crack open the door, wincing as it lets out the tiniest of creaks. Slowly, ever so slowly, I slip inside the dimly lit room, careful not to disturb anything.

"All right, Lillith," I mutter under my breath, my heart pounding in my chest, "time to see if your suspicions are correct."

I carefully scan the room, looking for anything out of the ordinary. The chamber is elegant and understated, with dark wood furniture and deep burgundy accents. Shadows dance across the walls, cast by flickering candlelight.

Does she know I suspect her? Am I walking right into a trap?

Shaking off my doubts, I continue my search, opening drawers and rifling through papers, looking for anything that could reveal who she is or if she knows about me.

The hairs on the back of my neck stand up, and I suppress a shudder. Are those shadows moving, or is it just my imagination?

Just as I am about to open the wardrobe, the room's shadows seem to coalesce into a single dark mass near the corner. From it, Mrs. Umbernuckle materializes, her willowy frame appearing as though she stepped out of the darkness itself. My heart seizes in my chest, and I instinctively duck behind a tall dressing screen.

My pulse races, and I try to control my breathing, praying she won't hear me. I peek around the edge of the screen, watching as Mrs. Umbernuckle calmly strides across the room. She seems to be searching for something as well, her movements deliberate and focused.

Maybe she's onto me, or maybe Prince Asher is the one who's suspicious, and he sent her to keep an eye on me.

As she moves closer to where I hide, I weigh my options—use my magic to escape or try to slip away undetected. Magic would be easier, but if Mrs. Umbernuckle catches even a glimpse of it, she'd know it's me. Besides, if she is as powerful as I am starting to suspect, she will sense my use of magic and possibly identity me. No, I can't risk it. I have to rely on my wits and agility.

Mrs. Umbernuckle pauses near the window, her back to me. This is my chance. With a deep breath, I silently step out from behind the screen and begin inching my way toward the exit. Every creak of the floorboards feels like a thunderclap, and my heart pounds so loudly that I'm sure she can hear it.

"Is someone there?" Mrs. Umbernuckle's voice cuts through the silence.

I freeze mid-step.

In a moment of sheer luck, Mrs. Umbernuckle turns her attention to the window, giving me the perfect opportunity to make my escape. I tiptoe across the room, each step more cautious than the last. My breath hitches in my throat, and beads of sweat form on my brow.

Finally, I reach the door. I grasp the handle tightly, praying that it will open without a sound. As if by magic, it opens with a barely audible click.

With one last glance over my shoulder at Mrs. Umbernuckle, I quietly open the door and slip out into the hallway.

I walk back to the room, my legs feeling like lead from a mixture of fatigue and disappointment. As I enter, I find my roommates sprawled on their beds, visibly exhausted from the cockroach cleanup ordeal we have just endured. Cherry is in the midst of scratching her arm furiously, no doubt due to the lingering sensation of tiny insect legs upon her skin.

"Ugh, I don't think I'll ever feel clean again," Mairelle groans, attempting to muster a smile despite her obvious discomfort. "Did you find what you were looking for, Lillith?"

"Unfortunately, no." I sigh, plopping down onto my bed.

That's not entirely true. I did learn that Mrs. Umbernuckle can move through shadows. That's not an ability that most people have, especially not those employed to work a lowly job such as being a maid. Why is someone with that sort of skillset working for Prince Asher?

I change out of my maid uniform and into my nightgown, my mind racing with possibilities. What is Mrs. Umbernuckle is up to? I have a feeling that there is much more going on than I can see.

The shadows dance across our room, their forms twisting and merging with one another. My mind is filled with visions of Mrs. Umbernuckle, drifting through the darkness like a wraith, her intentions hidden beneath her enigmatic exterior. I can't let this mystery lie unresolved, and as I drift into slumber, my determination to uncover the truth only grows stronger.

***

I hum lightly as I tidy Prince Asher's study, taking my time to ensure every surface is spotless. My thoughts idly drift between Mrs. Umbernuckle's mysterious shadow abilities and Asher's blissful ignorance to the threats within his own walls.

The prince works diligently at his desk, his quill scratching notes in tidy looping script. A half-empty teacup sits beside him, its remaining contents steadily cooling. As his cup empties, so too does the afternoon sunlight that fills the room. Perfect conditions.

"Need a refill, sire?" I ask sweetly, drifting over with teapot in hand.

He glances up with a tired smile, grateful for the brief distraction. "Please, Lilly. You have my thanks."

As steam rises from the freshly poured tea, I count out three precise drops from a small bottle in my apron pocket. Gugulipid, a part of the rose family, takes effect quickly and subtly when properly diluted. Soon enough, Asher's symptoms will begin in full force.

I hum a cheery tune while finishing my dusting, awaiting the herbs' results. Sure enough, within minutes of him drinking from the newly filled cup, Asher wipes his brow, the stress lines on his face deepening, and a small hiccup escapes his lips. Victory. Such a petty thing to find pleasure in a man's discomfort, yet who am I to deny myself simple pleasures?

"You seem weary. Care for a reading? My grandmother taught me how to read the leaves. I make no promises for accuracy, but it can be a bit of fun." I gaze at him through long lashes, keeping my expression guilelessly concerned.

He eyes me with a curious look and waves his hand at the cup with a nod.

Delicately collecting his empty cup, I peer within at the soggy brown leaves clinging to the porcelain. Meaningless images swirl together at first, as insignificant flotsam often does, but soon, a shape emerges clearer than the rest—a bleached skull staring back at me through the vapors. How intriguing.

Concealing my interest, I point out happier signs in the leaves' abstraction. "Why, here is a bouquet of roses foretelling new love! And this blob looks for all the world like a pile of gold coins." But then my smile turns sly. "This twisted branch, however... why, it resembles a bent woman with a heavy burden. Perhaps one of your servants will displease you." I tilt my head inquisitively.

Asher frowns, concerned for his people but unsure how to interpret my musing. Perfect.

"And these smudges could be ravens, a sign of ill fortune or deceit. Best watch your back, my prince."

A hiccup startles Asher mid-response, followed swiftly by another. The prince grimaces, clutching his aching head. My work here is done.

"It seems the leaves foretell a trying day," I say sweetly. "Best you rest and recover. I'll take my leave now."

As Asher excuses himself unsteadily, hiccups wracking his form, I watch with satisfaction. My poisons and portents have taken root deeper than he knows, and he is in for a rough night. Soon, this palace will be mine to reshape as I please, with Asher none the wiser to his imminent downfall.

But for now, I have seeds to sow and plots to nurture in preparation. The leaves have shown me but a glimpse of what is to come.

7

Lillith

A few days later I find myself at a gathering for heroes, the last place I would ever want to be, trying my best to blend into the background as a simple servant. The gardens are exquisite, from the marble statues that adorn the pathways to the crystal chandeliers that sparkle overhead. My pulse quickens with each passing moment, and I fear someone will recognize me and expose me as the infamous villain I am.

"Would you care for some wine, miss?" I ask a finely dressed woman, offering her a glass with a steady hand.

She regards me with a smile and takes the drink, apparently oblivious to my true identity.

The air is filled with laughter and conversation, while musicians play jaunty tunes that make it near impossible not to tap one's foot. The scent of lilacs wafts through the air, mixing with the mouthwatering aroma of roast meats and spiced vegetables. As I move among the guests, I marvel at the lavishness of the decorations. Vibrant banners in shades of gold and azure flutter in the breeze, bearing the Sunbash family crest.

Carrying a tray of hors d'oeuvres, I offer them to the guests with a forced smile, keenly aware of the weight of my secret. The plump, juicy grapes glisten like precious gems, while the tender morsels of meat are seasoned to perfection. Each bite is a delicacy, designed to impress even the most refined palates. My own mouth waters from the smells. I am half tempted to slip into the protection of the manicured shrubs and sneak a few of them myself.

"Thank you," says a man in ornate armor, reaching for a pastry on my tray.

I give a nod, attempting to maintain my composure as I recognize him as Sir Eldric, a renowned hero whose exploits I have often followed. My father had been trapped in Sir Eldric's dungeons for a time in his youth. He had been caught while stealing something completely unimportant, of course. My mother had to break him out before the noose became an acquaintance.

Try to breathe, Lillith.

Beads of sweat form on my brow. My hands tremble slightly while gripping the ornate teapot, and the warmth of the liquid inside does not help ease my anxiety. It is a careful dance I have to perform. I must appear confident and composed while internally battling the fear of being recognized by anyone at this gathering of heroes.

I chuckle at the ridiculousness of this. I am not one to become nervous. I've faced heroes greater than most of those present, albeit, I used my full powers then and only took on a few at a time. If it comes to it, I'm not sure I can take on everyone here at the same time. That thought is what truly scares me.

"Tea, milady?" I ask with an overly cheerful smile, offering the steaming cup to a regal-looking woman with dark hair.

She nods in thanks, and I quickly move on to the next guest, trying to avoid any prolonged conversations.

"Ah, tea! Just what I needed after that last thrilling tale," booms the voice of an older gentleman with an impressive beard. He reaches for the cup with a mischievous glint in his eye. "You know, young lady, a good cup of tea can do wonders for one's spirit."

"Indeed, sir," I reply, nodding along enthusiastically. Inwardly, I chastise myself for engaging in conversation when all I want is to keep a low profile.

"Are you familiar with the story of the Enchanted Teapot?" he asks, raising an eyebrow in curiosity.

"Can't say that I am, sir," I admit, pouring another cup for a nearby hero whose attire makes it apparent she is skilled in the arcane arts.

"Ah, well, perhaps another time then," he says with a wink before turning back to his group of fellow adventurers.

As I move through the room, I can't help but overhear snippets of their grand exploits, making my already-pounding heart race faster with each step. I continue serving food to the heroes in attendance. Despite the raucous laughter and lively conversations all around me, I can't shake the feeling that someone will recognize me at any moment.

"Excuse me, miss," says a burly man with a bushy beard and more muscles than I can count. "Could you bring some more of those delicious stuffed mushrooms?"

"Of course, sir." My voice shakes slightly as I glance at his sword, which is adorned with intricate engravings of past battles. He looks familiar, but I can't quite place him. Have we crossed paths before?

I hurry away, offering him a polite smile while praying he won't look too closely at my face and pass word along to another server to bring him mushrooms.

"Ooh, is that roasted pheasant?" a woman clad in gleaming armor asks, her eyes lighting up at the sight of the dish I hold. "You must give me the recipe!"

"Unfortunately, I'm just the server, not the cook," I reply with a nervous giggle, "but I'll pass along your compliments to the chef."

"Please do!" she exclaims, heaping a generous portion onto her plate.

She peers at me for a moment, her brow furrowing, and my heart nearly stops. Then, she shrugs and turns back to the feast, dismissing me from her thoughts as quickly as I'd entered them.

"More tea, please!" a familiar voice calls out, causing me to freeze in place.

I turn to see Triston Cross, the son of a long lost villain, sitting amongst a group of heroes. I shouldn't be surprised. Rumor is, his father died of a broken heart from Triston going good. If that is even possible. Triston's red hair and dark brown eyes stand out, making him impossible to miss.

He grins at me as I approach, oblivious to the potential danger he poses. "Ah, there you are," he says with a chuckle. "You've certainly perfected the art of brewing."

"Thank you, sir," I reply, desperately trying to keep my voice steady.

All I can think about is how close I am to having my secret revealed. Out of everyone here, he is the most likely to give me away. We went to the same school, but he was several years above me.

"Tell me, have we met before?" he asks, his gaze narrowing as if trying to place my face.

My heart leaps into my throat, and I fight the urge to bolt from the room.

"Perhaps in passing, sir," I answer, quickly filling his cup and moving away before he can inquire further.

As I continue serving tea to the guests, I feel as if I'm walking on a tightrope, teetering between anonymity and discovery. With each interaction, my anxiety grows, and I silently pray that I will make it through the night unscathed.

I return to the kitchen and retrieve a fresh pot of tea before heading back out.

My pulse quickens as I approach Prince Asher, his white hair a stark contrast against his dark attire. His blue eyes shimmer like sapphires. I am determined to serve him with the grace of a swan, but my hands can't stop shaking.

"Your Highness," I murmur, curtsying slightly before pouring tea into his cup. As I do so, a peculiar scent catches my attention. It is faint, nearly imperceptible, but I recognize it immediately.

The acrid tang of poison.

"Is something wrong?" Prince Asher asks, his eyes locked onto mine.

For a moment, I hesitate, unsure how to handle the situation without causing a scene.

"Your Highness, I'm so sorry," I say, feigning clumsiness as I accidentally-on-purpose spill the cup of tea all over his lap.

The garden goes quiet as gasps echo around us.

"Clumsy girl!" someone shouts from the crowd. "How dare you spill tea on the prince?"

"P-please forgive me," I stammer, my cheeks flushing with embarrassment.

Inside, I feel a surge of relief for having potentially saved the prince's life. No one can kill him before I do. I just hope no one will catch on to my ruse.

"Enough," the prince commands, silencing the crowd. He looks down at his now tea-stained trousers and sighs. "Accidents happen. Let's not make a fuss over a little spilled tea."

"Thank you, your highness," I whisper, avoiding his gaze.

"Bring me another cup, would you?" he asks, attempting to maintain an air of nonchalance.

I nod and hurry off.

As I prepare another cup of tea for the prince, I can't help but wonder who tried to poison him and why. Everyone here would have been vetted.

I return with a fresh cup of tea. This time, I make sure to smell it myself before handing it over. Satisfied that there is no trace of poison, I present it to him with a trembling hand.

"Here you are, sire," I say.

"Thank you," he says, his voice soft and sincere.

As he takes a sip, his eyes meet mine once more, and I can't help but feel a strange connection between us.

But that is impossible, isn't it?

"Your Highness," I murmur, bowing my head in reverence before continuing to serve the other guests.

Yet, as I move through the crowd, a lingering hunch tells me that something significant has just transpired, something that could change the course of both our lives forever.

PRINCE ASHER'S GARDEN GALA DAZZLES
BY SIR JUSTICE JAB

THE KINGDOM'S ELITE GATHERED FOR A DAZZLING GARDEN PARTY AT PRINCE ASHER'S ESTATE LAST EVENING. FESTIVITIES CARRIED ON LATE INTO THE NIGHT, WITH GUESTS PRAISING THE EVENT AS THE SOCIAL HIGHLIGHT OF THE SEASON.

AMONG THE ATTENDEES WERE MANY OF THE REALM'S GREATEST HEROES, WHO HAVE BEEN WORKING TIRELESSLY TO COMBAT THE RISING VILLAIN THREAT ACROSS THE KINGDOM. THOUGH SHADOWS GATHER, THE VALIANT PRINCE PROVIDED A WELCOMED RESPITE.

"ONE COULD FORGET THE TROUBLES BEYOND THE GARDEN WALLS FOR A NIGHT," SIR GALLANT REMARKED. "THE PRINCE BROUGHT TOGETHER LOYAL ALLIES TO RESTORE OUR SPIRIT."

Throughout the soiree, His Highness charmed guests with his refined manners and lively wit. All were struck by his meticulous attention to every detail for their comfort and pleasure.

"Prince Asher is the consummate host," Lord Heyward said. "He made sure each person felt welcome. His care for his people shows in everything he does."

Despite the late summer heat, the extensive gardens provided a cool, fragrant respite. Guests danced under twinkling lights and dined at floral-adorned tables. Even a minor mishap involving spilled tea on His Highness simply added to the convivial mood. The prince took it gracefully in stride, easing any tension.

As the night progressed, smiles and carefree laughter abounded. Lively music accompanied pleasant conversation between allies united against the spreading villainy. Many lingered long after sundown, reluctant for the magical evening of camaraderie to end, but at last, the happy guests bid their gracious host farewell, spirits lifted.

Prince Asher's gala will surely be the talk of noble circles for weeks to come. All who

ATTENDED FELT PRIVILEGED TO ENJOY THE HOSPITALITY OF THE KINGDOM'S MOST CHARMING ROYAL AND DISCUSS THEIR HEROIC CAMPAIGN.

DESPITE THE PERPETRATOR OF THE MYSTERIOUS BURNING OF THREE THIEVES REMAINING AT LARGE, THIS GATHERING SERVES AS INSPIRATION TO BRING MORE LIGHTHEARTED JOY TO THESE INCREASINGLY DARK TIMES. THE PRINCE'S SOIREE BLOSSOMED WITH LIFE'S SIMPLE PLEASURES—BEAUTY, COMMUNITY, AND KINSHIP.

8

Asher

As I scan the sea of guests, their laughter and chatter filling the air, I can't help but feel a twinge of unease. My eyes dart across the garden, eventually settling on Lilly as she moves gracefully between partygoers. I wonder if she knew about the poison in my tea, or if her spilling it was truly an accident. It was only after the liquid seared my skin that I noticed the telltale burn of the toxin.

"Your Highness," a voice interrupts my thoughts, snapping me back to the present.

A nearby guest raises their teacup in greeting, and I offer a polite nod before returning my attention to Lilly. Is it possible she knows something? Her demeanor seems too innocent to harbor any ill intentions, but something tells me that there is more to her than meets the eye. The way she carefully avoids conversation with the other servants, choosing instead to focus on her duties, intrigues me.

Though her actions could be chalked up to mere shyness, I find myself observing her every move. She is a wild card among my staff in a way I had not expected, especially considering the main core of my staff is of the more colorful sort.

"Prince Asher," someone else calls out, pulling me from my thoughts once more.

I smile and exchange pleasantries with another noble, all the while keeping an eye on Lilly as she continues to skirt around the edges of the party.

Her refusal of refreshments and cups of tea when they are offered catches my attention. Is it deliberate? Does she know something about the poison that I don't? I need information, but I can't confront her directly without arousing suspicion. I need someone to keep watch over her, someone who can blend into the background and report back to me.

"Rendfield," I whisper under my breath.

Within moments, my loyal butler appears at my side.

"I need you to keep an eye on Lilly," I instruct him in a hushed tone. "There's something... off about her behavior, and I want to know what's going on."

"Of course, Your Highness," Rendfield replies, his face betraying no judgment as he nods in understanding. He melts into the background, positioning himself where he can keep a watchful eye on Lilly without drawing attention.

I return to mingling with the guests, talking and laughing while maintaining a careful watch on both Lilly and Rendfield from the corner of my eye. As much as I want to dismiss my suspicions as unfounded, the nagging feeling that there is more to this situation than meets the eye refuses to dissipate.

"Prince Asher, your garden is absolutely delightful!" Lady Elspeth gushes as she fans herself with flourish, her emerald eyes twinkling. "And the tea is simply divine."

"Thank you, my lady," I reply, dipping my head in acknowledgment. "We take great pride in our gardens, and we're always pleased to share them with esteemed guests such as yourself."

Even as I chat with Lady Elspeth, my attention remains divided. Out of the corner of my eye, I continue to observe Lilly as she moves through the crowd, her steps seemingly lighter than before but still deliberate.

"Tell me, how do you manage to keep the roses so vibrant at this time of year?" Lady Elspeth inquires, her voice filled with genuine curiosity.

"Ah, that would be thanks to our dedicated team of gardeners," I answer smoothly, gesturing toward the abundance of blossoming flowers. "Their tireless efforts are what make this garden the jewel of the kingdom."

"Indeed, they have outdone themselves," she agrees, nodding appreciatively.

As our conversation flows like the gentle breeze that rustles the leaves above us, I steal glances at Lilly. There is something captivating about her, a mysterious allure that draws me in despite my many unanswered questions.

"Prince Asher?" Lady Elspeth's voice pulls me back into the moment, her brow furrowed in concern. "Are you feeling all right? You seem... distracted."

"Apologies, my lady," I say, offering her a sheepish grin. "I assure you, I am in excellent spirits. It's just that..." I trail off, not entirely certain how to explain my growing fascination with the peculiar new maid.

"Ah, say no more," Lady Elspeth replies with a knowing smile. "I believe I understand. The heart is a curious thing, is it not?"

"Indeed, it is," I agree, feeling a blush creep up my cheeks.

"Your Highness," Rendfield murmurs later, sidling up to me with a discreet update. "It appears that Lilly is avoiding the kitchen. She has not consumed any food or drink herself, only serving it to others. Additionally, she seems to be disposing of certain items without offering them to guests."

The news only serves to deepen my suspicions. Does Lilly have insight into the poisoning attempt? If so, why didn't she talk to me about her suspicions? The questions swirl around my mind, but I know I can't press her for answers just yet.

"Keep watch," I instruct Rendfield, "and report anything else you find."

"Of course, Your Highness," he says, melting back into the crowd.

I take a raspberry tart from the dessert table. The sweet, tangy flavor of the raspberry filling does little to dispel the unease churning within me. Lilly's strange behavior gnaws at my thoughts, and I know it won't be long before I have to confront her directly, consequences be damned. For now, though, I will play the part of the perfect prince, smiling and laughing with my guests while keeping a watchful eye on the mysterious maid who has captured my attention.

9

Lillith

With the poisoned tea incident fresh on my mind and Prince Asher seemingly unharmed, I keep a close eye on everything that runs through my fingers. Someone has tried to kill him, and that someone is still lurking among us. I have to find the culprit, not only for the prince's safety but because my own twisted plans for his corruption hinge on his survival.

As I continue to serve the guests, my eyes scan the crowd, searching for any sign of abnormal behavior or ill intent. That's when I spot him—Mister Rotting Hand. He stands near the edge of the party, dressed in a butler's uniform, a white glove covering his hands. I can see just the slightest bit of his injury peek above it on one hand.

"Excuse me," I murmur to the guest I'm serving.

I quickly set down the tray of pastries and follow the villain as he slips out of the grand hall. I trail him through the winding corridors of the palace, my palms sweaty as I try to keep up with his surprisingly nimble movements. Finally, he ducks into a secluded courtyard, the shadows casting eerie patterns on the cobblestones beneath our feet.

"Who are you?" I demand, stepping into the moonlit clearing. "And why did you try to poison Prince Asher?"

"Ah, Lillith," the rotten hand man hisses, his voice a low, raspy growl. "I should've known you'd be the one to foil my plan."

"Answer my questions!" I bark, my hands balling into fists at my sides.

"Now what fun would that be?" He grins wickedly. "If you think hard enough, you will remember me. I'm a bit offended that you've forgotten. And as for the prince, well, he's an obstacle in the grand scheme of things."

"An obstacle that only I'm allowed to tamper with," I retort, narrowing my eyes at him.

"Is that so?" the man sneers, raising his rotten hand and sending a blast of dark magic toward me.

I dodge the attack, leaping to the side as the energy crackles against the stone wall behind me. Despite my unwillingness to use my magical abilities I am determined to put up a fight. Magic will be my last resort. I lunge at him, aiming a swift kick at his midsection.

"Feisty, aren't you?" he taunts, blocking my kick with ease.

"More than you can handle, apparently," I shoot back, narrowly avoiding another blast of his dark magic.

We continue our dance of attacks and counters, each of us growing more frustrated with the other's persistence. I know I can't keep this up forever. Without magic, I am at a clear disadvantage, but I refuse to let him get the better of me or endanger my prey any further.

"Give it up, Lillith," he growls, panting from exertion. "You'll never win this battle."

"Never underestimate a woman who's got something to protect," I reply defiantly, even as my limbs grow heavy and my breath comes in gasps.

Just as I prepare for another assault, he throws down a smoke bomb, and a thick cloud of black mist envelops us. I cough and choke, my eyes stinging as I try to see through the haze.

"Where are you?" I scream, spinning around in search of my elusive enemy, but it is no use. By the time the smoke clears, the man has vanished.

"Damn it!" I spit, slamming my fist against the cold stone wall.

My frustration bubbles over like a cauldron left on the fire for too long, and I can't help but feel the sting of defeat. I have failed to catch the rotten hand man, and Prince Asher is still in danger.

But there is no time to wallow in self-pity. Clenching my teeth, I turn on my heel and sprint back toward the gathering.

Asher

I maintain a pleasant facade, mingling amongst the guests even as my mind swirls with questions about the poisoning attempt. Uplifting tunes from the string quartet and laughter float through the lush greenery while the guests enjoy the garden party.

Out of the corner of my eye, I notice Rendfield approaching swiftly, an alarmingly grave expression on his face. I excuse myself from the group of nobles and meet Rendfield in a shadowed alcove. This man is not one I usually see alarmed or really with any expression other than confidence and the mask of boredom he generally wears during work hours.

"Your Highness," Rendfield utters urgently, "there has been an incident with the maid, Lilly. I followed her as you requested and observed a confrontation between her and an unknown man near the eastern courtyard."

My brows furrow in concern. "Is she harmed?"

"I do not believe so, Your Highness, though the man utilized some form of magic against her before disappearing in a cloud of smoke."

My jaw clenches, anger simmering within me. "And where is Lilly now?"

"On her way back here, I presume. She gave chase, but he evaded her."

I place a hand firmly on Rendfield's shoulder. "Speak of this to no one else for now."

Rendfield nods. "Of course, Your Highness."

My mind races, thoughts swirling like a tempest. This strange new maid has nearly been assassinated on palace grounds after apparently saving my life. I need answers, and I suspect only Lilly holds the key.

11

Lillith

As I slip back into the garden, I notice that Prince Asher is watching me intently. His blue eyes seem to bore into my soul, making my heart race with a mix of fear and uncertainty. He doesn't look angry about the spilled tea, which I find odd considering his usual penchant for perfection.

"Your Highness," I say with a small curtsy, catching my breath as he approaches me. "I hope everything is well."

"Quite well, thank you," he replies, his voice warm and surprisingly gentle.

A slight smile plays on his lips, and it is difficult to read his emotions. Is he grateful or simply bemused at the chaos I have caused?

"Did you enjoy your tea?" I ask hesitantly, wondering if he has caught on to my little charade.

"Ah, yes, the tea," he muses, rubbing his chin thoughtfully. "It was certainly an... interesting experience." His eyes sparkle with amusement, though I can't tell if he is laughing at me or with me.

"Interesting?" My brow furrows in confusion. "I can assure you, Your Highness, my intentions were pure."

"Of that, I have no doubt," he says, his gaze never leaving mine, "but one must always be prepared for the unexpected, don't you think?"

"Indeed," I agree, swallowing hard.

I search his face for any sign of reproach or suspicion, but all I find is a strange sense of camaraderie, as if we are partners in some great adventure, bound together by a secret only we share.

"Your Highness," I whisper, daring to speak my true thoughts, "why are you not angry about the spilled tea?"

Prince Asher leans in closer, his breath warm against my ear. "Because, Lilly," he murmurs, "sometimes a little chaos is just what one needs to shake up the monotony."

When he pulls away, he winks conspiratorially, leaving me both flustered and relieved.

***

"Ah, freedom." I sigh, stepping into the bustling town market.

It's been nearly a week since the party and escaping the castle is surprisingly easy.The cacophony of vendors hawking their wares mixed with the lively conversations of townsfolk provides a welcome change from the stifling silence of the castle.

The familiar scents of coffee and baked goods waft through the air, furthering my determination to explore the town. I have no set destination in mind, but my nose seems to be guiding me toward a small cafe tucked away among the stalls of vendors selling fruits and vegetables.

I step inside the cafe and am immediately greeted by the warm atmosphere that seems inviting after my long walk. The smell of freshly brewed coffee permeates the room, making me crave a cup even more than before. After taking a seat near a window, I eye the menu with great interest.

My choices quickly narrow down to one item—a maple pecan latte with some sort of flaky pastry on the side. It arrives at my table within minutes after I place my order.

My eyes widen in delight as I take my first sip of the warm beverage. The smooth, creamy flavor swirls across my taste buds, and with each sip, I find myself wanting more.

"That was delicious," I exclaim to the barista behind the counter.

He gives me a friendly smile before thanking me for my order.

I continue to savor every last drop before turning my attention to the flaky pastry in front of me. Taking a bite, I am overwhelmed with joy at the sweetness and crunchy texture that fills my mouth.

"Wow this is amazing," I rave between bites, not caring who hears me.

My mouth waters with anticipation, and I quickly finish off the delectable treat and look out toward the bustling market.

I grab my things from the table and thank the barista again before heading into the market square.

This time, however, I am armed with an energy boost that allows me to take in all of the sights and sounds without feeling overwhelmed. It is easy to get lost in conversation with merchants or just admire their colorful displays of goods.

This is the life.

I watch vendors haggling over prices, children playing tag around their parents' stalls, and people bartering for goods they don't need but want anyway.

I laugh out loud as a little girl snatches fish from her father's basket and runs away cackling while he chases after her. "Come back here! You have to help me sell these!"

A nearby stall where two men are loudly debating over the price of an antique vase catches my eye. One man lowers his offer, while the other insists on a higher one until finally they agree on something in between both their prices and shake hands in agreement.

Behind it all, the little movements draw my attention the most. Sleight of hand slipping a coin pouch from one especially robust man whose hair appears almost glued back into a tight ponytail at the nape of his neck. Another hand slowly tucking an apple from a produce vendor into their pocket as they pass by. It feels like home for the first time since I have arrived at the prince's gates.

I'm drawn to a stall filled with an assortment of trinkets and baubles. The vendor, a plump woman with rosy cheeks, beckons me closer.

"Ah, Miss Grimsbane, right?" she asks.

I nod, wondering how she knows my name.

"I've seen you around the castle. My sister's a maid there, you see."

"Small world," I muse, picking up a delicate silver necklace with an intricate pendant.

"Isn't it just?" she replies, her eyes twinkling. "That one suits you, dear. Only five silver coins. What do you say?"

"Five? That seems a bit... steep." I hesitate, my fingers lingering on the pendant.

"Tell you what," she says, leaning in closer, "I'll give it to you for three but only because you room with my sister."

"Who's your sister?"

"Mairelle! She could have joined the family business but just had to go work for the prince."

After taking a second look at the woman, I can see a bit of resemblance. She has the same golden hair and delicate nose.

"Ah, Mairelle's positivity pays off, it seems." I chuckle. "Deal."

"Here you go, dear." She hands me the necklace, wrapped in a small cloth. "May it bring you as much joy as those two bring to others."

"Thank you," I reply, even though I don't know if bringing joy is what I would call my relationship with my roommates. If it saves me a few silvers, it's worth keeping my mouth shut.

As I continue to explore the market, A figure leaning against a nearby stall captures my attention. It is Mrs. Umbernuckle, the head maid of the castle. She is whispering to a mysterious man with an eyepatch. Curiosity piqued, I observe them from a safe distance.

"Mrs. Umbernuckle, fancy meeting you here," I mutter under my breath, hiding behind a stack of barrels filled with apples.

The two speak in hushed voices, and I strain to hear their conversation.

"Meet me in an hour at the old oak tree on the long dirt road back to the castle," the man says, his voice gruff, "and make sure you're not followed. We have business to take care of."

"Understood," Mrs. Umbernuckle replies curtly, her willowy frame tense.

Something inside me clicks. That man with the eye-patch—he had jumped out of a window to escape the castle just last week! They were working together? Did that mean they were working with Mister Rotting Hand?

"Long dirt road, huh?" I muse, my curiosity growing stronger. "Might as well see what's going on."

They part ways, and I trail after Mrs. Umbernuckle, careful to remain hidden. Keeping her just in sight but far enough away that if she turned around I would be difficult to identify. We venture down the long, winding road that leads back to the castle. I push through the thicket of gnarled and tangled branches, wisps of fabric from my shirt catching on their spines. While Mrs. Umbernuckle can stay on the well-cared-for road, I dare not. Every careful step I take threatens to send me toppling down the rocky incline as I keep hidden in the nearby forest, my target just in sight.

"Curse this blasted road," I grumble, swatting away a low-hanging branch. "Why couldn't they meet somewhere less... treacherous?"

Despite the obstacles, I persist in following Mrs. Umbernuckle.

Suddenly, the path is blocked by a throng of white-fleeced sheep, jostling and baaing. I spot her ahead of them, but the chaos quickly envelopes her.

Without thinking, I scramble up the nearest tree, managing to get a tall enough branch where I can see her struggling against the tide of wooly bodies. I have to stifle my laughter. This is too good. Every poke and snag was absolutely worth the scene before me.

Mrs. Umbernuckle stumbles through a sea of wooly backs, her arms flailing wildly as she desperately tries to keep her balance. Each time she regains it, though, the flock's solid booties push her further off balance. Eventually she emerges out the other side.

Time for me to climb down and follow. Of course I will avoid the sheep entirely.

As I near an old oak tree near the rot iron fence of Prince Asher's estate, I spot Mrs. Umbernuckle and the man with the eyepatch talking beneath its ancient branches. A stocky man I don't recognize cowers in front of them. The old oak tree's gnarled branches sway gently in the breeze, casting eerie shadows on the ground below.

Whatever this is, it must be important if they choose such a secluded spot.

I creep closer, staying low to the ground and moving as silently as possible. Hiding behind a bush, I strain to hear the conversation between Mrs. Umbernuckle and the one-eyed man. My heart pounds in my ears, making it nearly impossible to discern their words.

Speak up, you nincompoops! I mentally will them.

"P-please, milady," the man stammers, struggling against the ropes that bind him to the tree trunk. "I d-didn't mean any harm. I was only trying to feed my family."

"Your intentions matter little," Mrs. Umbernuckle says coldly, her voice cutting through the forest like a knife. "You stole from a member of the royal family. You must face the consequences."

Consequences? Since when did Mrs. Umbernuckle become an enforcer of justice? She's the head housekeeper.

As I watch, something strange begins to happen. Shadows pool around Mrs. Umbernuckle's feet, dark tendrils snaking up her body until she is wreathed in darkness. She raises an arm, and the shadows coalesce into a whip-like shape, crackling with an energy that makes the hairs on the back of my neck stand on end.

"Wait a minute," I mutter under my breath, my eyes widening. That's shadow magic. What I had seen in her bedroom wasn't a trick of the light.

Only one person can do that. Lamira the Wraith!

"Please, have mercy!" the thief cries out as the shadow-whip comes down upon him. He yelps in pain, but his pleas only seem to fuel Mrs. Umbernuckle's—or, rather, Lamira's—anger.

"Mercy? For a thief who sought to rob Prince Asher?" Lamira sneers, her voice dripping with contempt. "You should be grateful I'm not ending your life right here. Perhaps this punishment will teach you a valuable lesson."

"Oi, Mrs. Umbernuckle!" I shout without thinking. "That's enough!"

Lamira stops mid-strike, her shadowy form wavering as she turns to face me. A cold smile spreads across her lips while she regards me with amusement.

"Ah, Lilly," she coos, her voice dripping with false sweetness. "What brings you out here? Are you lost?"

"Hardly," I scoff, trying to appear braver than I feel. "I followed you and your one-eyed friend here, and now, it seems, I've discovered your dark secret."

Should I give away that I know who she really is?

"Indeed." Lamira sighs, her shadows dissipating as she resumes her guise as Mrs. Umbernuckle. "It appears you've seen I'm more than just a maid, but what do you intend to do with this knowledge?"

"Put an end to this charade, for one," I reply, my voice shaking slightly. "The people in the castle trust you, and you're taking advantage of them."

"Is that so?" Lamira asks, her eyes narrowing dangerously. "Well, then, it seems we have ourselves a bit of a... situation."

"Indeed. A situation that only one of us is going to walk away from," I say, feigning confidence as my mind races for a strategy. "Tell me, why are you here? Are you after Prince Asher?"

"Prince Asher?" Lamira laughs, the sound echoing eerily through the forest. "Oh, little Lilly, you give me far too much credit."

She steps closer, and I can feel the chill of her presence reaching out to me. My fingers twitch at my side, ready to summon my own magic if needed.

"Then what are your intentions?" I demand, refusing to back down despite my growing fear. "They deserve to know the truth."

"Ah, yes. The truth," she muses, her icy blue eyes locked onto mine. "Such a tricky thing, isn't it? So many layers, so many secrets. I suppose we all have our reasons for hiding them. My own is among the smallest on the castle grounds."

"Enough with your riddles!" I snap, my frustration boiling over. "Just tell me why you're here!"

"Very well." Lamira sighs, a malicious grin spreading across her face. "Call it a second chance. I'm here for the same reason any wraith would be. Power."

"Power?" I echo, my heart sinking as I consider the implications of her words. "Are you here to corrupt Prince Asher? Or has that already happened?"

"Perhaps," she replies cryptically, her smile never wavering. "Or perhaps not. It's all a matter of perspective, really. Maybe he's corrupted me."

"Your games won't work on me," I warn her, my resolve hardening. "Whatever you're planning, I'll stop you."

"Will you now?" she murmurs, her gaze drifting toward the thief still bound by her shadows. "You're hardly in a position to make such bold claims, little Lilly. You are nothing, and you know nothing."

She has no idea just how wrong she is. My fingers itch to wipe that smug smile off her face.

"Fine," I say, forcing myself to sound calm and collected. "We'll see if your perspective changes once Prince Asher and the others learn the truth about you."

"Ah, yes. The truth," Lamira repeats, her laughter filling the air once more. "Some already know the truth. Are you sure you do? But you forget, my dear, some truths are better left buried."

"Then consider me a gravedigger," I retort, my voice steady even as my heart races, "because I won't rest until you're exposed for the monster you truly are."

"Very well," she whispers, her eyes narrowing dangerously. "Just remember, little Lilly, some monsters are best left undisturbed."

With that chilling warning, Lamira and Eye Patch disappear into the shadows, leaving me alone with my thoughts and the thief who'd unwittingly become a pawn in our conflict. As I turn toward him, I can't help but wonder what other secrets lurk within the castle walls.

I grab the thief's shoulder and pull him up with me, my grip firm. He stumbles back in surprise, his eyes wide with fear, but I can see the fight still burning within them. I know that look all too well. He is ready to attack or run.

Mrs. Umbernuckle was a bit too irresponsible, leaving this thief alone after catching him. It will be up to me now to bring him before Prince Asher. I can only imagine the punishment Lamira will have for me if I don't, and I'm not sure I can withstand that punishment without giving myself away.

Holding tight to his arm, I begin to lead him away from the gardens toward the castle gates.

The thief thrashes about in my grasp, uttering angry outbursts as we near the entrance to the castle. "Why won't you listen?" he groans. "Let me go! I'm not your prisoner!"

I can feel his desperation for freedom seeping through my fingers, but little does he know I have no sympathy for anyone who gets in my way. He may have been trying to plead his case, but there is no turning back now.

"Stop struggling," I say firmly, maintaining my grip on his arm as we near the gatekeeper who stands guard at the entrance of the castle grounds.

The thief's protests are cut off as he takes in the sight of the towering gatekeeper, a hulking figure wearing armor and brandishing an impressive spear. He is no ordinary guard. Upon closer inspection, I have little doubt that he is also from the villain world. His gaze is stern and unforgiving as it falls upon us. How did I miss this when I first arrived?

"What business have you here?" the gatekeeper asks gruffly, his eyes never leaving us.

"This thief has been caught attempting to steal by Mrs. Umbernuckle," I say, my voice wavering despite my best efforts to stay composed. "I'm bringing him before Prince Asher."

The gatekeeper nods curtly in acknowledgment but makes no further comment on our mission when he opens the gates for us to enter.

We continue our march down the winding cobblestone path that leads from the entrance to the castle courtyard.

As we near the steps to the main entrance of the home, the thief twists in my grip. He thinks he can escape? From me? I sneer, jerking him back to face the door.

"Don't even think about it. There are things worse here than the woman you just dealt with."

The thief glances at me warily before turning away, his gaze fixed on something farther ahead of us as if he's found something else that interests him more than our conversation.

When we pass under the archway and into a long hall lined with portraits of past kings and queens, he stops short and gazes up at an old painting near the end of the hall, one depicting a young prince standing in front of a tall window overlooking a wide expanse of water far below us. The prince in this painting is none other than Prince

Asher himself. It must be a new one. It feels like new decor pops up in this place daily.

"Where is the prince?" I ask a passing footman.

"In his office," he replies in a gruff tone, pointing toward the door.

I nod and turn back to the thief. "Let's go," I say firmly, my voice echoing off the walls of the hallway as I tighten my grip on his arm and drag him toward the door.

When we enter, the prince sits behind his desk, flanked by Mrs. Umbernuckle who wears a frown of disapproval on her face. The thief finally stops struggling, and his eyes widen in fear.

Prince Asher stands up from his chair and studies both of us silently for a few moments before speaking. "Explain yourself," he says sternly, his gaze boring into the thief's soul.

The man glues his eyes to the floor, refusing to answer.

Mrs. Umbernuckle quickly recounts what she saw, adding her own personal dismissal of any kind-heartedness that might have been present in this situation for good measure.

The prince listens calmly before turning back to address us once more. "You are aware that theft is not tolerated here," he says gravely, his voice low but firm with authority. "Do you have anything else to add?"

The thief shakes his head miserably, unable or unwilling to speak in his own defense any longer, while I remain silent lest my words incriminate me due to our association together thus far in this matter.

After what feels like an eternity of silence broken only by our collective breathing, Prince Asher finally proceeds. "You may leave."

I'm confused. He wants the thief to leave? Nothing is going to happen? I stand dumbfounded.

"Lilly, he means you," Mrs. Umbernuckle adds.

I glance at the prince too. He offers a small nod confirming that yes, that is in fact what he meant.

I quickly leave the office without replying. Everything about this is suspicious. Are Prince Asher and Mrs. Umbernuckle working together? If they are, I know they will never tell me. Rule number eight of being a good villain—only reveal your evil plan if the person you are revealing it to is either needed to help fulfill it or will be the victim of it. I am clearly not in their little circle. Why does that bother me so much?

12

Lillith

"**S**crew this!" I mutter under my breath, attempting to smooth out the crumpled black hair that frames my face.

Today has been nothing short of exasperating between first Mrs. Umbernuckle's constant watch over every single thing I do and Prince Asher's constantly good attitude. I long for a reprieve from this charade. The Zibath Mountains beckon me with their promise of solitude and the freedom to exercise my magic without worry.

"All right," I say to myself as I walk off the grounds and into the forest, far enough away that my magic should be difficult to trace if it's noticed at all.

With a small grin, I close my eyes and feel the familiar warmth of my magic coursing through my veins. In an instant, the tedious world of my disguised life as Lilly Grimsbane, the maid, vanishes into thin air.

A floating sensation overtakes me as the ground reappears under my feet and I arrive at my secret hideaway, greeted by the cool mountain air and the comforting scent of pine. This is where I can truly be Lillith Shadowend without fear of discovery or judgment. Here, I can use my powers freely and relax, far away from the prying eyes of Mrs. Umbernuckle and the unnerving charm of Prince Asher Sunbash, with his white hair and captivating blue eyes.

"Sweet solitude." I sigh, making my way toward the entrance of my hidden sanctuary.

It is time to let loose and indulge in some much-needed relaxation. No more tea-reading or fire-controlling for now. Just pure, unadulterated magical bliss.

"Finally," I breathe, stepping inside with glee. "Time to let my hair down, so to speak."

My hideaway is nestled high in the Zibath Mountains, discreetly camouflaged amidst the towering trees and craggy rocks. The entrance is a simple wooden door concealed by an enchantment, visible only to those who know of its existence.

Inside, my secret lair is generously spacious, with ceilings high enough to accommodate the occasional burst of magical energy. The walls are lined with shelves filled with books and various trinkets I collected over time. A large window overlooks the breathtaking view of the mountains, allowing fresh air to circulate throughout my sanctuary. Ventilation, after all, is important when you dabble in magic, especially fire-based spells. Rule number three of being a good villain— ventilation must always be too small to crawl through.

Any good villain knows that security measures are paramount, and I have gone to great lengths to ensure the safety of my hideaway. Intricate runes are etched into the very foundation of the building, warding off unwanted visitors and keeping my magical experiments undetected. In addition, hidden traps are strategically placed throughout, ensuring that no intruder would make it far without regretting their trespass.

I think back to the time when my escape tunnel saved me from a particularly determined band of bounty hunters. They somehow managed to follow me to my sanctum, but thanks to my foresight, I slipped away unnoticed through a secret passage beneath the floorboards. Of course, those bounty hunters didn't exactly escape either. In fact, they were never seen again by anyone, including me. Just one of my many secrets.

"Chaos and destruction can be fun," I admit, "but they're also quite messy. Better to have multiple escape routes and backup plans than find yourself cornered without options." I chuckle to myself, feeling a sense of pride in my villainous wisdom.

I take a moment to relish the freedom that comes with being in my hideaway, surrounded by the tools of my craft and free from the watchful eyes of Mrs. Umbernuckle and Prince Asher. The weight of my disguise as Lilly Grimsbane begins to lift, replaced by the exhilarating thrill of power that comes with being Lillith Shadowend.

"Time for some magical indulgence," echoes in my hideaway as I stride over to the window, feeling the last vestiges of Lilly slip away.

The view from my mountain lair is breathtaking, the vibrant tapestry of green and gold trees swaying gently in the breeze below, the sparkling river winding its way through the valley like a silver ribbon.

"There it is," I murmur, spotting the now-empty dragon cave at the foot of the Zibath Mountains. The memory of my roommate bragging about Prince Asher slaying the great beast with his enchanted sword still sends a sense of loss in me. "Such a waste of a perfectly good dragon."

I sigh, shaking my head. My feelings are conflicted—admiration for the prince's skill tinged with frustration at losing an old friend. I didn't have many of them. Most of my life, I've lived alone, and even in the rare moments that I didn't, I tended to rub people the wrong way.

Well, most people. There was Silviana. Creatures of all types were always drawn to her, singling her out as both odd and in the way before she could start giving the animals directions. She was my only friend growing up. I was odd in my own way as a kid. Who wouldn't be if they were raised by two of the most feared villains who believed that showing any sign of compassion was a weakness? We became each other's best friends and confidants until I escaped the training facility my parents left me in. I've only heard of her in passing since.

"Enough of this," I mutter, deciding to focus on something more pleasant. "Time for food."

With a flick of my wrist, I summon a variety of ingredients from the hidden pantry—fresh bread, ripe tomatoes, crispy lettuce, and thinly sliced meats. One of the first spells I placed on my home after building it was a pantry that kept food fresh forever, and it appears this spell still holds strong.

Assembling the sandwich is an art form in itself, one that I take great pride in. I meticulously layer each ingredient, making sure they are evenly distributed.

"Perfection," I declare, admiring my handiwork. I take a moment to appreciate the array of colors and textures before me then hear my stomach growl impatiently. I chuckle to myself. "All right, all right. No need to be so eager."

I bite into the sandwich with gusto, savoring the crunch of the lettuce and the tang of the tomatoes. The smoky flavor of the deli meat dances on my tongue, while the bread serves as a soft, pillowy canvas for it all.

"Who knew magic could be so delicious?" I muse between bites. "Perhaps I should add 'sandwich artist' to my list of accomplishments."

At that moment, with the taste of victory and a well-crafted sandwich filling my senses, I feel at peace. It is so easy to forget about the challenges ahead and simply enjoy the pleasure of a meal prepared by my own magical hand.

"Soon," I whisper to myself, wiping crumbs from my lips. "Soon, Prince Asher will learn just what it means to cross paths with Lillith Shadowend."

But for now, I will savor the simple joys of an excellent sandwich and a priceless view.

After the last bite of my sandwich is savored, a chill creeps into my bones. My hideaway, nestled high in the Zibath Mountains, is known for its unpredictable weather. It's time to ignite a fire and bask in its warmth.

"Fire," I whisper, commanding the flames in the fireplace to leap to life.

They dance and swirl, casting flickering shadows on the cavernous walls of my library. The room is a treasure trove of knowledge, filled with books that have been collected over centuries, their spines worn and pages yellowed.

"Ah, now that's better," I murmur, allowing myself a small smile.

"Let's see... what shall I read today?" I muse, scanning the towering shelves. My fingers tingle with excitement as they always do when my magic responds to my whims. I reach out, willing a few choice volumes to float down from their perches and hover before me. "Hmm, perhaps something lighthearted."

I pluck a book from the air, its cover adorned with frolicking fairies, and settle into my plush armchair by the fire. Just as I am about to open the book, a small pop echoes through the room.

"Goodness!" I exclaim, dropping the book in surprise.

There, standing beside me, is the curious creature I've only seen twice before. Long ears twitch atop its head, and enormous eyes blink up at me.

"Who are you?" I ask, though I'm not sure if the little creature can understand me.

It tilts its head, seeming to ponder my question before letting out a soft trill.

"All right then, I'll call you Nargle," I decide, chuckling at the absurdity of it all. "Welcome to my secret lair, Nargle. Make yourself at home. I have no idea how you found me here, but as long as we keep this secret between just us two, you can stay."

Nargle hops onto my lap, nuzzling against me as if we are old friends. Its ears twitch with delight as I stroke its fur, and it emits another contented trill.

"Ah, Nargle, life would be so much simpler if everyone was like you." I sigh, picking up my book once more. "No schemes or betrayals, just cozy fires and good company."

As I begin reading, the weight of Nargle's presence on my lap serves as a reminder of the unexpected connections that exist even in the hidden corners of the world. And though my mind returns to the task at hand—corrupting Prince Asher—there is a part of me that revels in the simple joy of sharing this moment with a newfound friend.

I glance down at Nargle nestled in my lap and notice its complete lack of clothing. The thought strikes me as odd, given that the creature is obviously capable of magical feats like teleportation. Surely it must feel the chill of the mountain air on its exposed skin.

"Nargle," I say with a smile, "you must be freezing! Allow me to remedy that."

With a flick of my wrist, I conjure a tiny outfit for my newfound friend. A small vest and matching trousers materialize from thin air, both woven from the softest wool. As I dress Nargle, the creature's long ears perk up, and it blinks at me with those enormous eyes full of curiosity.

"Much better," I announce, placing Nargle back on my lap. "Now you won't catch a cold."

Nargle trills happily, snuggling into my warmth once more. It is a small act of kindness, one that I rarely afford to others, yet there is something about this gentle creature that stirs a sense of protectiveness in me.

The creature lets out a yawn as it settles onto a small cushion I conjure beside the fire. Its eyes droop, and within moments, it is fast asleep, its tiny chest rising and falling with each breath.

I smile as I watch Nargle slumber, the firelight casting dancing shadows across its peaceful face. The mix of emotions that stirs within me is unexpected. A warmth spreads through my chest, melting away the icy exterior I so carefully crafted over the years. For once, I feel something akin to happiness in the presence of another being, even if that being is an odd, two-legged creature with an affinity for teleportation.

An idea crosses my mind as I watch him sleep. Some mages acquire familiars. It's not something you can find on your own, but if you are among the most powerful, sometimes a familiar would choose you. Usually, it's something simple like an animal, but I truly have no idea what kind of creature Nargle is. He's short and sort of awkward. He clearly has some power and is intelligent even if he can't speak. A small elf? No, that's not quite right. A dwarf? He's not quite so stocky and is a bit more... floppy?

A small chuckle escapes me. That's it! Until I know better, Nargle is officially a dwarflop.

"Sleep well, little one," I whisper, turning my attention back to my book.

But as I read, my thoughts keep straying back to the innocence of the sleeping creature beside me, and I find myself wondering how long it has been since I've allowed myself to feel this way.

"Perhaps there's more to life than evil schemes and power plays," I muse, my fingers absently stroking Nargle's soft fur. "But for now, we'll keep that our little secret."

***

The moon's risen, casting a blanket of velvety darkness over the land. The fire in my hideaway dwindles to glowing embers and the comforting weight of Nargle's presence by my side makes it difficult to focus on my book. Might as well return to the prince's castle and resume my mission.

"Come on, Nargle," I whisper, carefully scooping the dozing creature into my arms.

My magic swirls around us, and with a soft pop, we stand just outside the castle walls. The moon casts its silvery glow over the ancient stones, making them shimmer like a pool of water under starlight.

"Back already?" I ask myself, trying to decipher the strange mix of emotions churning within me. "Why am I even here? Isn't this supposed to be my day off?"

Deep down, I know the answer. No one can take my prey away from me. I am the most powerful villain in three kingdoms, after all. Prince Asher is mine to corrupt, Mrs. Umbernuckle or any other meddling force be damned.

"Ah, well." I sigh, adjusting the tiny outfit I conjured for Nargle earlier. "No rest for the wicked, as they say."

"Grmph?" Nargle grumbles sleepily, rubbing its eyes with its fuzzy paws.

"Never mind, little one." I stroke its head affectionately. "Just some villainous musings."

With one final glance at the moonlit castle, I steel myself for the challenges ahead and magic us back to the forest outside of the castle, ready to figure out what Mrs. Umbernuckle and the prince are up to but with a newfound appreciation for the unexpected friendships that life can bring.

***

Stumbling into Prince Asher's private office I'm struggling under the weight of several large sacks overflowing with correspondence. Without access to my magic, tasks like lugging around heavy bags have become excruciatingly tedious, and I am over it.

"Just a little farther now," I grunt through gritted teeth, muscles burning as I haul the bulging sacks across the room. My shoes scuff against the polished stone floor with each labored step.

With a final grunt-inducing effort, I manage to hoist the mountain of mail onto the magnificent desk. No sooner have the sacks left my fingers than the overstuffed bag gives way, sending an avalanche of parchment spilling across the desktop and onto the floor.

"Seriously?" I sigh, tucking back the loose strands of dark hair that have slipped free of my cap. Kneeling down, I begin gathering up the strewn letters, muttering curses under my breath.

I gather the scattered parchment, fingers brushing over elegant scripts and ornate wax seals. What intimate thoughts are penned within these letters? Do the prince's admirers pour out their secret longings and wildest fantasies to the man they idolize? I trace over the broken seal of a rose-colored envelope, temptation creeping in. Before I can stop myself, I slide the letter free and unfold it.

My Dearest Prince Asher,

Words cannot express what you mean to me and the kingdom. From the moment I first saw you riding through the city, head held high and the sun gleaming off your silver armor, I knew you were special. They say you slew the dragon plaguing our lands single-handedly, though I know in my heart you must be too humble to admit it. A man of your valor and conviction only comes once in a generation. My days are spent longing for a chance to gaze upon your heroism once more. Please, brave prince, do not forget us common folk who look to your light in these dark times.

Eternally Yours,

Lady Amaryllis

I threw up in my mouth a little. This prince has armies of admirers ready to swoon over his every heroic deed, both real and imagined. How nauseating.

Unable to stop myself, I open another letter, skimming its intimate contents.

Your Highness,

I hope this letter finds you well. You do not know me, for I am just a humble baker's daughter from the village, yet I wanted to write and express my gratitude for your recent help upgrading our mill.

I know you faced resistance from some on your council who did not see our small village as worthy of the royal funds for repairs, yet you pushed ahead because it was right, not because it was popular. We now grind grain far faster, allowing my father to bake more bread to feed our people. You have filled many empty stomachs and warmed many hearts with your wise charity.

They say a true king has the heart of a servant. Your Highness, through your selfless service to communities like ours, you have proven this wisdom true. You could have ignored our remote village's plight, and none would have faulted you. Instead, you lifted us up when we were poor and powerless. The kingdoms need more leaders like you, my prince, those who lift the fallen and heal the hurting.

May your reign be long and blessed. You have my family's eternal gratitude and loyalty.

Sincerely,

Rosalind

Something hot and angry flickers in my core as I read these letters. I have spent weeks catering to His Royal Perfectness' every trivial whim, scrubbing chamber pots and waiting on him hand and foot, yet no matter what I do, the prince remains stubbornly noble. It is infuriating. He is supposed to be my prey, mine to manipulate and mold. Instead, Mr. Heroic Saint over there gets piles of adoring praise just for existing. Okay, maybe a bit more than just existing. I can at least appreciate him helping feed the people.

After a quick glance at the return address, I recognize that the village she speaks of is one where some of the villain community lives in secretly. Not everyone who is born into villain society wants to be a villain. Some just want to live a quiet life, but that isn't an option usually. The king has made sure of that. In his eyes, villains are born, not made. I'm not sure what makes me angrier, the fact that I have worked my ass off to become the villain I am today or that those who want an escape aren't allowed one.

I continue scanning letters, each more annoyingly worshipful than the last—young women begging for the chance to meet their noble prince, fathers offering their daughters' hands in marriage, children declaring him their idol.

It is too much. This prince, with his infuriating kindness and dashing good looks—I'm wicked, not blind—seems to have the entire kingdom, perhaps the entire world, enraptured.

An idea begins to form, slowly at first but quickly taking shape. Clearly, subtle methods are not enough to crack Prince Perfect. It is time for drastic measures.

I will use his gilded reputation against him. Surely underneath all this praise, he must have secrets, moments of weakness that would tarnish that gleaming heroic image. If such knowledge gets out, it could ruin him. Blackmail is dangerous, but cunningly executed, it may just do what pranks and tricks could not.

I open the desk and scribble out a letter on a blank piece of parchment from the top drawer, keeping the message intentionally vague:

Prince Asher,

It seems you have secrets that could destroy your sterling reputation should they get out. I know things about your past that could cause quite the scandal.

Of course, I would prefer this information remain between us. All I ask is that you obtain your father's enchanted emerald ring from the royal vault and discreetly deliver it to me. Do this small favor, and your secrets remain safe.

Should you refuse me, I cannot guarantee what tales may begin circulating or what evidence may come to light. Surely handing over one ring is preferable to the damage that could ensue?

Tell no one of this request. Speak of it, and you invite only trouble. Bring me the ring at dusk two days hence, when you take your evening ride by the old oak tree. Place it in the hollow there.

I trust we understand each other. I expect your utmost discretion in this matter, as I will show in kind by keeping your damaging secrets undisclosed once our bargain is struck. Do what is wise, Your Highness.

L.

P.S. My aim is only to help you avoid an unpleasant scandal. Once I have the ring, you need not trouble yourself further with me. Make the prudent choice, for your family's sake and your kingdom's. I await your delivery.

I fold the letter up and using a bit of a wax bar seal it without a stamp. Just a simple puddle. Let him try to maintain that saintly moral compass under the threat of total social ruin. Even heroes have weaknesses. I will find his and exploit it mercilessly until I finally bend him to my will.

I melt wax to reseal the opened letters, carefully covering any evidence of my tampering. With brisk efficiency, I neatly restack the correspondence on the polished desk. Finally, I slip my blackmail letter among the others.

Soon, these cloying words of praise will be replaced with shock and condemnation. I smirk. *Enjoy your glory while you still can, Your Highness.*

I tuck the letters into my apron and hurry out of the office, heart racing. If this scheme succeeds, the noble prince's reputation will be left in tatters. More importantly, it will prove that even the most golden hearts have shadows.

Let's see just how heroic you really are, Prince Perfect. No one denies Lillith Shadowend. No one.

13

Asher

Scanning over the pile of letters that have just been delivered to my desk, I prepare myself for what is sure to be an awkward yet fulfilling experience. It is my weekly tradition to read through correspondence from my subjects, one I look forward to each time.

As I break the wax seals and unfold the parchments, a mix of emotions swirls within me—gratitude for their kind words, humility from the effusive praise, and a tinge of embarrassment at some of the more amorous declarations. I appreciate their sentiments but never feel fully worthy of the admiration.

My Sweet Prince Asher,

Will you ever return to Fenton? I've missed seeing you as you pass through our small village while riding out to handle the horrible villains. I can help nurse any wounds you may receive. I've been training as a healer and would serve you well. How I wish I could see you again......

I skim the intimate letter, cheeks flushing slightly. The young maiden continues on to vividly describe her fervent longing to meet me in person, going into rather explicit detail about what she wished would happen between us. With an awkward chuckle, I neatly refolded the letter. Clearly the fanciful musings of a bored noblewoman.

Another letter catches my eye, this one bearing the seal of a farming village I had recently ordered repairs on their storm-damaged mill:

Your Highness,

I hope this letter finds you well. I wanted to express my gratitude for your help upgrading our mill. I know you faced resistance, yet still pushed ahead because it was rig ht...

I smile as I read the baker's earnest words of thanks, a sense of satisfaction warming me. Providing aid where it is needed, regardless of politics, is its own reward. If I could improve even one life, then the headaches of bureaucracy are worthwhile.

I continue reading, enjoying the glimpses into my people's daily lives, their struggles and small victories. Though many see me as perfect, I am just a man who tries his best, same as any other. Their belief in me is humbling, especially for a spare heir who has been given every opportunity possible for leadership in our kingdom.

Reaching the bottom of the pile, I pause at an unfamiliar letter sealed with dark wax and no sigil. I slide it open, brow furrowing as I scan the cryptic contents:

Prince Asher,

It seems you have secrets that could destroy your sterling reputation should they get out.

Secrets? I straighten in my chair. What is this anonymous accuser implying? I have no shady past to hide. Well, one thing, but there's no way they could know about it. An ominous opening but meaningless without substance.

I know things about your past that could cause quite the scandal.

My brow furrows, curiosity growing. Scandalous details about my past? Utterly false. My life has been an open book for all. This person clearly presumes too much.

Of course, I would prefer this information remain between us. All I ask is that you obtain your father's enchanted emerald ring from the royal vault and discreetly deliver it to me. Do this small favor, and your secrets remain safe.

I scoff aloud at the audacity. Hand over a priceless royal artifact to avoid unspecified consequences? Preposterous. This is no sinister figure.

Should you refuse me, I cannot guarantee what tales may begin circulating or what evidence may come to light. Surely handing over one ring is preferable to the damage that could ensue?

A hollow threat. Without truth behind their claims, I have nothing to fear from vicious rumors. However, this soul seems in turmoil. Redemption is still possible if nurtured.

Tell no one of this request. Speak of it, and you invite only trouble. Bring me the ring at dusk two days hence, when you take your evening ride by the old oak tree. Place it in the hollow there.

I trust we understand each other. I expect your utmost discretion in this matter, as I will show in kind by keeping your damaging secrets undisclosed, once our bargain is struck. Do what is wise, Your Highness.

L.

P.S. My aim is only to help you avoid an unpleasant scandal. Once I have the ring, you need not trouble yourself further with me. Make the prudent choice, for your family's sake and your kingdom's. I await your delivery.

Clearly this "friend" is grappling and has decided to lash out in desperation.

A knock sounds at the study door. "Enter," I call out.

Rendfield slips into the room. "Pardon me, Your Highness. I wished to discuss plans for the Willowsbrook festival."

"Of course," I reply, gesturing to the chair across from me. "Please, have a seat."

Rendfield settles into the plush chair, a subtle tension lingering in his posture—echoes of his villainous upbringing.

Though few know, he is born to notorious thieves. With villainy in his blood, his fate seemed sealed until I was tasked to finally capture him. Seeing the potential for change, I faked his death and hired him to be a member of my staff under a new identity . He has proven himself reformed over the years since.

"Renfield," I begin curiously, "what was it like, growing up destined for villainy?"

He considers the question thoughtfully. "It was all I knew. My parents trained me in the art of theft from the time I could walk and talk. I believed it was my birthright, that society would never accept me as anything else."

I nod solemnly. "Do you ever wonder what your life may have been, given a chance at an honest path at an earlier point in your life?"

Rendfield shrugs. "Idle speculation makes little difference. I have always made choices aligned with the hand fate dealt me."

I press gently. "If shown compassion and opportunity earlier, might you have walked differently?"

He hesitates, gazing into the distance. "Perhaps in a kinder world, but resentment feels justified for the scorn shown my kind."

"It is unjust," I agree, "to condemn a child for their blood before their character can take shape."

Rendfield meets my eyes. "You have been the rare few to recognize value beneath a villainous brand. Not all in power show such wisdom."

A statement, not condemnation.

"There are still good hearts worth nurturing, if we fight fear with compassion."

He bows his head graciously in acknowledgment.

"Ah, the festival. What did you need?"

"I needed to know if your appearance would be an overnight stay or if it would be a day trip? If I needed to make accommodations for everyone."

"Let's keep it short and leave them wanting more."

Renfield bows, "As you wish."

As Rendfield leaves, I consider the blackmail letter. Its author is not irredeemable. There is still conflict within, light wrestling shadow. My hands steady, resolve renewed. My response could plant seeds of hope that a better path exists.

I gather a fresh sheet of parchment and quill, contemplating how to encourage this struggling soul to their better self.

Dear Friend,

I understand you find yourself on difficult paths. The world can be harsh and past shadows painful, twisting us from who we hope to be, but your actions need not be bound by the past. The future remains unwritten.

Your talents could bring great good. There are always second chances for those seeking them. Know that you have potential for kindness and redemption, if you allow yourself to walk in light. Let go of bitterness and look to the good in human hearts, including your own.

I cannot in conscience give you the ring, but know I believe in you, my friend. Your choices define your destiny. May you find purpose and wisdom to guide your way. My door is open if you seek help escaping darkness. For now, take care and turn from anger toward hope.

With Faith in Your Future,

Prince Asher

I fold the letter carefully and drip wax to seal it. Come nightfall, I will leave it at the old oak tree as requested. Jewels I would not provide, but hopefully, some small light will shine through my words and guide this wayward soul to calmer seas.

My station grants authority, but true change comes from within. I can only plant seeds. Whether they bloom into something beautiful or withered untended is up to this conflicted individual.

14

Lillith

The sun sinks below the horizon as I slip through the castle gates, a cloak pulled tight around me to ward off the evening chill. Dusk's violet hues stretch across the sky, signaling the appointed time has come. Brimming with excitement, I hurry to the sheltering forest. Soon, the prince's enchanted emerald ring will be mine.

I have no doubts His Royal Highness will comply with my demands. The subtle implication of scandalous secrets has likely rattled his gilded cage enough to hand over a mere trinket to keep his sterling reputation intact. The fool probably thinks himself noble, making some trivial sacrifice for the greater good. Little does he realize he is simply my puppet, dancing to my strings.

The towering oak comes into view, branches draped like a cloak over the forest road. I scan the area, searching for any sign of the prince but see only an empty path stretching ahead. Good. He has sense enough not to linger.

Ducking under the curved boughs, I swiftly cross to the tree's far side where the designated hollow rests halfway up the trunk. Gripping ancient bark, I hoist myself up and reach inside, my fingers searching eagerly through dead leaves and moss. They brush not the hard cut of jewels, however, but the crisp dryness of paper.

Frowning, I extract the unexpected find, a sealed parchment addressed simply,

To My Friend.

Disappointment curdles in my stomach even as irritation prickles under my skin. I gave clear instructions—the emerald ring in exchange for discretion—and yet His Royal Stubbornness thinks to defy me?

The nerve. Does he take me for a fool? I should spread vicious lies from the highest rooftops and let his shining reputation crumble into dust. My fingers tighten around the sealed letter, prepared to shred it in fury.

Yet, some nagging curiosity stays my hand. What excuse has the high and mighty prince crafted to justify denying my demand? I ought to know his line of thinking before plotting my next move.

With a resigned huff, I drop to the ground and lean against the oak's trunk. Breaking the dark wax seal, I unfold the letter. The prince's elegant script curls across the page.

Dear Friend,

I understand you find yourself on difficult paths...

I scan ahead, scoffing under my breath at his condescending tone. Difficult paths, as though I am some misguided damsel who lost her way. I forge my own destiny through cunning and power. If the prince doesn't understand that, then naivety and hypocrisy blind him.

Let go of bitterness and look to the good in human hearts...

A bitter laugh escapes my lips. He thinks me embittered? The darkness in my core holds no room for anything so impotent as bitterness. And human hearts hold far greater potential for cruelty than kindness. If this prince clings to cheery delusions, I will take pleasure in showing him the truth.

Know that you have potential for kindness and redemption, if you allow yourself to walk in light.

Redemption? The word puzzles me, stirring an unwanted pang deep within my chest. I have no need for redemption. Villainy runs in my veins, and I embrace it fully.

...I believe in you, my friend. Your choices define your destiny.

My fingers crumple the letter reflexively. How dare he profess such faith in me, as though my destiny is some unwritten story waiting for his heroic intervention. I alone dictate my fate, bending all things to my will, prince and kingdom included. His naïve belief in my unseen "potential" means nothing.

Yet even as anger courses through me, I find myself smoothing out the letter's creases, unable to destroy it fully. Something unsettling stirs in my core, that silent pang deepening at this prince's willingness to see light in my darkness. I do not understand it.

No, it matters not whether he believes in redemption for a wayward soul. His cotton-cloud perceptions of the world will soon be torn asunder. I revealed a glimpse of myself by reaching out, and now, vulnerability nags at me, an unfamiliar feeling I do not care for. I must be more cunning if I wish to achieve my aims unscathed.

The prince assumes compassion can sway me, but he underestimates my resolve. I will use his precious faith against him, proving no heart stays untarnished forever, no matter how pure its intentions. Manipulation comes easily when someone thinks you worth saving.

Folding the letter neatly, I tuck it into my cloak—not destroying it but keeping it close. This is not an end but a beginning. I have my own beliefs to prove now, and I will see it done, no matter the cost.

***

The splintered wooden bench of the carriage digs into my thighs as we jostle down the forest road. I grimace, shifting to try and relieve the growing soreness. You would think a prince could get us a better carriage than this. My roommates are crammed onto the hard seat with me, yet they don't seem bothered by the uncomfortable transportation. Their incessant nattering fills the cramped space.

"Ooh, I can hardly wait to dance with the apprenticed blacksmith." Mairelle sighs dreamily, face flushed.

"You'll dance with everyone before the festival's end," Cherry teases. "Remember last year when you twirled about so much you collapsed in a dizzy heap?"

Mairelle's blush deepens as Cherry laughs. "Well, what about you, Cherry? Will you finally confess your love to the baker's son this year?"

Now it is Cherry's turn to redden and stammer. These foolish girls are consumed by thoughts of trysts with peasant boys and silly romantic fantasies. It is enough to make me retch.

Still, I plaster an indulgent smile on my face. "You all seem rather excited for this event," I remark. "Is it a special occasion?"

Mairelle nods eagerly, golden ringlets bobbing around her heart-shaped face. "Oh yes! The Willowsbrook Summer Festival is the highlight of the year."

"People travel from villages all around to join in the revelry," Cherry adds. "There's feasting, dancing, games—"

"And magic shows!" Mairelle pipes up excitedly.

Interesting. I file away that information for later.

Aloud, I say, "It sounds absolutely wonderful! And Prince Asher attends every year?"

Right on cue, the two sigh dreamily at the mention of the kingdom's favored son.

"He's the guest of honor," Cherry explains. "The festival is in celebration of when he saved Willowsbrook from destruction years ago."

This is news to me. I raise my eyebrows, inviting her to elaborate.

"Back when Asher was still a young prince, a deadly plague swept through Willowsbrook and most of the kingdom," Cherry continues. "The healers tried every remedy, but nothing could stop its spread. Thousands had already perished by the time Prince Asher arrived."

Mairelle chimes in, eyes distant as she recalls the tale. "They say he walked fearlessly among the sick, tending to them day and night. He poured all his strength and compassion into healing them, though many protested it was hopeless."

"For a fortnight, he labored without rest," Cherry takes up the story. "Until finally, the last of the plague faded from Willowsbrook. The prince had saved them all through his tireless efforts."

Mairelle clasps her hands to her chest. "Ever since then, Willowsbrook has held a festival each summer to honor Prince Asher's selfless courage and sacrifice. People see him as their hero."

I hold back an incredulous laugh. Of course these foolish girls would swoon over such ridiculous sentimentality. No doubt they picture the noble prince tending helpless peasants while haloed in heavenly light.

The urge to retch returns. Prince Asher's insufferable goodness is even more deeply rooted than I realized. Clearly, I will need to dig deep to uncover any shadows in his past, but they are there. No one harbors only light within them. I simply need to find the cracks in his gilded armor.

In truth, I remember the plague well. It nearly killed me. I only survived by sheer luck. No prince to come in on his white horse and save me. Not that a hero would have cared enough to save someone born a villain anyway.

We continue on toward Willowsbrook, the maidservants chattering about the festival as my mind turns with possibilities. I learned long ago that surfaces can conceal rotten cores beneath. What worms might be eating away at the prince's golden image from the inside? I will lay him bare, one way or another.

At last, our carriages roll through an archway adorned with flowers reading "Welcome!" in bright colors. We pass quaint cottages and rustic buildings decked in strings of ribbons and banners. Townsfolk wave eagerly at any carriage coming through, their faces alight with joy.

How I despise their simple contentment. I can almost taste the richness their pain and sorrow would provide if unleashed from beneath this sickeningly cheerful facade. Perhaps a bit of chaos is in order, but I must be careful not to expose myself just yet. I need more time to analyze the cracks in their gilded veneer first.

After our carriage jerks to a halt, I follow the other maidservants out, collecting my satchel of belongings. My fingers brush over the carefully packed potions and artifacts nested inside. While the girls have sewing kits and perfumed handkerchiefs, I carry more... unique party favors.

Up ahead, the crowds part to form an aisle. Prince Asher rides up on his gleaming white stallion, looking every inch the storybook hero in polished silver armor. He waves and smiles benevolently at the adoring faces. I roll my eyes.

The maidservants around me practically swoon as he dismounts gracefully and approaches the village elder, an ancient bearded man hunched with age.

"Greetings, Tobias! I'm happy to be here for the festival once more." The prince clasps the old man's gnarled hands warmly.

The elder smiles, deep creases lining his face. "The honor is ours, Your Highness. All because of your selfless actions does our village remain thriving all these long years later."

Prince Asher gives an awkward laugh, rubbing his neck. "I only did what anyone would have had they the means. The credit belongs to your people's resilient spirit."

I narrow my eyes, searching for any hint of dishonesty or deeper motive behind his words, but as far as I can tell, the fool means it genuinely. Interesting. The more layers I peel back, the purer his golden image remains. An increasingly frustrating revelation.

Yet, I know better than most that light casts shadows. The greater the virtue, the deeper they lurk. I simply need to slip past his blinding righteousness to uncover what rots beneath, and I am not known for my patience.

The crowds disperse as festivities begin in earnest. Everywhere, villagers dance and laugh to the lively music of fiddles and pipes. The scents of roasted meat, fresh bread, and pies fill the air.

I maintain my pleasant facade, like a wolf moving unnoticed amongst lambs, handing out the small bags of candies and coins the prince tasked all of his staff to distribute. I feel no joy observing their revels. These simple country folk know nothing of true power. They fritter away their short lives distracted by frivolity. The whole thing makes me sick.

As I wander the thoroughfare, a posted notice catches my eye. It is a wanted poster with a rough sketch of a young woman. At the top, it reads, "Wanted—Lillith Shadowend," in bold lettering.

I scan the list of outlandish crimes and misdeeds attributed to my name then have to refrain from laughing aloud. Robbing caravans? Poisoning wells? Absurd. The woman depicted looks only vaguely like me, and honestly, I am a go big or go home kind of woman. None of that small weak-minded stuff. Well, when I can do it in my own name. The things done to the prince have to be small considering I can't reveal my identity to him.

Before I can study the poster further, a deafening boom rends the air, the ground shuddering beneath my feet. Screams erupt as villagers begin fleeing from the thoroughfare in panic. I follow the tide, peering over heads to spot the source of the commotion. A large plume of dark smoke rises in the distance.

Making my way closer, I see that half of a barn has been reduced to flaming rubble. The fire roars, billowing thick black clouds into the sky. Townsfolk hurry to form bucket lines from the well.

That's when I notice two shapes seeming to materialize in the smoke high above. One is clearly a raven in flight, the other a name scrawled in looping script—Lillith Shadowend.

I cross my arms, eyes narrowing. Someone is trying to frame me for this infernal display, but why? The raven offers a clue, suggesting someone from my hidden past. I haven't spoken to him in years, though, and even when we ran in the same circles, we rarely interacted. For what purpose? Regardless, he will find I do not take kindly to being someone else's patsy. If I am to have a reputation, I will earn it on my own terms. He is messing with my brand. This isn't the kind of thing the most powerful villain would do.

The sounds of panic fade as I watch the smoking ruin, pondering this unexpected development. This could be the perfect opportunity to really put the prince to the test. If Lillith is already to blame for this event, it wouldn't be surprising for my magic to appear elsewhere.

It is time they get a taste of real magic, a reminder that true darkness cannot be ignored with smiles and merriment. Let this obnoxiously cheerful celebration see that shadows exist even in sunlight.

I slip away unnoticed down an alley between cottages and move swiftly through the village outskirts, searching for anything I can use to introduce a bit of delicious chaos. These foolish villagers deserve to choke on their complacency.

Then I spot it—a barn stacked high with freshly cut hay. No animals are inside, but that doesn't mean I can't use my magic to imitate the sounds of them or even a villager or two crying for help. Perfect.

With a muttered word, I send a spark onto the dry tinder. Within moments, crackling flames erupt, lighting the barn ablaze and sending acrid smoke into the sky.

Shouts ring out as villagers scramble to action, their cries of dismay like music. I watch hidden from the shadows, lips curling as fear replaces their earlier joy. Let their precious prince come save them from this.

But as the blaze strengthens, a light wind brushes my cheek carrying the scent of ash and... something else.

Before I can investigate further, a chorus of gasps draws my attention back to the flaming barn. Prince Asher comes galloping up on his white steed, gleaming armor dulled by a layer of soot. Murmurs ripple through the crowd at his sudden presence.

"But how...he was just..." I mutter under my breath, brow furrowing.

The prince had been clear across the village dealing with the other fire just moments ago. There is no way he could have ridden here so quickly, yet there he is, dismounting gracefully and striding toward the bucket line.

"Together now, pass them down!" he instructs, taking his place to help douse the flames. His assured voice strengthens the villagers' resolve as they work in unison.

Within minutes, the last smoldering embers are extinguished. Prince Asher clasps the shoulders of weary villagers, praising their efforts and ensuring no one is harmed after checking inside and finding it empty. They gaze at him with awe and gratitude, oblivious to the impossibility of his timing.

I stay hidden, watching the prince's soot-streaked face crease into a tired but satisfied smile. He shows no signs of exertion from presumably riding halfway across the village in the blink of an eye. There is more at work here than meets the eye.

As Asher confers with the village elder, my eyes catch on an ornate amulet hanging around the old man's neck, glinting in the sunlight. A teleportation charm, allowing the wearer to instantly transport to preset locations.

Comprehension dawns. The prince must have similar charms for times of crisis. That would explain his impossible punctuality. He hadn't ridden here directly but teleported from the other fire. A clever solution, I reluctantly admit.

I watch Prince Asher clap the elder's shoulder affectionately before remounting his steed and riding off to continue his festival duties. Once again, the insufferably perfect prince manages to be in two places at once for his adoring people. Why does he have to be so irritatingly perfect all of the time?

PRINCE ASHER SAVES WILLOWS-BROOK FROM ARSON ATTACK

By Sir Justice Jabs

WILLOWSBROOK—Prince Asher proved his unmatched heroism once more by saving Willowsbrook from a series of arson attacks during their annual festival yesterday.

The celebratory event, honoring the prince's past rescue of the kingdom from plague, turned to horror when buildings began erupting into flames throughout the afternoon. Prince Asher miraculously contained each inferno before it could spread, covering immense distances in the blink of an eye.

"Without the prince's swift actions, our homes and lives surely would have burned," Tobias, the village elder, declared.

By eyewitness accounts, His Highness displayed superhuman speed, somehow managing to be wherever flames broke out. Despite clear exhaustion, he fearlessly battled every blaze alongside panicked villagers to rescue those in jeopardy.

The locations destroyed have convinced locals a dark sorceress seen lurking nearby orchestrated the vicious attacks. Many reported sightings of a shadowy woman watching the festival with malice who fled once fires began. In the smoke above buildings, citizens saw signs of her evil magic along with the symbol of a raven believed to be her familiar.

"The witch Lilith Shadowend wished us ill from the start," one eyewitness asserted. "If not for Prince Asher, she would have left nothing but ashes behind."

The damage inflicted on Willowsbrook is heavy. The barn, tavern, chapel, and several homes now lie in ruins. Dozens suffered injuries from smoke, burns, and wounds.

Prince Asher remained afterward, tirelessly tending to the injured and displaced.

"Evil sought to tear our home asunder, but we endure thanks to our prince," a local said.

While the sorceress remains at large, Prince Asher vowed she will face justice soon for these "heinous deeds."

"Evil may wound us, but it will never triumph," he declared before departing.

All in the kingdom must rally against wickedness as our champion does—with courage, mercy and tireless spirit. Prince Asher stands as an example to all of the king's firm order to weed out and eliminate all traces of evil in the kingdom with no mercy.

Prince Asher's selfless example shall light our way forward through darkness. Though the hour seems grim, hope endures so long as hearts remain lit by fellowship's flame.

15

Lillith

I hum a merry tune as I hang the laundry in the newly prepared area of the garden. The tall bushes and stone wall provide me with the perfect little courtyard for clandestine clothes-drying, and I am reveling in this newfound privacy. Perhaps laundering can be a rather pleasant task after all.

"Miss Lilly," a footman calls, making me jump. "Prince Asher wishes to see you in his study."

"Of course." I hastily hang the last piece of clothing and wipe my hands on my apron.

Upon entering the study, I find Prince Asher deep in discussion with Mrs. Umbernuckle. Her willowy figure seems to tower over him despite their equal height. As soon as they notice me, they abruptly stop talking.

"Lilly, I'm glad you're here," he says as he walks toward me. He is dressed in a crisp uniform of dark navy and gold, and the blue of his eyes sparkles with intensity.

He gestures for me to sit, and I slowly comply.

His mouth curves into a slight smile. "I would like to have you be my traveling companion. I've taken on a job."

Mrs. Umbernuckle's eyes widen in shock, and for a moment, I see a flash of something darker lurking in their depths. "Your Highness, surely Lilly isn't the most suitable choice?" she protests.

"Of course she is. She's proven herself competent and clever. She's much more likely to return alive than if I brought any other maid to serve me while we traveled."

"Excuse me," I interject, unable to keep the confusion from my voice, "but what exactly is this job? Why do you need me?"

"Lilly." Prince Asher chuckles, leaning back in his chair. "All will be revealed in due time. For now, just know that your assistance will be invaluable."

If I wasn't already clenching to contain my irritation, my mouth would be wide open. He did not just say that. How did I ever think this man is the perfect hero? He's just another good guy who thinks they are better than everyone else.

"Your Highness, I must insist," Mrs. Umbernuckle presses on, her voice tight with barely concealed frustration. "Lilly is hardly equipped for such a task."

"Mrs. Umbernuckle, Lilly will do just fine. I have complete faith in her abilities," Prince Asher asserts, his tone leaving no room for argument.

"How long will we be gone?" I ask, nervously glancing between the two of them. "And where are we going?"

"Most of that is information you shall learn later," Prince Asher replies with a mysterious grin. "I've been assigned to find and stop a higher-ranking villain. We leave in the morning and will be gone for at least a week, if not longer. Your job will be to assist me. No fighting, just be my go-to for things."

"Your go-to? Basically assist your every whim while you travel?"

"Not every whim, but to a degree, yes. You are a maid in my employ. Do you not already do that here?"

One of these days, I'm going to make that man pay. The only plus side to traveling with the prince is that I won't be under Mrs. Umbernuckle's watchful eye for a few days.

"As you wish. I will prepare to leave as soon as you are ready."

"Wonderful. You are excused."

Avoiding Mrs. Umbernuckle's gaze, I curtsy and retreat out of the room, immediately heading to the only place that I might find peace at this time of day.

Upon closing the door to my chamber, I sigh with relief.

My thoughts race as I ponder the upcoming journey, the mystery around it, and the ever-looming threat of Lamira the Wraith. Shaking off my unease, I decide to focus on the task at hand—packing for a trip with an unknown destination.

"All right, Lillith," I say to myself, "time to get creative."

I reach into my dresser drawer, where I stashed the necklace I bought from Mairelle's sister in the market. The pendant features an intricate design that catches my eye, and now seems like the perfect time to put it to good use. Clasping the necklace in my hand, I whisper a small incantation under my breath, feeling the familiar tingle of magic activating, only the smallest bit of my magic being used to try and avoid detection.

"Let this pendant become a vessel, a safe haven for my belongings during our travels," I murmur, concentrating my energy on the spell.

I feel the enchantment take hold as I sense the magic working its way through the pendant.

"Time for a test run," I muse, reaching for a small stack of clothes.

With a flick of my wrist, the garments disappear, leaving no trace behind.

Satisfied with the results of my spell, I continue to pack, transferring my belongings into the enchanted necklace, careful not to leave anything important behind. If anyone questions me about the magic, I will simply claim the necklace came pre-enchanted—a little white lie to protect myself.

***

"Ah, much better." I sigh in relief as I adjust my new traveling attire.

The forest path underfoot is a welcome change from the stone floors of the palace. My necklace jingles softly with each step, a reminder of the magical items concealed within. Prince Asher walks beside me, his hair hidden beneath a hood. His rogue's outfit suits him well, though it is quite the departure from his usual princely garb.

"Indeed," he agrees, smirking. "Walking among the common folk has its advantages."

"Like hearing the juiciest gossip?" I tease, knowing full well that this journey is essential for gathering information.

"Exactly," he replies with a wink.

We continue on, my leather belt chiming as a tea cup, saucer, and various bottles held in a leather holster clink together. Tea, potions, poisons—all disguised as mundane necessities, unbeknownst to the prince. I can't afford to be unprepared.

As the sun dips below the tree line, Asher and I set about making camp in a small meadow nestled among the pines, hoping their branches will shield us from any wind.

Gathering brush proves tedious without magic to assist. I grab handfuls of fallen limbs and debris, some bundles contain greener twigs mixed in. I don't stop to separate them, eager to finish the task.

Constructing the firepit, I arrange the kindling in a pile of sorts. As long as they are all there, that's what really matters, right? The rocks I gather are uneven sizes, some small enough to leave gaps. While I work, niggling doubts emerge that this doesn't look quite right.

When it comes time to light the tinder, my flint sparks uselessly on the damp foliage sprinkled within. Frustration swells when light rapidly fades, and my kindling refuses to catch. This would be a million times easier if I could use my magic. I allow myself a quick glance at the prince to see if I can sneak in a touch of magic to get the fire started, but his gaze is focused on me.

Asher watches in growing concern until taking pity on me. "Allow me. I can help."

His efficient movements restructure my work, confirming my building suspicions I erred somewhere.

Once our accommodations are set, I pull dried meat, bread, and a salt satchel from my bag. While I work quietly to prepare our simple supper, Asher lounges in the grass nearby, absently plucking flowers. His fingers move gracefully as if playing an invisible instrument.

"Always finding beauty where others see only weeds," I remark with a small smile. "I guess that's what a hero should do."

Asher's mouth quirks up at the corners. "I could say the same of you. You have a way of doing something so ordinary in the most extraordinary ways." He rolls onto his back, gazing up at the first stars pricking through the dusky sky.

I hand him his portion and sit beside him waiting for him to continue and explain, but he doesn't. We eat in contented silence for a time, listening to the forest awakening around us.

At last, Asher breaks the quiet, his voice pensive. "As a second prince, I felt lost for much of my life," he admits, eyes distant. "The throne was a weight though no destiny I welcomed. I always yearned for adventure instead."

His expression darkens as old hurts reemerge. I stay quiet, sensing this confession releases long-buried feelings.

Asher takes a measured breath. "No one saw the person within, only the heirloom ruler they expected me to become. I was merely a spare they could bargain with or command mindlessly." He gazes toward the fading sunset, reliving painful memories only he can see. "Meant to be nothing but collateral yet required to shed this carefree spirit and fulfill obligations never meant for me."

His skilled fingers pluck absently at weeds, tearing them into pieces, mimicking how the stifling roles slowly unraveled his true self through childhood. My heart goes out to the lost boy still inside him yearning to break free once more.

The future seemed a gilded cage until he chose to shatter it, a feeling I understand well.

My silence urges Asher on, tacitly allowing him space to fully unearth long-held feelings. He meets my gaze, eyes luminous in the fading light. "That's why I left and became a hero, of course. For freedom. To find my true purpose beyond birthright expectations."

It is almost as if he is relieved to finally let those words out into the open.

I am very cautious about divulging the details of my own life. Suddenly uncomfortable with the direction of the conversation, I shift on the soft mossy ground. I have never shared the details of my past with anyone before, and it feels strange to do so now.

"My parents... they weren't often around," I say quietly, my voice barely above a whisper.

The prince nods sympathetically, seemingly understanding that I do not wish to elaborate further on the topic. He smiles kindly at me then, as if to offer comfort without speaking.

I swallow and nod in thanks.

"So, this person we're looking for," I begin cautiously, nibbling at a piece of bread, "who exactly are they?"

The prince's expression turns serious. "Rumor has a villain has been targeting villages in the mountains along the Rodel border. It's gotten bad enough that Rodan is threatening to shut down all trade."

"That would be devastating for both kingdoms."

"I agree."

I frown, taking another bite of my bread. "Do you know who it is? The villain, I mean."

The prince shakes his head. "No one does. It's part of why we are traveling like this. It's a long walk, but people will be much more willing to share rumors to a couple of typical travelers than someone traveling in a carriage."

"Sure, because traveling with a personal maid is something everyone can afford," I mumble under my breath.

The prince laughs, his gaze locked onto the fire. "You're right, of course, but safety always comes first when traveling through dangerous lands. If anything happened to me, I need to know there's someone who can get help even if they can't assist in the actual fight." He looks out into the night sky before continuing quietly, "Whoever is behind the attacks must be stopped before they cause any more destruction or take any more innocent lives."

I gulp and nod solemnly in agreement. Neither of us are strangers to violence and bloodshed, least of all me.

We sit in silence for a few moments before I finally find the courage to ask what has been on my mind since earlier that day, something that makes me hesitant to even think about it let alone say it out loud.

"What if... what if you fail? What if we can't put an end to these attacks?" My voice trembles as I speak, and I avoid the prince's gaze altogether, instead focusing on the almost empty cup of tea I cradle between my hands.

He takes his time responding, seemingly lost in thought as he stares off into the distance for several minutes. This time, his voice is low and resolute as he says firmly, "I won't fail..." He pauses once more before adding quietly, "I may not have all the answers yet, but I do know one thing. I find a way."

If that isn't a hero's answer, I don't know what is.

The campfire crackles and dances as I carefully balance the pot over the flames, hoping to speed up the process of boiling water for tea. Heat radiates from the fire, making me sweat in the chill evening air. I glance at Prince Asher, who is busying himself with unpacking our meager supplies. I can't help but roll my eyes as he struggles with a knot in one of the bags.

"Having trouble there?" I tease.

"Nothing I can't handle," he replies with a grin, finally managing to untie the stubborn knot.

"What's the point of bringing a maid along if you aren't going to even use her?" I shoot back, smirking.

The pot of water bubbles more vigorously than before, and in my hasty attempt to remove it from the fire, the pot slips from my grasp, spilling scalding liquid onto my arm.

"Ouch!" I cry out.

The pain flares up like a hundred tiny needles digging into my skin, and I can't help but gasp.

"Are you all right?" Prince Asher asks, rushing over to me with a look of concern. His eyes widen when he sees the angry red burn on my arm, and I can almost see him calculating how bad it is.

"Fine," I grit out through clenched teeth, trying to hide my pain.

But I'm not fine, and I know it. My arm throbs, and every time I shift even slightly, it feels like someone is pouring salt onto the wound.

"Here, let me help," Asher says, reaching out to steady me.

Instead of accepting his assistance, I grab a short dagger from my side, grip the end of his cloak, and rip a long strip of fabric from it without asking. Let's see him keep his cool after this.

His eyes widen as he watches me rip the fabric in one final jerk, breaking the last seam.

"Needed something to cover this," I say, gesturing to my burnt arm. "Thought you wouldn't mind sacrificing a bit of your precious cloak."

"Of course I don't mind," he replies, surprising me with his calm demeanor. "Let's just make sure we take care of that burn properly."

"Fine," I say again, frustration bubbling inside me.

Why doesn't he get angry? Any normal person would have been angry at this. I've killed people for less.

"Here," Asher says softly, gently taking the strip of fabric from me and wrapping it around my arm. "We'll clean it and find some medicine when we get into town."

"Thanks," I mumble, feeling conflicted.

His kindness is touching, but at the same time, it irritates me that he could be so composed in the face of my blatant attempt to provoke him.

"I'm just glad you're not more badly hurt," he says sincerely, meeting my eyes.

I nod, not knowing what else to say.

16

Lillith

The sun dips low in the sky, casting an orange and pink glow on the cobblestone streets of Shadowcrest, a small city nestled at the base of two imposing mountains. It is known far and wide for its peculiar charm as well as its hidden villain training arena.

I glance around, taking in the quaint shops with their whimsical signs shaped like potions or enchanted brooms. The townsfolk bustle about, their laughter tinkling like wind chimes in the crisp evening air.

"Quite the interesting place, isn't it?" Prince Asher remarks, his blue eyes sparkling with curiosity.

"Indeed," I agree, though my attention isn't on the city's beauty.

A nagging feeling starts to tug at my senses, telling me that someone or something is following us, but I say nothing, choosing to keep this information to myself for now.

The city's buildings are an eclectic mix of wood and stone, adorned with stained glass windows depicting creatures of myth and legend. A babbling brook flows through the heart of the town, creating a pleasantly soothing ambiance. Unlike other cities in the realm, Shadowcrest has a distinctive aura of secrecy that seems to whisper from every nook and cranny.

"Shall we find something to eat?" Prince Asher suggests, clearly eager to explore the city and its many delights. "I heard there's a tavern here that serves the best dragon egg omelets in the kingdom."

"Sounds delightful," I murmur, though my thoughts are still preoccupied with our unseen pursuer.

I can't shake the feeling that they are watching our every move, waiting for the perfect moment to strike. Not having the option of using my magic publicly leaves me feeling especially vulnerable.

As we walk down the cobblestone streets I feel a flutter of excitement despite my growing apprehension. There is something thrilling about being in the very city where I trained as a child, honing my skills in magic and dagger wielding. Not that I can let Prince Asher know that.

"Ah, here we are," Prince Asher exclaims as we approach a cozy-looking tavern with a sign depicting a fire-breathing dragon. "Let's see if these omelets live up to their reputation."

We enter the tavern, its warm, inviting atmosphere chasing away the chill of the evening air. Laughter fills the room, accompanied by the clinking of tankards and the strumming of a lute.

"Two omelets, please," Prince Asher orders when the barmaid approaches, flashing her a charming smile that makes her blush.

"Right away," she replies with a curtsy before scurrying off to the kitchen.

As we wait for our food, I glance over my shoulder, scanning the room for any signs of our mysterious follower, but there is nothing—just the happy chatter of patrons and the tantalizing aroma of sizzling eggs. Soon the woman returns with two plates that she sets in front of us.

I pick at my food as I watch the prince. His constant positivity is wearing thin. Something just doesn't add up.

"Is there something wrong with your omelet?" he asks, raising an eyebrow as he catches me staring at the plate.

I force a smile and shake my head, taking a small bite to prove my point. "No, it's delicious. I was just... thinking."

"About what?" His piercing blue eyes lock onto mine, and I feel my cheeks flush under the intensity of his gaze.

"About what your plans are once being a hero is no longer an option," I blurt out. "We all age. You've got a few good years left, I admit, but what then?"

He leans back in his chair, an amused grin playing on his lips. "You're a curious one, aren't you, Lilly? If I didn't know any better, I'd think you were trying to get to know me."

"Hardly," I scoff.

In truth, I do want to understand him, to figure out what drives him to have villains work for him and if he knows. More importantly, I need to protect my own secrets, like the fact that I trained in this very city as a child.

"Fine, I'll humor you," he says, taking a sip of his tea. "I plan to retire to a quiet life, away from politics and high society. It's all too stuffy."

"Can a prince do that?"

"I have siblings. As long as they stay alive, I don't see why not. I've never been one of the favorite children anyways."

None of this is adding up. Is it really possible for someone who has villains working for him to truly want that sort of retirement? It all feels too simple.

"Care for some more tea?" I ask, trying to sound innocent like the good little maid I am... for now.

"Do we have time?" Prince Asher replies, his blue eyes narrowing slightly as he studies me. "We should focus on gathering information."

"Everyone needs a break, Your Highness," I say, emphasizing his title with just the right amount of sarcasm. "Besides, I've heard that tea can help one relax and focus."

"Fine." He sighs, seemingly appeased by my explanation.

As I prepare the tea, I make sure to choose my grandmother's special blend—an exquisite mix of black tea, cocoa nibs, blackberry, dark chocolate, chicory, raspberry leaves, cocoa and blue cornflowers, and cream. It's perfect for reading tea leaves, a skill she taught me years ago. It will allow me to uncover any hidden truths behind Prince Asher's motives.

"Here you go." I hand him a cup, watching closely as he takes a sip. He seems lost in thought.

"Thanks," he mutters, not even bothering to meet my gaze.

I wait until he finishes his tea and gets up to relieve himself before swiftly collecting the cup, making sure he doesn't notice my eagerness. As I pour the remaining liquid out onto a flat surface, I begin to read the tea leaves, searching for any signs that might reveal his true intentions.

"Come on, tell me your secrets," I whisper under my breath, hoping the leaves will give me some insight into the enigmatic prince.

The leaves swirl around, forming a pattern I recognize all too well—a dagger piercing through a heart. The image signifies betrayal and heartache, warning me that someone close will let him down.

"Is everything all right?" Prince Asher asks, his voice tinged with concern as he returns to the table.

"Fine, just fine," I mumble, trying to hide my unease. "I thought tea would help us focus, but maybe I was wrong."

"Maybe," he agrees, an unreadable expression on his face.

An argument coming from the next table over catches my interest. Two people, a man and a woman, are arguing in hushed tones, their words filled with desperation.

"Please," the woman begs the man. "You don't have to do this. Stay home tonight."

The man laughs harshly and pushes away from the table. "You forget who I am," he says coldly. "Tonight might be my last chance at glory, and I'm not about to pass it up." He stands up and throws some coins on the table before storming out of the tavern.

I look over at Prince Asher and see him frowning in thought as he watches the man leave. After a moment, he reaches into his pocket and pulls out several silvers, laying them on top of what was already there.

He stands up and motions for me to follow him outside.

We quickly leave the tavern, slipping silently into an alleyway just across from where the man had gone. I crouch low behind a pile of trash next to the prince, peeking around as we watch him make his way down one of the city's back streets. I recognize the route.

Following the man, we walk through the city, making our way toward the villain training arena. The streets are bustling with activity as stalls are packing up, but my mind is elsewhere, going over every detail of my past in this place.

"Are you ready for this?" he asks as we approach the entrance, disguised as an inconspicuous door tucked between two buildings.

"Of course," I reply, trying to sound confident despite the churning in my stomach.

"I'll go first," he says, pushing the door open.

As we step into the dimly lit hallway, a sense of nostalgia washes over me. This is where it all began—where I transformed from a naïve child into the skilled villain I am today, and now, I am back, on the arm of a prince whose motives I can only guess.

***

We descend farther into the depths of the city, following a winding staircase that seems to go on forever. After so many turns, we lose our guide. I silently direct us away from the worst of the traps set in these tunnels to keep out people like us, taking the occasional wrong turn that would result in a quick dead end to backtrack from.

Finally, we stop in front of a heavy wooden door. Prince Asher glances down the empty hallway behind us before he opens the door and steps inside, followed closely by me. We enter a large chamber filled with people—mostly villains and criminals.

The prince tenses up. I chuckle to myself, watching this confident man suddenly freeze. I guess if I was a hero suddenly surrounded by over a hundred people who would take pleasure in torturing me before finally letting me die I would be slightly nervous as well. That will never be a problem for me, though.

The energy in the room is palpable, and the tension thickens as everyone sizes each other up. The prince is clearly out of place here. I can see it on his face as he looks around warily. Even so, he holds himself confidently and straightens his shoulders in an effort to appear unafraid.

However, even I can feel my own fear start to rise in that moment. After all, it wouldn't take much for someone to recognize me and expose me for who I truly am. Prince Asher looks over at me with determination in his eyes. If he notices my inner struggle, he doesn't show it.

"Enough dawdling," Prince Asher declares, his blue eyes shining with determination. "We need a plan."

"Fine." I sigh, trying to ignore the fluttering in my stomach. "First, we'll need to gather information on our villain's whereabouts, identity, and weaknesses."

"Agreed. Then, we'll devise a strategy to exploit those weaknesses and take him down."

"Shouldn't be too difficult," I muse, my thoughts drifting back to my training days. The arena taught me to adapt quickly and anticipate my opponents' moves. "I'm sure we'll find plenty of vulnerabilities to target."

"Good," he replies, "Now, let's focus on blending in. We don't want to attract unnecessary attention."

We barely take two steps when a tall, skinny man blocks our path. His beady eyes narrow suspiciously as he studies us.

"What are you two doing here?" he asks gruffly.

I snuggle up against the prince in an effort to appear like a loving couple and bat my eyelashes at the man. "We heard about the show," I say sweetly, "and we thought it would be fun to watch."

The man crosses his arms and shakes his head. "I'm sorry, but tonight's spectators are restricted to those participating in the challenge," he informs us sternly.

My stomach drops. We're going to have to participate in this challenge in order to stay alive.

Prince Asher seems unfazed as he steps forward and clears his throat. "How do we participate?" he asks confidently, not letting on that he has absolutely no idea what kind of challenge this is.

The man nods approvingly before turning around and motioning for us to follow him. We end up at a podium with an ornately decorated book upon it, and the man gestures for us both to sign it with a quill provided alongside the book.

Asher steps forward and signs first. I follow shortly thereafter by doing the same with my own signature for Lilly. Peter? He put down a lame name like Peter? Upon completion, we both prick our fingers with a special needle and stamp our bloodied fingerprints onto the page—officially committing ourselves to this challenge.

"This is the first night of The Challenges." The man gestures around to the crowd. "Each year during these Challenges, participants will be presented with various tasks or activities—physical feats of strength or endurance, intellectual riddles and puzzles, you name it—all designed to test your skills and ultimately determine each challenger's ranking upon completion." His eyes light up as he points around the room again for emphasis. "Not everyone makes it. Think you can?"

The look on the prince's face would have been encouraging if I didn't know exactly what we were in for. My fingers curl into tight fists as he replies, "I know I can."

More people approach to sign, and we wander away down a narrow tunnel carved of stone.

"Watch where you're going," I tease. "Wouldn't want to scuff those pristine boots of yours. I don't know if I will be able to care for them as your maid while disguised as a villain here. It may give us away."

Asher shoots me a sideways grin. "Have no fear. I'm far more graceful than your stumbling self."

No sooner are the words out of his mouth than the floor suddenly drops away before me. Heart in my throat, I slide sideways just in time to avoid the spiked pit that yawns open in the stone.

"Thanks for the assist," I mutter, pressing a hand to my racing pulse. Eyes narrowing, I turn to Asher. "I didn't expect you to actually be... helpful."

"And leave you to an untimely demise?" he asks lightly, though concern lingers in his gaze. "Like I said, we're in this together. Your survival enhances my own. Besides, a good maid is hard to find."

I snort. "How noble. Worried for your staff now, are you?"

Asher smiles ruefully. "Call it enlightened self-interest. With my skills and your guidance, our chances improve dramatically as a team."

My eyes narrow further, suspicion rising once more. What game is he playing at really? Trust does not come easily, yet in this place, remaining divided spells doom.

"All right, team it is for now." I arch a pointed brow. "But don't expect swooning when your antics land us in deep trouble."

Asher inclines his head graciously. "The lady's wisdom is as sharp as ever. I shall endeavor not to test its cutting edge unduly."

With that cryptic response and charming half-smile, he offers his arm to lead on into the shadows. Against my better judgment, I can't deny following comes easier than anticipated.

Finally, we arrive at the entrance of the arena where we are greeted by a tall, muscular man dressed in black. His face is stern as he eyes us up and down.

"Name," he barks, his voice deep and menacing.

"Peter Scarworth," the prince states firmly, straightening his shoulders, "and this is my partner, Lilly."

It takes everything I have not to laugh hearing the name Peter.

The guard looks us over once more before nodding curtly. "Proceed."

We step through the gate into the arena. It is massive, with towering walls that seem to stretch up to the vaulted ceiling. The ground beneath our feet is packed dirt, and there are rows upon rows of seats surrounding the central area. I can feel my heart pounding in my chest with anticipation. This arena still haunts my dreams.

Releasing Prince Asher's arm, I work my way through the crowd to look at the list. A groan escapes me. Of all the luck. We're up against someone who knew me when I was here as a child and I saw from time to time in the bit of villain society I grace with my presence when required, Xixor Shade.

I can feel Prince Asher's gaze on me as I stare at the parchment, my mind already thinking of strategies. I don't have the luxury of reminiscing about my past. Not anymore. This is a fight for survival, and I intend to win even if I can't use my magic. I know just about everything about

Prince Asher after waiting on the man hand and foot and can work as his sidekick.

As we move to await our time to enter the arena, I can't shake off the nagging feeling that something terrible is about to happen. The tea leaves have never been wrong before, and part of me knows deep down that I should brace myself for the storm that is coming.

Is it possible that Prince Asher is not what he seems? Or perhaps the leaves are warning me about my own secrets being revealed?

"Remember," Prince Asher whispers, his eyes scanning the area intently, "we're here to blend in, not draw attention."

"Right," I mutter. "Not getting killed would be great, too, though."

"You've got a point. I should go ask about the rules before this starts."

I bite my tongue as he leaves me on the edge of the arena. We are screwed. There are no rules.

17

Lillith

The underground arena is awash with the intoxicating scent of sweat, blood, and anticipation. Loud, dramatic battle music fills the air as shady characters slither their way into the dimly lit space.

I glance at Asher, who has taken it upon himself to leave my side for a moment. Who knows what for. As he disappears into the shadows, I begin casting a glamour spell to disguise myself. Not enough to make me unrecognizable—after all, the prince doesn't know that I can do this—but enough that it would be more difficult for anyone else to recognize me. Fortunately I don't spend much time in the villain circles and hadn't for several years.,

The music swells mysteriously as my appearance morphs, tendrils of magic weaving around me, changing my features.

Back to where it all began.

"Presenting... Grundle the Greedy!" booms the announcer's voice, cutting through the cacophony.

My heart skips a beat as I recognize the dwarf pit fighter from my past life in this wretched place. His dark shaggy hair is tied up into a messy bun showcasing the many scars he has earned, I imagine, from within this arena. He always did enjoy the fights here, not because he is truly the best, but this man's vice is gambling and I swear he gets off on betting on himself.

Grundle strolls into the arena, his spiked cestuses glinting dangerously under the flickering torchlight. A girl has to admire his armored glove reinforced with metal rings along the joints and fingers as well as protective spikes protruding from the knuckles. The material is leather and adorned with runes and symbols, most of which I do not recognize. I wonder what those can do.

Triumphant music accompanies his entrance, and the crowd roars in approval.

I continue to work my glamour as I watch Grundle strut and play to the crowd. He certainly seems to have improved his showmanship.

"Oi, pretty face! You new 'round here?"

The gruff voice jolts me back to the present, and I turn to see a burly man leering at what he assumes is my true visage. Surprisingly, he's not someone I recognize.

Suppressing a shudder, I force a coy smile onto my lips and nod demurely. "Indeed, sir. This is my first time," I reply in a sweet tone that belies my true feelings.

The man laughs, slaps my back a bit too hard, and saunters off to join the throng of spectators.

"Ugh," I mutter inwardly, rubbing my aching shoulder. It is bad enough having to be here, but to endure the company of these vile creatures? It is almost too much. Still, I have a mission, and maintaining my glamour is crucial.

The atmosphere in the underground arena shifts, as though an icy wind blows through the crowd. I glance around and spot Gorthak the Executioner stepping into the ring. The creeping, ominous music that accompanies his arrival sends shivers down my spine.

I vaguely remember the day he shaved his head claiming it was to prevent his victims from being able to grip him, a ridiculous notion considering his wardrobe is full of things they could grab anyways.

Grundle might've changed little, but Gorthak appears as cruel as ever.

A murmur of anticipation spreads through the crowd as Grundle and Gorthak examine each other, sizing up their opponent. The anticipatory music builds suspense, drowning out the nervous chatter.

Seeing Asher working his way back through the crowd toward me, I hurry to finish my glamour. My nose is just a little larger, my eyes a smidge farther apart, and my jaw is now less defined. Not much of a difference but hopefully enough.

"Ah, there you are," Asher murmurs as he takes the empty seat beside me. He scrutinizes my face for a moment before offering a small shrug and turning his attention to the fight. "Quite the show, isn't it?" he whispers, leaning closer.

His breath tickles my ear, making me shiver involuntarily.

"Indeed," I reply, trying to sound innocent and awed. "I've never seen anything quite like it."

"Ah, you're still so young," he says, chuckling softly. "This is the kind of stuff I deal with all the time, usually in a less structured way. Stick with me, and I will keep you safe."

I cover my snort with a cough at how ridiculous this entire thing is. In the end, I wouldn't be surprised if I end up saving him.

Grundle and Gorthak continue to size each other up. It is only a matter of time before one of them makes the first move, and then the real carnage will begin.

"Let's make a wager," Asher suggests suddenly, his eyes alight with mischievous glee. "Who do you think will emerge victorious?"

"Um..." I hesitate. Gorthak is at a disadvantage since his expertise doesn't involve opponents who are quite so mobile. "I... I don't know. They both seem so... fierce."

"Ah, playing it safe." He says with a nod. "Wise choice, my dear. Wise choice indeed."

I force a smile onto my lips and nod demurely. My dear? Who does he think he is?

"Thank you," I reply in a sweet tone that belies my true feelings.

The sound of the chime echoes through the underground arena, silencing the excited chatter and anticipatory music. I take a deep breath, steeling myself for the brutal spectacle that is about to unfold.

Let the fun begin.

"Place your bets!" a goblin bookie cries, scampering between spectators with his parchment in hand.

"I've changed my mind," I declare, turning to the prince. "I want to bet on Grundle."

Prince Asher's eyebrows shoot up in surprise, but he smiles approvingly. "Very well then. What shall we wager?"

"A foot rub," I blurt out before I can even think about it. "Since I'm always doing things for you, it would be nice if you did something for me for a change."

Asher lets out a laugh and then leans forward to shake my hand in agreement. "You have yourself a deal."

The crowd roars with anticipation as Grundle and Gorthak square off in the center of the arena. They move carefully at first, each gauging their opponent's strength and abilities.

Grundle is the first to make a move, launching himself at Gorthak with a flurry of strikes.

"Come on, Grundle!" I whisper, clenching my fists at my side. Though I don't care much for the dwarf's pursuit of riches, he is the lesser of the two evils facing off before me.

"Such violence." Prince Asher sighs, shaking his head. "A shame there isn't a more civilized way to settle disputes in this place. This would never happen in our circle."

"Perhaps you should start a debate club, " I quip, allowing myself a small smile.

He chuckles, but his eyes remain focused on the battle. Gorthak lunges at Grundle, swinging his barbed whip with deadly precision.

"Watch out!" I shout involuntarily, unable to suppress my concern for the dwarf pit fighter.

Grundle manages to dodge the attack, rolling to safety just in time.

I take a deep breath and try to regain my composure, schooling my features into a mask of indifference, but inside, my heart races as Gorthak unleashes a gruesome new torture move, wrapping his whip around Grundle's legs and yanking him off balance.

"By the gods," I breathe, unable to tear my eyes away from the scene. "Some things never change."

As the battle rages on, a chant erupts from the crowd, their voices blending into a familiar rhyme I haven't heard in years. It's the same cheer that was once reserved for me, back when this dark place held sway over my life. The rous-ing, rhythmic music swells around us, filling the air with a strange mixture of hope and bloodlust. I can't help but feel a pang of nostalgia despite my best efforts to remain detached.

I turn to find Prince Asher scrutinizing my expression with narrowed eyes. The music shifts, adding an under-current of suspicion to the atmosphere.

"How are you holding up?" he asks quietly, his gaze never leaving my face.

"Fine," I lie, forcing a smile. "Just enjoying the show."

"We're next. Our opponent will be Xixor Shade," he informs me. "I trust you'll be prepared? Remember just let me handle most of this."

"Of course," I reply, trying to keep my voice steady.

I can't let the prince see how much the prospect of facing my old tutor shakes me or, worse, how worried I am about fighting him without revealing my true identity.

We both turn our attention back to the arena. Surviving this place—and each other—just might be the most diffi-cult challenge we'll ever face.

The music slashes through the air like a knife as Grun-dle, with surprising agility for a dwarf, counters Gorthak's attack using his spiked cestuses. The crowd gasps and cheers at the impressive maneuver.

"All right, so here are the rules," Asher says, leaning in closer to me, his voice barely audible over the cacophony of the arena. "Each team must fight three rounds against different opponents." He ticks off each rule on his fingers as he speaks.

"Got it," I reply tersely, trying to focus on the battle before us.

Gorthak swings his weapon toward Grundle, but the dwarf manages to dodge it by mere inches. The crowd erupts in cheers at the close call. Swelling music accompanies their excitement.

My mind briefly flashes back to when I was just eleven years old, standing in the center of this very arena. My small, bruised fists clenched the top-ranking trophy tightly, and the roars of the crowd washed over me like an intoxicating tidal wave. How proud I had been and how much I had yet to learn about the true nature of this place.

"Pay attention, Lilly," Asher admonishes gently, snapping me out of my reverie. "We need to study their moves, find their weaknesses."

"Right," I mutter, forcing myself to watch the brutal spectacle unfolding before us.

Grundle and Gorthak trade blow after blow, their faces twisted in both pain and determination.

The final blow lands with a sickening crunch. Grundle has emerged victorious, standing over Gorthak's crumpled form as the crowd erupts into deafening cheers. Triumphant music swells, matching the intensity of the scene. I can't help but feel a twinge of relief for the dwarf pit fighter despite the gruesome nature of his victory.

"Next up!" booms the announcer's voice, cutting through the cacophony. "Peter Scarworth and Lilly versus Xixor Shade!"

My blood runs cold at the mention of the name, my heart pounding in my chest like a trapped bird. Tense, dramatic music begins to play, heightening the sense of dread that washes over me.

As we make our way down to the arena floor, I try to focus on the task at hand, but the memories of Xixor Shade's cruel tutelage haunt me, each one more painful than the last.

"Remember," Asher whispers in my ear as we step into the arena, "we're in this together. We've got each other's backs."

"Right," I murmur, taking a deep breath to steady my nerves.

The thought of having someone by my side, someone who genuinely cares about me, is both comforting and disconcerting. It is unfamiliar territory for me, but perhaps it is just what I need to face my demons head-on.

Xixor Shade strides to the arena, a sneer curling his lips, I feel a surge of anger mixed with dread rise up within me. There is no turning back now. It is time to confront my past and fight for my future, and maybe, just maybe, I can do so without revealing who I really am.

18

Lillith

A knot forms in my stomach as I enter the arena. The roaring crowd seems to close in on Asher and me, their excitement palpable. My eyes scan the room before locking onto our opponent, Xixor Shade. He is massive, muscular, and exudes an air of confidence that sends a shiver down my spine.

"All right, Lilly," Asher whispers, leaning in close. His white hair brushes against my cheek, his blue eyes twinkling with mischief. "I know you're worried, but we've got this. Just follow my lead."

"I hope you have a plan," I mutter, my gaze never leaving Xixor.

"Of course I do," Asher replies, puffing out his chest in a playful manner. "When have I ever let you down?"

"Never," I admit, begrudgingly, trying to stifle a smile. "We haven't really known each other all that long, and there's always a first time. All right, Peter Scarworth." I roll my eyes at his fake villain name. "Let's see what you've got up your sleeve."

"Trust me," he says, giving me a confident grin. "We'll make it through this together."

The bell rings, signaling the start of the match. Xixor wastes no time in launching himself toward us, his movements surprisingly swift for a man of his size and age. I dive to the left while Asher jumps right, nearly colliding with each other as we fumble our dodge of his attack. This is so incredibly frustrating. I don't work well with others. I'm a one woman team!

"Whoops, sorry!" Asher calls as we scramble to regain our footing. Our first attempt at moving in sync clearly needs some work.

Xixor presses his advantage, swinging towards me.. I barely manage to roll out of the way.

"Stay focused!" Asher warns. "Watch me and follow my lead."

I nod, turning my full attention to my partner. As Xixor charges again, Asher subtly gestures left then leaps right. I mirror his movements, and this time we flow smoothly together, evading Xixor's blow.

"Yes! Just like that," Asher says.

Bit by bit, we start to find our rhythm, using hand signals and body language to coordinate our attacks and defenses. Though my heart is still racing, I can't help but grin as Asher and I duck and weave in perfect sync, driving Xixor back.

"See?" Asher calls, his voice barely audible over the roar of the crowd. "We've got him right where we want him!"

"Sure," I think, my heart pounding as I catch sight of Magmog the Minotaur and the Magus Maleficus watching from the sidelines. "Just a walk in the park."

"Keep your eyes on Xixor," Asher warns, his tone suddenly serious. He must've noticed my momentary distraction. "We can't afford to slip up."

"Right," I agree, focusing my attention back on our opponent.

Xixor's eyes narrow, and I know he is trying to figure us out—how we are able to anticipate his moves and counter them so effectively. I can only hope that Asher's plan will continue to work, that we can keep him guessing long enough to win.

"Let's do this," I whisper, turning to Asher with a determined smile.

Time seems to slow down as Asher and I move in sync somehow. He raises his hand, fingers splayed wide, and a burst of white-hot flames shoots toward Xixor. The spell catches our opponent off-guard, singeing the edges of his cloak and forcing him to stagger back.

Xixor snarls in frustration, clearly not expecting such resistance from the two of us. He charges again and attacks with a low sweeping kick that I've seen him use countless times before.

"Look out!" Asher shouts, but I don't need the warning.

Though I know how to counter the move easily, I feign surprise, allowing myself to be knocked off-balance. I stumble, pretending to struggle to regain my footing.

"Are you okay?" Asher asks, his voice laced with concern as he grabs my arm, steadying me.

"Fine," I lie through gritted teeth, my pride stinging more than any physical pain. "Just didn't see it coming."

"Of course," Asher agrees, though I can tell from the glint in his eye that he suspects the truth. His eyes dart between the powerful figure and me. "Xixor is faster than I expected. We need to find a way to slow him down."

I rack my brain, trying to remember any details from our shared past that might give me an advantage. Then, it hits me. Xixor's old knee injury. It never fully healed, leaving him with a slight weakness he has always tried to conceal.

"Leave it to me," I whisper, a mischievous grin playing at the corners of my lips.

"Are you sure?" Asher asks, concern etched on his face.

"Trust me," I reply, meeting his eyes for a moment before turning my attention back to Xixor.

As we engage in a flurry of attacks and counters, I keep my focus on Xixor's movements, waiting for the perfect opportunity. Xixor charges at me and I feign a clumsy stumble, luring Xixor into overextending himself.

"Watch out!" Asher cries.

With a swift, precise kick, I target Xixor's injured knee. He lets out a surprised grunt, stumbling as tears rim his eyes.

"Impossible," he growls, looking at me with shock and suspicion. "How did you know?"

"Just a lucky guess," I reply airily, forcing a laugh to keep up the charade.

Internally, I chastise myself for not being more careful. If Xixor becomes too suspicious, everything could unravel.

"Nice move," Asher quips. "Now, let's press our advantage!"

"Right." My heart pounds in my chest, a mix of adrenaline and fear that I might have revealed too much.

For now, we have the upper hand, and I can't let my past get in the way. Asher is depending on me, and together, we'll find a way to win. No matter what it takes.

With Xixor still limping from the pain in his knee, Asher and I launch a coordinated attack. Our movements are synchronized, like a dance we practiced for ages, even though we haven't. As our strikes connect, it is clear that Xixor's strength is waning.

"Yield!" Asher shouts, his voice booming through the arena as he delivers one final blow to Xixor's chest.

The large man stumbles back, clearly defeated, but his eyes remain locked on me, suspicion clouding them.

The crowd erupts into cheers, their enthusiasm shaking me out of my thoughts. The announcer's voice booms through the stadium. "Lilly and Peter Scarworth take the match!" The entire arena seems to be vibrating with euphoria as I lock eyes with Asher, a smile on both of our faces. Against all odds, we won.

"We did it!" Asher cheers, momentarily dropping his villainous persona.

His arms envelop me in a sudden hug, and without thinking, I hug him back. It is a brief moment of elation and relief, our bodies pressed together, celebrating the triumph over our enemy.

Just as quickly as it began, we both seem to realize our proximity and pull away from each other, awkwardness settling between us.

"Right. Um, good job, Lilly," he says, rubbing the back of his neck and forcing a grin. "We make quite the team."

"Indeed," I reply, trying to sound casual but feeling my cheeks flush, "but we shouldn't get too comfortable. We have more battles to face."

Leaving the arena, I head toward a nearby hall desperate for a moment to compose myself.

Ahser follows. After a few moments of silence he rubs the back of his head and says, "I'm going to grab us some drinks. Refuel after the match. Do you want anything in particular?

"Water. Thank you."

Lost in thought, I barely notice the figure approaching me until she speaks. "Lillith? Is that you?"

The voice is sweet and familiar, like honey mixed with a touch of nostalgia.

"Silviana," my mind whispers, my heart skipping a beat. My pulse quickens as I turn to face her. Silviana... after so long... but I can't let her know me now.

I attempt a casual smile. "You have me mistaken. I'm Lilly."

The elven woman before me is unmistakable. Silviana the Beastmaster. Her dark hair cascades down her back in an intricate braid. Her eyes sparkle like emerald fire, and her posture exudes grace and confidence, yet there is no mistaking the fondness in her gaze as it settles on me.

Silviana's eyes narrow slightly, her voice firm. "I would know my Lillith anywhere no matter how much time has passed," she insists.

I shake my head and force a small smile, trying to play it off. "You're very kind, but I assure you that I'm just Lilly," I say, desperately hoping she won't press the issue further.

"If you say so," Silviana replies hesitantly, but the doubt in her eyes is clear as day.

As she glances around the hallway, seemingly searching for an excuse to stay by my side, I can't help but reflect on the friendship we lost. Late nights spent talking under the stars, sharing secrets we thought would bind us together forever. Dreams of our future, when we would rise above our humble beginnings and take the world by storm. Those memories feel like another lifetime, one where I could be open and honest with the only person I've ever been able to trust.

My heart aches with the longing to tell Silviana the truth, to pull her close and let her know that I am right here, but I can't. We haven't been in each other's lives since I left the arena at thirteen. The past is gone, and I have to protect what little I have left. The stakes are too high now, even if the risks seem low.

"Actually, I have to go check on my beasts," Silviana announces suddenly, her gaze locked onto mine, "but I'll see you around, won't I, Lilly?"

"Of course," I reply, forcing a cheerful tone. "We'll be here until the end of the competition."

"Good." She flashes me a smile tinged with sadness before turning away, her footsteps echoing down the hall.

As Silviana disappears from view, I lean back against the cold stone wall, my chest constricting with each ragged breath. The secrets and lies weigh heavily on me now, casting a shadow over my earlier lighthearted banter with Asher and the excitement of the arena. This all feels wrong. This isn't me. I am hardened and cold. I don't reminisce and have emotions toward other people. Something is wrong with me.

"Are you all right?" Asher's voice cuts through my thoughts as he returns, two drinks in hand. "You look like you've seen a ghost."

"Nothing I can't handle," I mutter, taking one of the drinks from him and sipping it absently. "Just... thinking about the past."

"Ah, the past has a way of sneaking up on us, doesn't it?" He grins, but his eyes search mine, maybe looking for any sign of distress. "Well, let's focus on the present, then. We have more important things to worry about, like our next match in the arena."

I smile back at him, grateful for his unwavering support. "You're right. Let's make sure we're ready for whatever they throw at us."

Together, we toast to our future battles, hoping that our fake dating facade will hold up just a little bit longer, but deep down, I know that the truth can't stay hidden forever, and when it finally comes to light, I can only hope that we'll all be able to pick up the pieces.

"Cheers to your foot rub," Asher says, a wide grin on his face and raised cup in hand. "They better be cleaned first."

MYSTERIOUS NEW VILLAIN PAIR DEFEATS ARENA CHAMPION
By Maud Malcontent

A new villain duo calling themselves Peter Scarworth and Lilly has taken the underground arena by storm, defeating the previously undefeated champion Xixor Shade in a stunning upset last night.

The pair executed a series of flawlessly coordinated attacks, anticipating Xixor's moves as if they could read his mind. Their combination of powerful magic and martial arts skills overwhelmed the muscular brute.

Though little is known about the duo, witnesses describe a handsome rogue with white hair and a fierce dark-haired sorceress fighting in perfect sync.

They moved "like two pieces of a well-oiled machine," one spectator said.

The woman in particular displayed uncanny knowledge of Xixor's weaknesses, targeting an old knee injury to bring the giant down. Their flawless teamwork suggests these two share a mysterious past, perhaps growing up and training together.

Xixor clearly recognized the female villain. "How did you know?" he demanded after she exploited his weak knee, but Lilly skillfully evaded answering, keeping their origins concealed. I think at this point we all want to know the answer to how she knew.

In the end, Xixor had no choice but to yield to the upstart pair now claiming his crown as arena champions. Their meteoric rise has electrified the underground community starved for fresh hope.

Many see these young villains as a sign of changing times in the kingdom. Where once caped "heroes" like Prince Asher and his ilk could dispatch undesirables with impunity, now the oppressed are fighting back.

"The Golden Prince and his lackeys may think they've snuffed us out, but new flames are rising from the ashes," Anton Vipera, leader of

THE SERPENT SYNDICATE, DECLARED. "LET THEM KEEP CELEBRATING ATOP THEIR IVORY TOWERS. A STORM IS GATHERING BELOW."

OTHERS URGE CAUTION, WARNING THAT THE RUTHLESS KING WILL SURELY SEEK TO MAKE EXAMPLES OF ANY VILLAINS GROWING TOO BOLD, BUT AFTER LIFETIMES LURKING FEARFULLY IN SHADOWS, PEOPLE ARE DESPERATE FOR SOMEONE TO RALLY BEHIND.

THE VICTORIES OF SCARWORTH AND LILLY HAVE LIT THAT SPARK. THEIR SKILL AND TEAMWORK SYMBOLIZE THE GREATER STRENGTH POSSIBLE IF VILLAINS STAND UNDIVIDED. UNITED, NO "HERO" CAN WITHSTAND THEIR COMBINED MIGHT.

"THEY'RE STILL YOUNG, BARELY MORE THAN KIDS," GRIZZLED ARENA REGULAR JAX NOTED, "BUT MARK MY WORDS, THAT PAIR IS DESTINED FOR GREATNESS. THE SHADOW PRINCE MAY HAVE MET HIS MATCH AT LAST."

UNTIL NOW, PRINCE ASHER AND HIS HEROIC ORDER HAVE HELD UNQUESTIONED SWAY, ENFORCING THE KING'S HARSH DECREES. MANY FAMILIES CAN TESTIFY TO LOVED ONES EXILED OR EXECUTED AT THE PRINCE'S WORD, NO MERCY ALLOWED.

ONLY UNITED RESISTANCE CAN END THIS APARTHEID, SEPARATING THE KINGDOM INTO THE DESERVING AND UNDESERVING. AS SCARWORTH AND

LILLY DEMONSTRATED, TEAMWORK AND COMMUNITY CAN OVERCOME EVEN THE STRONGEST FOE.

THESE TWO HAVE BECOME THE FACES OF A NEW MOVEMENT, PROOF THE TIME IS RIPE FOR CHANGE. THEIR COURAGE HAS INSPIRED EVEN TIRED CYNICS TO NURTURE FRAGILE HOPES FOR FREEDOM FROM PERSECUTION.

BUT RISKS REMAIN. THE CROWN DOES NOT TAKE DEFIANCE LIGHTLY, AS THE HEADLESS CORPSES OF PAST AGITATORS ILLUSTRATE. MYSTERIOUS DISAPPEARANCES SILENCE ANY WHO GROW TOO VOCAL. THE GOLDEN PRINCE'S REACH IS LONG.

YET PERHAPS THESE NEW CHAMPIONS CAN SUCCEED WHERE OTHERS FAILED. AS THEIR FAME SPREADS, MORE RALLY TO THE CAUSE, EAGER TO ADD THEIR MIGHT. IF HEROES LIKE ASHER CAN GATHER LEGIONS OF DEVOTEES, WHY NOT VILLAINS?

THE SHADOWED STANDARD ENCOURAGES ALL TO HEED THE LESSON OF PETER SCARWORTH AND LILLY, THE LESSON THAT THERE IS POWER IN NUMBERS, POWER IN REFUSING TO BOW. A GRAND DESTINY AWAITS IF THEY SEIZE IT TOGETHER.

OUR KINGDOM'S HISTORY NEED NOT BE WRITTEN ONLY BY THE VICTORS. THE TIME NEARS WHEN THE IGNORED VOICES FROM BELOW RISE UP AS ONE TO DEMAND THEY BE HEARD.

Let the Golden Prince and his cronies tremble in their gilded towers. A new era dawns.

19

Lillith

The sun dips low over the horizon as Prince Asher and I wander the market square. Asher insists we take rooms at the inn for a few days while we hunt for the information we need.

"We've had little enough time away," he says, "and you deserve a proper rest after your victory in the arena today."

I flush at his praise. "It was nothing."

Asher shakes his head. "Don't discount your skills, Lilly. That was a hard fought match, and you showed great courage and cunning. I was quite impressed! I didn't know you knew how to fight."

I look at him in surprise. His compliments are as unlooked for as they are kind.

A yawn creeps up on me. Arms full of packages of food and books, I refuse to even attempt to cover it.

"Lilly," he says, a teasing glint in his blue eyes, "you can't possibly be tired already."

"Of course not," I huff, adjusting my grip on the packages. "It's just that these parcels seem to have gained weight since we started."

"Ah, my apologies," he says with mock seriousness. "I forgot to warn you about the magical properties of shopping bags."

I can't help but chuckle at his jest, shaking my head in amusement.

We stop at a stall selling an assortment of roasted nuts and fruits, the fragrant aroma wafting through the air.

"Would you like some?" Asher asks, gesturing toward the treats.

"Thank you," I reply, shifting the packages to one hand.

I gratefully accept a handful of the sweet-smelling snacks, and we continue browsing the stalls, munching on our treats while exploring.

As we meander through the crowded square, I can feel the tension that has been building all day. Despite the light-hearted banter between us, there is an undercurrent of danger lurking beneath the surface. If he is discovered, it would cause serious trouble.

"Have you ever tried candied figs, Lilly?" Asher asks suddenly, pulling me from my thoughts.

"Can't say that I have," I reply, curious about the sudden change in topic.

"Then you must try one," he insists, purchasing a small bag and offering it to me.

"Thank you," I say.

I take a bite of the sticky-sweet treat. It's delicious, but I can't help but feel uneasy. Is this just another one of Asher's playful distractions, or is there something he isn't telling me?

"Ah, Asher, my boy!" a voice booms through the market square.

I glance up and see Bronn, one of Prince Asher's closest friends, making his way toward us. His arms are open wide for an embrace, and Asher sets down his bag to return the gesture.

As the two men continue their conversation, I notice someone watching us. A quick scan of the bustling market reveals Xixor Shade, lurking in the shadows of a nearby stall. My heart races and I subtly elbow Asher and nod in Xixor's direction.

"Anyway, Bronn," Asher continues, raising his voice slightly. "Would you care to join us for a drink? We were just about to stop at the tavern."

"Sounds delightful," Bronn replies.

We make our way to the tavern. I keep an eye on Xixor. He continues to watch us, his eyes narrowed in suspicion. I try to focus on Asher's light-hearted banter with Bronn.

The tavern is a cozy little place, filled with laughter and the scent of roasted meats. The warm glow of the fireplace illuminates the faces of patrons while they clink their mugs together in celebration. My fingers twitch nervously against the parcels I carry as I try to focus on anything but the danger that potentially lurks outside.

"Ah, this place brings back memories, doesn't it?" Asher asks, clearly attempting to lighten the mood as he pulls out a chair for Bronn. "The last time we were here, we were barely fifteen."

Bronn grins widely. "Remember that time you started a bar fight just because someone insulted your hair?"

"In my defense, they called it 'the color of a sickly pigeon'," Asher retorts, feigning offense.

I let out a small chuckle despite the tension coiling in my stomach. After taking a deep breath, I excuse myself to fetch some drinks for the three of us, all the while keeping my eyes peeled for any signs of danger.

"Be on alert," Asher whispers into my ear as I pass him. His warmth sends shivers down my spine, but I quickly nod and focus on my task.

As I approach the bar, I feel eyes on me.

"Three ales, please," I say to the barkeep, plastering a smile on my face even though my heart races like a runaway carriage.

"Coming right up, miss," he replies cheerily, filling the mugs with frothy ale.

"Thank you," I murmur, taking the drinks and carefully weaving my way back to our table, trying not to spill a single drop.

I slide into the open seat next to Asher and bring the ale to my lips, hoping the bitter drink will calm my nerves. The boisterous laughter of the tavern patrons rings out around us.

"Remember that time we borrowed the blacksmith's horses and rode them through town?" Bronn asks with a mischievous grin.

Asher chuckles. "I thought the blacksmith was going to tan our hides! His face went as red as a ripe tomato when he caught us."

I sip my ale silently, keeping my eyes trained on the tavern door. The shadows seem to shift and morph as patrons enter and exit. I search for any sign of Xixor, but see nothing amiss yet.

"More memories from your unruly youth?" I ask lightly, hoping to mask the tension thrumming through me.

"You know us too well, Lilly," Asher replies with a wink.

I manage a thin smile in return. The ale warms me, but does little to abate the unease coiling in my stomach. Xixor could be lurking just outside, waiting to catch Asher unawares. We cannot stay long.

Asher seems to sense my discomfort. "Ready, Lilly?" Asher asks, offering me his arm.

"Ready as I'll ever be," I reply, taking his arm with a small smile.

Together, we step out into the bustling market square, the cool air a welcome relief from the stuffy tavern.

"He's coming," I whisper, spotting his imposing figure just a few stalls away and closing in on us.

"Quick. Act natural," Asher says, barely containing the panic in his voice.

"Natural? How?"

"Like this!"

Without another word, Asher pulls me into his arms and presses his lips against mine. My eyes widen in surprise, but I realize his plan and close them and lean into the passionate kiss.

Is this natural enough for you? A hint of amusement breaks through my nerves.

I feel Xixor's presence nearing, his heavy footsteps on the cobblestone ground. As he passes by, I steal a glance and see him determinedly staring straight ahead, visibly uncomfortable with our unexpected intimacy on display.

"Lovebirds," he mutters under his breath, shaking his head before he continues walking away from us.

We hold onto each other until he is out of sight. Breaking apart, both of us are visibly flustered and relieved that our impromptu performance worked.

"Phew, that was close!" I manage a giggle, trying to shake off the awkwardness of our staged kiss. "I didn't think you'd go for that."

"Desperate times call for desperate measures," Asher replies, his cheeks still flushed.

We navigate the crowded streets, and I can't help giggling to myself or eyeing the prince.

"Seriously, Lilly, you're enjoying my embarrassment far too much," Asher grumbles, shooting me a sidelong glance.

"Forgive me," I tease, unable to resist poking fun at him, "but your flustered expression is rather endearing."

"Endearing, huh?" Asher raises an eyebrow, a playful smirk tugging at the corners of his mouth. "Well, just remember who came up with the plan in the first place."

"Of course. Your brilliant mind never ceases to impress me," I reply sarcastically, earning a snort of laughter from Asher. Because this was all his idea, obviously.

As we hurry through the bustling market, our hearts still race from the adrenaline and the lingering embarrassment of our stolen moment. We can't deny that something has shifted between us—a new understanding and, perhaps, the spark of something more. For now, we simply focus on the task at hand, leaving the memory of our embrace behind us in the colorful chaos of the market square.

20

Asher

I stride purposefully through the inn's corridors, Lilly trailing behind while carrying our parcels and luggage. The events of the day weigh heavily on my mind, from our victory in the arena to our close call with Xixor in the crowded market.

Upon reaching my chamber, I unlock the heavy oak door and usher Lilly inside. "Have a seat. Rest your feet. I'll fetch us refreshments."

Leaving no room for argument, I depart swiftly, eager to lighten the palpable tension between us.

When I return, Lilly's settled stiffly into an over-stuffed armchair by the crackling hearth. Her posture speaks volumes despite our practiced camaraderie. An undercurrent of uncertainty has lingered since our staged kiss in the square. Have we crossed an invisible line?

Determined to dispel the awkwardness, I try lightening the mood. "I trust I served you well in the arena, fierce champion?"

Her lips quirk up ever so slightly. "As well as could be expected for royalty. I suppose I should be grateful you can wield weapons between your weekly manicures."

"Manicures? Perish the thought. There's a reason I mostly use magic," I scoff in mock offense while positioning myself in front of her, grateful for her familiar teasing retort. Her feet are already bare and she wiggles her toes inviting me to fulfill our bet. "Comfortable?" I ask, kneading Lillith's tense feet.

She sighs, eyes drifting shut. "Don't let it go to your head, Prince, but you've magic fingers."

Emboldened, I dig deeper into tired muscles, coaxing further hints of pleasure.

Her unexpected giggles catch me off guard.

I glance up in wonder. "Ticklish, are we?"

"Don't you dare—" Lilly chokes, squirming as I wiggle probing fingers along her sole.

Laughter escapes unchecked, carefree and charming where icy composure reigned before.

I persist in my tactless attacks till tears shine in her eyes.

"Please, no more!" she begs through gasps.

Relenting, I flash a cheeky grin. "Who knew my fierce maid had such vulnerabilities?"

She swats me, color staining her cheeks. "And who knew the noble prince such a tease! Consider yourself fortunate I spare you for such antics."

"Ah, but it lifts my heart to see you like this." I speak without thinking, sobering as truth laid bare.

We stare at each other, all humor gone, understanding blooming where once stood only wary skepticism.

Friends or more, in this tender moment's clarity, all feels... right.

***

The dream pulls me back into a vivid recollection of that fateful night long ago. I find myself in my mother's bedchamber, the lavish space lit only by a few trembling candles. Shadows dance across the elegant furniture and ornate tapestries that adorn the walls.

My mother, the queen, lies upon her grand four-poster bed. Her normally lustrous golden curls are plastered to her damp brow by the fever's cruel grasp. Dark circles beneath her closed eyes stand out starkly against her ashen, hollowed cheeks.

Desperation claws at my heart. The mystifying illness has ravaged her over countless days and nights while the baffled physicians try every remedy to no avail. I cannot bear to lose my mother. She is the light to the shadow my father is in my life.

This is why I delve, by the thin light of a single candle, into the forbidden world of blood magic, an art so sinister it is the domain of only the most wretched villains, but I am determined to save my mother, whatever the cost.

My hands tremble as I draw the silver ritual blade across my own palm. Crimson blood, black in the candlelight, wells up and drips into the prepared bowl. I whisper the twisted incantation, fighting revulsion at the infernal words. This perverse sorcery is my final gambit to cheat the merciless fate threatening to rob my mother of life.

As the ritual crescendos, the swirling blood erupts upwards in writhing, snake-like tendrils. They surge through the air over my mother's frail body and plunge into her flesh. She jerks and convulses violently, locked in the magic's throes.

I watch in mingled awe and horror as the pulsing crimson cords fade, their work done. With a gasp, my mother goes still. The room is silent except for the thunder of my heart. Did the ritual work...or kill her?

Then, she draws a shuddering breath, color returning to her pallid cheeks. Her eyelids flutter open, and she whispers my name.

I fly to her side, weeping with relief, a secret thrill coursing through me at the triumph of this forbidden act.

With a start, I awake, my sleep clothes soaked in cold sweat, pulse racing. As my chambers materialize in the muted dawn light, unease stirs within me. Why has slumber dredged up that dire memory now after so many years undisturbed in their crypt?

Perhaps pretending to be a villain on this mission has awoken past ghosts I thought long laid to rest. My father, the staunchly righteous king, would never have understood the love that drove me to blood magic's abyss. Some stains, no matter how righteously earned, can never be fully cleansed.

Lillith

The roar of the crowd shakes the walls of the arena as our next opponent emerges from the gate opposite us. I peer across the space, straining to get a glimpse of the figure approaching, but his features are obscured beneath a voluminous, hooded black robe. An enchanted aura seems to cling to the fabric, writhing like serpents made of shadow.

Curious. This is no ordinary mage we face.

Prince Asher strides forward confidently, raising his sword in salute to the spectators, but I catch his sleeve, tugging him back. "Careful, my lord," I murmur. "This one is not like the others."

Asher frowns, studying the robed man gliding soundlessly across the stone. "How so?"

"I don't know, but I sense a darkness about him. Powerful magic cloaks his form." I glance around the familiar oval of the arena I fought in many times, but now, all seems strange and threatening. "He comes for more than glory or gold. Be on your guard."

Asher hesitates, then nods.

We step forward together as our opponent halts before us, invisible beneath his robes. An expectant hush falls over the crowd.

From the shadows of his cowl, a single red eye gleams like a hot coal, fixing us with a piercing stare. When he speaks, his voice seems to slither into my mind, cold and malignant.

"So these are my contenders? Fresh meat and his girl? You're not even a challenge." A gnarled gray hand emerges, pulling back the hood to reveal a face from night-mares—granite skin, twisting horns, and a smile full of malice. "I am the Magus Maleficus. You face powers be-yond your comprehension. That book is the door through which you might slip away, if your wits can uncover where it's hidden before your strength gives out. " He waves his hand and we are transported to a place of illusion. I can sense his magic surrounding us.

As he disappears, leaving us alone in a library, I feel a surge of determination. Asher must have felt it too, be-cause he flashes me a grin and says, "Well, Lilly, let's show this pompous mage what we're made of."

"Agreed," I reply, returning his smile. "Maleficus won't know what hit him."

We begin our ascent, one stair at a time, anchoring each other as we go. It isn't easy; the staircase seems to delight in trying to throw us off balance, flipping upside down or sideways without warning, but with each near-miss, our teamwork improves, our movements becoming more fluid and in sync.

"Last one," Asher says, panting slightly as we reach the top of the stairs. "I hope."

"Me too," I agree, my muscles aching but my spirits buoyed by our success.

We enter a vast hall filled with identical-looking doors stretching out as far as the eye can see.

"Next challenge? Doors," I announce. "Maleficus really has a flair for the dramatic, doesn't he?"

"Seems that way," Asher replies, eyeing the doors warily. "How do we know which one to choose?"

"Trial and error?" I suggest, only half-joking.

"Let's mark the doors we've tried with symbols so we don't get lost," Asher proposes, pulling a piece of chalk from his pocket.

"Good thinking," I praise him as we approach the first door.

We work our way through the doors, marking each one with a symbol to keep track of our progress. Some lead to dead ends, others to rooms filled with more traps and illusions, but none hold the book we seek.

"Maybe it's behind this one," Asher muses, opening yet another door.

"Or maybe it's behind the next one," I counter, a teasing lilt to my voice, "but we'll find it eventually, right?"

"Right," Asher agrees, offering me a warm smile, "because we make a pretty formidable team, don't we?"

"Absolutely," I reply, rolling my eyes.

"Wait, do you hear that?" Asher asks, halting our progress through the labyrinth of bookcases and doors.

I strain my ears, trying to discern what has caught his attention. "I...I think so," I whisper, as a low, eerie growl echoes through the library.

Almost immediately, an oppressive sense of dread settles over me like a cold, damp blanket.

We move cautiously, following the source of the sound while trying to avoid drawing its attention. As we round a corner, we find ourselves face to face with a monstrous creature resembling a mix between a wolf and a dragon.

"Any ideas?" I shout, my voice sounding distant even to myself.

"Run!" Asher suggests, grabbing my arm and pulling me along as we dart through the maze-like corridors and throw ourselves through one of the doors.

We work together to evade traps and illusions at every turn.

"Remember when I said we make a formidable team?" Asher asks, grinning. "I think I underestimated us. We're downright unstoppable."

"Agreed," I reply, smiling back at him.

A familiar wide-eyed face peers around a shelf, and my heart leaps.

"Nargle!" I cry, crouching down to greet the little creature.

We follow my little friend through the twists and turns of the shelves at a rapid pace. His help is uncanny, as if summoned by our need.

At last, Nargle halts before a wooden door obscured behind cobwebs and debris.

Nargle scampers over to a cobwebbed alcove, and scratches at something within.

"What is it, Nargle?" I kneel beside him. He has found a hidden shelf, and there glows the book we seek.

The moment I grasp the ancient tome, I know we've won. Its title shimmers, "The Perfect Relationship." Asher's eyes lock onto mine in triumph.

Maleficus suddenly appears and whirls, dark robes billowing, hurling bolts of black energy at Asher and me. We dodge and weave, fighting back with sword and magic.

Asher and I exchange a look, seeing the strain in each other's eyes. If we do not end this soon, we will fall. Our only hope lays in a final gambit.

I begin to whisper an incantation to weaken Maleficus.

Asher charges forward, flaming sword raised high.

Seeing my opening, I finish my spell. Maleficus freezes in place, defenses crumbling. The crowd gasps. Asher raises his sword and strikes Maleficus down.

He runs to me, catching me up in a fierce embrace. I cling to him, overcome with relief and joy.

The crowd chants our names.

I gaze at Asher, heart swelling.

"Impossible!" Maleficus gasps, his voice barely a whisper.

"Believe it," I tell the villain, my heart swelling with pride and affection for the man beside me.

Asher and I amble through the arena halls after our latest victory. Only one fight remains in the arena, and we are no closer to uncovering the identity of the villain we seek.

"Remind me again why I agreed to this?" Asher groans, his white hair matted against his forehead, the blue eyes that make my heart race hidden beneath a weary grimace.

"Because, Peter Scarworth," I tease, using his ludicrous fake villain name, "we're doing this for the greater good." I feign a noble air, but my voice cracks from exhaustion.

"Ah, yes, the greater good." Asher sighs, rolling his eyes. "The things we do for love."

"Love?" I raise an eyebrow, trying not to let my surprise show. "I thought it was just for money. What does love have to do with this?"

We turn a corner and stumble upon a magnificent hall adorned with intricate tapestries and ornate chandeliers casting an ethereal glow upon the portraits lining the walls. The faces of champions past stare back at us, their expressions a mixture of anger, determination, and—most notably—triumph.

One image, however, makes me halt in my tracks, that of a pale woman dressed in black, her wicked gaze frozen in time as she brandishes a dagger.

"Who's this?" Asher asks, his eyes narrowing as he studies the portrait. "She looks... dangerous."

"Her name is Lamira the Wraith," I murmur, trying to keep my voice steady. "They say she was once a powerful sorceress who turned her back on the light and embraced darkness."

An invitation dangles from the bottom of Lamira's portrait, catching my eye. Asher must have noticed it, too, because he leans in to read the flowery script aloud.

"'Join the celebration of the life of the Wraith at midnight's ball,'" he says, furrowing his brows. His eyes light up with excitement. "Ah, a masquerade. I've always loved dressing up and hiding behind masks. It adds an air of mystery, don't you think?"

"Sure," I agree half-heartedly, concerned about what lay ahead. "But we shouldn't let the allure of the event distract us from our mission."

As we wander farther down the hall of champions, a particular portrait catches my eye—myself. My heart skips a beat as I recognize my own face, framed by dark curls and a knowing smile.

"Hey, what about this one?" Asher asks, drawing my attention to a nearby painting of a fierce warrior.

"Ah, yes," I say quickly, hastening him away before he marks the familiarity in the portrait of my former self. My knowledge here must stay hidden, even from him.

As we continue on about sweet treats and other frivolous topics, I can't shake the feeling that the stakes are higher than ever. For now, I have to keep Asher in the dark, protect him from the secrets that threaten to bring us both down. And so, with each step we take farther into the hall of champions, I resolve to enjoy our time together even as darker forces lurk just out of sight.

***

I tap my foot impatiently on the worn wooden floor of my room in the inn, the rhythm echoing through the small chamber like some sort of restless heartbeat. The scent of lavender mingles with the low hum of distant laughter. The sun has already begun to set, bathing the room in an ethereal golden glow as my thoughts turn toward a certain prince and the many secrets I've so carefully hidden.

"Rule number thirteen," I mutter under my breath, the words a mantra meant to keep me focused. "No matter how attractive a hero may be, there is always someone just as attractive who doesn't want to kill you."

As the minutes drag on, I find myself pacing the length of the room, my nerves fraying at the edges. Prince Asher will arrive any moment now with my wardrobe for the ball. He promised to take care of everything. The longer I wait, the more my thoughts seem to betray me, images of his white hair and piercing blue eyes filling my mind.

When I open the door, I find not the prince but a timid-looking servant girl, her arms laden with boxes filled with what I assume are garments and accessories.

"Are you all right, miss?" the girl asks, her brow furrowed in concern, her gaze on my fidgety hands.

"Of course," I lie through gritted teeth. "Just... eager for tonight."

She giggles, her eyes darting around the room like a sparrow. "Aren't we all! Prince Asher is quite the catch, isn't he?"

"Indeed," I mumble, feeling an unfamiliar twinge of jealousy.

I'm not here to catch him. I'm here to corrupt him. Yet, as I watch the servant girl carefully unpack my things, I can't help but entertain the thought of what it would be like to dance with him under the moonlight.

She nods to me and leaves me in peace.

My fingers graze over the delicate lace of my gown, a shiver of anticipation running down my spine at the thought of wearing it to the masquerade. What would his fingers feel like around my waist over this lace?

"Focus, Lillith," I admonish myself, shaking the distracting thoughts from my head.

My gaze wanders to the polished surface of the dressing table where the mask lays, its intricate beading casting tiny golden reflections around the room as the last rays of the day disappear. It taunts me.

After dressing myself in the gown, I reach for the mask, feeling the weight of its beads in my hand as I loop the thin black ribbon around my head. The lace clings to the contours of my face, transforming me into an enigmatic stranger who will dance with Asher yet remain hidden beneath a veil of secrecy.

A knock on the door startles me from my reverie, and I quickly smooth out my gown before opening it. Prince Asher stands before me, dressed in an immaculate black suit that complements his white hair and piercing blue eyes. The sight of him sends an unexpected thrill through me.

"You look radiant tonight," Asher says.

I try not to blush. "Thank you."

As we walk together toward the masquerade, I struggle to maintain my facade. My thoughts are a whirlwind of conflicting emotions, and I can't help but be acutely aware of the warmth of his arm pressed against mine.

22

Lillith

I enter the dimly lit ballroom on Prince Asher's arm, a thrill of trepidation and excitement coursing through me. The ballroom is lit only by a few flickering candles and the eerie green glow of the chandeliers, crafted from human bones and shards of jade.

Villains and rogues of all kinds fill the room, decked in elaborate costumes that flaunt their sins. A string quartet of hooded musicians plays a sinister melody in a shadowed alcove.

A thick haze of smoke hangs in the air, fragrant with opium and tobacco. Along one wall is a buffet of strange and exotic foods—platters of figs drizzled in blood, sugared violets, chocolate truffles filled with a liqueur so strong it causes hallucinations.

"Quite the motley crew, isn't it?" Asher murmurs, leaning close so only I can hear.

I nod, tightening my grip on his arm. My scarlet gown and jewels feel out of place among so many miscreants, my innocent act unraveling.

We make our way through the crowd, many villains nodding respectfully to Asher and eyeing me with interest and suspicion.

Asher procures two glasses of absinthe from a serving girl, the green liquor sloshing ominously. "To keeping up appearances," he says quietly, and we both drink deeply, wincing at the bitter taste.

"Let's get this over with," I mutter under my breath.

Asher gazes down at me, eyes gleaming in the greenish light, a cunning smile twisting his lips. "Let's give them a show they won't forget." He bows and offers his hand. "May I have this dance?"

I curtsy, slipping seamlessly into my role though my heart pounds. "You may."

I place my gloved hand in his, and Asher whirls me into the sea of villains, our act beginning in earnest. Little do I know the danger and treachery the night holds in store or how fiercely Asher will fight to protect me from it.

We begin dancing stiffly, but as the music swells, a dark and passionate tango, I find myself swept away. Asher leads me confidently across the floor, spinning and dipping me with practiced ease. Our gazes lock, and the rest of the room fades away. It is only us, caught in the rhythm of the dance.

My scarlet skirts swish and spin, feet flying over the floor. The music is sultry and mesmerizing, played by unseen musicians in a shadowed alcove. How strange that I once thought I belonged in this world, I think, heart pounding as Asher dips me low, when I feel so out of place now.

Asher pulls me upright and draws me close, our bodies nearly touching. "You're enchanting tonight," he murmurs in my ear. His breath is warm, his arm sure around my waist.

I feel dizzy with the rush of the dance and his nearness.

This is all part of the act, I remind myself. I am playing a role, but as I gaze into Asher's eyes, for a moment, I can believe this deception we play is real. I see a fire in his eyes that seems to hint at hidden depths of feeling.

The music reaches a crescendo, and Asher bends me back in a deep, dramatic dip, surely stealing the breath of any who watch. As the final notes sound, he draws me up slowly until our faces are inches apart.

My heartbeat echoes the finish of the tango. The line between my true self and this role I play is becoming blurred. Pretending to be Asher's woman is dangerous. For, in this moment, held tight in Asher's embrace, I wish for nothing more than for this dance to never end.

As the music ends, Asher gazes down at me with something like wonder. "You were exquisite," he says softly.

I feel myself blushing and glance away, suddenly shy.

Asher places a finger under my chin and tilts my face back to his. "There's my Lilly," he murmurs with a smile.

My guard comes down in the wake of his tender smile and earnest gaze. It terrifies me that I enjoy letting my act fall away in his presence.

A new song begins, but we linger there, caught in a moment apart from the revelry around us. Villains and rogues spin on, oblivious to our stillness.

"Must we continue this charade all evening?" Asher asks lightly, though I glimpse a flash of longing in his eyes.

My own heartbeat quickens at the unspoken suggestion in his words.

But I sigh, grasping for my role once more like a cloak. "You know as well as I the danger we'd court by revealing the truth." I glance pointedly at those around us, a sea of potential threats.

Asher's eyes darken. "Then, let's continue the performance, my villainous lady," he says, slipping back into the act.

He spins me into another dramatic dance, leading me through practiced steps, though I feel the change in him—the subtle tension in his shoulders, the way his smile doesn't quite reach his eyes.

I follow his lead across the floor once more, donning my role, but my thoughts are in a whirl. The charade had fallen away in that tender moment, and I saw Asher's true feelings as clearly as he saw mine. The game we play is altering into something else entirely, and there will be no going back.

But do I really want it to go back?

We dance for what feels like hours, caught in a whirl of music and movement, never once dropping our act. When a waltz fades, we leave the floor, I feel utterly breathless and lightheaded.

Asher grasps my hand and bows. "I'll fetch us some drinks." He brushes his lips across my knuckles before disappearing into the crowd.

Alone, I sigh, relishing a moment's rest from the charade.

Internally, I laugh a bit. When I went here, I was too young to go to these events, and it was all I wanted to do. Now here I am, in disguise, hoping no one will recognize me.

"Well, if it isn't Amethyst Eyes," a voice says softly in my ear.

I spin around to find Silviana behind me, a sly smile upon her lips. I give a sharp intake of breath, and my heart clenches at the old nickname... and at her cunning. After so many years, she finally caught me unawares.

Silviana's smile only widens at my sharp intake of breath. "Did you think I wouldn't recognize you, Lillith? No matter how many times you denied it in the hall, I would never not recognize my old friend."

My true name slips from her lips softly as a shadow, laced with secrets from long ago.

I grasp her hands, pulse racing. "Silviana, please. It's too dangerous for this deception to be unwoven now."

She arches an eyebrow, gazing down at me with eyes which miss little. "Dangerous? Or are you simply not yet ready for your charming young prince to know the truth about his villainous lover?"

I shake my head, hoping my alarm isn't written plainly on my face. Silviana has always been able to read my thoughts as easily as words upon a page.

"Promise me you'll keep this secret, for now at least." I squeeze her hands, pleading. "Like old times?"

Silviana studies me. I glimpse a flicker of our past friendship behind her eyes, softening her resolve.

She sighs. "For now, your secret remains concealed." She leans close to murmur, "But be cautious, Amethyst Eyes. The higher the climb, the more perilous the fall, and you, my dear, have climbed to the peak."

I embrace her in thanks, relieved to feel her arms around me as they had been so often in our youth. For a fleeting moment, the burden of pretense and power falls away, and we are simply two girls sharing secrets once again.

Silviana pulls back to gaze at me searchingly. "There are none in this den of trickery that can be trusted, other than myself of course." Her eyes gleam harshly. "Wear your disguise well, and keep your true self hidden, or you will find even this palace of rogues will turn against you."

"I would love to see them try, but thank you. I will refresh my glamour and keep my eyes open."

With that, Silviana turns and vanishes into the shadows, leaving me shaken. My deception remains unbroken, but Silviana's warning echoes in my mind like some refrain.

The higher I climb, the more perilous my downfall will inevitably be.

The prince has still not returned with our drinks, leaving me uncomfortably alone once more among the sea of hidden faces. Walking around the edge of the room, I mentally list off the faces I recognize and take note of the ones I don't. I idly study the intricate mural on the ceiling, depicting images of demons and destruction.

"Why waste your time with the likes of him, my pet?" The voice is smooth as silk. "You belong on the arm of someone who can truly appreciate you."

I turn to find a tall, broad-shouldered man looming over me, garbed all in black, his face obscured by an ornate raven mask. He smells of leather and spice, with an undertone of something metallic, blood perhaps. My instincts prickle warily.

"That boy can offer you nothing," the stranger continues, stepping closer. "He is but a trifle for you to toy with, unworthy of your talents." His gaze travels over me slowly. "You need a partner of your caliber, little raven, someone who knows the darkness you hide behind that pretty mask."

No name comes to mind. He must be new and unimportant in the villain world. At least for now.

I stand straighter and meet his gaze levelly, irritation rising. "You presume much, sir. My loyalties are not so easily swayed by pretty words and false promises."

The man chuckles, a low dangerous sound. He grasps my hand and lifts it to his lips, breath hot against my skin. "Loyalties change in time. When you tire of playing pretend with your lover, seek me out." He slips something small and hard into my palm—a jet-black feather etched with a raven's skull. "Ask for Raven at the Crimson Door tavern."

My temper rises, and I feel my magic tingle in my fingertips. Before I can lash out at him, however, a hand wraps around my wrist, tugging me away from the man. My gaze follows up the arm to find Prince Asher glaring at the stranger, his expression a mix of anger and protectiveness.

"I suggest you leave," he growls, his voice barely more than a whisper. "Now."

The stranger steps back and gives us both a mocking bow before turning and disappearing into the crowd.

My heart racing with fear and adrenaline, I exhale shakily and look up at Asher.

He slowly releases my wrist. "Are you all right?" he asks gruffly, eyes still searching the room for any sign of danger.

I nod mutely and hold out my hand to show that it is empty. The card with Raven's name is gone.

ANNUAL VILLAIN MASQUERADE BALL DRAWS NOTORIOUS ROGUES

By Maud Malcontent

The annual villain masquerade ball was held last night at the Blackthorn Estate, drawing infamous rogues and scoundrels from across the kingdom. Hosted by the notorious crime lord Theron Blackthorn, the lavish event featured debauchery and scheming in equal measure.

Villains turned out in dramatic costumes and masks, mingling and making deals over lavish foods and drinks. A menacing string quartet played throughout the night, accompanied by exotic dancers and other scandalous entertainment.

"It was a delightfully wicked affair, as always," Anton Vipera, head of the Serpent Syndicate, commented. "So many opportunities to network and forge advantageous partnerships."

The ball has become an important event for networking among villain circles. With the tyrannical king cracking down on their activities, these social events allow them to meet safely.

Notable attendees included Magmog the Minotaur, Jaxor the fierce, the illusionist warlock Rasmodius, vile necromancer Sir Bedivere, and the assassin twins Castor and Pollux.

However, the legendary sorceress Lillith Shadowend was absent once again. Though undisputedly the most powerful villain in the kingdom, she rarely makes public appearances anymore. Her fearsome reputation alone maintains her status.

The highlight of the evening was an impromptu duel between Rasmodius and Sir Bedivere over a business dispute. Their magic shook the hall threatening to tear down the cave system as each tried to destroy the other in in-

VENTIVE WAYS. FORTUNATELY, THERON INTERVENED BEFORE IT COULD TURN DEADLY.

IN ADDITION TO SUCH CHAOTIC ENTERTAINMENT, BACKROOM DEALS WERE STRUCK OVER BLACK MARKET GOODS, SMUGGLING ROUTES, AND MORE NEFARIOUS SCHEMES. THE MASQUERADE BALL IS NOT JUST DECADENCE BUT AN OPPORTUNITY FOR VILLAINS TO FURTHER THEIR AIMS FREE FROM MEDDLING "HEROES."

WHETHER FOR BUSINESS OR PLEASURE, THE ANNUAL EVENT CEMENTS BONDS AND RIVALRIES AMONG THE KINGDOM'S VILLAINS. THEY EMERGE REINVIGORATED IN THEIR OPPOSITION TO THE OPPRESSIVE LAWS CONSTRAINING THEIR KIND.

"THE PATHETIC KING AND HIS TAME PRINCES CANNOT SUPPRESS US MUCH LONGER," THERON DECLARED IN A TOAST. "A NEW AGE IS DAWNING, MY FRIENDS. OUR TIME COMES SWIFTLY!"

23

Asher

Guiding Lilly out of the ballroom with an iron grip on her arm, a hot surge of jealousy courses through me. I try to keep my cool, but that proves difficult, and my grip on my drink tightens. I tell myself that I am just keeping up appearances – after all, we are undercover – but the anger swells in my chest, and I can't stand the idea of anyone touching her.

"Really, you could loosen your grip a bit," Lilly chides. Despite her complaint, she doesn't try to pull away. Instead, she leans into me, as if trying to prove a point.

"Sorry," I mutter, reluctantly releasing her arm, "but you have to admit, that guy was getting a little too friendly."

"I don't know if friendly is a term I would use for the people here. Jealous much?" Lilly teases, a mischievous glint in her eyes.

"Of course not," I retort, trying to brush off the comment. "I'm just... protective, that's all."

"Protective, huh?" Her laughter fills the air like wind chimes. "Well, thank you for coming to my rescue, Prince Charming."

"Hey, I'm no prince here," I remind her, trying to suppress my own grin. "Peter Scarworth, remember?"

"Right, right," she agrees, still smirking. "Well, either way, you're quite the dashing hero."

"Flattery will get you nowhere, Lilly," I warn playfully.

We continue down the corridor, the sounds of laughter and music from the ballroom fading behind us. I can't help but feel a little smug at having rescued Lilly from that persistent flirt. Still, we have more important things to focus on—like finding our elusive target.

As we pass by an ornate door slightly ajar, the unmistakable smell of pipe smoke wafts out along with a drunken voice complaining loudly.

I raise a hand, signaling Lilly to pause and listen.

"That coward Lexir Crow! How dare he steal from me!" slurs the voice from within the dimly lit room.

Curiosity piqued, I take a cautious step closer to the door, peering through the haze of smoke to try to see who is speaking. The man's hunched over in a plush armchair, clutching a glass of something amber and clearly intoxicating. As his face swings into view, I recognize him as Theron, a notorious crime lord whose reputation for ruthlessness is legendary.

"Can you believe it?" Theron rants, seemingly to no one in particular. "After everything I've done for him, the ungrateful snake turns on me! That rotten crow had better watch his back because I'm coming for him. I don't care if he's hiding in the mountains with his friends."

"Lexir Crow, huh?" I murmur under my breath, surprised at the revelation.

If even someone as dangerous as Theron has been betrayed by Lexir, he is likely up to no good.

"Over the years, I've given that man everything! And this is how he repays me?" Theron's voice booms through the smoke-filled room, his face flushed with anger and too much drink. "Ambushing my men and taking the chest of gold I'd plundered!"

Lilly and I exchange a shocked glance. This Lexir has grown bold enough to steal from fellow villains. He is probably the one we are looking for.

Lilly's expression, however, holds a look I can't quite place. It seems as if she is more shocked and worried than I am.

"Can you believe it?" I whisper to her, trying to gauge her reaction.

"Lexir always had a knack for getting in over his head," she murmurs, her amethyst eyes clouded with concern, "but I never thought he'd be this reckless."

"You sound as if you know him personally."

Eyes wide, she shakes her head, "Nothing like that. Just off of his reputation. I didn't think he would be foolish enough to backstab someone within his inner circle."

"Neither did I," I admit, "but now we know who we're dealing with." I pause, staring at the opulent chandelier above us, its crystals casting a kaleidoscope of light across the room. "We just need to find him before things get worse."

"Agreed," Lilly says, her gaze flitting back to Theron.

Theron continues, his voice rising with each word, "Three days ago, on a mountain pass, Lexir's men ambushed mine! They trapped us with a forest fire and made off with the chest of gold!" He pounds his fist on the table, sloshing his drink. "And every time we tried to retrieve it, the damn fire reappeared!"

Lilly and I exchange another glance, our shock morphing into understanding. Lexir's affinity for fire magic is well-known. He has burned down many villages, and even my own brother has scars from his last encounter with Lexir.

"Are you thinking what I'm thinking?" Lilly whispers, her green eyes sparking with determination.

"Head to the forest and take him down there while avoiding any unnecessary casualties?"

"Exactly," she agrees, her grip on my arm tightening slightly.

I can sense the worry that still lingers in her eyes. But there is no turning back now. We have to put an end to his schemes before things get even worse.

I'm about to turn away, intent on quietly leaving and planning our next move when Theron's voice booms through the room again. "Mark my words, I'll see Lexir Crow hang for this!"

His shout draws attention from everyone in the vicinity. Theron's eyes narrow as they land on Lilly and me. Still standing in the doorway, I can practically feel the suspicion radiating off of him.

I barely have a second to think before my arm loops around Lilly's waist, drawing her close as I slosh the drink in my hand for effect. It is an impulsive move, but two can play at the game of deception, and it seems our best chance of escaping Theron's notice without arousing suspicion.

Lilly plays along beautifully. She leans into me with a giggle that is both alluring and slightly tipsy, batting her eyes at Theron as if she, too, is caught up in the moment. "Please forgive us," she chimes in, her voice breathy and flirtatious. "We didn't mean to intrude. We were looking for an empty room. Not that I mind any witnesses..."

Lilly's act catches me off guard, but a spark shoots through me as she leans into my embrace. Despite the danger, having her so close feels right.

I grin roguishly, though my pulse races. "Apologies," I echo smoothly, our eyes locking in understanding.

"Next time, mind where you're going," Theron grumbles, his gaze suspicious but ultimately unfocused. From the glazed look in his eyes, it's clear the alcohol is getting the better of him. He waves a dismissive hand at us before turning back to his conversation.

"Of course!" I reply, still maintaining my pretense of drunken cheer.

As soon as Theron's attention is elsewhere, I gently urge Lilly away from the door and back into the crowded ballroom. We put some distance between ourselves and the smoking room before we finally dare to relax.

"Nice improvisation," Lilly whispers, amusement dancing in her eyes. "I didn't know you had it in you."

"Neither did I," I admit with a rueful smile, "but desperate times call for desperate measures."

"Indeed," she agrees, her expression growing more serious as she considers what we've learned. "Now we have another clue on where exactly to find Lexir Crow. We need to locate him before getting caught ourselves."

"Or attracting the attention of any more crime lords," I add wryly. "I think we've had enough close calls for one evening, don't you?"

"Definitely," Lilly nods, her laughter bubbling up once more, "but at least now we know we make a convincing pair of drunken lovers when the need arises."

"True," I concede, feeling an odd mixture of pride and embarrassment at the realization. "I suppose every cloud has its silver lining."

"Indeed it does," she agrees, a mischievous glint in her eye as she pats my arm.

24

Lillith

My heart pounds in my chest as I enter the secret underground lair, using the shadows as a cloak for my disguise.

After the masquerade last night, I struggled to sleep. My interactions with the prince had been confusing and the reemergence of my ex, Lexir, has me on edge still, honestly. First light, I gave up on sleep entirely and opted to see if any still-inebriated villains were up for spilling the beans on the location of Lexir. We need to get out of here before everything falls apart.

"Oi! Watch where you stand!" a gruff voice suddenly snaps, pulling me from my thoughts.

I look down to see Grundle the Greedy glaring up at me as he counts his latest winnings. His thick brows scrunch with irritation, but there's a glint of humor in his eyes.

"Apologies," I say, injecting a hint of haughtiness into my voice as I shift my weight away from his coin purse. "I was merely admiring your success."

"Ha! Well, you'd better get used to it, lassie!" Grundle retorts, puffing out his broad chest proudly. "Ain't no one gonna bring me down!"

"Is that so?" I tease, allowing myself a small, secretive smile. "Well, best of luck to you then."

"Thanks, but I don't need luck!" he scoffs before returning to his mountain of gold.

"Ah, there you are!" exclaims a voice I recognize all too well.

Kade, one of Lexir's top men, saunters toward me with a smug grin plastered on his tanned face. His dark hair thrown back in a messy bun probably from the aftereffects of a highly inebriated night.

"I thought I smelled the stench of failure," he adds.

"Charming as always, Kade," I retort, rolling my eyes. "What do you want?"

"Nothing from you," he sneers, "but I thought I would come and see what you've been up to. I spotted you the moment you came into town and found it interesting that you arrived under a different name."

"Is that so?" I feign disinterest.

"Indeed," Kade confirms, his eyes narrowing suspiciously. "I've been following you since you got here. What are you up to, Lillith?"

I bat my lashes. "Just trying to reconnect with my old fling."

"Why? Hoping for a romantic reunion?"

"Hardly," I scoff, folding my arms across my chest, "but if I were to find him, it would be to settle some unfinished business."

"Ha! Well, good luck with that, sweetheart," Kade taunts before stalking away.

"Fine," I shout, swallowing my pride. "I really am here to see Lexir. Will you take me to him?"

"Really?" Kade walks back, eyes narrow, suspicion in his voice. "Why would Lexir want to see you after all this time?"

"Because he still owes me a favor. Besides, I thought we could catch up on old times." I force a laugh, trying to sound casual. "You know how it is."

"Indeed," Kade replies, his skepticism evident. "Very well. Follow me."

As we navigate the shadowy corridors, I keep a close eye on the various rogues and miscreants lurking in the corners. Their stares follow us, making me uneasy. I can't help but feel like a lamb being led to slaughter.

"Are we almost there?" I ask, struggling to keep the growing anxiety from my voice.

"Patience," Kade chides. "We'll get there when we get there."

"Of course," I reply, biting back a sarcastic retort. "How silly of me to forget the secret underground lair etiquette."

"Ah, your wit hasn't changed," Kade muses, a hint of amusement in his voice. "It's one thing I actually missed about you."

"Missed?" I raise an eyebrow. "Well, I'd say that makes two of us, but that would be a lie."

"Ouch," Kade feigns hurt, chuckling as he pushes open a heavy wooden door. "Here we are."

The small, empty room is filled with mismatched furniture and dimly lit by flickering candles. It looks like a makeshift study or meeting place, not the kind of space my ex would spend his time.

"Is Lexir not here?" I ask, masking my relief with disappointment.

"Sadly, no. He's up near the Rodel border taking care of some business," Kade admits, leaning against the doorframe, "but don't worry. I'll let him know you stopped by."

"Thanks," I say, trying to sound grateful while inwardly cursing the fact that my plan hit another snag. "I suppose I should get going then."

"Wait," Kade calls out as I turn to leave. "You can't just walk in and out of here without raising suspicions. It's dangerous."

"Then what do you suggest?" I ask, exasperated.

"Stay a while," he replies with a grin. "We could always use more... resourceful members like yourself."

"Very funny," I retort, rolling my eyes.

"I've always been known for my humor, or did you forget that? Follow me. We're almost there."

We leave the room through the same door and head further down the hall.

"Where are you taking me now?" I ask Kade, trying to keep my voice steady as we continued down a dimly lit corridor.

"Patience," he replies with a sly grin. "You'll see soon enough."

As we round a corner, my heart skips a beat when I see who awaits me in the next room. Seated at an elegant chess table is none other than Lord Azantor himself, his fingers drumming lazily on the polished wood. The flickering candlelight casts eerie shadows across his face, yet he seems perfectly at ease in this underground lair.

"Ah, Lillith, so nice of you to finally join us," Azantor greets me with a sneer, his eyes twinkling with mischief. "Please, have a seat. It seems we have much to discuss."

"Lord Azantor," I reply coolly, trying to hide my surprise and apprehension. "I didn't expect to find you here."

Lord Azantor is a man I hoped to never cross again. He's a close friend of Lexir's, and during my time here as a child, he had been my tormentor. His version of competing was to completely take out his adversaries or render them useless unless he had a use for them. I thought I was free of him when I escaped, but years later, when I was dating

Lexir, Azantor decided we were competing once again. Little did he know, I had no intention of ever competing with him. By that point, I could already kill him on a whim , but I didn't for the sake of the man I loved.

There is no love anymore, though, and that will protect this man from my revenge. Perhaps, though, I can get some information from him instead if he is still connected to my ex.

"Life is full of surprises, my dear," he says, gesturing for me to sit opposite him. "Now, shall we play?"

"Play?" I echo, looking at the chessboard in confusion. "I haven't played chess in years, and I'm afraid I don't have the time. If you would excuse me..."

I turn to leave but find the door closed behind me and locked. While I could just blow it open, I decide to wait it out and see what exactly he wants.

"What's the point of playing chess right now?" I ask, my tone indifferent.

"Consider it a friendly game between old acquaintances," Azantor suggests, his smile not quite reaching his eyes. "Besides, I'm curious to see how well you've honed your strategic skills since we last met."

"Very well," I agree reluctantly, taking a seat and eyeing the chess pieces carefully.

What does Azantor possibly want from me? And why did he choose to confront me here, of all places?

"Let the game begin," he announces grandly. He always was overly dramatic. "First move's yours," he adds, clearly enjoying the power he held over me in this moment.

"Fine." I grimace, moving one of my pawns.

As we play, exchanging moves and countermoves, the tension between us grows heavier. Despite my best efforts to keep up, it's clear that Azantor has the upper hand.

"Your mind seems to be elsewhere, Lillith," he taunts, capturing one of my pieces. "Are you perhaps worried about someone?"

"Hardly," I snap back, taking out one of his knights with a hasty move. "I'm just wondering why you're wasting both our time with this game."

"Ah, but time is a luxury we villains can afford, don't you think?" Azantor smirks as he advances his queen. "Besides, it's been so long since we last crossed paths. It's only natural to want to catch up."

"Is that all this is? A friendly chat over chess?" I ask, my thoughts racing as I try to predict his next move.

"Of course not," he replied, leaning back in his chair and steepling his fingers, "but you'll have to play along if you want to find out what else I have in store for you."

"Fine," I muttered, forcing a smile onto my face. "Let's keep playing, then."

As we continue, I can't shake the feeling that there's more to Azantor's intentions than he lets on. I have no choice but to focus on the chessboard and hope I can uncover his true motives before it's too late.

"Your move," Azantor says, his eyes never leaving mine as I stare at the chessboard.

With a sinking feeling in my stomach, I notice something engraved on the base of each piece.

"Is that..." I lean in closer, squinting to read the tiny letters etched into the wood.

I can't believe it. Each piece bears the name of someone I care for or at least had at one point in time of my life. My parents, Silviana, even Mrs. Umbernuckle...

"Surprised, Lillith?" Azantor smirks, enjoying my reaction. "I told you we have much to discuss."

How did I not immediately expect this? It's so very predictable of him.

"Let me guess." I sigh, trying to keep my composure. "If I lose this game, those people die?"

"Very perceptive," he replies, tapping his fingers on the table, "and if you win, they live. Simple as that. I thought I would work with your most recent interactions. Figured at least a few of them would be people you care about."

"Fine." I grit my teeth, forcing myself to focus on the game. "But remember, Azantor, two can play at this game."

"Of course," he purrs. "That's what makes it so thrilling."

The tension mounts with every move. For the first time in my life, I'm playing a game I actually want to win but doubt I will. The names I've seen so far, I wouldn't be too upset if they're killed. Of course I would be sad, but I don't let just anyone actually matter to me. That would give me a weakness and absolutely is not something a villain can get away with having.

We exchange pieces like old friends trading insults, each capture a small victory or defeat.

"Check," Azantor announces, moving one of his bishops.

I frown, shifting my king to safety. There's no time to waste. I need to find a way to turn the tables before it's too late.

"Ah, you're putting up quite a fight, Lillith." He leans back in his chair. "But will it be enough?"

"Quit the theatrics," I snap, capturing another of his pawns. "We'll see who has the last laugh when this is over."

"Indeed, we shall," Azantor agrees, moving his queen to threaten my remaining knight.

I hesitate, weighing my options. Is it worth sacrificing the piece to gain a better position? Or should I try a more defensive approach?

"Ticktock, Lillith," he taunts, tapping the table impatiently. "Time waits for no one, not even you."

"Fine," I mutter, moving my knight out of harm's way.

It isn't the most aggressive move, but it could buy me time to regroup and plan my next attack.

"Very cautious." Azantor smirks as he takes another of my pieces. "But will caution save your friends or simply prolong their suffering?"

"Enough," I growl, pushing aside my doubts and fears as I make a bold bid to turn the tide of the game. "Check."

"Ah, well played," he admits, shifting his king to safety, "but don't get too cocky, Lillith. The game is far from over."

"Then let's finish this." My voice is shaking with barely restrained fury. "For once and for all."

"Indeed," Azantor agrees, his eyes narrowing as the final moves unfold before us. "Let's see who truly deserves the title of top villain, shall we? Check," he announces with a triumphant grin, his rook putting my king in peril.

I quickly move my king to escape the threat, but it's becoming clear that I'm cornered. The cold sweat trickles down my back as I try to maintain my composure and strategize.

"Feeling the pressure, Lillith?" Azantor taunts, delighting in my struggle. "Don't worry. It'll all be over soon."

"Stop talking," I snap, focusing my attention on the board.

My desperation is mounting, and I can't afford any more distractions.

Why do I care this much? Does it really matter if I win?

I move a bishop, hoping to create an opening for a counterattack.

"Ah, clever girl," he says, mockingly clapping his hands, "but not clever enough."

He slides his queen across the board, forcing me to sacrifice my last knight to protect my king.

"Checkmate," Azantor declares triumphantly, his eyes gleaming with malice.

I stare at the board in disbelief. He's trapped me.

"Time to face the consequences, Lillith," he sneers.

He flips over the fallen chess pieces one by one to reveal the names of those I care or cared about. Each name feels like a dagger in my chest, and I clench my fists, struggling to contain my anger. I hate losing.

"Prince Asher Sunbash," he reads aloud, holding up the knight I just sacrificed.

My breath hitches, and panic wells up inside me. How could I have let this happen? If anything happens to Asher...

"Angry, are we?" Azantor mocks, relishing in my pain. "Well, you should have thought about that before you lost."

"Shut up!" I yell, my voice cracking with emotion. "You don't get to gloat! This was a twisted game, and you know it!"

"Perhaps," he concedes, his grin never wavering, "but in the end, Lillith, you were the one who played along and lost."

The last straw has been placed on my back, and I will not stand for it any longer. Fury burns within me like a wildfire, consuming every bit of restraint I have left.

"Your twisted games end here! Rule number eight of being a good villain, Azantor, only reveal your evil plan if the person you are revealing it to is either needed to help fulfill it or will be the victim of it. I refuse to be either. Take your monologues and shove it," I scream.

I raise my hand to unleash a simple but devastatingly powerful spell. A surge of raw magic flows through me, and I channel it into a concentrated blast aimed directly at Azantor's smug face.

"W-Wha..." he stammers, his eyes widening in shock as the spell hits him with full force.

His body crumples to the ground, lifeless and broken before disappearing entirely.

"Trust no one," I whisper, swallowing the lump in my throat, "especially not in this villainous world."

I turn away from Azantor's corpse and stride toward the exit, determined to leave this wretched place behind. With each step, I focus my lingering rage into another spell, one that will bring this lair crumbling down around me.

"Time to bury this den of snakes," I mutter, releasing my magic into the walls.

The stone groans and shifts, cracks spiderwebbing outward as the tunnels began to collapse.

As the destruction unfolds around me, I think of Asher. There may be no place for me in his world, but the realization that I have feelings for him—real, genuine feelings—is both terrifying and exhilarating. It fuels my resolve to protect him at all costs, even if it means facing my past and seeking out Lexir myself. Having an excuse to take on both the villain and hero parts of Necia's society is just a perk.

Lexir Crow, you won't know what's coming for you. I narrowly dodge a falling chunk of rock. *And when I find you, you'll wish you'd never crossed me*

The world outside seems impossibly bright and open as I emerge from the collapsing lair, dusting off my clothes and tucking away the last remnants of my fury for another day. Even as I step into the sunlight, I remind myself, steeling my resolve, "Trust no one, Lillith, not even yourself."

25

Asher

A sudden, deafening noise jolts me awake. The ground beneath the inn shakes violently, and I shield my face from the debris falling all around me. My mind races as panic surges through my veins.

"Earthquake?" I mutter to myself, attempting to regain my bearings. Just as quickly as the thought came, it's replaced by a more pressing concern. "Lilly!"

Panic sets in as I scramble out of bed and throw open the door to the hallway, still shouting her name. It's pure chaos outside of the room—people running, screaming, trying to escape the collapsing building.

"Lilly!" I cry out again, hoping against hope that she's safe.

I make my way through the panic-stricken crowd and find myself at her door. It's wide open, revealing an empty room. Dread consumes me. She's not here.

"Where are you?" I whisper to myself, feeling urgency and protectiveness at a level I never expected. I can't leave without knowing she's safe.

"Sir, we have to go!" a voice shouts at me, snapping me back to reality. A fellow patron of the inn is urging me to follow him to safety.

I hesitate, torn between finding Lilly and escaping the imminent collapse of the inn. She's smart. She's probably safe, but what if she's trapped somewhere in here?

"Go on without me," I tell the man, determination settling into my bones. "I can't leave without Lilly."

"Good luck," he replies, clearly thinking I'm crazy. He disappears down the hall, leaving me to fend for myself.

"Come on, Asher, think," I mutter to myself, trying to come up with a plan.

Desperation courses through me as I continue calling for Lilly amidst the chaos, praying that she's unharmed and within earshot.

Stay safe, Lilly. I won't let anything happen to you.

I stumble over the rubble that once was the entrance to the inn, palms sweaty as I scan the chaotic scene for any sign of Lilly. The street's littered with debris and injured townspeople, their cries for help echoing through the air like a haunting melody.

"Where are you, Lilly?" I mutter under my breath, desperately hoping she's safe.

My gaze darts from one side of the street to the other, searching for her familiar figure amidst the chaos.

"Hey, watch out!" calls a voice behind me.

I turn just in time to dodge a falling piece of wood. It crashes onto the ground, sending up a cloud of dust that made me cough and squint.

"Thanks," I manage to wheeze.

My heart rate increases as the fear for Lilly's safety gnaws at me. I can't bear the thought of something happening to her because of me. She is only here because I insisted on her coming with me. I don't usually travel with a maid or really anyone when fulfilling jobs. Most of my staff are retired villains, and I can't risk their identities being discovered. On my own property, I use my magic to prevent it, but when dealing with other villains, the risk is too high. I've been selfish. This is entirely my fault.

"Damn it, where are you?" I whisper, more to myself than anyone else.

Desperation fills every fiber of my being, urging me to keep looking.

"Sir, have you seen a young woman with black hair?" I ask a passing couple.

"No, we haven't seen her," the man replies, his eyes filled with worry, most likely for their own safety rather than for a stranger.

"Thank you," I say, releasing a heavy sigh as they disappear into the crowd.

My heart pounds loudly in my ears as I call out her name, hoping she'd respond, but all I hear are the chaotic sounds of people in distress outside. My stomach clenches with worry. I have to find her.

"Please, let her be safe," I mutter under my breath, my voice barely audible over the chaos unfolding around me.

There she is, emerging from an opening, her clothes covered in dust. Even better, she appears to be unharmed.

Relief washes over me like a cool wave. I can hardly contain my emotions at the sight of her safe and sound.

"Lilly!" I cry out, running toward her without hesitation. "Are you all right?"

"Of course, I am," she replies, attempting to brush off my concern with a dismissive wave of her hand. "You didn't think a little explosion would be enough to take me down, did you?"

"Maybe not," I admit, unable to suppress a smile at her usual wit, "but I couldn't help but worry."

"Sweet of you, really," she says, her voice dripping with sarcasm, "but there's no time for that now."

She's right. Now that I found her, my instinct is to rush to the wounded's aid, using my healing magic to mend their wounds.

Lilly grabs my arm. "Your Highness, we must leave now before your identity is discovered."

I hesitate, torn between helping these desperate people and heeding her warning. The weight of responsibility feels heavy on my shoulders, but deep down, I know she's right.

"On our way. I will help them while we leave. That's the best I can do."

She nods and follows me as I begin making my way through the town.

My heart twists painfully when I look around, trying to locate the source of the frightened voices. Everywhere I turn, there are people in need—some injured, others trapped under debris. It's a sobering sight, one that leaves me feeling both helpless and responsible as a hero and their prince.

"Peter," Lilly calls out, using my fake villain name, "we need to do something."

"I know," I say, looking all around to see who needs help the fastest."Start with what you can," she urges, placing a reassuring hand on my arm. "We may not be able to save everyone, but we can still make a difference."

Nodding, I take a deep breath and lock gazes with a small child huddled beneath an overturned cart. I run toward the frightened child. As I approach, I can see the fear in her eyes, and it only strengthens my resolve. Carefully, I lift the cart off of her, my muscles straining with the effort.

"Are you all right?" I ask gently putting down the cart. I reach out a hand to help her up.

"Y-Yes..." she stammers, tears streaming down her face. "Thank you..."

"Stay close," I tell her, glancing around for any other immediate dangers, "and try to find your family."

"Okay," she whispers, gripping my hand tightly as we move through the debris-strewn street.

"Good job," Lilly says, appearing at my side with a young man limping beside her. "We need to keep going, though. There's still so much to do, and we have to get out of here."

"I know. If we see someone from the underground, we will leave immediately." I hand off the child. "Stay here," I tell Lilly firmly, ignoring her protests as I rush toward the nearest injured person, an elderly man clutching his bloodied arm.

"Please, help me," he begs, his eyes filled with terror.

My heart breaks for him and all the others who are suffering, but I can't let my emotions cloud my focus. I need to act quickly and efficiently.

"Of course," I reply, trying to keep my voice steady.

I gently take hold of the man's arm and close my eyes, focusing on the healing energy that resides within me, and begin to recite the ancient words that will mend his wounds.

As the magic surges through my veins, the man's pained expression gradually eases, and the blood on his arm disappears, replaced by fresh, unblemished skin. When I'm certain he is healed, I release him and move on to a young woman with tears streaming down her face as she clutches her broken leg.

"Thank you," she whispers, her eyes wide with gratitude as my magic works its wonders on her injury.

I merely nod in response, unable to find the words to express my own relief at being able to help.

"Where did you learn to do that?" a nearby voice asks, causing me to look up from my work. A small boy, no older than ten, watches me with curiosity.

"From my master," I answer truthfully, careful not to reveal too much. "He taught me everything I know."

"Wow," the boy breathes, clearly impressed. "You must be really powerful."

"Powerful enough to make a difference," I reply, returning my attention to the injured townspeople.

The boy's words weighs heavily on my conscience, and I can't help but question whether I am truly doing enough.

As I continue to heal the wounded, my thoughts stray to Lilly. Yes, my powers will bring more danger if they are discovered, but I owe it to these people to do whatever I can to alleviate their pain.

"Keep going, Asher," Lilly urges, reappearing beside me, pulling me out of my thoughts. "We need to put as much distance between us and this chaos as possible."

I want to do more, but there is only so much one person can do in the face of such destruction. I've been in similar situations more times than I can count and know that no one person can take care of everything at once. My kingdom's broken, and there is nothing I can do about it, not without eliminating my father, which is a line I am unwilling to cross. When my brother inherits the throne, I can only hope things will get better.

"Thank you," an elderly woman whispers, clutching my hand as I heal her broken arm. Her eyes fill with tears of relief.

"Of course," I reply, offering her a small smile. "It's the least I can do."

As the woman hobbles away. I glance around for anyone else in need of assistance. My gaze falls upon a young girl, no older than ten, lying amidst the rubble. She's unconscious, bleeding profusely from a gash on her forehead.

My heart races as I rushed over to her, carefully lifting her fragile body into my arms. "Hold on, little one," I murmur, channeling my healing magic into her wound.

Slowly, the blood stops flowing and the gash begins to close, leaving behind only a faint scar.

"Is she going to be okay?" a frantic voice asks beside me.

I turn to see who I assume to be the girl's mother, her face etched with worry.

"She'll be fine," I assure her, gently handing the now-stirring child back to her mother. "Just let her rest for a bit."

"Thank you," the mother sobs, hugging her daughter tightly. "Thank you so much."

"It's the least I can do," I said softly, my chest tightening at the sight of their embrace.

As grateful as I am to be able to help these people, it pains me to know that there are countless others who won't be so lucky. Hopefully other heroes of the kingdom are near and will arrive to assist soon.

"Sir," a man calls out, running up to me with a look of desperation on his face. "My wife, she's trapped under that beam over there! Please, you have to help her!"

"Of course," I reply without hesitation.

I follow him to where the woman is pinned beneath a heavy wooden beam. With a grunt, I lift the beam off of her and use my healing magic on her crushed leg.

"Thank you," the man mumbles, tears streaming down his face as he embraces his wife. "Thank you so much."

"Please," I insist, offering them a weary smile. "Just doing what I can."

As I continue to work, helping anyone I can on my way out of the city, I can't shake the feeling that there has to be more I could do. These people are relying on me, and I want nothing more than to make their lives better, even if it is only in some small way.

My thoughts are briefly interrupted as a strong grip suddenly clamps onto my arm, pulling me from my contemplation. It's Lilly, her eyes wide and urgent. I try to hide my concern for her own safety. The destruction has left her covered in dust, but she seems otherwise unharmed.

"Sir, we must leave now," she whispers, glancing around anxiously. "If the villains realize who you are, they'll attack and put the townspeople in even more danger."

Her words send a shudder down my spine. Is the situation really that dire?

"Are you sure?" I ask.

"Absolutely," she insists, tightening her grip on my arm. "We need to get out of here before they figure it out."

I hesitate for a moment more, weighing my options. As much as I want to stay and help these people, I can't argue with Lilly. If my true identity is discovered, it will only bring more devastation to this already suffering town.

"All right," I say finally, nodding in agreement. "Let's go."

Lilly leads me away from the chaos, weaving through the rubble-strewn streets with surprising agility. I feel a twinge of guilt at leaving the townspeople behind, but I have to remind myself that stopping Lexir is my ultimate priority and the best way to protect them in the long run.

"Where do we go from here?" Lilly asks.

"Somewhere safe, where we can regroup and plan our next move."

As we hurry out of the town, the sounds of crying and panic slowly fade behind us. My heart aches at the thought of the suffering we are leaving behind, but I force myself to focus on the task at hand. Stopping Lexir is all that matters now.

"Thank you, Lilly," I say softly as we continue onward, "for everything."

"Of course, sire," she replies, a hint of warmth in her voice. "It's my duty to serve you."

As we press forward, I glance back one last time at the town we are leaving behind. It is then that I see it, a fleeting moment of empathy on Lilly's face before she quickly hides it away. In that brief instant, I can see the goodness within her that she so often conceals.

MYSTERIOUS COLLAPSE REVEALS HIDDEN TUNNELS AND VILLAIN LAIR

By Sir Justice Jabs

A massive, unexplained collapse has decimated the town of Rockhaven, reducing half the village to rubble. The catastrophic event also unearthed a network of hidden tunnels and what appears to be the ruins of an underground lair used by villains.

Around midnight three nights ago, a deafening rumble shook the earth as the ground gave way, swallowing over a dozen buildings on the town's south side. The violent quake left many residents buried in debris. When the dust settled, emergency crews discovered a maze of secret passageways and chambers beneath the

RUBBLE. SINISTER OBJECTS RECOVERED REVEAL THESE TUNNELS WERE USED FOR DARK PURPOSES.

"THERE WERE TORTURE DEVICES, FORBIDDEN TEXTS, AND HUMAN REMAINS SCATTERED IN THE DEBRIS," CAPTAIN RORIK, HEAD OF THE EXCAVATION EFFORT, SAID. "THIS WAS CLEARLY THE LAIR OF SOME VILE GROUP."

THOUGH THE CULPRITS REMAIN UNKNOWN, EVIDENCE SUGGESTS POWERFUL MAGIC WAS INVOLVED IN THE CATACLYSMIC COLLAPSE. EXPLOSIVE RESIDUES FOUND NEARBY POINT TO SABOTAGE OF LOAD-BEARING SUPPORTS UNDER THE TOWN.

WHILE THE CAUSE REMAINS UNDER INVESTIGATION, ONE THING IS CERTAIN—A GREAT EVIL LURKED BENEATH THE UNSUSPECTING VILLAGE ABOVE. WHAT DIABOLICAL PLOTS WERE HATCHED IN THOSE BURIED HALLS MAY NEVER FULLY BE KNOWN.

IN THE AFTERMATH, HEROES FROM ACROSS THE KINGDOM JOURNEYED TO THE DECIMATED TOWN TO OFFER AID. PRINCE REDRICK, THE HEIR APPARENT, WAS AMONG THOSE WHO TRAVELED TO AID IN THE RECOVERY. USING THEIR MAGICAL GIFTS, THEY WORKED TIRELESSLY TO RESCUE TRAPPED SURVIVORS AND TEND TO THE MANY INJURED TOWNSFOLK. THEIR TIMELY INTERVENTION PREVENTED FURTHER LOSS OF LIFE IN THE WAKE OF THE COLLAPSE.

"IF NOT FOR THE HEROES' ASSISTANCE, WE SURELY WOULD HAVE LOST MANY MORE," TABITHA, A LOCAL HERBALIST, SAID. "THEIR SELFLESS ACTIONS GAVE US HOPE AMIDST THE CHAOS."

THOUGH IDENTITIES WERE KEPT DISCREET, EYE-WITNESSES DESCRIBED BOTH SEASONED WARRIORS AND YOUNGER NEWCOMERS ALIKE PUTTING ASIDE ANY RIVALRY TO WORK TOGETHER. THEIR COMMANDING YET COMPASSIONATE PRESENCE MAINTAINED MORALE DESPITE THE DESTRUCTION. LIKE ANGELS OF MERCY, THE HEROES TOILED THROUGH THE NIGHT TO HELP ANYONE THEY COULD.

"IT WAS A BLESSING THEY CAME WHEN THEY DID," ELDER MIRIAM SAID. "WORKING HAND IN HAND, THEY ACCOMPLISHED WHAT WE NEVER COULD HAVE ALONE."

WHILE THE HEROES' INTERVENTION PREVENTED MORE CASUALTIES, THE DEVASTATION REMAINS HEAVY. THEIR EFFORTS NOW TURN TOWARD AIDING REBUILDING EFFORTS AND SUPPORTING THOSE DISPLACED BY THE LOSS OF HOMES AND LIVELIHOODS.

ADDITIONALLY, INVESTIGATION CONTINUES INTO FINDING THOSE RESPONSIBLE FOR ORCHESTRATING THE COLLAPSE. THE BEHAVIOR OF THE HEROES SERVES AS A MODEL FOR UNITING AGAINST THE FORCES OF WICKEDNESS TO PREVENT FURTHER TRAGEDIES.

As the rubble is cleared, the people of Rockhaven are heartened knowing champions of justice stand ready to thwart the lurking shadows.

Lillith

The forest is still and quiet as Asher and I make our way beneath the spreading boughs of oak and elm. Shafts of late afternoon sunlight filter through the canopy, dappling the leaf-strewn path in front of us. The only sounds are our footsteps and the occasional rustling of small creatures amidst the underbrush.

I'm grateful for the serenity. My thoughts have been in turmoil since fleeing the collapsed underground lair this morning. The confrontation with Azantor rattled me, but not as much as the realization that I feared for Asher's life when he was threatened.

I risk a sidelong glance at Asher walking beside me on the path. His handsome profile is lined with golden light, his stride steady and tireless. Did I seriously just think handsome? When did I start seeing him as something other than a target? A mark to be manipulated? The unwanted affection growing inside me feels like vines creeping stealthily upward, wrapping themselves around my heart before I realize what's happening.

Asher notices me looking at him and smiles, his eyes crinkling at the corners. I swiftly turn my gaze forward again, an unwelcome heat rising in my cheeks. I don't know how to interpret these new feelings blossoming within me. I only know that being close to Asher stirs them dangerously near the surface. He's a hero. Even if the thought of being romantically involved with a hero didn't make me uneasy, the way our society works, it can never work. It legally isn't allowed. If I really want this relationship, there's no way Prince Perfect would go for it, not when it would mean breaking the very foundation of the kingdom and defying his own father.

We continue on in silence beneath the sheltering trees. I focus on putting one foot in front of the other, avoiding stumbled steps or wayward roots—simple actions requiring no thought, no bothersome sentiments.

But when Asher brushes against me, reaching out to help steady me over a tricky bit of terrain, my pulse leaps at his brief touch. I mumble my thanks, hating how flustered he makes me with such innocent contact.

Get control over yourself! You are playing with fire with a man sworn to oppose all you are.

I force more distance between us, needing space to shore up my defenses once more. Out here alone with him, things have shifted. The thought of what might happen if I surrender to these tender feelings terrifies me. I'm not some naive girl, blind to the reality of our different worlds. There is no future for an upstanding prince and a cunning villainess who trusts no one.

Even now, part of me worries this growing closeness could be a cleverly laid trap. With villains, affection is too often used as a weapon for manipulation rather than given freely. Lexir is proof of that. While my instincts tell me Asher's heart holds only sincerity, old habits of mistrust die hard.

Letting my guard down again could prove more perilous than facing Azantor's wrath. At least pain caused by those who make no pretense of caring for you lacks the sharp sting of betrayal. Those wounds cut deepest of all.

No, it's far safer to play my part flawlessly, giving nothing of my true self away. I am ice—beautiful but cold and untouchable. The tempting warmth of Asher's kindness cannot reach my core.

"Lillith." Asher's voice breaks the silence, startling me from my brooding thoughts. "Let's stop here a while."

I follow his gaze to the creek up ahead, its water glinting invitingly in the slanted sunlight.

Suddenly aware of my thirst after the day's long walk, I nod. "A good plan. We should refill our waterskins as well."

We make our way down the sloping bank to the creek's pebbled edge in unspoken harmony. I kneel on a flat rock and splash the bracing water on my face before filling my skin. The chill helps sharpen my focus, washing away the haze threatening to descend over my judgment when Asher is near.

As we linger by the burbling creek, some of the tension eases from my shoulders. Away from the pressures and pretenses of society, I can almost forget the implacable differences dividing us. Out here, we are simply two travelers making our way together through the wilderness.

Who am I kidding? The prince could never be just a traveler.

Asher removes his boots and socks and steps into the creek, closing his eyes blissfully as the water eddies around his calves. The open joy on his face makes something catch in my throat. In moments like this, his gentle spirit shines through so clearly.

"It's freezing but feels wonderful." He laughs. "You should join me."

Before I can reject him, he playfully splashes water in my direction. I gasp as the cold droplets strike my face and arms. "Sire!"

He grins, unrepentant. "Yes?"

I want to cling to my composure, but his smile is irresistible. This new side of him is a delight.

"Just for that..." Moving quickly, I dip my hands in the creek and send a splash of my own directly at his chest.

Asher blinks in surprise then lets out a deep, full-bodied laugh. The sound warms me like honeyed mead.

He holds up his hands in a gesture of defeat. "Truce, truce! Unless you'd like to continue this water battle?" A competitive gleam enters his eyes.

"A tempting offer," I reply, lips quirking, "but we really should keep moving if we want to find shelter before nightfall."

The spark of mischief fades from Asher's face. "You're right, of course." He steps back onto the bank and sits on a boulder to put his boots back on.

I feel a pang of remorse, worried I disappointed him by declining to prolong our playful moment, but the day is quickly passing, and wandering unknown woods after dark would be unwise.

Rising to my feet, I hold out a hand to help Asher up. He grasps it firmly, his callused palm warm against my skin. Our eyes meet, and something passes between us, a flickering current I cannot name.

I let go hastily, flustered by the intensity of his gaze. "We should go," I mumble, avoiding looking at him directly again.

Every small connection only complicates matters further in my conflicted heart. I want to cling to this afternoon's easy joy yet dread what deeper entanglement might follow. For now, putting distance between us seems the safest choice.

Asher studies me for a long moment before nodding. "Lead on." His voice holds no judgment or demands, only patience.

It would be easier if he pressured me for more than I can give. Instead, he seems content with what little of myself I share, asking for nothing beyond the present moment.

I walk on along the leaf-strewn path, torn between gratitude for his consideration and frustration that I cannot shake my wariness, even with someone as kind as him. I crave the relief of fully trusting, of melting like a frost under spring's first light.

Yet, old habits of doubt wrap me in their chilly embrace, whispering words of warning in my ear. Many before have seemed virtuous on the surface, only to shatter faith when it suited them. I must protect the fragile hope now taking root inside me until I can be certain it is safe to let it bloom.

So I continue erecting walls between us, piece by piece, even as a deeper part of me yearns to tear them down. I act the part of the aloof villainess playing him false while secretly counting every smile he coaxes from me as a treasure.

For now, this dance of push and pull between wariness and wanting must suffice. My feelings for Asher are still too new and tender to expose without care, like a budding shoot emerging after winter's thaw. Time will reveal whether my feelings can endure past the first blush of blossoming.

Until then, I will relish the sweetness of this awakening within me, even as I shield it behind thorns and
hope beyond hope that perhaps the warmth of spring
will finally thaw the ice encasing my hesitant heart.

***

It is getting late as the prince and I come upon a small
cottage nestled in the forest. Constructed from weathered gray stone and timber, it has the rustic, worn appearance of a structure that endured countless seasons.
A simple thatched roof tops the building, with a lone
stone chimney rising from its center.

I pause to inspect the dwelling, noting the heavy
wooden door set into the front facade. Thick vines
creep up the side of the cottage, weaving their way
under the eaves like the tangled threads of an unkempt
tapestry. Stepping closer, I press my hand against the
sturdy oak door, comforted by its solidity.

"We should rest here awhile," Prince Asher suggests
behind me, a note of relief in his voice.

I hesitate, eying the tree line warily for any threats.
The forest is still, filled only with the muted sounds
of birdsong and rustling leaves. Finding no immediate
danger, I nod in acquiescence.

Inside, shafts of waning sunlight filter through dusty windows, illuminating the single-room interior. Faded wool blankets and a lumpy straw mattress occupy one corner, while a plain wooden table and chairs serve as the cottage's sole furnishings. The cracked hearth contains remnants of old ash, long cold. It will provide much-needed warmth when relit.

While crude and worn by time, the cottage has a certain rustic charm. As I run my fingers over the rough-hewn table, I imagine simple folk taking their meals here, perhaps laughing and sharing stories before the fire. For a brief moment, I wonder what it might be like to live a quiet, uncomplicated life in a place like this, but the thought quickly fades. I have a mission and a prince to keep alive, although dedication to the mission seems far less important to me now.

"I'll start a fire," Prince Asher offers.

"Thank you," I reply with a weary nod.

The day's events weigh heavily, leaving my limbs leaden and thoughts muddled. It's bad enough my mind is running in directions about the prince that I can't afford to allow to happen. I'm suddenly nervous about staying in a single room with him alone. Glancing around our shelter once more, I say, "I will fetch us some water from the nearby creek. I need to wash up anyway."

Ever gallant, Prince Asher begins to object.

I wave him off. "I'm unharmed, sire, merely fatigued as are you. After all, am I not here as your maid? Please, rest while I gather supplies."

After retrieving the battered pail from beside the door, I step back into the muted glow of dusk. The babbling creek beckons, just beyond sight but still within earshot. As I follow the sound over moss-strewn rocks and gnarled roots, I breathe deeply of the pine-scented air, allowing my racing thoughts to settle.

Since destroying the collapsed lair and leaving that chaos behind, I avoided pondering the ramifications too closely. Now, alone amidst the ancient trees, doubts creep in. Had I acted rashly?

Distracted by my thoughts, I nearly stumble over the creek's rocky bank. Righting myself with a murmured curse, I dip the pail into the crystal water, relishing its bracing chill. As I stand, movement sounds in the nearby brush. I tense, senses honed, prepared to defend myself.

From the brush lumbers an enormous shadowed shape easily three times my size. My breath catches in my throat, magic ready on my lips to strike whatever horror approaches, but as the beast steps into a shaft of fading light, dread turns to disbelief.

"Basilisk?" I gasp, immediately recognizing the scaled behemoth.

He is one of Silviana's creatures, carrying a leather satchel upon his back. How did he find me all the way out here?

With a rumbling grunt, Basilisk ambles closer, regarding me with one great amber eye.

I reach out slowly to stroke his snout, reassured by familiarity. "However did you come to be so far from home, my friend?"

In response, Basilisk dips his head, granting me access to the satchel. My fingers tremble slightly as I unfasten its ties and draw out a parchment sealed in wax. Unfolding the letter reveals Silviana's elegant script, infusing me with both relief and renewed worry.

Lillith,

I survived the destruction of our old romping grounds and hope that Basilisk finds you safe and sound as well. There's rumors that the all-powerful Lillith Shadowend may have been behind it but no one can prove it or figure out why exactly. If only they knew...

Be safe and know that I am here if you ever need me. I've missed you, dear friend.

Yours, in friendship eternal,

Silviana

My vision blurs, eyes stinging with emotion I dare not give name to. Across all these years and falsehoods, Silviana still cares for me. The realization stirs both joy and sorrow within my breast.

Basilisk huffs, nudging at my shoulder until I stroke his scaly brow once more.

"Thank you, dear one," I murmur thickly, "for delivering hope when I needed it most."

I continue to rub Basilisk as I consider who I'm becoming. I don't know if I entirely like the softer edges I seem to be forming the longer I am around the prince. It's almost as if his goodness is rubbing off on me. A sickening thought, especially when I'm suppose to be corrupting him.

Basilisk nuzzles me and I chuckle as I remember my mother when messages would arrive for her. She had a nasty habit of killing all messengers no matter the news delivered. She was always a suspicious villain, convinced everyone was out to get her. To be fair, in the villain society, that's generally how things work. Her unseemly habit did help me create rule number fourteen of how to be a good villain—don't fly into a rage and kill messengers of bad news. Good messengers are hard to come by.

I fold Silviana's letter and return it safely to the satchel. After a final fond pat to Basilisk's snout, I bid the loyal creature farewell and turn back toward the cottage, water bucket in hand.

My steps feel lighter now despite the creeping shadows of dusk. Winding my way along the wooded path, I notice details that had escaped me before. Delicate crimson fungus sprout from a rotting log, crimson caps glowing faintly in the fading light. I kneel to gather a few, knowing their earthy flavor will enrich a humble forest stew.

Farther along, I spy clumps of emerald sorrel leaves peeking from the underbrush, tart and lemony once boiled down. I pluck a generous handful, savoring their vibrancy. Tiny wild onions present themselves next, pungent and savory, which I harvest along with sprigs of thyme and sage. As I select the herbs, I remind myself these are merely tasks to help the prince recover and feed us. Nothing more. I'm allowed to want my food to taste good as well. I don't care if he finds dinner delicious, right?

A sudden sharp pain explodes against the back of my head.

"Ouch!" I cry out, whirling around.

Had something struck me? Squinting into the gloomy forest, I freeze as a flicker of movement catches my eye. Is that... No, it can't be, but for a moment, I could have sworn Mister Rotten Hand was lurking amongst the trees.

Heart pounding, I scramble in his direction, searching for any sign of my nemesis, but the woods are still and silent now, filled only with lengthening shadows.

Cursing under my breath, I rub the tender spot on my head. Perhaps a wayward pine cone struck me, and my mind is simply playing tricks on me. With the dangers we've faced, I'm jumping at shadows.

Shaking off a lingering sense of unease, I finish gathering ingredients, the last being a handful of wild radishes, their spicy kick sure to accent the stew. Bucket brimming with forest treasures, I hurry onward through the gloom, eager to return to the cottage.

The fire's welcoming glow guides me inside, where Prince Asher awaits, and I step into the cottage, the warmth from the crackling fire a welcome respite after the chill creeping into the night outside. Prince Asher sits slumped at the rough-hewn wooden table, weariness etched in the lines of his face. Dark circles ring his kind eyes, and his shoulders sag under some invisible weight. The day's healing magic has clearly drained his energy.

"Lilly, thank goodness you're back," he says, mustering a tired smile that doesn't quite reach his eyes.

"I found some ingredients for a humble forest stew," I explain, holding up the brimming bucket. The pungent aroma of crushed herbs and earthy vegetables fills the small room.

"Wonderful," Asher replies, though without his usual enthusiasm.

He slowly helps carry the ingredients to the table, each movement betraying his fatigue. The prince sinks back onto the bench with a heavy sigh.

I set to work chopping the assortment of roots and leaves by firelight, my knife rhythmically thudding against the weathered wood. The sage's heady fragrance mingles with the onion's bite as I work, conjuring memories of my mother's own rustic stews from childhood, back when she tolerated my presence enough to occasionally feed me.

A contemplative silence falls between us, interrupted only by the scrape of my knife and the crackling fire's sporadic pops. Prince Asher adds another log to the flames, stoking their glow before returning to his seat.

"Were you in the village when the collapse happened?" he asks after a stretch, his voice raspy with exhaustion. "It must've been frightening to witness."

I tense, the knife nearly slipping to slice my thumb open. Where had I been as the underground lair crumbled? Right at the epicenter, unleashing explosive magic fueled by rage.

"I... I had just slipped out to fetch water," I lie, scrambling for a plausible story. "Utter chaos trying to get back and ensure you were unharmed."

Asher simply nods, seemingly too spent to detect the hesitation in my words, and I release a small breath, grateful to avoid further questions for the moment.

I continue preparing the meal in companionable quiet, the fire's sporadic crackles underscoring the silence.

"Whatever caused the collapse, I'm thankful you're unscathed," Asher says later, mustering a gentle smile despite his visible weariness.

His sincerity sends a pang through my chest, an ache from secrets untold.

Soon, aromatic steam rises from the bubbling pot suspended over the flames. I ladle the chunky stew into wooden bowls, and we sit across from one another at the humble table to eat.

I take a sip of the hearty broth, letting the stew's warmth spread through my body. "This is quite flavorful for foraged fare. What do you think, Your Highness?"

Asher blows on a spoonful before tasting it. "It's delicious! You have a skill for transforming humble ingredients into something special. Perhaps your talents would be better suited in the kitchen than washing my undergarments."

"You flatter me," I reply, unused to such sincere compliments. "My mother teaches me what little cooking I know when she is so inclined."

"I rarely see my mother as she usually is busy with royal duties," Asher says thoughtfully, "but our palace cook takes me under her wing at times. We'd sneak into the kitchens at night, baking honey cakes and seeing how tall we can stack them before they topple."

I laugh, picturing a mischievous young prince covered in flour and honey. It is the first unrestrained laugh I can remember in ages, surprising myself.

"We all have cherished memories, don't we?" I muse, my own rare happy recollections rising to mind.

Asher regards me with intrigue. "Indeed we do. Even in dark times, preserving those memories helps nourish the soul."

I meet his earnest gaze, feeling strangely seen. With a small nod, I raise my spoon again, savoring the stew's simple nourishment.

"What other talents are you hiding from me?" Asher asks before sampling more. "When you're not busy wi th... maid duties," he adds tactfully.

I consider his question. I have few hobbies besides scheming and magic, neither of which I can safely share.

"I enjoy reading when I can," I say after a moment. Tales offer brief escape from harsh realities. "And some-times needlework, though I'm not very skilled. And you?"

"Reading is a favorite pastime of mine too," Asher replies.

His smile catches me off guard, stirring an unwel-come warmth inside. I tamp it down, annoyed at this unwarranted reaction.

"I used to get lost for hours in our library as a boy," he continues, "but my chief joy is music. I taught myself to play the lyre and often compose songs."

I find myself intrigued by this new detail, trying to picture his calloused hands gently strumming.

He gives a self-conscious chuckle. "Not very heroic, I suppose, but we all need beauty as well as bravery."

"Beauty takes many forms," I muse. "My mother disdains all things artistic, but there's power in creativity and vulnerability in sharing it."

The notion resonates with my own hidden talents. Perhaps we aren't so different after all.

27

Asher

I awake to filtered sunlight and swirling dust motes, my mind fuzzy with sleep. As awareness returns, I realize two identical figures lie peacefully on either side of me. Two Lillys. Why are there two Lillys?

As they begin to stir, I notice with confusion that one exudes an air of sweetness and light, but the other seethes with a sinister darkness. Before I can make sense of this, the one with rage in her eyes rises and leaps toward me with alarming speed. Dark tendrils of energy coil around her, pulsing with venom. I brace for impact, but a blast of fiery magic throws her back.

My eyes widen in shock as the gentle Lilly steps forward, wisps of light fading around her palms. Lilly has magic? How have I never noticed before? Both women's magic practically roll off of them.

Clearly these two possess great power, though their reasons for battling elude me. I struggle to understand the scene unfolding as mystical forces erupt around the cottage.

I scramble back in alarm, my hand instinctively reaching for a weapon. "What's going on?"

The vengeful Lilly's lip curls in disgust. "So much for the prince's bravery. Can't handle seeing my true self, weakling?"

With preternatural speed, she lunges at me, pinning me against the cottage wall by the throat. I gasp for breath as her grip tightens, magic constricting my lungs.

"Stop!" the other cries, distraught. She grabs her vicious double's arm in vain.

The dark Lilly backhands her without even glancing over. "Silence, you simpering fool. You may wear my face, but you're weak."

I struggle helplessly in her iron hold, spots swimming across my vision. Through the haze, I focus on the anguished eyes of the gentle Lilly still pulling at her counterpart's sleeve. Eyes full of light... and love.

As the dark Lilly chokes me against the wall, the gentle version's eyes suddenly blaze with white light. Magic gathers around her hands as she calls out, "I won't let you harm him!"

A burst of energy knocks the vicious Lilly aside, breaking her stranglehold on me. I collapse, gasping gratefully for breath. The two Lillys now face off, circling each other warily.

"Still weak, I see," the shadowy one taunts. She hurls a bolt of smoky energy, but it fizzles uselessly against a shimmering shield now surrounding the luminous Lilly.

"I protect those I care for," she replies firmly. More radiant magic builds around her fingers, casting the room in a soft glow.

She cares for me? I know this shouldn't be what I get from this entire experience, but I can't help the glimmer of hope those words have just given me.

With a feral scream, the dark Lilly unleashes a torrent of power, but her counterpart meets it head-on with her own blazing beam. The opposing energies collide in a shockwave that shatters the cottage windows, bathing us in shards of glass.

I shield my eyes from the blinding collision. When I can see again, the gentle Lilly is slumped on the floor, clearly drained from the magical duel. The darker version looms closer, murder in her coal black eyes.

"Now you perish, weakling!" she cries, swirling darkness gathering in her palms. Time seems to slow as lethal magic flies toward the exhausted Lilly.

Suddenly, the air shimmers, and a small, spindly creature appears before her. With a quick gesture, it throws up a glowing magical barrier. The killing blast disperses harmlessly, inches from Lilly's face.

I blink in astonishment at the unexpected guardian. It is only knee-high, with bat-like ears and bulging eyes. Nargle. Though lacking speech, its intent is clear—to protect the gentle Lilly from harm.

As I stare at the unlikely pair, comprehension dawns. A faint shimmering cord of light connects the two Lillys. These are not duplicates but split aspects of the same conflicted being—her inner darkness and light made flesh. I've never seen something quite like this, but I once had encountered a similar situation in a village spelled by an unknown villain creating duplicates of much of the population.

I know what must be done.

I rise unsteadily, broken glass crunching under my boots. Stepping through the tension thick as fog, I come before them. The creature watches me warily as I reach out a hand.

Taking a deep breath, I begin weaving strands of magic and emotion into the air. Memories of our time together, glimpses beneath her walls, my feelings left unvoiced... I channel it all into glistening threads, binding us heart and soul.

"You are my redemption as I am yours. Deny me, demonize me, but I will never forsake you for only together may we find the better parts of ourselves."

The charm pulls at the luminous cord between them. As the words fade, their forms melt together into one.

Lilly collapses forward with a ragged gasp, and I catch her tightly, our knees hitting the hard floor.

She trembles against me. I cradle her, instinctively offering soft consolations. I smooth back her hair and press a feather-light kiss to her forehead, allowing myself that small intimacy.

As I hold the trembling Lillith, a storm of emotion rages within me. Seeing her so broken feels like shards of glass piercing my heart. This woman, who has always exuded such strength and composure, now seems so fragile in my arms.

Unthinking, I whisper, "I can't lose you, my love." The endearment slips out before I can contain it.

She stills against me, and panic rises in my chest. What have I just done?

Lilly pulls back slowly to search my face, eyes glistening. "What... did you call me?" she asks hesitantly.

I take a deep, steadying breath. We've drifted far from pretense. Now, it is time for truth.

"My love," I repeat, willing my voice not to shake. She looks at me with an unreadable expression as I add, "Through our journey, you've become so much more than a traveling companion or maid. I've come to care for you, deeply."

There. I have given voice to feelings kept hidden even from myself until this moment.

Her lips part in surprise, but she does not pull away.

"Your light called to me from the beginning," I say softly, tenderly brushing a strand of hair from her cheek. "But today, I fully realized the depths of my affection for you. When I thought we'd never have this chance..."

I trail off, overcome with the memory of nearly losing her.

She searches my face, her eyes clouded with confusion, tentative hope, and no small amount of fear. My own heart pounds as I will her to understand.

"Forgive my presumptuousness," I murmur. "I don't fully grasp the magic that drew us together, but I know the truth in my heart now. I have fallen in love with you, Lilly."

Uttering those words aloud both terrifies and relieves me.

For several thudding heartbeats, she simply searches my face in silence. Doubt creeps in, causing me to worry that I have overstepped our unspoken bounds.

28

Lillith

Asher's confession echoes in my mind, even as he holds me close. The prince loves me? After witnessing the violent darkness within, how can he? I am a storm. I destroy all I touch. I have to protect him from me.

"You cannot love me," I whisper, pulling back to search his kind eyes... eyes that still look at me with affection, even after everything. "If you knew the truth..."

Asher silences me by pressing his forehead to mine. "I know your heart," he murmurs. "The battle I just witnessed only shows the depth of your spirit."

His earnest words ignite a fragile hope in my own troubled heart. Perhaps he sees something in me that I cannot.

"Do not be ashamed," Asher says gently. "All people have darkness within. Yours does not define you." He lifts my chin so our eyes meet fully. "I have seen your compassion, felt your warmth. The light in you called to me from the beginning. I love you, Lilly, in all your facets."

His conviction washes over me. He may not truly know me, but he has just seen a very dark side of me yet still cares deeply.

Perhaps I can become more than what I always hoped to achieve. After all, I have already become the most powerful villain in three kingdoms. What else is there for me to do? How else can I grow? But do I really want to become... good?

"If you can accept me as I am, then I love you as well, Asher," I confess. "You give me hope I can overcome the shadows yet still be who I want to be."

He draws me close once more. Together, we have awakened something pure.

I turn to Nargle, who watches us contentedly. "Thank you."

He gives a gracious bow before popping out of sight, leaving us alone but both less alone than before.

My mind tries to process what just happened. How did I just get divided in two? I could feel the other part of me missing, an invisible thread between us telling me that she was a part of me and not a copy. The only thing that comes to mind is my encounter with Mister Rotten Hand yesterday. What exactly did he hit me with?

The morning sun filters through the broken cottage windows, bathing everything in a hazy golden glow. Asher and I finally pull apart, though a new connection now hums between us. I study his face, committing every line and contour to memory.

"We should be going," Asher says gently, his thumb tracing small circles on my hand, "but I wish we could stay like this a little longer."

I nod reluctantly. Continuing our quest to stop Lexir feels less urgent when I am wrapped in Asher's arms.

To be fair, I'm not exactly in a rush. This is the prince's mission. I'm just as happy to leave my ex to his own devices forever and never see that egotistical prick again. I wish we could linger in this moment forever—just the two of us and this fragile new love we have kindled—but the outside world waits.

With a sigh, I gather up my few belongings.

Asher gives me a sympathetic smile and squeezes my shoulder. "Someday, this will be our life, nothing but time together ahead," he says, ever the optimist.

My heart swells, imagining that future. I never hoped for something like that before, but perhaps I can do it... for him.

I almost throw up in my mouth. This isn't me. I worked for too long and far too hard to give up everything I earned, but I have to admit, if I ever give up my real life, I can see it being for him.

Outside the cottage, I lift my face to the patches of blue beyond the forest canopy. Birds swoop from branch to branch, trilling joyful songs. It all seems brighter now, the world reborn through the lens of love.

We walk leisurely all morning, no particular destination in mind, simply enjoying each other's company is enough. Asher regales me with playful childhood stories that bring a smile to my face. In turn, I open up about my own past, tales I'd never shared with another soul. With him, the words flow freely.

By midday, we come upon a sun-dappled meadow dotted with wildflowers. It is too lovely a setting not to pause and rest. I sink down among the soft grass and herbs, closing my eyes contentedly as the sunlight washes over me.

After gathering some berries for us to snack on, Asher settles beside me. He begins fussing with something in his hands, brow furrowed in concentration.

"What are you up to?" I ask curiously.

"You'll see," he replies with a secretive grin.

I peer over his shoulder, catching glimpses of green stems and purple blossoms.

After a few more moments, he spins to face me with a triumphant, "Ta-da!" In his hands is a flower crown, expertly woven together.

"For you, my queen," he says, eyes dancing playfully as he places the circlet atop my head.

I laugh in surprise and pleasure. His fingertips linger against my hair, sending a shiver down my spine.

"How does it look?" I ask self-consciously, though I can't keep the smile from my face.

Asher's expression grows serious, his gaze tender. "Like it was made for you," he says, "though you'd be beautiful to me if you were wearing naught but rags."

Heat rushes to my cheeks at his words. I glance down, unexpectedly overcome with emotion.

Gently, Asher tilts my chin up until our eyes meet once more. "I mean it," he says earnestly. "Even when you don't see it yourself, know that, to me, you are everything graceful and good in this world."

My vision swims with tears I blink back. No one has ever declared such feelings for me. I want to scoff at the sheer sappiness of it, but instead, I find it simply makes me love him more.

"You have a rare gift for seeing light within the darkness," I manage unevenly. I caress his cheek, still hardly believing this man is mine. "With you, I feel... worthy. Whole."

The admission leaves me vulnerable, exposed, but Asher's eyes reflect only tenderness and awe.

"No greater honor than having won your heart," he replies softly.

He draws me into his arms then, and I go willingly, melting against him. We stay entwined in the meadow for some time, the rest of the world fading away.

When we finally part, Asher spies more wildflowers, and his eyes light up. "I'll make you a matching bracelet!" he proclaims.

I laugh, heart lighter than it has been for longer than I care to admit. "Only if I can make you one in return."

And so we while away the golden afternoon together, fingers intertwined, transmuting fragile blooms into symbols of our love. By the time we are done, I am bedecked in floral crowns, bracelets, and anklets. We must have looked a silly pair—a prince and sorceress adorned in wildflowers like woodland sprites—but when Asher pulls me in for another lingering kiss, I realize I won't trade this moment for all the power in the world.

We stay for hours, basking in joy and possibility. As the sun begins to set, we gather firewood, and I use magic to spark a small campfire. It's a bit strange to be able to use magic in front of him freely. The flames soon crackle merrily, holding off the evening's chill. We lay out our bedrolls side by side, so close my arm brushes Asher's when I recline back to gaze up at the darkening sky. One by one, stars blink into being, like scattered diamonds against velvet.

Glancing over, I find Asher watching me, eyes soft. "What are you thinking about?" he asks.

I smile shyly. "How I never want this day to end."

It is the simple truth. Tomorrow, we will continue our quest, but under this vast sky alone together, no darkness can touch us.

Asher shifts onto his side and reaches out to tuck a lock of hair behind my ear. "I was thinking the same," he admits. "If only we could stay in this meadow forever."

I catch his hand and press it against my cheek. "Maybe we can," I suggest impulsively.

Asher's eyebrows shoot up in surprise. Then, his expression melts into a grin. "What did you have in mind?"

In answer, I sit up and hold out my hands, concentrating as I trace them through the air. A dome of pale light springs up around us, enclosing our little campsite in a protective bubble.

Asher's eyes widen in understanding. "A barrier spell?"

I nod, suddenly shy. "We can be safe here, just for a night. No one can touch us."

Perhaps it is foolish, delaying our quest over a fanciful notion, but Asher's face lights up with joy.

"It's perfect," he proclaims, pulling me back down beside him. "One night where it's just you and me under the stars."

My heart swells, and I nestle contentedly against Asher's side as we gaze upward. He points out constellations and tells the stories behind them. I conjure small illusory images to accompany the tales—heroes vanquishing monsters, lovers reuniting.

Laughing together, we forget everything beyond this bubble universe. Tomorrow can wait. Tonight, we simply revel in each other and the magical realm we have woven from light, story, and shared dreams.

When the fire eventually burns down to glowing embers, Asher stokes it gently back to life. The flames cast shifting patterns over his handsome features. Unable to resist, I trail feather-light kisses along his jaw and down his neck.

Asher inhales sharply, arms tightening around me. When he claims my lips a moment later, the kiss lights an entirely different kind of fire within me.

My skin heats, and my heart drums a wild rhythm as I eagerly open to him. His hands move down my back and linger at my waist, tugging lightly at the straps of my leather armor.

He breaks away from our kiss with a low chuckle, his breath warm against my neck. "You're wearing far too much," he murmurs, voice husky with desire.

His fingers move deftly over the buckles and straps, loosening them one by one until the armor falls away from my body in a whisper-soft rustle of leather.

Finally free of the restrictive garment, I feel exposed but not uncomfortable, not with Asher's hands caressing me as if he memorized every curve and hollow of my body through some unseen touch.

A moan escapes me when Asher's lips close over one hardened nipple, sending a thrill straight through to my very core. He pauses to look up at me then, eyes dark with an emotion I can't name but want to explore more deeply.

Without a word, Asher shifts his attention to my other breast, teasing and caressing both until I writhe beneath him in pleasure. His hands glide down my body, exploring every inch of me as if searching for something he lost long ago.

Desperate for more contact, I grab the laces of his leather armor and tug it open with eager fingers. Beneath the heavy hide is a smooth expanse of skin that begs to be touched. With a silent request, Asher kicks the garment away and lies before me completely exposed.

My gaze flickers hungrily over his muscled chest and stomach, trailing lower still before coming to rest on his erect cock. Aroused by the sight, I reach out and slowly run one finger along its length. His sharp intake of breath only encourages me further, and soon, my hand closes around him possessively as I stroke faster with increasing pressure.

He groans in approval, pushing against my grip as he brings our mouths back together in a passionate kiss that leaves us both trembling with need.

Asher breaks away from our kiss just long enough to flip me onto my back before tugging off the last remaining pieces of leather armor. The cool air of the meadow brushes across my heated skin as he straddles me, his gaze hungry and full of desire.

He lowers himself down until I can feel the length of his hard body pressed against mine, and I moan in pleasure as his lips find my own again. His hands roam over my curves with renewed urgency while one thigh snakes between mine, pressing against my throbbing sex.

His skilled fingers find their way between my legs and start to stroke lightly at my clit. I gasp at the sensation, arching into him as wave after wave of pleasure ripples through me. His low chuckle is all the warning I have before he slides two fingers inside me with a single smooth thrust that leaves me breathless.

"You're so wet," he murmurs, his voice thick with need as his thrusts intensify.

Every movement feels like a direct assault on my senses, driving me closer and closer to sweet oblivion until finally I can't take anymore.

I reach between us and grab onto his cock, guiding it to line up perfectly with my opening. He groans in anticipation as I slowly lower him down until the tip is just barely inside me.

His sure hands move from my hips up along my sides and over my breasts. His lips trail kisses over my neck and chest as he moves faster and deeper, stealing all the air from my lungs.

The rhythmic movements combined with his skilled touches quickly bring me right to the edge of ecstasy until I am begging him for more, panting out his name.

Suddenly, he increases the speed of his thrust as an orgasm unlike anything I have ever experienced crashes over me in glorious waves of pleasure that leave me trembling beneath him in its wake. With a guttural growl, Asher follows suit a few seconds later, collapsing onto the bed of grass and flowers as we both gasp for air.

Afterward, I rest my head over his heart, drifting in sublime contentment. I have never felt so cherished.

"You are my light in the darkness," Asher murmurs, trailing his fingers idly through my hair.

My eyes grow heavy, and I let sleep slowly claim me.

I awake sometime later to silvery predawn light and birdsong, tucked securely in Asher's embrace. Last night comes back to me in a rush, and I smile, heartbeat quickening.

By unspoken agreement, we move slowly that morning, neither eager to shatter the spell of our hidden world. We bathe in the nearby stream then eat a leisurely breakfast in each other's arms.

Eventually, we can delay no longer. As the sun rises higher, I dissolve the barrier with a wistful sigh. Our one perfect night has ended.

Asher pulls me close and kisses my forehead. "We'll make more of these memories, I promise."

Together, we pack up camp and continue on our quest, hearts lighter after even so brief a respite.

As we walk, Asher gives me a considering look. "We should reach the edge of the area Lexir is rumored to occupy by tomorrow," he remarks.

My smile fades slightly. Of course reality would intrude again soon. At least we stole a moment of magic for ourselves. That will have to sustain me in the trials ahead.

29

Lillith

The forest shows no change as we enter the area that Lexir claims as his own domain. I feel at peace as Asher and I stroll along the leafy path. A playful breeze ruffles his white hair, and I smile, heart full. After our idyllic time together, the larger quest feels distant but a bigger threat still looms over me. Should I tell him who I really am? He seems to have accepted every other part of me. Could he accept this too?

Lost in thought, I stumble over an exposed root.

Asher's steadying hand goes to my back, eyes crinkling with amusement. "Careful. As graceful as you are in battle, perhaps we should avoid outright war with the forest floor today."

I roll my eyes but squeeze his hand in wordless affection. His teasing means the world to me. It is a side only I get to see.

A child's frantic cries suddenly shatter the birdsong. "Please, help! They've taken my brother!" A young boy bursts from the underbrush, eyes wide with terror. He clutches at Asher's tunic with dirty hands. "You must help, sir! The bandits came at dawn and dragged him away!"

Asher grips the boy's shoulder, eyes grave. "Calm yourself, lad. Just point us toward these villains." His commanding, princely tone leaves no room for doubt.

I frown as we follow the child through the tangled woods. Something in his shrill voice rings false to my senses, but Asher charges heedlessly ahead, one hand on his sword hilt, ever the righteous hero. With a resigned sigh, I summon magic to my palms and trail behind them.

We trail the young boy through the dense forest until we reach a rocky outcropping dotted with dark cave mouths. The river churns nearby, but no sounds emerge from the shadowy tunnels. Unease pricks my neck.

"Stay behind me," Asher murmurs, unsheathing his sword.

I bite back a retort. Does he think me some helpless damsel? Still, his protectiveness ignites a warm glow in my chest, much as I hate to admit it.

We creep into the earthen darkness. The cavern slopes downward, the only sound our muted footfalls and dripping water.

Then, a chorus of unearthly shrieks erupts ahead. Bony hands burst from crevices, clawing and grasping. The stench of rotting flesh chokes the air. Ghouls!

"Back!" I cry, throwing up a barrier to force the fiends away.

More claw from the shadows. Asher slashes fiercely even as they overwhelm him.

A menacing chuckle echoes through the tunnel. "Enjoy my trap?" A hulking figure emerges, his right hand nothing but bone.

I scowl. Mister Rotting Hand himself. We've been expertly played, but why?

"Let the boy go!" Asher commands.

Mister Rotting Hand just sneers as more ghouls pour in. Fear lances my heart seeing Asher pinned beneath gnashing teeth.

I blast the creatures away in a rage. Several shatter completely, my fury fueling the dark magic. I rush to help Asher stand, gasping. "The boy can wait. Watch yourself first!" I twine protective magic around us.

Mister Rotting Hand grows frustrated by my shields. He sends two brutish lackeys barreling at me. Tactical but foolish. With a blast, I rip the air from their lungs and watch dispassionately as they collapse.

"Lilly, no!" Asher shouts

Fury roars in my ears. These worms had threatened us. They will suffer!

I stalk toward Mister Rotting Hand, magic roiling.

Suddenly, he cowers. "Mercy, m'lady! I only serve Lord Lexir! Someone you once served or should I say serviced, Lillith?"

I freeze. Lexir. My heart turns to ice at the name. This minor villain is in league with the powerful wizard who ruined my life? Rage and pain clash within me. I tremble with the effort to restrain my darker impulses.

Sensing weakness, Mister Rotting Hand attacks, hands glowing ominously. I brace for impact, but Asher intervenes, sword flashing. Mister Rotting Hand howls, severed hand thudding to the floor.

"You will pay for helping Lexir," Asher growls, blade leveled at the warlock's heart.

My prince will kill in cold blood for me as I would for him. What does that make us?

Mister Rotting Hand's eyes bulge as Asher's hand clamps around his throat like a vice.

"Where is Lexir hiding?" my prince growls, tightening his grip.

The warlock gasps and chokes, face purpling.

Asher's hand begins to glow with sinister magic, pressing Mister Rotting Hand against the cavern wall. "Tell me what you know, and your end will be swift," he threatens.

Dark tendrils snake from his fingers, worming under the warlock's skin.

Mister Rotting Hand screams hoarsely as the dark spell burrows deeper, probing his mind. Asher's eyes are merciless. His jaw is clenched with concentration as he brutally extracts the information he seeks.

At last, Mister Rotting Hand goes limp, mind broken by the agonizing assault. Asher lets his body drop carelessly.

Inside, I recoil from this ruthlessness while also admiring his willingness to use any means for our cause.

He turns to me, eyes still glowing with fell magic. "The warlock's mind revealed a lot more than I expected before his end," Asher says coldly. "Now tell me who you really are, Lillith."

30

Asher

Lillith's outstretched hand trembles in the space between us, her eyes glistening with barely restrained tears. My pulse thunders in my ears as I await her response.

Finally, voice scarcely a whisper, she answers, "I am Lillith Shadowend."

The admission lands like a blow. My mind reels, grappling to reconcile this woman with the terrible villain of legend. She seems so unlike the ruthless manipulator from whispered tales of dread. Perhaps that is merely evidence of how utterly she deceived me. I saw everything that this man knew about her. The acts she committed as a villain with Lexir, their relationship, and their breakup. The worst part is that the one thing I really care about is that she lied to me.

I recoil, anger and disbelief warring within me. "You lied about who you were this whole time!" I accuse harshly. "You mean to betray me. Admit it!"

Anguish floods her face. "I never meant you harm. I swear it!" She reaches for me desperately. "Please, Asher, you have to believe me—"

"Believe you?" I snarl, pulling away. "You posed as an innocent to get close to me. For all I know, you mean to slit my throat as I sleep!"

Fury blazes in her eyes. She rises to her feet, voice whip-sharp. "Do not presume to know my intentions. If I wanted you dead, you would be."

I raise my sword, leveling it at her chest while she stares at me unflinchingly. "Give me one reason why I should not cut you down here and now, villain."

Her fierce look softens then, eyes shining with emotion as she steps toward me and grasps my arm. "Because you've felt what grows between us," she says softly. "As have I."

I recoil from her touch. "You lied about who you were. Why?" I demand harshly.

Lillith flinches at my tone but does not retreat. "It was never to harm you. I swear! I just wanted to see if I could make you a little bit less good. You've got to believe me." Her voice breaks. "I never had a chance at goodness, but with you... for the first time I feel hope."

The anguish in her eyes gives me pause. Could she truly have been forced into evil? Still, doubts gnaw at me.

"You hid your identity because you meant to betray me."

"No!" Desperation floods her face. "I hid because I knew if you discovered who I was, you would have killed me. Any hero would." She falls to her knees before me, gripping my hands even as I try to pull away. "Please don't give up on us."

Her raw sincerity brings me up short. She seems a different woman than the ruthless sorceress of legend. I want to believe redemption is possible, even for her, but reservations still plague me.

"Please. I don't know what our future would look like, but I know I want you to be part of it. You've shown me that being good isn't quite so bad," she entreats.

I search her face, finding no deception there. Could she truly be ready to abandon her villainous nature? It seems impossible, yet her anguish appears genuine.

"I know you find it hard to trust me," she concedes brokenly, "but I beg you, give me a chance to prove myself. I may have the title of the most powerful villain in three kingdoms, but I've never been called the most evil."

Everything in me wants to pull her close, to believe we can overcome her dark past if she is willing, but my duty demands caution. She deceived me once already. I cannot afford to be blinded by sentiment.

"You will have your chance," I say heavily, "but it will take time to know your heart is true."

Hope and fear war in her eyes. "That's all I ask," she whispers. "A chance to show you I want to be made anew."

My own heart is in turmoil, pulled between affection for the woman I thought I knew and wariness for the infamous villain she has proven to be.

I extend a hand to her. She clings to it like a lifeline, as though terrified I will cast her back into darkness alone.

"We should head out," I tell her gruffly. "We aren't far from Lexir's camp."

Silent, she nods and leaves the cave.

It is true that I long to trust that redemption can flower even in the most corrupted soul, but only time will tell if she is ready to step fully into the light. The light that I now fear blinded me to the viper I clasped to my breast…

***

The forest seems to close in oppressively as Lillith and I continue toward Lexir's camp. Ever since she reveals her true identity back in the cave, Lillith hasn't spoken a word. I can't blame her. Learning she is Lillith Shadowend, the infamous dark enchantress, rattled me pretty hard too. All this time I've trusted her, even started to… care for her. Now, I don't know if anything between us had been real.

I sneak a glance at Lillith as we hike. Her gaze is distant, lost in thought. How can I ever trust her again after she lies to my face? Yet, part of me wants to believe she has changed over our journey together, that what we share means something, no matter her past sins.

After about a league on the forest trail, Lillith pauses, frowning at the surrounding woods. "This area looks familiar," she murmurs. "Like a different lifetime, yet also just yesterday."

She steps off the worn path, picking her way among the dense underbrush and beckoning for me to follow. I trail after her warily, one hand resting on the hilt of my sheathed sword. What is she doing?

We hack through prickly thickets and duck under low-hanging boughs until the forest opens up into a tiny clearing, little more than a break in the trees. Kneeling, Lillith carefully brushes away the carpet of fallen leaves from a patch of bare stone. Carved deeply into its surface is an elaborate, curling letter "L."

"My childish signature," she remarks, a bitter twist to her mouth. "Etched here on the day I swore none would ever make me feel powerless again."

Her words give me pause. Powerless? What happened to her as a child to elicit such a vow?

Before I can ask, Lillith rises swiftly to her feet and plunges onward into the gloom beneath the forest eaves. Mystified, I scramble after her.

We pass a decrepit wooden shack, its roof sunken in and walls green with moss. The remains of a firepit lie before it.

In a nearby copse, scorch marks blacken the bark of several ancient oaks. An entire pond we come upon is strangely frozen over, glistening ice coating its surface despite the late summer warmth.

As we pass the crumbling shack, melancholy flashes across Lillith's face.

"I took shelter here after first escaping the underground training facility at eleven. My parents sent me there. They were convinced it was for the best. Train me into the ruthless villain they wanted to be themselves and get me out of their hair all in one go." Her voice drops to a haunted whisper. "I still hear their screams sometimes in my dreams. That place hollowed out my innocence, so I fled here to the forest determined to regain control." She ducks inside the shack, running her hands over the moss-covered walls. "Cold comfort but the solitude was a balm. No more punishments or forced deeds. For the first time, I could breathe."

In a nearby copse, scorch marks blacken several ancient oaks.

Lillith walks over and rests her palm on one charred trunk. "I was trying to master a fire spell using lightning as the spark," she explains. "I underestimated the intensity. The flames raged wildly, consuming half the copse before I regained command." She shakes her head ruefully. "I lived on roots and berries until I could hunt. An important lesson in respecting elemental power."

Each thing she shows me breaks my heart a little bit more. If this is what her life was like, how could she have become anything other than a villain?

As we pass the frozen pond, Lillith grimaces, her eyes brimming with painful memories. "An early attempt at morphing water into ice. As you can see, I hadn't yet mastered reversing my own spells." She gazes out at the sparkling expanse. "I was stranded for two frigid nights, nearly dying of hypothermia before it finally melted enough for me to escape." Lillith slowly shakes her head, eyes clouded with old hurts. "I chose this path myself to escape their neglect and claim the power over magic.." Her voice holds echoes of deep-seated pain.

Her eyes go out of focus as if seeing something I can't.

"One winter, I fell desperately ill," Lillith continues, her voice distant. "It came on suddenly... violent chills, searing fever. I could barely gather the strength to stoke the fire." She gestures around the dilapidated shack. "For three days, I lay here alone with no one to aid me. The snow piled high outside, cutting off any hope of seeking help. Little did I know, the entire kingdom was sick with the plague." Lillith shakes her head. "I was sure those empty walls would be the last thing I saw."

My heart aches at the thought of her suffering through such a harrowing ordeal with no comfort or care. She endured only because of her sheer resilience.

A sliver of guilt creeps its way into me. I made some mistakes in my youth that had horrible consequences. Some still give me nightmares. I can't help but wonder if this is connected to one of my worst, but I am too afraid to ask.

"But the fever finally broke," Lillith says, "and when it did, my resolve to survive only strengthened. I had only myself to rely on so I vowed to grow stronger whatever it took."

Her candid words take me aback, the sincerity in them resonating within my heart. She was just a frightened, lonely child trying to survive the only way she knew—by seizing control of her own destiny through training her gifts.

It strikes me how foolish I have been to judge her so rashly, forgetting that even the most fearsome villains were innocent babes once. Lillith hid truths about her identity, true, but the spirit I have come to know over our journey has been real. Standing here, surrounded by the ghosts of her past training, I see at last the glimmers of light she clutches to even in the smothering darkness she knew.

Lillith turns to me then, her eyes pools of uncertainty and shame, as if my thoughts are scribed plainly on my face for her to read.

"I know you must think me a monster after all I've done..." she begins haltingly.

I raise a hand, stopping her. "You became what circumstances forced you to be. How could a child shown only cruelty know kindness?"

Lillith looks surprised and hesitant to accept my words. "Still, the choices were mine," she insists. "I let anger and pain twist me into something hardened and dark."

"And yet your humanity remained," I counter gently, "buried but not destroyed. You used your magic to protect me, did you not?"

Lillith nods slowly. "I suppose I did." She is silent for a long moment.

After a moment, I take a deep breath. There is a confession of my own that must be made if we are to truly understand one another.

"The illness you described nearly claiming your life...I am responsible for unleashing it." I admit heavily.

Lillith's eyes widen in surprise and confusion. I force myself to continue.

"When I was young and reckless, I delved into dark magic, seeking the power to cure my mother's terminal disease. But I lost control of the spell and inflicted the kingdom with that deadly plague instead."

I meet Lillith's gaze solemnly. "So you see, I too know the bitter taste of regret. In my ignorance and pride, I brought only suffering while trying vainly to conquer death."

"So the only reason you could help heal the people of this kingdom is because you first made them sick and dying. You became a hero because you were fixing a mistake you made out of a selfish desire," she said at last. There is no accusation in her tone, only dawning comprehension.

I nod heavily. "I understand the desperation that drives one to such darkness. I know there is a piece of me capable of those same evils under the right circumstances." I meet Lillith's gaze. "Perhaps that is why I find it easier to forgive the shadowed parts of your past. In you, I see a reflection of myself and the mistakes I, too, am capable of when fear and love drive me beyond reason."

Lillith steps forward then and takes my hands in her own. "The past cannot be changed," she says softly. "We can only let it teach us how to go forward with more wisdom and compassion... although I admit it's nice to see you a bit less perfect." She shakes her head. "Blood magic... it's something even I was never willing to mess with."

Tears sting my eyes. With her gentle absolution, it feels as though a festering shard of guilt has finally been lanced from my heart. Perhaps together, two wounded souls can find the redemption we both so desperately seek.

# 31

Lillith

"How much farther until we reach his camp?" I finally ask, unable to bear the tense quiet any longer.

Asher glances at me, his expression unreadable. "Another few miles or so."

I suppress a frustrated sigh. Ever since my identity came to light, our easy camaraderie has evaporated. I long to find some way to regain Asher's trust, to prove I am no longer the villain of old, but so far, he remains stubbornly on his guard around me.

We trudge onward down the forest road, the uneasy quiet hanging over us like a pall. Though Asher walks beside me, a chasm may as well stretch between us.

The calls of birds and chittering of insects only amplify the tense silence. I rack my mind for some way to bridge this yawning gulf, to regain even a shred of his trust, but no magical words come to restore what has been shattered.

Without warning, faint screams pierce the air, drifting through the trees ahead. Asher and I exchange a swift, startled look, our quarrel briefly forgotten. Together, we rush down the road, the sounds of chaos growing louder. Then, the acrid stench of smoke hits my nose.

We round a bend, and a horrific scene lies before us. An overturned merchant caravan and strewn-about burning bodies are under assault by an enormous emerald-scaled dragon. Blood pools slickly under corpses with limbs bent at unnatural angles. A horse thrashes madly, pierced through by a wooden shaft.

Surviving men desperately try to battle the rampaging beast. One man swings his sword valiantly. The dragon seizes him in its jaws and flings his limp form aside.

As we freeze in horror, the creature rears back and unleashes a torrent of flames from its maw, engulfing a wagon in an inferno.

The metallic tang of blood and the stench of charred flesh choke the air. Screams rent the air as the survivors plead for mercy while the dragon tirelessly slaughters them. This is no longer a tranquil forest road but a vision of hell itself.

Asher charges forward, sword drawn, just as the dragon opens its jaws to unleash flaming breath upon a frightened woman.

With lightning speed, Asher cuts through the air between them. In one swift motion, he grabs the woman and swiftly pulls her to safety, just as the dragon's fire scorches the earth where she once stood.

Asher turns to face the dragon, ready to defend the rest of the caravan.

Before he can charge again, I step forward. "No!" I cry, placing a hand on Asher's arm.

Asher looks at me in confusion. "But it will attack again!"

"It attacks out of fear, not evil," I say, gazing at the dragon. "It does not see us as we see it."

"Lillith, stand aside," he commands. "This beast threatens innocent lives."

He tries to step past me, but I grab his arm, halting him.

"I won't let you slaughter this one too," I say fiercely, remembering the dragon whose death paid for his new palace.

Magic gathers in my palms, fueled by desperation. I have to stop further bloodshed. With a guttural cry, I release the energy toward the dragon.

The blast hits the ground at the dragon's feet in a spray of dirt and rock. The dragon rears back, roaring in anger and surprise. I do not let up, continuing to bombard the area around the creature with flashes of light and explosive magic. The dragon spreads its wings, snarling, but takes to the air to retreat.

I hold my breath, braced for it to turn back and unleash its fury upon us, but the dragon only gives an offended huff before disappearing over the trees.

My shoulders slump in relief. I drove it off without causing lasting harm. Let Asher call me a monster, but I will not stand by to see more innocent lives lost. There has been enough death already.

A crowd of merchants and travelers have emerged cautiously from their hiding places now that the attack is over. I scan their faces for malice or judgment but see only grateful awe at being saved.

One young woman with flowing brown hair and a pretty face breaks from the group and runs toward us or, more specifically, toward Asher.

"You saved us!" she cries, catching hold of his hands earnestly. "We would have surely all perished if not for your swift arrival." She gazes up at him adoringly while he shifts in faint embarrassment.

"It was really my companion who scared off the beast," he demurs awkwardly.

The woman is not to be deterred. "Nonsense. You must have fought it bravely for it to flee so quickly." She leans closer, delicately inspecting his arm. "Why, you're injured! Please, allow me to tend it."

I clench my jaw so hard it hurts as I watch this simpering girl fawn over Asher, even though his "wound" is no more than a shallow scratch. He barely raised his sword before

I intervened, yet now this stranger gazes at him as though he is the greatest of heroes.

It pricks at my deepest insecurities, reminding me I can never hope for the admiration and accolades heroes like Asher receive. I will always be mistrusted and feared for my dark powers no matter the good I try to do.

With great effort, I swallow my bitter jealousy. Now is my chance to prove I can be selfless, not allowing petty envy to sway me. I will not win back Asher's esteem through trickery or malice.

I assist in tending to the wounded and burned, repairing what damage I can by binding the wounds until the caravan leader pronounces they are fit to travel again. I avoid looking at Asher and his new admirer, not trusting myself to hold composure. Her musical laughter grates at my ears.

As we walk away from the ravaged caravan, I try to ignore the jealousy still simmering inside me. That fool girl had clearly been dazzled by Asher's bravery, even though I drove off the dragon. Did anyone thank the dark villainess? Of course not.

I sigh, reminding myself that petty envy won't help my case with Asher. I need to take the high road if I want to prove I've changed. Be the better woman and all that nonsense.

Just then, Asher grimaces and rubs his shoulder. "Blast, that dragon's claws caught me deeper than I thought. Have any healing potions left, Lillith?"

I resist the urge to roll my eyes. His "wound" is barely a scratch, yet he is carrying on as if it is a mortal gash. I guess nearly dying makes everyone dramatic.

"I believe I have one," I reply politely, recalling a vial from my necklace.

As I hand it to him, a wicked impulse strikes. Before I can think better of it, I subtly cast a spell, turning the red liquid into hot sauce.

Just a harmless prank to take the edge off my envy.

"You have a magic necklace?" Asher asks.

"Technically, I made a magic necklace. Quite a simple spell if you read a little."

"Anything I need to be worried about in there?"

I only smile in return. Let him think what he wants.

"Many thanks," Asher says gratefully. He tilts back the vial and immediately erupts into violent choking. "Gods be damned, woman!" he sputters accusingly. "Is this your idea of a joke?"

I try and fail to look innocent. "Oh, dear, my mistake. Let me fix you a real potion."

But Asher has none of it. "This is exactly why I can't trust you!" he snaps. "Pranks and deceit. What else should I expect from a dark enchantress?"

His words sting, and my smile fades. "It was just a bit of fun," I say weakly.

"Fun?" Asher looks incredulous. "You call childish tricks fun while people lie dead back there? Do you care nothing for them?"

Now it is my turn to snap. "Of course I care! I saved those people, not you!" Angrily, I shove the real potion at him. "Drink it, and stop whining over a little hot sauce."

Asher regards me coldly. "I see this spree of good deeds hasn't rid you of your dark heart."

His scorn cuts deeply. For a moment, we just glare at each other. Then, Asher turns and stalks off down the road. I stand there, cursing myself for slipping back into petty malice. Why is it so hard to just be good?

With a heavy heart, I trail after Asher's retreating figure, keeping a careful distance. The long road to redemption seems longer than ever, but I have to keep trying, for both our sakes.

The light mood from earlier has vanished entirely, leaving tense silence hanging between us once more. So much for redeeming myself in his eyes.We continue on as ominous gray clouds roll in overhead. Soon, fat raindrops begin splashing down sporadically. Asher doesn't even glance back at me as he presses onward, shoulders tensed.

Before long, the sporadic drops turn into a drizzling downpour. I conjure up an umbrella with my magic, more out of reflex than conscious thought, but I don't offer to shield Asher from the rain. Let the fool get soaked for all I care.

The icy droplets seep through my clothes and trickle down my neck, but I ignore the discomfort. We've certainly endured far worse than a bit of rain. Still, the muddy road has become treacherous to navigate. More than once, my foot nearly slides out from under me. Up ahead, Asher is similarly struggling not to slip in the muck.

A particularly deep puddle lies directly in his path. I open my mouth to warn him but stop myself. Why should I help after the way he's treated me? Let him fall on his royal behind.

Sure enough, his foot sinks into the deceptively deep puddle up to his ankle. With a startled cry, Asher pitches forward face-first into the muddy water.

I freeze, momentarily stunned. Despite myself, a small smirk tugs at my lips. The sight of the normally poised prince floundering about in the mud like a clumsy ox is too absurd. Before I can stop it, a tiny snicker escapes me.

Asher's head jerks up, his face dripping and smeared with mud. His eyes narrow. "You think this is funny, do you?" he demands, clambering back to his feet with as much dignity as he can muster.

I press my lips together, but another laugh bubbles out regardless. "Forgive me, Your Highness. I never imagined you'd be one to take a mud bath so eagerly."

"As if you foresaw that pit in the road," Asher retorts, swiping at the mud clinging to his tunic in vain. "Admit it. You enjoyed watching me fall."

I incline my head in acquiescence. "Perhaps a little," I admit with a smirk.

Asher scoops up a handful of the wet soil. "I hope you'll also enjoy sharing in it!"

He tosses the mudball at me catching me off guard. It splatters across my shoulder, flecks of it hitting my cheek.

I gasp, more outraged than harmed by the childish attack. "How dare you!"

But Asher only laughs, the sound ringing out over the steady patter of raindrops. "Now who's the one covered in muck?"

My eyes narrow at the challenge. "You clearly have a death wish today."

I gather up my own dripping glob of mud. Asher's eyes widen. He attempts to dodge, but my missile catches him squarely in the chest.

"You'll pay for that one!"

He reaches for more ammunition, but I am quicker. With a hissed spell, a wave of mud rises up and crashes over him.

Asher splutters, wiping the sludge from his face. "That's cheating!"

"All's fair in mud and war!" I cackle.

Soon, we are both slipping and sliding about, lobbing mud and insults with equal fury. Asher's white hair hangs in dripping soiled strands, his fine cloak abandoned. I know I must look equally bedraggled and filthy but can't bring myself to care.

For the first time since my identity reveal, Asher's smile meets his eyes. The sound of our laughter drowns out the falling rain. I find myself grinning too, breathless between muddy assaults.

At last, sides aching, we mutually call a truce.

Still chuckling, Asher wipes pointlessly at the layers of caked grime coating his skin. "Well fought," he concedes, "though we both emerge the losers in this battle."

I glance down at my mud-coated leathers and stained hands, my hair dripping. "Perhaps, but I couldn't remember the last time I so thoroughly enjoyed losing ."

Asher's grin softens. Thunder cracks ominously above us before he can reply.

"We should find shelter," I suggest. Spotting a rocky overhang in the distance, I point. "There's a cave. We can wait out the storm there."

Asher follows my gaze and nods.

We set off toward the cave, our steps slowing on the muddy slope. Halfway up, my foot slips out from under me.

Asher's hand darts out instantly to grab my arm, steadying me. "Careful."

His touch lingers a moment before withdrawing.

Together, we reach the cave safely. While Asher gathers kindling, I use magic to start a fire. We clean up with conjured water as best we can, though grime still clings stubbornly.

As we settle in to wait out the rain, I glance sidelong at Asher. "For what it's worth... I am sorry about the hot sauce and for letting jealousy get the better of me."

He raises an eyebrow wryly. "Jealous? Of that silly girl?" At my abashed look, he chuckles. "She meant nothing to me, Lillith, but your actions did. I need to know I can trust you."

I nod, gaze lowered. "I know."

"Perhaps you already have my trust." Asher nudges me gently. "The past is the past, and I prefer laughing with you to fighting."

I meet his eyes, touched by the olive branch extended. There is hope for reconciliation yet. Outside the storm rages on, but here in this cave, a fragile peace has emerged from the mud and rain.

The firelight dances across Asher's handsome features as he gazes at me, his earlier anger faded. My heart flutters at his closeness and the intimacy of this moment sheltered from the storm.

On impulse, I rise to my feet and stretch, joints stiff from the damp cold. As I reach my arms overhead, I feel Asher's eyes follow me. Turning, I find him standing mere inches away, his expression unreadable.

"Lillith..." he murmurs, voice low.

Before I can react, his hands are cradling my face, and his lips claim mine in a searing kiss.

For a moment, I freeze, stunned by the sudden passion. Then, I melt against him, kissing him back fiercely, the outside world forgotten. Our misunderstandings don't matter now, only this connection between us that goes beyond words.

We break apart at last, breathing raggedly.

Asher's thumbs gently caress my cheeks as he searches my gaze. "I'm sorry too," he whispers. "Sorry I doubted you. Your heart is changed. I see that now."

My eyes prickle with emotion at his trust so freely given, and I lay a hand over his. "There is goodness in you that I don't deserve, but I swear to spend my life trying to."

Asher silences me with another deep kiss that steals my breath away. There is no need for further vows or explanations between us. The past is washed clean by rain, the future bright with hope's first light.

We stand there in the flickering firelight, our bodies mere inches apart. I feel as though I have crossed some sacred threshold, one that my heart has yearned for without realizing it.

Asher moves closer, his gaze fixed on mine with a hunger that makes my knees weak. His hands cup my face tenderly before moving down to stroke the bare skin at the base of my neck. A shiver runs through me at his touch, and he smiles knowingly, clearly enjoying my reaction. He leans forward, nuzzling my neck as he caresses the curves of my body hungrily.

With trembling fingers, I begin to unlace his leather armor, pushing it down his arms and onto the ground around us. His own hands move to do the same for me, carefully but eagerly undressing me until we are both exposed and vulnerable. Completely naked.

Asher steps back and looks at me with desire. His eyes travel up and down my body in appreciation before settling on mine again with an intensity that makes me catch my breath. He pulls me close with one hand while the other moves to cradle my head as he captures my lips in a passionate kiss that promises intimacy beyond anything I have ever known before.

Asher's kiss is wild, uninhibited, and full of desire. I feel as if I am melting into him, our bodies pressing together in a way that seems to connect us on a level deeper than just physical. His hands roam my body, gliding along the swell of my hips and tracing along my back before coming to rest against my buttocks. His lips leave mine and travel down the column of my neck as he nibbles and kisses his way along its length.

My head falls back against the stone as ecstasy courses through me. Asher lifts me off the ground, pressing me against the cave wall. His strong arms hold me there as his lips seek out every inch of exposed skin, driving my desire higher and higher until it consumes me completely.

Asher deftly moves one of his hands between us, guiding himself into me. Our bodies join in a single swift movement, and I gasp at the sheer intensity of it. A flood of sensations overwhelms me, and I cling to him desperately, my body trembling and quaking with euphoria.

He moves slowly at first, savoring each thrust as our moans echo off the walls. Our movements begin to quicken, both of us lost in a passionate whirlwind where time seems to stand still. Asher's powerful body moves in perfect harmony with mine as we reach for something greater than either of us could understand or comprehend alone.

We ride each wave together until we both reach a dizzying peak before collapsing into each other's arms in an exhausted but blissful embrace. Our breathing gradually returns to normal, our hearts frantically beating as we lie there locked in an embrace that speaks volumes without the need for words or explanation.

I may not know what exactly the future holds for us, two people on opposite sides of a moral war, but I know that right now this feels like perfection.

32

Lillith

Dusk drapes over the forest as Asher and I approach the distant firelight of Lexir's camp. We expect a ragtag crew of twenty at most—no match for Asher's sword and my sorcery combined.

Yet, as we creep nearer, glimpses between the trees suggest the intel is wrong. Ringing the camp are crude iron cages, not for holding goods but prisoners.

I freeze, unexpected sympathy rising within me. Once, I'd have turned a blind eye to such suffering, but now, injustice kindles my temper.

Asher's jaw clenches, hand resting on his pommel. "Free the captives while I deal with Lexir," he instructs tersely.

I mutely nod, magic already sparking at my fingertips—not for destruction but salvation.

Before parting, Asher and I share a searing kiss, wordlessly praying for the other's safety. Then, we slip into the shadows.

While Asher storms the camp head-on, every eye drawn to his bold challenge, I dart swiftly between the crude iron cages, focused on my task of freeing the wretched prisoners within.

As I slip unseen between crowded cages, my mind drifts to tangled recollections amid grim duty. Seven years past, a bitter teenage orphan alone in the world, I stumbled upon a striking figure practicing elemental spells deep in a glen. Lexir exuded charisma beyond his twenty years, silver tongue and charming wit entrancing my wrath-filled heart. His jet hair fell in tousled waves, contrasting pale skin and dancing coal eyes that promise untold delights.

Where others scorned my magics, Lexir claimed to understand my thirst for empowerment and freely teaches forbidden arts. Soon, we were inseparable, two alienated souls bonding over glorious visions of mayhem and anarchy wrought across the land, but beneath silken words lurked darker hungers, his "experiments" growing depraved as madness took root.

Shaking free of the past, I dissolve a lock. A haggard woman's eyes glisten with disbelieving relief, and I offer a fleeting smile.

"Go, run. You're free," I whisper.

She cringes back, holding up trembling hands. "Please, no more tricks..." she croaks, voice rough.

My heart twists, imagining what torments these people have endured to make them fear even an offer of freedom.

I soften my voice further, like calming a spooked animal. "No tricks. I swear it. I'm here to help you escape this place." I hold out my hand slowly.

The woman hesitates then takes it with a skeletal grip. I gently help her climb from the cage. As soon as her feet touch earth, her eyes go wide with disbelief.

"It's real?" she breathes. "I'm free?"

I nod and conjure a glowing orb to light her way into the woods. "Hurry now before they notice."

As she stumbles away, I hear a faint sob of joy. The helpless gratitude on her thin face is payment enough, steeling my resolve. I will free every prisoner here if it takes all night.

In the next enclosure, a pair of children cling to each other, large eyes blinking owlishly. My heart clenches, remembering pleas to Lexir falling upon deaf ears as "subjects" begged pitifully for release from new torments. He hoped seeds of doubt would take root which would bear bitter fruit in time.

My magic melts rusted iron, and the siblings hurry into safe woods, tiny hands clasped tight. Scattered cheers and Asher's grunts spur me onward, memory chased by grim duty.

For moons, Lexir and my band tore across the realm unrestrained, reveling in the havoc sown. But where I sought empowerment, Lexir desired only domination over all. Our philosophies collided as darkness consumed him, wrathful temper growing violent without provocation.

When his conquest over a small village who had offered everything yet he still slaughtered them all broke me at last, mad eyes revealed his ghastly true self, a monster craving only pain and power over others. We dueled for hours beneath the waxing moonlight, survival mere chance against venomous vengeance. Fleeing into isolation, I thought never to see those twisted features again, banishing all recollection to distance emotion.

Now, magic flows readily yet differently, no longer governed by wrath or passion but focused only on salvation. Asher's encroaching grunts keep demons at bay, rekindling flickering courage to see duty through. Another lock dissolves, and a bandaged man hobbles free with a teary nod, grin tugging despite agony plainly etched upon gaunt features.

"You're safe now," I murmur.

As I weave between the cages, I pause often to watch the duel unfolding fiercely by the bonfire's light. Lexir moves with serpentine speed, lips curled cruelly, but blow for deadly blow, Asher matches him, muscles gleaming. Their ringing blades set my heart lurching, frozen in place.

The next cage holds an elderly man with a bloody gash across his forehead. His rheumy eyes fill with tears as I dissolve his chains. "Bless you..." he rasps, patting my hand with his gnarled one before hobbling away.

Cage by cage, my magic and soft words free captive after captive from their nightmare. Each time, their disbelieving joy upon escape renews my dedication. However long it takes, I will free them all.

I dart between the cages, melting locks and freeing prisoners as quickly as I can. Most shrink back in fear until they realize freedom is at hand. Then, their eyes light up with dizzying gratitude.

Too focused on my task, I don't notice the approach of footsteps until too late. I weave between cages lost in grim focus, memories rising unbidden between. Another lock melts away to free hollow eyes blinking back to life, but my reprieve ends as armor glints between oaks.

"You there, halt!" a harsh voice rings out.

I turn to see two of Lexir's men advancing, scimitars drawn. They finally noticed the escaping prisoners.

With a snarl, I fling scorching flames outward. Curses spill forth. Those armored giants are familiar. As they retreat ablaze, recognition strikes.

"Karn! Balthus!" I call.

The larger peers up blearily from singed armor. Recognition sparks, and Balthus growls, "Lillith? Traitorous witch!"

His oathbound partner nods grimly. "Aye, betrayed us for pretty words and false power."

I sneer. "Prettier than pillaging villages at Lexir's whim. I chose a nobler path."

Karn spits. "Noble? You're as twisted as he, demon-girl."

I only laugh. He isn't wrong.

Memories resurge—nights spent pushing boundaries of ravaged farms, bonding over spilled lifeblood beneath the changing moon, but where I sought empowerment, they craved only spilling more. Our philosophies clashed, and I fled, realizing the darkness growing within me, mirroring Lexir's all-consuming madness. Now, full circle brings only grim resolution against the shadow of passion corrupted utterly. Tonight, justice's flame will purge all traces of infatuation once so fiercely held.

Steel arms heft, and I settle into an offensive stance, meeting old "friends" with flinty eyes holding no quarter. Magic surges defiant, fueled by my vows' unbending will against the horrors birthed from innocence ruined.

The larger charges with a bellow that shakes skeletal cages. I sidestep as flames engulf his frame.

His partner follows in berserker charge, spiked club arcing heavenward, only to freeze inches from my forehead. Pained eyes meet mine, finding no mercy as fingers clench. Bone cracks audibly, and he crumples, releasing his weapon for younger hands once molded by his own. My stare pierces steel casings, searing visages stained with cruelties inflicted when camaraderie meant something pure.

Exhaling slowly, I turn from ghosts now banished. My mind refocuses grim purpose, stirring flickers of hope amid nightmares seared too deeply ever to truly fade. For now, living souls remain trapped while the axe falls elsewhere, demanding swift mercy's release against horrors' creeping grip.

Yet, my attention keeps darting back to the main duel. Lexir moves with preternatural speed, deftly deflecting Asher's furious swings while lashing out with tendrils of flame from his palms. Asher's cloak is badly singed, but still, he presses the attack.

With a roar, Lexir unleashes a molten fireball toward Asher's face. At the last second, Asher twists away, the projectile exploding against a tree instead. In the same motion, Asher lunges forward and slices a deep gash across Lexir's thigh.

Howling in pain, Lexir stumbles back. I can see the fury blazing in his eyes from across the camp. He will not underestimate Asher again.

I long to aid Asher directly, but the endless waves of Lexir's men keep me occupied. After blasting two more aside, I risk a glance back to the duel. What I see makes my heart drop into my stomach.

Lexir has disarmed Asher and now has him pinned down, a flaming dagger at his throat. Even over the din, I hear Lexir growl, "Yield or die, princeling."

Asher will never surrender.

"No!"

The scream tears from my lips unbidden as I hurtle magic desperately at the man I once loved. It catches Lexir in the shoulder, spinning him away before the blow can land.

Asher's head jerks up at my shout. I think I see a flash of gratitude before Lexir presses the attack once more. Back and forth, they trade thunderous blows, though Asher now clearly favors his left leg. My heart drops into my stomach like a stone.

This time, there is no triumphant rally. Lexir batters aside Asher's weakening defenses until finally, terribly, he slips past Asher's guard entirely to bury his sword to the hilt in my beloved's gut.

Time fractures. Disbelief freezes me in place as Asher slides off the blade and topples forward, blood pooling beneath him.

Rage boils through me at the sight of my prince run through by Lexir's blade. Even as the hero's blood pools on the hard ground, fury overcomes my grief. I will make Lexir suffer for this unforgivable betrayal.

"You'll die screaming for this," I vow, magic already crackling at my fingertips.

Lexir blanches but quickly composes himself. "Come now, Lillith. We both know you won't kill me. You still love me deep down, despite this little hero fling of yours."

His arrogance fuels the tempest within me. He thinks our past will stay my hand, but his cruelty severed those bonds forever.

"You lost my love when you decided to become the most evil villain," I snarl.

He laughs. "Wasn't that your goal as well, Lillith?"

"Never. I want to become the most powerful. Make myself untouchable to the likes of you."

I unleash a devastating bolt of lightning, but Lexir deflects it barely in time. We sparred together for years. He can anticipate my moves to a degree most foes cannot, but he does not know the depths of agony he has awakened in me.

We trade blows that would level cities, the forest around us disintegrating from the collided forces, yet we both remain unscathed, our knowledge of the other's power perfectly balanced. I keep the most important thing to me—Asher—protected in his own little bubble of magic. Never again will I let Lexir touch anything I love.

I scream my grief and fury to the heavens, channeling it all into one final strike. The landscape warps and cracks beneath the sheer magical strength I summon.

Lexir's eyes widen in sudden fear. He raises his hands to counter, but my wrathful power smashes through his defenses like a tsunami. His body comes apart under the onslaught, shredded into nothingness.

Panting and trembling, I fall to my knees beside my beloved prince. Cradling his broken form, I weep bitterly over hopes forever lost and love found too late.

At least Lexir will never harm another soul. I have made certain of that in his last agonizing moments. Small consolation but vengeance nonetheless.

The storm within calms, concern finally conquering retribution.

"No, hang on, please..." I beg, tears streaming down my cheeks.

I press my palms over the gruesome wound, reaching for my power instinctively. This time, instead of wielding it as a destructive force, I focus solely on mending the ravaged flesh and restoring life.

My magic surges upward, but now, it feels subtly different—warmer, gentler. It flows through me into Asher's body, knitting together torn muscle and vessels, staunching the bleeding. I guide it tenderly, like threading a needle, no trace of fury or vengeance.

Under my palms, the ugly gash slowly closes, the skin smoothing over. It is delicate work. A small mistake could cost Asher's life if I rush or falter. I channel all my concentration into the delicate healing spell, brow furrowed with effort.

Drop by drop, the angry red of spilled blood fades as Asher's body is made whole once more. Yet, he lies lifeless, no breath stirring his chest. I pour ever more power into the spell, ignoring the weariness creeping into my limbs.

"Come back to me," I plead, wetting his pale cheeks with my tears.

Never has my magic felt so heavy and at the same time so right. For the first time, I am wielding it not to destroy but to create, to turn back death itself and coax new life from what has been broken.

Tears stream down my cheeks, falling on his skin as I clutch him close. I bend over him, shielding him and willing breath back into his lungs through hope alone.

At last, when I fear I can give no more, Asher's chest rises weakly.

Time crawls impossibly slow before finally, blessedly, he stirs weakly in my arms.

Relief sweeps through me. He will live.

I gather Asher's limp body in my arms, weeping with relief that his chest still rises and falls weakly. The healing spell has worked. He will live to see another dawn, though it has drained the last of my magic and strength.

But if I continue to be close to him, those from my world will never give him peace, and I can't guarantee that I will be there to save him again. I don't want to admit it, but I need to give him up to ensure that I don't entirely lose him.

With trembling limbs, I focus my will and somehow trace a teleportation spell through the air, picturing Asher's royal bedchambers. In a whirl of light, we leave the destruction behind and reappear within the palace walls.

Gently, I lay Asher atop the plush blankets of his canopied bed. His face seems more peaceful in sleep, the pained lines smoothed away.

I linger a moment, brushing a white strand of hair from his forehead. He is safe now, far from the bloodshed in the woods. Perhaps in time he can forgive me for bringing such violence to his doorstep.

A soft gasp draws my attention to the doorway, where the head maid Mrs. Umbernuckle stands, staring wide-eyed between myself and the unconscious prince.

"You..." she breathes. "What did you do?"

I hold up my hands pleadingly. "No evil, I swear it. Asher was wounded fighting Lexir Crow. Lexir was defeated, but Asher almost didn't make it. Please, he needs rest and care to recover."

Mrs. Umbernuckle's eyes only narrow further. "You expect me to believe you did not cause his injuries yourself? I know who you are, Lillith," she hisses. "I warned His Highness against trusting you. See the ruin you have brought upon him!"

Her accusations sting, but I can hardly blame her wariness. As villains, we aren't known for being understanding and patient with others.

"Believe what you will," I say wearily, "but he clings to life by a thread. I beg you, put aside your doubts and help him heal. For his sake."

The maid's face remains hard, unmoved. "Leave before I put you in a worse state than you brought him. He isn't awake to be able to protect you from me."

My heart cracks. I cannot force her to aid Asher nor linger here myself much longer without risking more lives. Perhaps it is better this way. Asher deserves to recover surrounded only by those loyal to him, not someone who only knows how to destroy everything she touches.

Blinking back tears, I bend to press one last kiss to Asher's brow, smoothing back his hair. "Recover your strength," I whisper. "When you wake, know that I will always watch over you, even from afar."

Rising slowly, I turn my gaze back to Mrs. Umbernuckle's flinty stare.

"Heal him well," I command, letting steel enter my voice, "or you will discover powers darker than you can fathom. Asher's welfare is now in your hands."

I let malice flash across my face, if only for a second, to ensure she understands the warning is no idle threat. Then, I dissolve into shadows, disappearing from the palace.

My magic carries me back to my home in the mountains. Tears spill down my cheeks. Each step away feels like leaving a piece of my heart behind, but this is the only way. Asher deserves a life of light after the darkness I have brought down upon him, a life free of the enemies forever hounding my steps.

Perhaps one day, when redemption no longer feels so far off, our paths will cross again beneath the sun's gracious light.

Collapsing beneath a broad oak, I weep freely, letting grief pour out until no more tears remain. I cry for the injured man I love, the redemption just out of reach, and the future we might have shared in a gentler world.

33

Asher

I drift slowly back to consciousness, my mind fogged with confusion. As awareness returns, so does the deep ache throbbing through my body. I blink open bleary eyes and find myself staring up at the familiar carved wood canopy of my bedchamber. How have I gotten here? The last thing I remember is...

The battle. Lexir's dagger plunging toward me. Searing pain as the blade pierces my gut.

My breath quickens as fragmented memories flash through my mind. The clash of steel, the sting of Lexir's fire magic, the crimson soak of blood on the forest leaves. Surely a wound so grave should have killed me. Am I in the afterlife then?

With a soft groan, I try to rise, only for the ache in my stomach to flare sharply at the movement. No, not dead then, unless the heavens are far more painful than promised.

Gingerly, I lift my head just enough to examine my torso under the blankets. Beneath my nightshirt, thick bandages are wrapped tightly around my abdomen. The blood has been cleaned away, the mortal gash now only a traumatic memory.

I collapse back against the pillows, exhausted even from that small effort, but my mind still churns in bewilderment. However I have survived, surely more than just medicine has healed me. Magic has been at work here.

"Lillith," I croak out hoarsely.

She had been there, fighting alongside me. The last image in my mind is of her stricken face over me as darkness took me. Did she somehow bring me back from death's door with her power? Where is she now?

Hurried footsteps approach from the hallway outside. The bedchamber door bursts open to reveal Mrs. Umbernuckle, my head maid, her face creased with concern.

"Your Highness!" she cries, rushing to my bedside. "Thank the stars you've awakened at last!"

"How... How long?" I rasp out through parched lips.

My maid quickly fetches a goblet of water from my bedside table and helps prop me up just enough to sip at it.

"Nearly two days since that wicked woman dropped you off here half dead," Mrs. Umbernuckle says, wringing her hands. "We all feared the worst when she carried you in covered in blood, pale as a ghost!"

My thoughts snap back into focus at the mention of a mysterious woman. "It was Lillith, wasn't it?" I demand hoarsely. "The one who brought me here. Did she say where she went?"

Mrs. Umbernuckle's face creases further with disapproval. "Indeed, the dark enchantress herself," she confirms with a cluck of her tongue. "Slunk off before the guards could seize her after leaving you at death's door. You're fortunate to have escaped her clutches alive."

I shake my head impatiently before the motion makes my temples pound. "You don't understand what happened. She's not who you think she is. She saved me. Brought me back from death's gate."

My insistence only deepens my maid's frown. "Your loyalty is admirable, sire, but is misplaced. That woman has bewitched far stronger minds than yours before." She smooths the bedcovers needlessly, avoiding my gaze. "I hope, when you are well, you will see reason and let her go."

Frustration simmers in my chest. I hoped Mrs. Umbernuckle would look beyond her prejudices at last and see Lillith's true heart, but if even near death in her arms does not convince the woman, nothing will.

"The mistake was mine for bringing her in the first place," I say grimly. "I must find her, ensure she wasn't harmed escaping."

I make again to rise, only to fall back with a choked gasp as the ache in my body flares anew.

Clucking reprovingly, Mrs. Umbernuckle gently presses me back against the pillows. "You must rest now, my lord. Regain your strength before chasing after phantoms." Her voice drops, almost to a plea. "I beg you, for the sake of your people who need you, let this obsession with the woman fade. She will only bring you more suffering."

My jaw tightens obstinately. "I will rest," I acquiesce. The truth is I can do little else in my weakened state. "But I will find her again once I am able. She did not abandon me freely. I know it."

Perhaps seeing the resolve in my eyes, Mrs. Umbernuckle sighs but says no more, smoothing the covers over me. My mind drifts as she quietly tends to me, lulling me back to much-needed sleep.

Before slumber claims me fully, I swear a silent oath. As soon as I am able, I will seek out Lillith once more. The depth of my care for her frightens the old maid, I know. She fears what vulnerability it brings me, but Lillith has proven herself true in the end. She deserves my trust. The shadows of her past cannot change who she is now—a woman capable of profound light when she so chooses.

Whatever her reasons for fleeing, I am certain she has not abandoned me completely. Lillith would not simply leave me to die, not after striving so hard to save me from death's grasp. No, some other force must have driven her away after that battle.

I have to ensure she is safe and help protect her from the shadows that no doubt hunt her still for the choice she made. Until I can hold her again, I will put my faith in the goodness she has shown and the love we share. She has saved my life. Now, I must do the same for her.

***

The bedchamber doors suddenly crash open. I jolt awake, disoriented, as rough hands grab me and start dragging me out of bed.

"What's happening?" I cry out.

I struggle to resist as my foggy mind tries to make sense of it, but I am still weak as a kitten from my injuries. I can't break their grip as they haul me to my feet.

They are royal guards, their faces like stone as they flank me on both sides. Without a word, they start marching me toward the doors.

"Unhand me!" I shout, digging in my heels.

They are unmoved, their pace unrelenting. As they force me stumbling through the manor halls, shock slowly turns to dread. The staff peers out of their rooms, faces drained of color at the sight of my being manhandled like a criminal.

"Someone tell me what this is about!" I demand, craning my head around.

The guards stare straight ahead in silence.

"Sir?" Mrs. Umbernuckle asks as she begins to follow the procession.

"Stay here!" I yell back as they drag me down the steps. "No one is to do anything. Do you understand?"

"Yes. I will make sure myself."

It isn't until they drag me outside into the crisp night air that I see our destination. A royal prison carriage waits, torchlight flickering ominously off its black iron bars.

"You can't do this! I'm a prince!" I yell hoarsely as they bring me to the carriage door.

One guard finally meets my eyes, his gaze cold as winter. "You lost that right when you betrayed your duty and harbored the kingdom's enemies."

Their words wound me almost as much as my being flung into the barred compartment. The door clangs shut with a note of chilling finality, sealing my fate. I am ruined.

This is about the villains I secretly spared instead of killing as ordered, the ones I tried to rehabilitate to lives of good. My deception has been discovered somehow.

Fury and fear war within me as my prison begins to roll.

The carriage rolls swiftly through the night, carrying me farther from my home with each turn of the wheels. I sit slumped on the narrow bench watching the moonlit countryside pass by through the small barred window.

My initial shock and outrage have faded, leaving me hollow inside. I know with grim certainty where this midnight journey ends—the royal palace dungeons. Once behind those sunless stone walls, I will likely never again see the sun.

I should have expected this reckoning eventually. I knew the risk I took by concealing the villains I'd shown mercy. It was a risk I accepted gladly, believing that saving lives mattered more than blind obedience.

Perhaps that belief has been my downfall. I always trusted that redemption is possible for even the worst souls, if given the chance. My heart saw the humanity haunting their eyes, and I could not end them when it would be snuffed out forever.

Yet, despite my good intentions, here I sit in chains. I ruined myself and likely condemned the very souls I tried to save. Perhaps I had been naive to think I could deceive the crown and succeed where generations of "heroes" had failed.

My thoughts turn to Lillith. Our time together had been fleeting, yet she sparked a change in me and showed me the world is not as clear as I thought. In her eyes, I glimpsed the woman she might become.

Yet even now, staring into the darkness of my own future, I cannot make myself regret the choice I've made. Better to fall knowing I stayed true to my conscience than rise upon so many unjust deaths.

The carriage wheels echo beneath me as we cross a bridge into the city. I gaze out at the torch-lit streets I once patrolled proudly as a champion of the realm. It cuts deeply to now pass through them as a condemned prisoner.

At last, the gilded spires of the palace come into view. My pulse quickens despite my efforts to steady it. I will not cower or beg before my accusers no matter what awaits me within those walls. I will speak the truth and accept my fate with dignity.

The carriage descends through a stone archway into the palace undercroft then lurches to a halt. The door is flung open, and guards grab me roughly, their torchlight blinding after the darkness. I wince as my half-healed wounds protest the rough handling.

Wordlessly, they march me through a maze of damp corridors, each step taking me farther from light and life. The fetid chill of the place seeps into my bones. So this will be my tomb.

We reach the deepest dungeons, reserved for the worst offenders. With callous indifference, the guards hurl me into a lightless cell barely large enough for me to lie down in. I stumble but catch myself against the cold stone wall as the door clangs shut behind me.

For a moment, I can only stand here, breaths coming raggedly as I stare at the rust-barred door that seals my fate. The guards' footsteps echo away, leaving me in absolute darkness. I am utterly alone now, with only my thoughts for company.

Slowly, I sink down onto the pile of filthy straw that is to be my bed. I bury my head in my hands, the full weight of despair threatening to crush me. Is this to be the unjust end of my quest to show mercy over malice?

I grind my fists into my eyes until colors burst across the darkness. No. I cannot—will not—regret the choice I made though it brings me here. I walked the honest path, followed the whisperings of my heart. That knowledge must sustain me now.

I believed redemption was possible for anyone and was willing to risk all to grant that chance. Whatever comes next, they can imprison my body but not my unconquered spirit.

I will face my accusers with courage and accept my fate with head held high.

Let them cast me as a criminal, a cautionary tale. I know the truth in my heart. I chose the just path, though it was harder. Perhaps someday, actions of goodness will speak louder than any lies told against me. Justice will prevail.

Until that day, I will not waver in my beliefs. My chance will come to finish my mission, to reveal the deceptions told against me and those I tried to save. I only pray the price will not be more innocent lives.

This is my burden to bear, and I will not falter.

PRINCE ASHER ARRESTED ON CHARGES OF TREASON

By Sir Justice Jabs

THE KINGDOM WAS ROCKED THIS WEEK BY THE SHOCKING ARREST OF PRINCE ASHER ON ALLEGATIONS OF TREASON AND CONSPIRING WITH VILLAINOUS ENEMIES OF THE CROWN.

GUARDS DESCENDED ON THE PRINCE'S ESTATE IN THE DEAD OF NIGHT, DRAGGING HIS HIGHNESS AWAY IN CHAINS TO THE CAPITAL. HE NOW AWAITS TRIAL IN THE PALACE DUNGEONS.

THE CHARGES CLAIM PRINCE ASHER KNOWINGLY HARBORED AND ALIGNED WITH VILLAINS, DECEIVING BOTH THE KING AND THE HEROIC ORDER DEDICATED TO VANQUISHING EVIL. IF CONVICTED, HE COULD FACE EXECUTION. EVIDENCE SHOWS THE PRINCE LIED

FOR YEARS ABOUT CARRYING OUT RIGHTEOUS EX-ECUTIONS, INSTEAD KEEPING DANGEROUS CRIMI-NALS ALIVE IN SECRET AND ALLOWING THEM TO AC-CUMULATE POWER.

"I LAMENT MY SON'S TREASONOUS BETRAYAL," THE KING SAID IN A STATEMENT. "THOUGH IT PAINS ME, JUSTICE DEMANDS HE PAY THE PRICE IF PROVEN GUILTY BEYOND DOUBT."

PRINCE ASHER'S CONTROVERSIAL PAST ACTIONS HAVE LONG RAISED SUSPICIONS THAT HE SYMPA-THIZES TOO READILY WITH VILLAINS. DESPITE BE-ING THE KINGDOM'S CHAMPION, HE HAS AVOID-ED DIRECTLY CONFRONTING THREATS ON MULTIPLE OCCASIONS WHEN EXPECTED, BUT NONE SUSPECT-ED THE EXTENT OF HIS DECEPTION UNTIL GUARDS APPREHENDED A SUPPOSEDLY SLAIN VILLAIN HID-ING RIGHT UNDER THE PRINCE'S ROOF. THIS DIS-COVERY HAS SHATTERED TRUST IN THE ACCUSED'S PROCLAIMED MOTIVES.

"HE SWORE OATHS TO PROTECT THIS REALM FROM WICKEDNESS," LORD GREGOR, HEAD OF THE HEROIC ORDER, SAID. "TO THINK OUR PRINCE WOULD SPIT UPON THOSE SACRED VOWS AND CON-SPIRE WITH MONSTERS LEAVES ME ILL."

WHILE PRINCE ASHER HAS EARNED DEVOTION THROUGH PAST HEROICS, MANY NOW FEEL DEEPLY BETRAYED BY HIS ALLEGED DOUBLE LIFE. THOSE

WHO PRAISED HIS MERCY TOWARD VILLAINS HAVE CHANGED THEIR TUNE SWIFTLY.

"I SAW HIM SHOW KINDNESS TO THE FOULEST OF PRISONERS," BRANTON, AN EX-SOLDIER, SAID. "AT THE TIME, I THOUGHT IT COMPASSION, BUT NOW I KNOW. HE WAS SIMPLY HELPING HIS ALLIES."

IF THE SHOCKING ALLEGATIONS PROVE FACTUAL, IT WOULD MEAN THE PRINCE UNDERMINED KINGDOM SECURITY FOR YEARS WHILE PRETENDING TO CHAMPION ITS PEOPLE. SUCH TREACHERY FROM ONE SO REVERED HAS LEFT CITIZENS REELING.

THE KING HAS CALLED UPON ALL TRUE HEROES TO TESTIFY AGAINST PRINCE ASHER'S MISDEEDS AT TRIAL. "THOUGH MY HEART GRIEVES, JUSTICE MUST BE SERVED," THE KING PROCLAIMED GRAVELY. "NONE CAN STAND ABOVE THE LAW, EVEN MY OWN BLOOD."

WHILE THE PRINCE AWAITS HIS RECKONING, THE PALACE HAS INCREASED SECURITY TENFOLD. CHECKPOINTS SCRUTINIZE ALL VISITORS TO PREVENT CONSPIRATORS FROM REACHING THE ACCUSED TRAITOR AS HE ROTS IN THE DUNGEONS BELOW. PRINCE ASHER'S ALLEGED BETRAYAL REMAINS FRESH AGONY FOR A KINGDOM THAT REVERED HIM. THE JUSTICE SYSTEM WILL RUN ITS COURSE, UNHINDERED BY SENTIMENTALITY.

IF GUILTY, THE DISGRACED ROYAL WILL PAY THE ULTIMATE PRICE FOR CONSPIRING WITH VILLAINY.

Hɪs legacy will stand not as heroism but the dangers of mercy taken to reckless extremes. Let his fate serve as a cautionary tale. The wicked cannot be reasoned with, only eliminated for the greater good. The king's justice comes for all equally under the law's harsh but fair light. None are exempt.

34

Lillith

Brumble nuzzles against my side, his warmth comforting as we sit curled up in the library of my hidden mountain castle. My fingers idly stroke his leathery ears while my gaze remains fixed on the flickering flames in the fireplace. Their soothing dance does little to calm the storm raging within me.

My heart feels shattered, torn the moment I left Asher in his bedchamber. I had to leave him, yet each step felt like walking on shards of glass.

I console myself that at least he will live. The spell's magic would've continued to knit his body back together in my absence. Mrs. Umbernuckle would ensure that the healing would continue if anything went wrong. He will return safely behind palace walls and, in time, forget this strange encounter with an infamous villainess. My reputation will keep him from seeking me out again. He will be safe.

But such hollow reassurances bring me no peace. I yearn to see his smile once more, hear him call me by name in that tender tone that pierces my tattered soul. No one ever looked upon me as he had. Usually, it was as if I would destroy them and everything they cared for. But not Asher. I dared to reveal my true self to him, and he met me not with disgust but wonder.

Now, I sit alone but for Brumble, my only friend in these isolated walls of stone and magic. My existence had returned to how it was before—roaming empty halls, talking only to fire and books—yet now, it feels so much colder. I tasted sunlight's warmth upon my skin, but that has been snuffed out.

Brumble nestles closer against me, his wide eyes brimming with concern. Asher is the only one who knows the full truth of who I am beneath the fearsome legend. Without him, I will again bear my secrets alone. That dark thought hollows me like wind whistling through a cavern.

Restless energy tingles through my veins. I need to escape these stifling walls, if only briefly, to walk beneath open skies and fill my lungs with crisp night air untainted by dust and sorrow.

"Come, Brumble," I say, rising to my feet. "Let's stretch our legs."

The little creature's eyes light up eagerly, and he grasps my outstretched hand. I weave the spell to transform our appearance, his large bat-like ears becoming small and rounded, rugged green skin smoothed to a rosy complexion. My wild dark tresses are wrapped neatly beneath a modest bonnet, the plain cloak concealing my elegant black gown. We seem peasant women now, harmless and unremarkable.

Another flick of magic whisks us from the hidden castle. We emerge atop a secluded mountain pass overlooking a humble village in the valley below. Its windows glow warm with hearth fires, smoke twining lazily up into the night sky.

I inhale deeply, conjuring an image of Asher safe in his own halls. Perhaps he, too, now gazes out at this same moon, its light bathing us both in a gentle veil. Foolish fancy but it eases the ache of our parting nonetheless.

"Come along," I murmur to Brumble, picking my way carefully down the steep winding trail.

He follows dutifully, eyes round with curiosity about these dwellings of men. I also feel strangely drawn to walk among them, if only as a ghost, to pretend, just for a moment, that I belong beneath the same sky.

We pause at the village outskirts, watching peasants laugh and chat on their way home or to the tavern. None give us more than a passing glance. After all, we're just two ladies out for an evening stroll, bracing against the night's chill.

My steps slow as we pass the village message board in the square. Normally, I completely ignore it, but tonight, my gaze catches on a vivid poster pinned front and center.

A portrait of a handsome, familiar visage stares out at me. Prince Asher. My breath stalls at the sight of his rakish grin. How I miss him already, with a longing that startles me.

Then, my eyes drop to the words below the portrait, and dread seizes my heart with icy claws.

PRINCE ASHER, CHAMPION OF THE REALM, CONDEMNED TO DEATH FOR TREASONOUS CRIMES

No. It can't be, but the poster spells out in bold lettering the date set for Asher's execution by beheading.

Today.

My pulse roars in my ears. How could he go from lauded prince and hero of the kingdom to condemned traitor?

I read on in disbelief as the charges are listed—harboring villains, disregard of duty, failure to carry out righteous executions.

Sudden understanding pierces me cruelly. He knows exactly who the villains are working in his home. He put them there to protect them and spread the rumor of their deaths. He really is a hero and not just for the supposed good guys.

Around me, villagers studying the poster cluck their tongues and shake their heads.

"Shameful business, that."

"Thought him a hero, but he's just another coward unwilling to get blood on 'is hands."

"Good riddance. Any man who coddles monsters deserves the axe, prince or not."

Their callous words ignite sparks of fury within me, even as shame floods my veins. I misjudged him and left him to this doom because I feared others would go after him to get to me. I thought I spared him further pain, but instead, I abandoned him to the wolves.

I want to tear the vile poster down and set this entire rotten village ablaze, but I cannot reveal myself now when Asher needs me most.

My turbulent thoughts churn as Brumble leans against my leg.

A gnarled hand squeezes my shoulder, jolting me from despair's claws. "A tragedy indeed, eh?" rasps a familiar voice.

I turn to find Mrs. Umbernuckle regarding me keenly beneath her hood, eyes swimming with sympathy and concern.

Before I can reply, she takes my arm gently. "Walk with me. We have much to discuss, you and I."

Her kind tone leaves no room for refusal.

As we amble from the square, she peers at me sidelong like a mother seeking truth from a daughter. "No need for tricks now, girl. I know who you are, Lillith."

I start. "How?"

She chuckles lightly. "The prince was asking for you when he woke up. I had my suspicions, but I admit you kept your secret well. That's not why I'm here, though. You are going to get him out, right?"

My heart clenches as I imagine his grief.

Mrs. Umbernuckle eyes me deeply. "He's been asking for you. I've never seen him care for another in the way he does you. While he's forbidden any of the villains working under him from saving him, you are not part of that command."

I hang my head, tears threatening to fall. "I thought to spare further pain. Instead, I doomed him by leaving."

Her palm squeezes mine fondly. "Then make things right! You're the most powerful villain in three kingdoms. Act like it."

Her earnest eyes renew my weary soul's flame. I will not abandon him again to face the executioner alone.

A smile spreads across my face. "That's the plan."

With that, I sweep Brumble into my arms and disappear in a whirl of magic. Brumble pats my arm anxiously, his eyes pools of concern as we reappear back in my home, his concealment gone.

"I need for you to stay here," I murmur, caressing his wrinkled head. "I can't let him die, and I don't want you to get caught up in the fight."

Pacing restlessly before the fire, I rack my mind for anything that can save Asher. A daring rescue would be suicide with the palace doubtless on high alert, but perhaps stealth and cunning can succeed where brute force is doomed to fail.

My eyes land on the towering bookshelves lining the library walls. Yes, there lies the solution. Within these pages dwell ancient magics long forgotten to mortal minds. While everyone has magic, some things require particular movements or focus to work correctly. I need only refresh my memory.

Frantically, I begin pulling down heavy leather tomes, sending up plumes of dust. I require something that will immobilize most of the people there. While I have more power at my fingertips than most people could dream of, I can still be overpowered by sheer numbers, and in the king's castle I will undoubtedly be outnumbered. If I don't do it exactly right, this spell won't hold as many people as I need, only those nearest me.

My mind wanders to Asher for a moment. How is he holding up? He can't be fully healed yet, and I doubt his health is at the top of his father's list since he condemned his son to death. I will not fail my prince again.

Brumble brings me text after ancient text as I seek just the right enchantments. I am so absorbed I nearly miss his small hand tugging at my sleeve until he does so more insistently.

"What is it?" I ask gently.

He points to a faded page in a book left open on a table. Leaning closer, I see it describes magics that can temporarily alter one's appearance only for those who you wish. This could let me do this without being recognized by anyone other than the prince.

"Brumble, you clever thing!" I cry, sweeping him up into an embrace.

The little fellow grins, nuzzling against me happily that he can help.

I set Brumble down gently then flip back through the book, committing the spell to memory. This magic is too powerful for a sustained spell, but it should serve well enough for a mission that I intend to take only a few minutes.

I kneel so my eyes are level with Brumble's own orb-like gaze. "I must go before it's too late," I explain, "but I promise we'll be together again soon, my friend."

He mewls softly in understanding then waves his little hand encouragingly. My heart swells with gratitude, and I pull him close, blinking back tears. Then, I steel myself and repeat the spell from memory. My raven hair turns to a fiery red, my skin ages and I feel myself stretch a bit.

With a final pat on Brumble's head, I whisper the teleportation spell and brace myself as magic tugs me across the void. The soaring castle library is replaced in a blink by a bustling crowd that nearly knocks me over. Steadying myself, I stare around in wonder at the colorful chaos of the packed market square. My isolated tower feels a world away from this sunlit revelry.

For a moment, I stand frozen, overwhelmed by the sights and noises. Then, a passing crier's bellow about Prince Asher's execution shatters my paralysis.

Lifting my chin, I square my shoulders and make my way forward.

Joining the somber queue, I file into the great hall behind a trickle of peasants being granted entry to witness the trial. My nerves thrum beneath my illusion spell as we are directed to the public gallery overlooking the expansive chamber. I have to get closer to Asher but dare not break from the passive herd yet.

The cavernous space echoes with low murmurs, the air thick with tension and incense. My gaze fixes on the far end upon a raised dais where two ornate thrones stand. The king has not yet arrived, but soon, he will sit there in judgment over his son. The thought sparks flames within my chest.

Beneath the shadowed dais is a simple wooden platform draped in black. A bloodstained stump awaits, executioner's blade glinting cruelly beside it. Bile rises in my throat at such a cold, indifferent end prepared for my dear Asher. How can these people possibly claim to be good when this is the type of thing they find acceptable?

A shoulder bumps into me, and I jump.

"I thought I would find you here."

To my surprise, Silviana stands beside me, the hood of her cloak hiding most of her face.

"Oh?" I murmur.

"I knew you wouldn't let him die. I saw the way you two looked at each other in the arena."

I don't dare look at her directly. Instead, I keep an eye on the rest of the crowd and lower my voice. How could she recognize me? My first instinct is to tell her to leave, but if she can see me as myself a small part of me must want her by my side. To have the help I so rarely ask for. "I'm sorry I didn't tell you."

"No worries. I understand why. I'm here now, though, so what's the plan? You're not doing this alone."

"Freeze everyone that I can and rampage."

Silviana snorts. "You're serious? That's the plan?"

"Did I mention the word everyone? I'll be fine."

"I'm sure you will be until they start to break free of the spell. I will be your backup and try to take care of people as they break free so you can get your prince out of here. Deal?"

"Deal."

A fanfare of horns announces the king's arrival, the grave notes trumpeted by heralds on the balcony above. The king sweeps into the hall, ermine-lined robes trailing behind him. The crowd bows low, myself reluctantly with them. I peek through my lashes as he takes his seat upon the throne. His stony gaze holds no hint of paternal warmth for the accused traitor. His son he might be, yet today, he will die the same.

The horns sound again, and a side door is flung open. Flanked by armored guards, Asher is led stumbling into the chamber. I suck in a sharp breath at the sight of him—face pale and drawn, rakish stubble covering his strong jaw. He appears even thinner than expected, the toll of weeks imprisoned clear, but strength still radiates from him as he holds his head high, defiance flashing in his sea-foam eyes. The shackles at his wrists cannot contain his indomitable spirit.

He is forced to kneel before the dais, an attendant reading out a lengthy list of his alleged crimes as Asher gazes calmly up at his sire. I yearn to run to him then, crush him close, and spirit him away from this horrific farce, but I hold myself taut, watching... waiting.

"Prince Asher, you have been found guilty of treason and sentenced to die this day," the king pronounces once the charges conclude. His voice echoes coldly off the stones. "Do you deny these crimes or repent your actions against the crown?"

A tense hush falls over the hall.

Asher lifts his battered but unbowed head and addresses his father and king. "I deny nothing and repent even less," he declares firmly. "I accept the price for my choices but will never recant my effort to show mercy over malice.

There are yet glimmers of light if we but strive to find them."

Shaken murmurs greet this bold response, but his father's face only hardens to flint. With a curt nod, he gestures the executioner forward.

My pulse roars as the hulking man strides up to the platform, double-bladed axe glinting ominously. This cannot come to pass!

I begin weaving magic swiftly between my fingers but keep it muted for now. A few moments more...

Asher is forced down, his neck positioned over the scarred stump. The entire hall holds its breath. The executioner raises his axe high, his muscles bulging.

Now!

I whisper a word and unleash my spell. Silvery light ripples out in a wave from my hands raised high. Time slows as my magic takes hold, the executioner's axe suspended mid-swing.

I rush onto the dais amidst the frozen forms of the king, prince, and executioner. All attempts at hiding are gone. I am only Lillith now.

My hands tremble in combined relief and fury as I gently lift Asher's head from that dreadful block. His sea-glass eyes blink up at me in wonder. He's unaffected by my spell.

"Lillith?" he rasps out. "You came for me?"

"Of course I did. Now hush," I murmur, smoothing back his hair with quaking fingers. "Let's get you free of this place."

With a wave of my hand, I sever his chains, then help him rise on unsteady feet. He leans heavily against me, still shaken.

"I thought you were gone," he says hoarsely. "You shouldn't be here. It's not safe."

I shake my head, shame and joy warring within me. "Anyone who stands in my way isn't safe."

As I turn to usher Asher from the dais, warning prickles dance across my skin. My spell has affected most of the hall's occupants, but something still stirs. I glance around warily just as yelling erupts from the gallery.

"Watch out!" I yell as Sylviana's beasts begin to materialize around me.

Gorgons, hippogriffs, and chimera materialize, fixing the guards in place with their hypnotic gazes. I stand calmly amid the monsters, silvery wings extending from my back.

A handful of royal guards are fighting against the paralyzing magic, their movements slowed as if underwater, but they're gradually regaining control. One has drawn his sword and is struggling toward the dais in jerky steps. More will surely follow.

Cursing under my breath, I swiftly draw Asher behind me. "Stay close," I warn.

We retreat until our backs hit the cold stone wall. The freed guard lumbers ever nearer, his blade finally swinging freely. He barks something unintelligible, spit flying from his lips.

I raise my hands, magic sparking at my fingertips, but I hesitate to strike. Killing the king's men will make us irredeemable outlaws. Perhaps I can instead immobilize him…

My moment of indecision costs me. With surprising speed, the guard surges forward and swings his sword at my head. I throw up a hasty shield, the blade rebounding off it with a flash of light. The force of the blow sends me staggering back into Asher.

From the corner of my eye, I see more guards breaking free, lumbering onto the dais with weapons drawn. We are out of time.

Silviana gracefully descends onto the dais, pointing at the men. Her beasts rush forward with supernatural speed, knocking the guards aside with claws and wings. Their screams echo through the chamber.

With a growled curse, I unleash a bolt of purple energy at the attacking guard. It strikes him square in the chest, flinging him halfway across the hall where he crumples, unmoving. Dark magic but needs must.

I turn swiftly, ready to attack the other guards, but they hesitate now, staring wide-eyed at their fallen comrade.

Their courage is fleeting without the king to command them.

"Stand down if you wish to see tomorrow!" I warn, magic flaring.

To my surprise and relief, they lower their weapons, cowed by my display of power.

I seize the advantage and grab Asher's wrist, pulling him toward the steps. We have to flee this cursed place before the spell breaks entirely.

But our path is suddenly blocked by an imposing figure. The king himself, face mottled with rage, fights against my magic. Of course, one of true royal blood would resist longer than his guards. His hand creeps toward the jeweled pommel of his sword, inch by strained inch.

Cold purpose floods my veins. I cannot allow him to raise that blade against us.

Asher's breath catches as he realizes my intent. "No, Lillith!" he cries, seizing my wrist. "He is still my father!"

I meet his beseeching eyes steadily. "He means to kill us both. He gave you no choice. I will not let him harm you again."

With that, I tear my hand from Asher's grasp and stride to meet his sire. The king's visage contorts, paralyzed muscles straining as he battles my spell. His eyes convey the depth of his hatred and fury.

Halting before him, I raise my palm, magic swirling. "For the sake of the son you betrayed, I will make this quick."

Dark lightning erupts from my hand, engulfing the king. There is a terrible roar... then silence. What remains of him collapses boneless to the floor, smoke rising from his charred finery. The tyrant who condemned his own blood is no more.

I stand over the corpse, breathing hard. A part of me relishes having felled the monster who brought such suffering to Asher and countless others, but a larger part grieves that it has come to such bloody vengeance.

A strangled gasp breaks my dark reverie. The executioner! In the fray, I nearly forgot about him.

I whirl to find the brawny man mobile once more, axe raised high to cleave me in two.

Desperately, I throw up my hands. A lethal spell will take too long.

But the expected bite of the blade never comes. Instead, the executioner's bearded face registers only shock before he topples stiffly to the side like a felled oak.

My mouth falls open as I see the jeweled hilt of King Adinar's sword jutting from the man's chest.

I turn to see Asher standing unsteadily behind the corpse, his expression tormented. He took the sword from his father's body before the executioner could strike.

"Asher," I begin softly, heart wrenching at his anguish, but further words flee as the spell breaks entirely in a violent rush.

Chaos erupts in the hall. Guards surge toward us as the crowd screams, only now grasping what has transpired. We are out of time.

I run to Asher, pulling him close. Before the guards can reach us, I summon my power and picture my sanctuary, wrapping us in magic.

The great hall blurs into streaming shadows and light, reforming swiftly into blessedly familiar surroundings. My library materializes around us, and I sink to my knees on the carpet, weak from exertion and relief.

We have made it. We are home.

I glance up to share the triumphant realization with Asher, but my elation dims at the shell-shocked grief haunting his eyes.

Of course. I callously slew his father before him, no matter how deserved. What demons must now torment his noble heart? I acted in haste, failing to foresee the damage left in my wake.

Rising on still-unsteady feet, I go to Asher, gently taking his hands in mine. His gaze remains distant, lost in sorrow and memories.

"I'm sorry."

A single tear rolls down his cheek. "I know it's for the best. Things couldn't change if he wasn't gone, but he was still my father."

I hold him close, understanding exactly how he feels. While my own parents have never shown me parental love, I, too, would feel their loss. I wish I could take away his pain for now, but I feel powerless, an unusual feeling for me. All I can do is be here for the person I love, never abandon him again, and wait and see what our future holds together.

35

Lillith

I stroll leisurely through the palace gardens, Asher's hand clasped in mine. After the events of the past weeks, it feels surreal to simply relax beneath blue skies untroubled by turmoil. A gentle breeze stirs the neatly trimmed hedges and wafts the sweet scent of blooming flowers. For the first time in forever, it seems peace is within my grasp.

Asher gives my hand a gentle squeeze, as if sensing my thoughts. I turn to find him gazing at me, sea-glass eyes soft with contentment. Though faint scars still mark his face, the haunted shadow that lingers after his imprisonment has finally begun to lift, allowing his natural optimism to shine through once more.

"What's on your mind?" he asks.

I smile. "Nothing much. Just how happy I am."

He chuckles knowingly but does not press me.

We continue along the gracefully curving path in a comfortable silence. I struggle to suppress a laugh as we pass a familiar heart-shaped bush. I can very clearly remember exactly how it looked with a certain someone's pair of underwear draped over it.

My thoughts drift ahead to the future. With Asher's brother newly crowned, long overdue reforms are coming to the kingdom. New ideas are being presented to help those who want to leave a life of crime behind. There is, of course, prejudice to overcome, but the first small steps appear to finally be happening.

The tranquil moment is broken by approaching footsteps accompanied by the rustling of skirts. I tense instinctively before forcing myself to relax. Whatever awaits, I need not face it alone anymore.

To my surprise, the newcomer is Mrs. Umbernuckle, emerging from an arched trellis covered in twining roses. I frown guardedly, memories of our past clashes still vivid, but rather than her usual stern expression, the matronly housekeeper looks oddly hesitant, twisting a handkerchief between her hands.

"Pardon my intrusion, miss... I mean, Lillith," she begins.

I raise a quizzical eyebrow at the use of my true name. "Yes?"

Mrs. Umbernuckle draws in a steadying breath. "I wish to speak with you. To apologize for the assumptions I made about your character." She flushes slightly. "Seeing how you risked all to rescue Prince Asher made me realize you are more than the name you've created for yourself. I hope you can forgive this stubborn old woman for misjudging you so terribly."

I study her uncertain face and sense her sincerity. Asher gives my hand a reassuring squeeze. After a moment's thought, I incline my head graciously.

"You had reason for doubt based on my reputation," I reply. "Your change of heart now is apology enough."

Mrs. Umbernuckle's expression floods with relief, and she takes my free hand between both of hers. "You are too kind! Please, let us put the past behind us for good." Glancing between Asher and me, she adds brightly, "In fact, would you do me the honor of taking tea together here in the gardens? I prepared some cakes earlier, and it's too fine a day to waste indoors!"

I smile, moved by her gesture of friendship. "That sounds perfect."

Soon, we are seated at a metal table engraved with vines, a matching umbrella shading us from the mellow sun. The tea is delicately fragrant, the cakes light and moist. Birds chirp merrily in the hedges around us. Despite our rocky history, I feel utterly at peace.

Between bites, Asher speaks animatedly of his older brother's coronation and plans to reform unjust laws targeting magic users.

Mrs. Umbernuckle sets down her teacup, gazing at the dregs pensively. "Long overdue changes," she remarks.

I study her thoughtful face, feeling a new kinship with this woman who has also been forced to conceal her talents. "I suspect you and I are not so different, Mrs. Umbernuckle," I muse. "Both judged harshly for our uncommon gifts."

Her expression turns sympathetic. "Indeed. I should have extended a hand in shared understanding, not suspicion."

Asher leans forward eagerly. "Just think of all we can build now that we are freed from outdated constraints! For instance, I envision a school where those of all magical bloodlines can gather to develop their talents in community without stigma."

My heart swells at his infectious optimism. "A place of belonging for outcasts. What a truly visionary idea!"

A throat clears from a bush nearby. "That's a most innovative concept," Rendfield remarks as he approaches with a tray of cookies. "I aim to support all progress under this new regime. Please let me know if any assistance is needed to bring such an institution to fruition."

At Asher's proposal, Mrs. Umbernuckle gazes into her tea, eyes distant as if surveying a darker past. As head maid, discretion is key, though she'd be remiss not offering counsel where able.

"This place has weathered much, as have we all," she notes, voice steady despite any stirring memories. "Once I, too, saw the world through a shadowed lens and aided those who kept folk afraid, but lessons were learned." Her stare lifts, and she meets Asher's hopeful gaze with a look that conveys both warning and wish for change. "A school could aid redemption's path for others walking in night, just as your reforms lift shadows realm-wide. I've experience to share, if my counsel proves useful to your vision in any way."

Impulsively, I reach across the table and squeeze her hand. "The past is behind us all. What matters now is the future."

At that moment, we hear the shuffle of feet on the pebble walkway and excited voices approaching. I look over to see Mairelle and Cherry round the corner. They both halt in surprise before Mairelle breaks into a radiant smile and hurries forward.

"We heard your happy voices and had to see what was happening!" Mairelle bounces on the balls of my feet, unable to stand in one place.

Laughing, I meet Mairelle's guileless smile, guilt twinges within me over the callous way I once treated her. Taking her hands earnestly, I say, "Mairelle, Cherry, I owe you both an apology for my coldness when we first met. I hope you can forgive me and we might start anew as true friends."

Mairelle's eyes shine. "Friends may be stretching it. After all, you will be the new mistress! But if you insist, friends it is. The past is past."

Cherry nods agreement, her usually stoic face breaking into a smile.

Watching my former adversaries now laugh together, I marvel at the unexpected blessings life can bring. I catch Asher's eye, and we exchange a smile brimming with promise. The future lays before us, bright and full of hope.

NEW SCHOOL OPENS FOR MAGICAL YOUTH ACROSS FACTIONS

BY MAUD MALCONTENT

IN A HISTORIC MOVE TOWARD UNITY, A NEW ACADEMY HAS OPENED ITS DOORS FOR YOUTH OF ALL MAGICAL BACKGROUNDS, REGARDLESS OF PREVIOUS AFFILIATIONS.

FOUNDED THROUGH THE EFFORTS OF PRINCE ASHER AND LADY LILLITH, THE SCHOOL AIMS TO FOSTER FRIENDSHIP BETWEEN CHILDREN FROM BOTH SIDES OF THE LAW. INSTRUCTION IS OPEN TO ANY STUDENT WITH MAGICAL ABILITIES, VILLAIN OR HERO ORIGINS ALIKE.

"FOR TOO LONG, THOSE OF UNCOMMON TALENTS HAVE BEEN DIVIDED BY FEAR AND MISTRUST," LADY LILLITH DECLARED AT THE RIBBON-CUTTING CEREmony. "Here, we can nurture the next generation beyond outdated prejudices."

Prince Asher echoed this sentiment in his rousing speech to students and families. "Through cooperation and community, you will see the goodness in every heart," he proclaimed. "Your shared gifts make you kindred spirits learning together."

Mrs. Umbernuckle, the headmistress, assured families that redemption is possible for past wrongdoers. "With compassion guiding our youth, the future will be brighter for all," she stated warmly.

In addition to core magical subjects, the curriculum includes ethics training, equality lessons, and community building. Students also rotate co-teaching classes to learn teamwork.

The faculty itself sets an example, blending reformed villains, established heroes, and various magical practitioners united under one roof.

Headmaster Rendfield, a powerful illusionist, described the school as "a vision of how strong we become without dividing lines." He expressed hope students will form lifelong bonds transcending old social barriers.

Many see the academy as the first step toward lasting change. Children studying magic together under an egalitarian model may reshape society's views.

"Seeing kids from all walks learn and play together does an old heart good," Grimsley, a groundskeeper, said. "Gives me hope for the days ahead when they're grown."

While some families remain hesitant, enrollment is robust for the inaugural semester. Students hail from across the kingdom, arriving eagerly to develop their talents without stigma. The enthusiastic reception speaks to a generational shift toward inclusivity.

"My parents say change is dangerous, but I want to make friends with everyone," Marigold, fourteen, a new student, said.

Prince Asher has issued an open invitation for all youth gifted with magic to apply. The school doors remain open, with the only requirement being a willingness to learn collaboratively.

For many, this academy represents a long-awaited sanctuary where magical children can grow into their powers safely and without judgment, a chance to move beyond the divisions of the past.

I shift uncomfortably in my seat as the carriage jostles down the uneven forest road. Across from me, Draven leans back against the velvet cushions, seemingly unbothered by the bumpy ride.

"We must be getting close," he remarks, peering out the window at the thickening trees. "Are you ready for this?"

I bite my lip, fingers worrying the hem of my cloak. "I think so. It's just... these people may not exactly welcome a vampire on their doorstep, even if I come bearing gifts."

Draven reaches over and gives my hand a reassuring squeeze. "Hey, it'll be okay. Prince Asher and Lillith extended the invitation themselves. They want to help the vampire students feel comfortable at their academy."

"I hope you're right," I murmur. In truth, the thought of facing the infamous ex-villain Lillith Shadowend makes my stomach twist into anxious knots.

When the invitation arrived requesting I provide my special asrbloom tea to aid some struggling vampire pupils at the Academy of Magical Learning, I hesitated. Why would these legendary heroes want me, a lowly vampire alchemist, visiting their elite school?

But Asher and Lillith's academy is the first of its kind—created to teach both heroes and reformed villains side by side. Such a radical concept intrigues me, as does the chance to potentially help young vampires in need.

So here I am, jostling through the forest with a carriage loaded down with crates of asrbloom tea. I only hope my gift will be accepted graciously by the students and not regarded with suspicion.

The trees gradually thin, revealing an immense stone edifice nestled between rolling green hills. Towering turrets top its impressive façade, and even from a distance, I can see students milling about its grounds. My nerves redouble at the sight.

"We're here," Draven announces needlessly. He gives me an encouraging smile. "I'll be right by your side."

I muster a weak smile in return. In truth, I am grateful Draven insisted on accompanying me. His steadfast presence always gives me strength.

The carriage rolls to a stop before the sheer cliff face edging the rear of the academy. As I exit the stuffy cabin, I gaze up at the soaring towers, intimidated by the castle-like structure. This building does not look like a school.

"Thorn. Welcome."

I turn to see Prince Asher striding toward us, his handsome face crinkling into a friendly smile. His white hair shines like a beacon in the afternoon sunlight. Beside him walks a petite, dark-haired woman who can only be the notorious Lillith Shadowend. My knees nearly buckles.

"Your Highness," I manage to utter with a shaky curtsy. "Thank you for inviting me."

"The pleasure is ours," Asher replies warmly, "and please, call me Asher. Anyone who tries to let those who are made to feel outcast live a normal life is a friend of ours."

Lillith gives me a measuring look but keeps silent. I squirm under the intense scrutiny of those violet eyes. The enchantress's fearsome reputation sends a sliver of unease through me.

Sensing my discomfort, Draven steps forward. "Hi!" he says with an elegant bow. "I'm Draven."

"Welcome, Prince Draven," Asher says, shaking his hand vigorously. "We appreciate you escorting Thorn and these supplies for our students."

Lillith continues studying the pair of us, eyes lingering on the subtle way Draven shields me protectively with his body. A small smile curves her ruby lips.

"Yes, thank you both for making this journey," she says at last, her voice surprisingly warm and musical. "Your gift will make a difference. We have several children who have sought refuge in our school who could use a bit of help. I think the others will be much less afraid of them with time if they have this resource."

"Of course, My Lady," I say. "I remember how difficult those early years were. If this brew can help them even a little, I'm happy to provide it."

"Please, call me Lillith," the sorceress says with a kind smile. She gestures toward the tower doors. "Come inside and see what we've built here."

Draven and I exchange a look before following Asher and Lillith into the academy. The interior is even more impressive than the exterior, with soaring arched ceilings and intricate stained glass windows filtering rainbow light.

As we walk, I take in the sights and sounds—young voices chattering excitedly, footsteps echoing down stone corridors, and distant shouts and clangs from combat practice. It resounds with the controlled chaos of an active school.

Some students stop to gaze curiously at me as I pass. I try not to wither under their scrutiny, taking comfort from Draven's steady presence beside me.

"Our mandate is to teach empathy and redemption as much as magical and fighting skills," Asher explains as we walk. "Too often, those with villainous bloodlines face judgment and isolation. We want to change that."

Lillith nods solemnly. "Cruelty and persecution often breed cruelty. If we cannot break that cycle, peace is but a fantasy."

Her fierce conviction surprises me. This is not the merciless villainess from whispered legends but someone committed to forging a brighter future. "I absolutely agree. It's something we are working on in our kingdom as well."

As we continue down a long corridor, a young boy comes hurtling around the corner and nearly crashes right into Lillith. The child's eyes go wide with alarm, and he stumbles back, clutching a training sword that is far too large for his skinny arms.

"S-Sorry Mistress Shadowend!" he squeaks, shaking like a leaf.

But Lillith only smiles and gently touches the boy's head. "No harm done, Timothy," she assures him. "Just mind your speed in the hallways, all right?"

"Yes, ma'am!" Timothy promises breathlessly before scampering off.

I raise an eyebrow. The gentle exchange is not what I expected, but I am relieved to see it.

Noticing my surprise, Lillith gives a small, almost sad smile. "I know what you must think of me," she remarks softly, "but I take no pleasure in causing fear or pain needlessly, especially in children."

Unsure how to respond, I simply return the smile hesitantly. More and more, this place is unraveling my preconceived notions.

At last, we come to a set of carved oak doors that Asher pushes open to reveal the dining hall. Four young vampires sit at one of the long tables, looking rather glum. They perk up at the sight of me.

"Students, I want to introduce you to someone special," Lillith announces. "This is Thorn and Draven. They are vampires like you and have brought something to help with your transition to school."

The vampires gaze at me with a mixture of curiosity and shy hope that makes my heart ache in recognition. I know all too well the isolation of being different.

"Thorn is not just a vampire. She's also part witch," Asher explains to the pupils. "She brews a special medicinal tea to help satisfy blood cravings and provide nourishment. Please show your gratitude for her generosity."

"Thank you, Miss Thorn," the small group choruses dutifully.

"You're very welcome," I reply, suddenly feeling quite self-conscious with all eyes upon me. "I hope it brings some comfort while you adjust to school life."

"Shall we have a taste?" Lillith suggests, conjuring several teacups out of thin air with a wave of her hand. The students' eyes widen at the casual display of magic.

Soon, we are all sipping the fragrant ruby-hued tea amid enthusiastic slurping sounds. I hold my breath anxiously, hoping for positive reactions.

"This is delicious!" pipes up a blonde girl, fangs poking from her grin.

The other vampires chime in with equally positive reviews between long sips. I exhale in relief. The asrbloom is a hit.

"I'm so glad you like it," I say, smiling back at the group.

"This was most kind of you, Thorn," Asher praises, squeezing my shoulder. "Your gift will help these students immensely. We would love to create a schedule of delivery. Perhaps we can find something that we can trade or purchase with gold if that's preferred."

I duck my head, unused to such effusive thanks. "I'm just happy I could help a bit. I know it isn't easy being different."

Lillith's expression softens with empathy. "You understand our mission well," she says. "We aim to make this academy a safe haven for all."

As the four vampires finish their tea, I feel a swell of purpose. Already, my small gesture has brought these vulnerable youths some comfort. Perhaps I can do more.

Perhaps noticing Draven hanging back silently, Lillith turns to him with a penetrating look. "And what do you think of our little establishment so far, Draven?"

"I'll admit I had my doubts," Draven says. "Would people of such different backgrounds cooperate or just come to blows? But seeing you build common ground through compassion... it gives me hope. It's something we are trying to do as well."

Lillith tips her head graciously at the praise. "High ideals must be matched by daily empathy and forgiveness, mundane as such efforts may seem. That is how lasting change is forged."

Asher nods. "Well said, my dear. We have seen hearts transformed here through relationships built over shared meals, lessons, and chores rather than pompous lectures." He gives Draven a measuring look. "Your perspective would add an important voice on our council."

Draven's eyebrows shoot up. "Me? Serve on the council?"

"We could use someone with experience bridging the gap between vampire and human societies," Asher elaborates. "As the first academy of its kind, we value diverse viewpoints."

Draven glances at me.

I offer him an encouraging smile. "I think it's a wonderful idea. Your knowledge would help so many."

Draven rubs his neck thoughtfully before meeting Asher's eyes. "I am honored by the offer. Let me consider it carefully. The distance would be difficult, but if we could possibly consider sending students your way as well, especially those who aren't vampires, it could be beneficial for us as well. Most of our population are vampires as well so the resources for other magical aptitudes are weak."

"Of course. We could make something along those lines work," Asher says, clapping his shoulder. "Now please, allow us to show you more of the academy."

As we leave the dining hall, I feel as if a weight has lifted from my chest. The warm reception from Asher and

Lillith has cast away my initial doubts. This truly is a place of safety, community, and purpose.

Asher and Lillith proceed to show Draven and I the full grounds—the advanced magical laboratories, the gardens where mixed groups tend plants together, and the training arena where we observe good-natured sparring between young heroes and villains. Everywhere, the vision of harmony in diversity takes shape through cooperation and friendship.

"Incredible," Draven remarks as we watch an archery lesson.

Lillith follows his gaze to where a vampire girl is coaching a wood elf on his technique. "When labels are stripped away, people are simply people," she muses. "Our students teach us that every day."

As the tour concludes back in the main hall, Asher turns to us with a smile. "Thank you again for delivering the asrbloom tea. We are deeply grateful."

"Of course," I reply. "This is a wonderful thing you are doing here. I look forward to working together more."

"Indeed." Draven nods. "You have shown the real possibility of reconciliation beyond just hollow words. That brings hope."

Lillith smiles, her severe reputation belied by the warmth in her eyes. "Then our efforts are achieving their purpose. Know you both will always have a place here should you feel called to join us."

Draven and I both bow graciously, touched by the unexpected gesture of goodwill.

As we turn to depart down the cliff face steps, my outlook shifts. The future seems brighter, possibilities opening up where once lay only stagnant habits and divisions. If Asher and Lillith can build this radical community, perhaps one day, vampires will be welcomed everywhere without judgment or fear.

Glancing back up at the academy's soaring spires now wreathed in sunset hues, I silently thank the powers that be for this glimpse of a world reborn through understanding. I will share the hope I found here with any who would listen.

Seated beside me as our carriage rumbles away, Draven seems lost in thought too.

"Quite a place, wasn't it?" I remark after a while. "Makes you think change is really possible."

Draven nods slowly. "Seeing what Asher and Lillith built, how they're shaping young hearts and minds..." He gazes out the window pensively. "It's the sort of school I wish existed when I was growing up. Would have spared me years of anger. Possibly saved my brother and father if they had had it when they were young."

I cover his hand with mine, knowing that old resentments still pain him at times. "The future will be different because Asher and Lillith dared imagine something better," I say gently.

Draven turns his hand over to squeeze mine. "With more bridges built like you built today with your tea," he muses, "perhaps we will come to judge others on their character rather than their kind."

I nestle close to him as the carriage ambles down the wooded lane. For once, I feel no bitterness at my vampirism, only hope that our shared efforts will improve the lives of others carrying that same burden.

As the academy's spires fade into the distance, I silently vow to myself that one day, I, too, will work to build bridges between divides.

It won't be an easy task, but a new sense of purpose kindling inside me. In small acts like my gift of blood brew and Draven's potential role on the council, the way forward reveals itself—not through grand pronouncements but daily compassion and courage to create change from within.

Together with allies like Asher and Lillith, I believe we can forge a new era of cooperation and understanding between all people of the kingdom, no matter their powers or origins. The wheels of transformation has begun turning at last.

Maple Pecan Latte

1/2 cup pecan halves

1 1/4 cup milk

2 Tablespoons maple syrup

1 Tablespoon brown sugar

1 teaspoon cinnamon

4 shots brewed espresso or strong coffee

Soak the pecan halves and milk for at least 5-10 minutes.

Blend the pecans and milk together until smooth.

Use a nut milk bag or a mesh colander to strain the pecans (optional, but recommended to prevent a grainy texture. Pecan butter can be used too).

Heat up the strained pecan milk in a saucepan over medium heat.

Add in the maple syrup, brown sugar (optional), and cinnamon.

Cook for about 5 minutes, whisking often.

Pour the mixture into 2 coffee mugs.

Brew 2 shots of espresso for each latte.

Pour into the milk and enjoy!

Mushroom Stew

2 tablespoons butter
1 large onion, diced
1 ½ lb mushrooms
3-4 garlic cloves, crushed
2 tablespoons Hungarian paprika
1 tablespoon dried dill

1 tablespoon tamari soy sauce (or worcestershire)
2 cups vegetable stock
1 cup milk
2 tablespoons plain flour
1 tablespoon lemon juice
½ cup sour cream

In a large cauldron (or pan), add the butter and let it melt over the flames of a medium-sized fire. Toss in the diced onion and let it dance in the pot for about 5 minutes until it softens. Add the sliced mushrooms and let them simmer for 5-10 minutes, or until they release their moisture and start to turn a golden brown.

Sprinkle in the crushed garlic, paprika, dried dill, and soy sauce. Let the mixture brew for another 2 minutes, stirring occasionally with a spoon. Pour in the stock, bring the stew to a boil, then reduce the heat and let it simmer for 5 minutes. In a separate bowl, whisk together the milk and plain flour using a magic whisk until the mixture is as smooth as silk. Slowly pour the milk and flour mixture into the simmering soup, stirring constantly with a spoon to combine. Let the soup cook for another 5-10 minutes until it thickens to the desired consistency. Remove the cauldron from the heat and stir in 1 tablespoon of lemon juice.

In a small bowl, mix together the sour cream with a few spoonfuls of the hot soup to temper the cream. This will prevent it from curdling when added to the soup. You can skip this step if the sour cream is at room temperature.

Gradually stir the tempered sour cream mixture back into the soup, combining well with a magic whisk.

Serve in a bowl as soup, over mashed potoatoes or noodles.

CLASSIFIED ADS

DARK ARTS CATALOGUE SUMMER EDITION NOW AVAILABLE!

GREETINGS, FELLOW MISCREANTS AND MISCHIEF-MAKERS! THE LATEST ISSUE OF THE EXCLUSIVE DARK ARTS CATALOGUE HAS ARRIVED, CRAMMED FULL OF RARE ARTIFACTS, SINISTER SPELL TOMES, AND POTIONS TO FUEL ALL YOUR NEFARIOUS NEEDS.

THIS SEASON, OUR INVENTORY INCLUDES:

ENCHANTED RUNE DAGGERS OF SOUL TRAPPING! HARVEST LIFE ESSENCES TO EMPOWER YOUR RITUALS!

ROBES OF FEAR AURIFICATION! SPREAD TERROR WITH THESE ARMOR-WARDED SHADOW MAGICS.

DISINTEGRATION DRAUGHT! INSTANTLY REDUCE FOES OR FORTIFICATIONS TO ASHES FROM A SINGLE DROP!

Necronomicon of the Damned! Secrets of forbidden fleshcraft and bone magic are within these cursed pages.

Chains of Enslavement! Bind even the mightiest beasts or champions to your malignant will.

Plus many more items for the villain with discerning tastes! As always, we offer discounts for cursed artifacts fresh from past "adventures." Delivery via unmarked crested carriage guaranteed.

Don't delay. Supplies are limited! Send inquiries and deposits to our hidden alcove drop-box. We take gold, souls, or firstborn as payment and promise full detachment should pursuers trace transactions back. The future of villainy is in your hands, so grab it while it's hot!

***

WANTED: Fighters for Hire

Tired of going it alone in your villainous schemes? Let Nefarious Ned and his Band of Brigands take care of all your strongarm needs!

Since our exile from the kingdom, we've been building our renown in the underworld. Now, we've recruiting the best cutthroats, warlocks, and reavers for hire to help further your nefarious goals.

Need some heroes kidnapped? We'll snatch 'em in the night! A dark ritual requires guarding? We'll spill the blood of any who oppose! A rival needs eliminating? Just say the word. One bolt from our master assassin and the job's done without a trace.

Pay is a quarter up front, the rest upon completion. No contract too dirty. We live outside the law's reach! Generous bonuses are also offered for any jobs involving the torment of do-gooders.

Leave a message at any tavern for Ned, and a meeting will be arranged post-haste. Discretion and success guaranteed. Not even the Mage's Guild could trace our signature mayhem. Dark times call for darker allies, so give us a shout if you need real results!

***

End Your Suffering! Curses Cured Here!

FED UP WITH THAT BOTHERSOME HERO'S BRAND BURNING YOUR FLESH OR LUCKLESS GEAS THWARTING YOUR SCHEMES? COME TO WITCH HAZEL'S WARDS. WE'LL LIFT ANY CURSE FOR A PRICE!

WHILE LESS SKILLED "HEALERS" MAY PROMISE RE-MOVAL, ONLY OUR COVEN OF CURSEBREAKERS OFFERS A 100% SUCCESS RATE.* WITH OUR COMBINED TAL-ENTS OF DARK DIVINATION, WITCHCRAFT, AND DE-MONOLOGY, NO JINX IS TOO POWERFUL OR PAINFUL TO UNDO.

TIRED OF CONSTANTLY SPOILING PERFECT ASSASSI-NATIONS DUE TO THAT MANDATE OF MERCY? WAST-ING AWAY UNDER A ROYAL FAMILY'S AGE-OLD HEX? WHATEVER PLAGUES YOU, A VISIT TO OUR SECRET GROVE IS SURE TO REMEDY WOES.

POTIONS, RITUALS, AND SACRILEGIOUS SOR-CERIES—NO METHOD IS TOO TABOO IN OUR QUEST TO FREE CLIENTS FROM HEROIC HINDRANCES. WALK AWAY LIGHT AND CURSE-CLEAR, READY TO FULLY EM-BRACE YOUR SINISTER TALENTS ONCE MORE!

RATES VARY BASED ON CURSE SEVERITY, BUT PAY-MENT PLANS ARE AVAILABLE. SIMPLY FOLLOW THE SMOKE AT THE CROSSROADS AT MIDNIGHT TO FIND OUR SANCTUARY. WE GUARANTEE SATISFACTION... OR YOU NEED NOT PAY!*

*LIFTING OF GEASA, COMPULSIONS, AND OTHER HEROIC HINDRANCES NOT FULLY GUARANTEED. SIDE

EFFECTS MAY INCLUDE INCREASED MALEVOLENCE, BLOODLUST OR DEMONIC POSSESSION.

*****

RARE TOXINS FOR THE DISCERNING VILLAIN!

IN NEED OF A FAST-ACTING POISON FOR AN IRRITATING KNIGHT? A PLAGUE TO SPREAD IN THE REALM'S WELLS? WE'VE THE REMEDY FOR ANY MURDEROUS IMPULSE AT TOXIC TOMES!

IMPORTING ONLY THE RAREST VENOMS, OUR APOTHECARY STOCKS LIMITLESS ELIXIRS TO FUEL MISDEEDS. NIGHTSHADES TO INDUCE LIVING NIGHTMARES, SCORPION MILKS TO STOP A HEART IN SECONDS... WE'VE TOXINS FOR ALL NEFARIOUS TASTES. LEAVE INCONVENIENT HEROES SLEEPING FOREVER.

NEW IN STOCK—THE PRIZED BLACK LOTUS BILE! SMUGGLED FROM THE WARRING KINGDOMS, JUST A FEW DROPS GUARANTEE A GRIZZLY, HALLUCINATORY DEMISE. PERFECT FOR COWARDLY ASSASSINS OR MERCILESS MAGIC-USERS.

SPECIAL DISCOUNTS FOR MEMBERS OF THE CULT OF SHADOWS. SIMPLY PRESENT THEIR INFERNAL SYMBOL FOR 20% OFF ALL WARES AND CONFIDENTIAL DELIVERIES VIA UNHOLY RAVEN.

Walk-ins welcome at our new villa front! We keep business discreet for lifetime clients. Who could refuse such villainous value?

***

Commission Nightmare Devices and Receive 20% Off!

Tired of run-of-the-mill daggers and staves? Veldaran's Forge crafts uniquely sinister arms for villains seeking the edge in power and fearsome mystique.

Through our blood sorcery and demon-pacts, any item can be imbued with shadow magics, whether soul-stealing swords, staves that render flesh to ash, or armor that spreads plagues at a touch.

Access to rare essences allows augmentations no mortal smith could achieve. Swords that swallow magic, helms that can uncover even the best-laid deceptions... Anything your dark heart desires can be made real.

For a limited time only, receive 20% off all custom-enchanted arms. Designs imbued with curses also welcome. The more depraved, the better the discount!

Struggling dark lords and ambitious underlings, come to us for the weapons that will help topple heroes and kingdoms. What diabolical device will you commission to terrorize the realm?

Contact the forgeMASTER via our private portals. Discretion and the veil of night ensure full anonymity for clients. The future of evil starts with the right tools.

***

Villainous Vacations:

Escape to The Shadow Isles!

Growing weary from your efforts to plunge the world into chaos? Need an escape from prying heroes and their ilk? Then look no further than The Shadow Isles Resort!

Located deep in the cursed archipelago, our remote private islands cater exclusively to villains seeking sun, sex, and sacrifices away from watchful eyes. Indulge to your black hearts' content without moralizing interference.

A variety of sinister activities await! Join coven rituals under the full moon. Hunt

CORRUPTED BEASTS THROUGH MISTED FORESTS OR EXPLORE LONG-ABANDONED TEMPLES OF ELDRITCH POWERS WHERE DARK MAGICS STILL SLUMBER.

LUXURIOUS BLACK-MARBLE VILLAS AND FORMIDABLE WARDED PROTECTION ENSURE ABSOLUTE PRIVACY AND DISCRETION FOR GUESTS. FRESH SACRIFICES DAILY, WITH AN EXCLUSIVE SUMMONER ON STAFF TO SATE MORE ESOTERIC HUNGERS.

BOOK YOUR STAY TODAY AND RECEIVE TWO COMPLIMENTARY DOSES OF VENOM BLOOM ELIXIR—PERFECT FOR ENHANCING YOUR ALREADY DEPRAVED PLEASURES! SPOTS ARE LIMITED, SO DON'T DELAY YOUR MUCH-NEEDED R&R IN THE ISLES' EMBRACE!

***

CUSTOM LAIRS TO ECLIPSE EVEN DRAGONS' HOARDS!

GROWING TIRED OF SUBTERRANEAN LAIRS OR HOVELS IN REMOTE FORESTS? LOOKING FOR A LAVISH REDOUBT TO STRIKE FEAR INTO ANY WHO WOULD OPPOSE YOU? VELDARAN ARCHITECTS DESIGNS MOBILE MOUNTAIN CITADELS, SWAMP HIDEAWAYS, AND UNDERGROUND COMPLEXES TO OUTDO ALL OTHERS!

OUR MASTER SCHEMERS HAVE DECADES OF EXPERIENCE CRAFTING INDESTRUCTIBLE FORTRESSES. MOUNTAIN REDOUBTS HEWN FROM LIVING ROCK ARE

AS IMPREGNABLE AS THE MASSIFS THEMSELVES! SIMPLE VILLAS SECRETED AWAY IN SWAMPLAND ARE SURROUNDED BY DEADLY FLORA AND PLAGUES. SPRAWLING UNDERGROUND COMPLEXES RIVAL DWARVEN DELVING WITH DEFENSES AND SECRET PASSAGEWAYS.

PLUS, ALL MODELS COME EQUIPPED WITH BARRACKS, TROPHY HALLS, ARMORIES, RITUALS CHAMBERS... EVERYTHING TO ESTABLISH YOUR DOMINION! CUSTOM TRAPS, AUTONOMOUS SENTRIES, AND INBUILT WARDS ARE AVAILABLE. LET OUR SAVANTS ENSURE NONE WILL EVER DESPOIL YOUR LAIR UNINVITED!

ORDER NOW AND RECEIVE A COMPLIMENTARY DESIGN CONSULT. YOUR CITADEL WILL BE THE WONDER OF THE DARK WORLD, THE ENVY OF KINGS AND VILLAINS ALIKE! STRENGTH, SUBTLETY AND SECURITY, TAILORED FOR MAXIMUM EVIL... WHAT MORE COULD A WARLORD DESIRE?

THIS IS AN INVESTMENT FOR THE AGES. CONTACT VELDARAN FOR A FORTRESS TO WITHSTAND EPOCHS! LEGACIES ARE BUILT ON FOUNDATIONS AS STRONG AS STONE AND STEEL.

***

SECRETS FOR SALE—DIRT CHEAP!

Tired of being in the dark while paltry "spymasters" demand exorbitant prices? Veldaran's hidden brokers offer underground intelligence for the most competitive rates.

Need kings' battle plans? We have cartloads of intercepted letters. Seeking heroes' true names or locations of loved ones? Just name your price. Want blackmail on corrupt lords? Look no further.

With operatives embedded in every court and tavern, we collect the crown jewels of subterfuge easily overlooked by lesser talent. Plus, with new Telepathic Translators, even mind-reader detection is obsolete!

This season's hot goods included:

- Royal bastard lines kept in shadows

- Paladins' darkest vices and hypocrisies

- Secret societies and heretical covens

Pay what you want. We just want your patronage. Discounts offered to villains willing to trade their own "acquired" materials. See how the mighty fall when secrets are sold! Knowledge is power, and we provide cheap enough for all.

VISIT OUR CATACOMB ARCHIVES TODAY. WALK OUT KNOWING ENEMIES' DEEPEST SHAMES AND HEROES' ACHILLES HEELS. YOU'LL BE GLAD YOU DID, AND THEY'LL BE WISHING YOU NEVER DID!

***

RARE AND MERCILESS BEASTS FOR SALE!

GUARDIAN LIONS AND HUNTING HAWKS TOO MUNDANE FOR YOUR MENAGERIE? SEARCHING FOR THE PERFECT MOUNT TO COW PETTY LORDS INTO SUBMISSION? COME TO VELDARAN EXOTICS, WHERE ONLY THE DEADLIEST OF CREATURES WILL DO!

THIS SEASON, WE OFFER:

- CHIMERA KITS, PERFECT TO RAISE AS LOYAL FLAME-BREATHING SENTINELS

- WYVERNS, DURABLE FLIERS TO SURVEIL FROM THE SKIES

- YOUNG COCKATRICES, WHOSE GAZE WILL PETRIFY ALL WHO CROSS THEIR MASTER

- WYRMLINGS PLUCKED FRESH FROM THEIR HATCHING PITS

All crested in hardened scales or fangs, with potent venom gland extra. Trained from an early age to bond for life with their dark lord.

Open daily for viewing and purchases. Experts on hand to advise feeding, housing, and training your new terror. Remember, with great power comes great fear and respect! Invest in YOUR future today.

Discounts for members of the Villainous Vagrants. Join our breeding program and receive one free beast per year! The choice is obvious. Bolster your forces with only the deadliest specimens. Come see for yourself!

***

Bid for Infamy at the Dark Market!

Connoisseurs of villainy, the next gathering of Veldaran's notorious black market is upon us! As always, we've scoured the darkest corners of the realm to procure our most exclusive and unlawful inventory for public ~~sacrifice~~ bidding.

Featured lots include:

- Set of goblin triplets, raised in murder

AND STEALTH. STARTING BID: 5 SOULS.

- BLOOD-RUSTED RELIC OF THE BETRAYER GOD. MINIMUM OFFER: 100,000 GOLD OR A POLITICAL FAVOR.

- CURSED ROSE GOLD CIRCLET, ENHANCES ILLUSIONS BUT SLOWLY MADDENS THE WEARER. BID WISELY!

- HEIR TO A FALLEN NOBLE HOUSE. INDEBTED TO THE NEW "PATRON" FOR LIFE.

PLUS, ALL YOUR STANDARD ILLICIT WARES—POISONS, SMUGGLED GOODS, HANDCRAFTED ARMS, AND MORE! REFRESHMENTS AND ENTREATMENTS ARE PROVIDED FOR WAITING PATRONS.

NEW THIS CYCLE—LIVE ENTERTAINMENT! WATCH AS CRIMINAL SCUM BATTLE TO THE DEATH EACH NIGHT. PLACE WAGERS AND EARN FAVOR WITH THE UNDERWORLD ELITE.

BIDDING OPENS AT MIDNIGHT'S TOLL UNDER THE NEW MOON. DISCRETION IS GUARANTEED FOR ALL TRANSACTIONS IN THE DARK. SEE YOU ON THE AUCTION FLOOR, AND MAY FORTUNE FAVOR THE BOLDEST VILLAIN!

CLASSIFIED ADS

HERO'S HAVEN RETIREMENT VILLAGE SEEKS YOUR GENEROUS SUPPORT

FOR THREE DECADES, HERO'S HAVEN HAS PROVIDED SANCTUARY FOR BRAVE SOULS WHO SACRIFICED ALL TO DEFEND PEACE IN THE REALM. OUR RESIDENTS ARE VETERANS OF A HUNDRED BATTLES, KNIGHTS WHO LOST LIMBS IN THE THICK OF COMBAT, MAGES DRAINED BY BINDING FELL MAGICS, AND MORE.

THOUGH THEIR GLORY DAYS OF HEROISM MAY BE BEHIND THEM, THEIR SPIRIT REMAINS. AT HERO'S HAVEN, THEY FIND COMMUNITY AMONG FELLOW SURVIVORS, CRAFTING TOGETHER, TENDING OUR GARDENS, AND SHARING TALES BY THE HEARTH, BUT AGE AND INJURIES NOW TAKE THEIR TOLL ON EVEN THE STAUNCHEST SOULS.

WE STRIVE TO MAKE THEIR GOLDEN YEARS AS COMFORTABLE AS POSSIBLE THROUGH SMALL COMFORTS, BUT SUPPLIES AND FUNDS GROW SHORT, AS MORE RETIRE HERE EACH SEASON. OUR INFIRMARIES NEED ADDITIONAL COTS AND HEALERS TO EASE THEIR PAINS. CRAFT SHOPS REQUIRE NEW MATERIALS TO KEEP MINDS AND HANDS BUSY.

WON'T YOU CONTRIBUTE TO THEIR LEGACY IN THEIR TWILIGHT? A SINGLE SILVER CAN SUPPLY YARN FOR MANY SHAWLS TO WARM THE ELDERLY. TEN GOLD WILL FURNISH THE APOTHECARY FOR A MOON. LARGER DONATIONS GO EVEN FURTHER. YOU MAY EVEN SPONSOR THE REMODELING OF THE HOSPICE WING IN A LOVED ONE'S NAME.

EVERY ACT OF GOODWILL, WHETHER COIN OR SUPPLIES, LIFTS THESE HEROES' SPIRITS IMMEASURABLY. THOUGH THE BATTLES ARE WON, THE COSTS OF VICTORY REMAIN. SHOW YOUR GRATITUDE FOR LIVES LIVED IN SERVICE BY ENSURING THEIR NEEDS ARE MET WITH GRACE IN THEIR FINAL YEARS. IN THEIR DAY, THEY GAVE ALL TO YOU. NOW, REPAY THEIR SACRIFICES WITH YOUR MERCY.

DROP DONATIONS AT ANY TOWN HALL OR VISIT HERO'S HAVEN DIRECTLY AT THE EDGE OF THE HIGH WOOD. THE RESIDENTS AND I THANK YOU DEEPLY FOR ANY GENEROSITY THAT EASES THEIR DAYS REMAINING UNDER THE SUN. YOUR SUPPORT HONORS THEIR

INDOMITABLE SPIRIT EVEN AS THEIR BODIES WEAR DOWN.

***

LOST SOMETHING? WE MAY HAVE FOUND IT!

ITEMS ASTRAY ARE FREQUENTLY RECOVERED AT THE TOWNSHIP HALL. COME VIEW OUR COLLECTION OF DISCOVERED TREASURES. YOU MAY BE REUNITED AT LONG LAST!

RECENT ADDITIONS INCLUDE:

- A MAN'S SILVER SIGNET RING ENGRAVED WITH TWISTING VINES. FOUND IN THE MARKET SQUARE.

- A LADY'S LACE HANDKERCHIEF, STAINED BUT FINELY MADE. DISCOVERED IN THE MEADOW.

- A CHILD'S CLOTH DOLL WITH YARN HAIR AND BUTTON EYES. ABANDONED ON THE WESTERN ROAD.

- A LEATHER-BOUND NOTEBOOK FILLED WITH DIAGRAMS AND NOTES. LEFT BEHIND AT THE SHINDIG.

- A GENTLEMAN'S TOBACCO PIPE OF DARK-

WOOD AND AGING BONE. RECOVERED BESIDE THE WELL.

WE KEEP LOST ITEMS FOR TWO MOON CYCLES BEFORE DONATING PROCEEDS TO CHARITY, SO IF YOU'RE MISSING A PRIZED POSSESSION, COME SEE IF LUCK HAS BROUGHT IT OUR WAY!

IN THE MEANTIME, OTHERS CAN ALSO BROWSE FOR SERENDIPITOUS FINDS. ALL UNCLAIMED BELONGINGS WILL BRING JOY TO THE ORPHANAGE COME LAMMAS. LET'S REUNITE AS MANY TOWNSFOLK WITH THEIR TREASURED THINGS AS WE CAN!

POP INTO THE TOWNSHIP HALL DURING BUSINESS HOURS. HONESTY IS THE BEST POLICY, AND SOMETIMES IT'S REWARDED TOO!

***

WORK WANTED ON ANY FARM NEAR OR FAR

STRONG BACKS AND SPARE HANDS SEEK HONEST WORK ON THE LAND. WITH HARVEST UPON US, ANY BIT OF LABOR IS APPRECIATED.

THIS FORMER FOOTMAN AND FARRIER'S APPRENTICE WILL PLOW, PLANT, WEED, HARVEST, AND HAY OR MUCK YOUR STABLES AS NEEDED. NOT AFRAID OF HARD YAKKA FROM DAWN TILL DUSK. CAN MEND

FENCES, THATCH ROOFS, AND CHOP FIREWOOD TOO IF YOU'RE SHORTHANDED.

GOOD WITH ANIMALS AS WELL. HELPED BIRTH LAMBS, FOALS, AND PIGLETS IN ME PRIOR ROLE. KNOW MEDICINES TO KEEP YOUR STOCK FAT AND HEALTHY TOO.

WILL WORK FOR FAIR WAGE, HOT MEALS, AND A DRY BARN CORNER TO LAY ME HEAD. ROOM AND BOARD IS ALSO WELCOME BUT NOT REQUIRED. YOU'LL FIND ME AN HONEST WORKER EAGER TO PULL ME WEIGHT.

REFERENCES CAN BE PROVIDED FROM ME PREVIOUS POSTS. JUST ASK THE WAYBOURNE HOMESTEAD OR HIGGINS FARM, WHERE I EARNED ME KEEP FOR YEARS.

LOOKING TO SIGN ON LONG-TERM IF IT'S A MUTU-ALLY GOOD FIT, BUT HAPPY WITH TEMP WORK TOO. YOUR CROPS WON'T GROW THEMSELVES. PUT ME TO USE! COME SEE ME AT THE INN IF INTERESTED. THE HARVEST WON'T WAIT.

***

APPRENTICE WIZARDS WANTED

THE ESTEEMED ARCHMAGUS ACADEMY SEEKS EN-THUSIASTIC STUDENTS TO LEARN THE MYSTICAL ARTS. WHETHER YOUR TALENTS INCLINE TO ELE-MENTAL MAGICKS, ILLUSION, DIVINATION, OR ARCANE

ARTS, UNLOCK YOUR POTENTIAL AMONG LIKE-MINDED PEERS!

YEARS OF STUDY UNDER ACCOMPLISHED MAGES WILL HONE YOUR ABILITIES, FROM BASIC RUNECRAFT TO SUMMONING FEY. MASTER SPELLS OF PROTECTION, HEALING, AND UTILITY. LEARN OUR ORDER'S HIGHEST SECRETS, FROM THE PRIMORDIAL FORCES THAT SHAPE THIS WORLD TO PATHWAYS BETWEEN THE PLANES THEMSELVES.

BEING AN APPRENTICE IS NO LIGHT TASK, BUT REWARDS ARE PLENTIFUL. REGULAR UPKEEP OF THE LIBRARY AND TEACHING GARDENS IN EXCHANGE FOR ROOM AND BOARD WITHIN THE ACADEMY'S MAGICALLY WARDED WALLS IS AN OPTION. ADDITIONAL TRAINING IN COMPLEMENTARY SKILLS LIKE ALCHEMY, LANGUAGES, AND HISTORY IS POSSIBLE.

SUCCESSFUL NOVICES MAY EVEN ACCOMPANY MASTERS ON RARE WILDLIFE OBSERVATION OR PATROLS OF WILD MAGIC ZONES. DEFEND VILLAGES FROM OTHERWORLDLY INCURSIONS. REST ASSURED, ALL EXPEDITIONS ARE STRICTLY OVERSEEN FOR YOUR SAFETY.

WHEN STUDIED PROPERLY, MAGIC AUGMENTS ALL CALLINGS, FROM COMMERCIAL ENCHANTMENT TO SAFEGUARDING COMMUNITIES. SHAPE YOUR TALENTS TO UPLIFT LIVES THROUGH THE MIRACULOUS ARTS.

APPLY AT THE ARCHMAGUS GATEHOUSE THIS MOON. LESSONS BEGIN AT THE FALL EQUINOX. YOUR MAGICAL EDUCATION AWAITS!

***

LOST MY LITTLE ONE! DRAGON PUP MISSING!

I'M BESIDE MYSELF WITH WORRY FOR MY DARLING HAMMOND. MY BELOVED WHELP WENT MISSING LAST NIGHT WHILE WE WERE STARGAZING IN THE EASTERN FIELDS.

HAMMOND IS A BLUE-SCALED DRAGON PUP, ONLY TEN MONTHS OLD, ABOUT THE SIZE OF A LARGE DOG, WITH SOFT SPIKES DOWN HIS BACK AND LITTLE NUB HORNS. HE HAS GREEN EYES AND LIKES TO PLAY WITH SHINY ROCKS I'VE COLLECTED.

WHEN LAST SEEN, HAMMOND HAD A COLD SO WAS SNIFFLING QUITE LOUDLY. HE MAY BE FRIGHTENED AND HIDING SOMEWHERE DAMP AND COOL. PLEASE CHECK ANY BARNS, CULVERTS, OR FOREST THICKETS HE COULD HAVE CRAWLED INTO TO REST.

I'VE SEARCHED THROUGH THE NIGHT WITH NO SIGN AND AM TOO DISTRAUGHT TO KEEP LOOKING ALONE. A HANDSOME REWARD IS OFFERED TO WHO-EVER FINDS MY SWEETLING AND RETURNS HIM HOME, NO QUESTIONS ASKED.

HAMMOND IS VERY AFFECTIONATE BUT WILL LIKELY BE SCARED WITHOUT HIS MAMA. IF YOU HAVE HIM OR ANY CLUES AS TO WHERE HE COULD BE, PLEASE CONTACT ME AT ONCE AT THE MOUNTAIN ESTATE. SAFE RETURN OF MY BABY IS ALL I ASK.

***

CALLING ALL THREAD BEARERS! LEND YOUR SKILLS!

THE FABRIC OF REALITY GROWS THIN IN REMOTE CORNERS OF THE REALM, RENT BY DARK FORCES MEDDLING WHERE THEY OUGHT NOT. YOUR ABILITIES ARE NEEDED TO REPAIR RUPTURES BEFORE THEY SPREAD FURTHER!

AS A THREAD BEARER, YOU CAN MEND TEARS IN THE WEAVE THAT DIVIDES THIS WORLD FROM BEYOND. MAINTAIN BALANCE AS AN AGENT OF THE ARCHMAGI. LEARN DEEPER SECRETS OF MAGIC IN THE PROCESS.

ROAD WARRIORS WILLING TO TRAVEL TO FAR-FLUNG LOCALES WHERE FRINGE INVASIONS WEAKEN BARRIERS ARE SOUGHT. DISCERN REASON AND REMEDY. SOMETIMES, A SIMPLE INCANTATION OR BURNT HERB CLOSES WOUNDS THAT COULD FESTER. OTHER INCURSIONS REQUIRE AURAMANTIC BINDINGS OR BANISHMENT RITUALS.

Your efforts are crucial but not lonesome. More senior Menders provide wisdom and watch your backs. Fortnightly reports earn modest stipend or room at the Academy if repairs take moons.

This is serious work, but rewards abound. The Archmagi's libraries are yours to peruse in leisure hours. Join expeditions to mystic glades or remedy curses. For those extending service, apprenticeships in higher mysteries may follow in time.

If you possess an affinity for the Weave, join our roving bands of menders. Shore up weaknesses before rifts grow too large to mend. Help maintain the shimmering strands that keep encroaching shadows at bay. Your talents are sorely needed!

***

Trees For Tomorrow—Hands Needed!

Have you a green thumb and care for future generations? Then join our vital reforestation efforts!

Our woodlands face pressures—overharvest, blight, unnatural wildfires. To sustain

WOOD SUPPLIES, WILD GAME, AND OXYGEN FOR OUR CHILDREN, SAPLINGS MUST BE SEEDED.

VOLUNTEER MORNINGS PLANTING ACORNS, PINECONES, HAZELNUTS, AND MORE ACROSS CLEARINGS. LEARN ARBORISM FROM SEASONED FORESTERS—SELECT HEARTY BREEDS, IDEAL SPACING, SUPPLEMENTAL WATERING.

EARN CORNERSTONE EXPERIENCE WILL WIDEN YOUR SKILLS. EVENSONG MEALS AND CAMPING AMIDST NATURE'S BEAUTY ARE YOURS. KNOWLEDGE BLEEDS THROUGH IN LEISURELY HOURS IDENTIFYING FLORA/FAUNA.

MULTI-MONTH STINTS WELCOME, BUT ALL CONTRIBUTIONS AID MOTHER NATURE'S REPLENISHMENT. FROM FURROWING SOIL TO TENDING SPROUTS TAKES COMMUNITY AND STEWARDS ALL THROUGH DECADES TO COME!

SHARE THIS BOUNTY FOR GENERATIONS YET UNSEEN. LET YOUR GRANDCHILDREN WALK TALL TREES THAT YOU NURTURED FROM SEED. APPLY AT TRAILHEAD NOTICEBOARDS OR LOCAL PARLORS. ROOTS BEGIN WHERE YOU PLANT YOUR SOLES. THE FOREST CALLS FAITHFUL LABORERS!

***

WANTED: LOVING RETIREMENT FOR MAGICAL STEED

HECTOR THE GELDING SEEKS PASTURE FOR HIS GOLDEN YEARS. WITH A HINT OF MAGIC IN HIS NOBLE BLOOD, THIS NOBLE WHITE STALLION HAS FAITHFULLY SERVED THE KINGDOM FOR DECADES.

A DESCENDANT OF MYSTICAL UNICORN STEEDS, HECTOR POSSESSES A GENTLE SOUL AND A HEALING TOUCH. A PAT ON THE NECK FROM THIS STEED CAN EASE ACHES AND LIFT WEARY SPIRITS. HIS GENTLE PRESENCE HELPS NOURISH THE LAND AND ALL WHO DWELL UPON IT.

NOW IN HIS ELDER YEARS, HECTOR'S BATTLE DAYS ARE BEHIND HIM, BUT HIS GIFTS REMAIN. HE SEEKS ONLY QUIET FIELDS TO GRAZE AND A KIND MASTER TO KEEP HIM COMPANY IN HIS RETIREMENT.

IN EXCHANGE FOR AMPLE GRAZING AND SIMPLE STABLES, HECTOR WILL BLESS YOUR LAND WITH ABUNDANCE AND WARD OFF ILLNESSES FROM MAN AND BEAST ALIKE WITH HIS LIGHT. CHILDREN ESPECIALLY FIND JOY IN HIS COMPANY.

IF YOU CAN OFFER THIS MAGICAL STEED A HOME FOR THE REMAINDER OF HIS DAYS, YOU'LL FIND HIS PRESENCE REWARDS ITSELF. SEND WORD TO THE SUMMER

VILLAGE BY SEASON'S END IF YOUR HUSBANDRY HEART HAS ROOM FOR ONE MORE. HECTOR WILL REPAY YOUR GENEROSITY TENFOLD WITH THE GIFTS HE SHARES.

Behind the Scenes

I always love doing a little behind the scenes to show some of the inspiration behind the book. How to Be a Good Villain started as all of my books do, a wouldn't it be funny if moment, but this time I blame it entirely on Eastern dramas and anime. Wouldn't it be funny if there was a villain who was One Punch Man level of overpowered and they were bored out of their mind because nothing is a challenge anymore? What would she do? Disguise themself as a maid and try to corrupt a hero? Yes please!

From there it slowly evolved into a list of ways that a villain would do normal things that would seem a bit out of the ordinary and how exactly would someone who was a villain but not necessarily evil go about doing things? For example, how would a villain clean dirty underwear?

The idea of the split kingdom between a villain and a hero society really didn't start forming until around halfway through writing the book. Everything was still in Lillith's point of view only and written in 1st person past tense other than the first few paragraphs which were written in 1st person present because I struggle to stay in the same tense as I write. An idea started form about a villain secret underground training facility and why exactly did they need to have that? Why did Prince Asher need to keep his secret about him saving villains and helping hide them? At this point I planned on that being the big reveal later in the book and when I added in his point of view I had to do some major recalculating on how exactly the book was going to go.

It wasn't until after a few rounds with beta readers (you guys are the best!!!) and a sample edit from a new to me editor (thank you for the advice Nicole!) that I realized I wanted to completely rewrite the book from first person past tense to first person present tense in two days and add in the newspaper snippets to help flesh out the world and let the reader see what the different parts of society were like and why it needed to be fixed.

During the rewrite, a meme floated around facebook, and when I tell you that I was tagged over and over again by my beta readers for this meme I'm not exaggerating. It was a snippet of text that involved the phrasing of "Excuse me? I beg your pardon?" and "Then beg" and they were tagging me because it immediately made them think of Lillith. So of course I had to add it into the new intro I was writing for the book. Initially, the opening scene was Lillith being interviewed for the job, but I felt like I wanted the reader to get a feeling for who she was first. Something that screamed villain so it was clear what her personality was like and just how powerful she could be.